Time's Tempest

Part One of The Chronicles of Xannia

M.J. Moores

Time's Tempest: The Chronicles of Xannia

Copyright © M.J. Moores, 2014

Published by Infinite Pathways Press 2015
P.O. Box 4, Caledon Village, ON Canada L7K 3L3
Produced in Canada

ISBN 978-0-9921168-8-0 Paperback Edition

First Published in 2014
By GWL Publishing
An imprint of Great War Literature Publishing LLP
Produced in United Kingdom

Dedication

For my husband, without whom this story would not have been possible.

Acknowledgements

For any writer there are innumerable people who help make a manuscript come to life. However, just as recipients of an Academy Award will prepare a speech to make sure everyone gets thanked, invariably a name or two is missed.

I'd like to start by thanking those who've helped me cross the finish line with grace and style: my original GWL editor Wendy Lawrance, my independent editor Morgen Bailey, my most recent beta readers/critiquers Mark Arnold and Susannah Daugharty and my writing/critique/support groups.

Before I got to the stage where I could actually benefit from the wisdom of these professionals, I had the support of my estended family as early readers, my two best friends Teresa Cline, OCT and Dr. Sean Palmer, PhD, as well as the never ending love and support given by my mother.

A final nod goes to Serguei Tchertok, a university friend who helped make the incredible science of Xannia possible by grounding it in plausible modern technology.

Build a strong foundation and you can reach even the most unthinking heights.

Thank you all.

Chapter One
A Fine Line

Ducking through one of the large, back double doors of Professor Denali's cube-rider, I second-guessed myself as I scanned the open shelves. Every fibre of my training as a Contractor with the Facility tore at the ethical implications of digging through a client's personal files. *But this is important, Taya. It goes way beyond job ethics. Silence is not an option.*

I forced my breathing to deepen, slowing my heart rate, to clear the adrenaline from my body. It was one of the first techniques taught at the CTF – Contractor Training Facility. The idea of 'mind over matter' had not been easy in practice, but once I learned it, nothing could stop me.

The files themselves were pristine red folders of varying thickness located in chaotic and random stacks on the clear shelving unit. They looked identical, save one with a thin vertical black mark on the base. The paranoid professor did not want anyone going through his research. He almost fired me, the day I started on the project, for trying to categorise and organise his haphazard stacks, but not before I noticed the file with the mark and looked at it.

A crackling sounded outside. *Dammit! He's supposed to be across the lake.* My shoulders stiffened. I listened carefully for any other sign of the professor's reappearance. The wind shifted and a faint rasp wavered in the mid-morning heat from the dry grasses surrounding the smallest of three lakes in this region.

No one appeared.

I turned from the shelving and strode back to the double doors. If I was caught, I needed a good excuse for being in here. I pocketed one of the stoppered vials I needed for the research from a rack by the doors. The reflective metal above the triple row of individually-suspended samples caught the edge of my sightline. For a fraction of an instant, I stared back into my large black eyes beneath my work cap, framed by bronze skin and red s-shaped tattoo-like birth markings of various sizes, known as coliths. It was an imperfect reflection, but then again, so was I.

My eyes asked the questions I fought to ignore. *So then, what are you doing? Do you realise the consequences?* I snapped my head away from the reflection and returned to rifling through the wall of folders.

Three weeks ago, when I'd learned that Professor Denali registered with the office for a Contractor to fill a three-fer, a position equal to three lab technicians, my radar for the unusual triggered. Less than a year ago, the professor had been discredited in court and his ecological research into the stability of verrin, the life- sustaining liquid for all Xannians, was deemed compromised, due to report falsification. The scientific community ostracised him. Only the Facility knew he'd reactivated his research into the natural sources of verrin and the liquid's chemical makeup. I capitalised on his request for a Contractor willing to enter the Expanse on a daily basis. The controversy surrounding the work, and the man himself, bothered me from the start.

The fact that Denali was taking his theories so far beyond civilization and so near the death zone of the Deserts, made even the top Contractors nervous. With my habit of craving challenging assignments, this not only gave me the opportunity to work in one of the scientific fields I excelled at, but also to learn the truth about his research.

I moved from one stack of files to the next, from one shelf to another. *He never puts it in the same place twice.*

The Press hadn't been permitted into court hearings, and the Kronik, the governing body of councillors and the honorific term used for the head ruler of Xannia – made the final ruling on Denali's case behind closed doors. I allowed myself a brief smile as I thought of Zaith, my best friend, who happened to be one of a few reporters to interview the professor after the trial. She too believed a cover-up was in play, and she knew the right way to break a story. My contract forbade me from discussing work-related issues with non- Facility personnel but Zaith had taught me when to bend the rules.

Zaith didn't know it yet, but she needed this information.

The thin black mark called to me like verrin to a dying man. Gingerly, I slid the file out from the bottom of one of the precarious stacks, past the raised base of the clear Plexiglas cabinet. Shifting through previously scanned pages, I spotted fresh ink in the middle of the folder. With Vitexid's Lakes lying so close to the Deserts' border, the professor did not want to risk losing any data stored electronically, should a pocket of charged magnetism blast through the Expanse. I never thought I would have need of the old skill of writing without a stylus and responsive screen, but here it was a daily occurrence.

Yes. This is it – he's getting closer to the truth. I scanned the new notes, committing to memory each paragraph as a separate picture and internalizing my sense of the current atmosphere as a trigger.

As the weight of Denali's words registered in my mind, I rasped air into my throat. The letters swam on the page. A convulsion shivered its way from the base of my neck down through my arms and into my fingers. The pages I held echoed my shudder.

"Holy Trinity," I whispered.

A twig snapped. I shoved the file back in place, steadying those above it, closed the protective door, and backed out of the vehicle. Taking the vial from my pocket, I held it up to the bright rays of the second sun, Beta, to better illuminate the thick pearly-orange liquid inside. Although I faced the tube, my eyes tracked the professor as he flattened more of the reeds and grasses between the current verrin sampling station and the rider.

I walked several paces back to my spot by the lake, the smallest site we'd visited during our first week out here, and set the vial on the trampled grasses. I made comparison notes between the sample and the lake before me.

I heard the crisp sound of a page turn as Denali flipped through the report I'd printed for him that morning. A grimace crawled across my face as I thought about riding to work with the professor. He was usually late, and he was always grumpy. It was so much easier to get lost in a crowd on public transport and be left to my own thoughts, than ride with a miserable old photon who wanted nothing to do with me. Owning my own rider wasn't practical. Contractors had free access to public transportation, and usually the jobs I took were within city limits.

The rider creaked as he entered the back. I sighed, shaking the tension from my shoulders. Trailing my fingers back and forth in the verrin, I created deep swirls in the viscous liquid. I hadn't realised just how thin the verrin back home was becoming. Looking at the thick, life-sustaining ripples, I leaned closer for a better view. Denali had said to check for darker, muted patches of orange.

Scanning the surface, I focused on the hazy reflection bobbing back. The natural hue of the verrin distorted my Matin heritage by washing out the bronze skin and turning my deep-red coliths a hue closer to rusty orange. There were few colith markings on my face, as was normal for most Xannians, but a particularly long thick wave extended from the right side of my chin and down the length of my neck. A shorter, thinner squiggle nestled by my left ear along my jaw line.

I marvelled at how the loose strands of black hair escaping my cap and the unique black tracings around the red coliths stood out bold and clear. *Strange how the colour black is altered so little by verrin.*

I stared at the reflection of the embossed emblem on my black hat. A light-grey inverted triangle sat beneath the outline of a dark-green circle that crossed the tips of the triangle. What caught most people's attention though was the thin, three-sided natural bolt of red lightning crashing through each side of the triangle. The red capped letters, CTF, were more a formality than a necessity. Every citizen learned to distinguish that symbol from a young age. It represented more than its slogan of Strength, Power and Unity.

As a member of the Contractor Training Facility, I represented less than one-percent of Xannians who were capable, both mentally and physically, of graduating the daunting prerequisite training in order to work for the government's most esteemed public service outlet. Held to a higher standard than most people, I still managed to fight my way through the trials at the Facility faster than anyone before me.

My mind flashed images of the pages I'd just scanned, taunting me. Don't get me wrong, I respect the code but sometimes interpreting the ethics of a situation were far greyer than I liked. Even so, I would never compromise a Contract.

I took a shallow sample of the darker patch of verrin and wiped the excess drips from the tube onto my dark-green, Facility-issue work pants. I labelled the newest sample, making sure to keep a steady hand for clear and legible letters. The professor and I collected data from various sites in and around the Expanse, with particular attention to the natural verrin lakes first discovered by the early immigrants travelling from the Ancient City. Vitexid the Waylayer was the first to map this area, and so the lakes and this region were named after him.

As Denali and I studied the local flora and fauna, we extracted verrin samples on a regular basis, not only from the main lakes but via exploratory holes, using compact boring machines to get to areas where the underground springs and rivers flowed closest to the surface. This week we were back at the third lake – the most dramatic data coming from this site.

Holding the two vials against the arm of my lab coat, I compared colour and viscosity. Lifting both tubes up to Beta, I squinted. The back door of the rider slammed shut, and the crackling of dry grasses drew nearer. Another page flipped.

I could sense what was coming by the way Denali held his body and the aura of tension clinging to him, but I tried to analyse the two tubes anyway. With so much information vying for precedence in my head, it was no surprise that I couldn't concentrate. Besides, if I didn't look at him, he might not speak to me. I could only hope.

I had learned not to converse with the professor for any reason, shy of a major revelation in the research. A guarded and fickle man, his suspicions of everyone and everything irritated me from the moment we met. He constantly hovered over me as I worked; an irritation I managed to deal with, so long as he didn't actually call my efforts into question.

Setting down the vials, I hastily wrote out my notes. Denali's double shadow crossed over me as I set down the clipboard beside my knees. I could imagine his mind buzzing as he flipped through the report. *Stay calm. Breathe.*

"Ms Jutaya," he blustered moments later. "You failed to state in this summary the development of new life forms in the surrounding soil bed."

I stood up.

"Professor Denali—"

He shook the report at me, inches from my nose. I did not flinch. Being shorter than this middle-aged man nearing his seventies, he often attempted to use his height as an intimidation tactic.

Usually, I could meditate through it, zone out. But the file with the black mark changed all that.

"I can't afford mistakes. There can be no question of authenticity. You have no idea the severity of the situation face…"

"On the bottom of page—"

"I should have known you weren't old enough…" His vocalised thought trailed to a murmur.

"Professor, if you would—"

But he wouldn't listen. He turned from me and stalked away, grumbling about the current state of the planet and the impertinence of youth today.

I frowned. I knew very well what he was up against, but he was mistaken about that report. He's mistaken about me.

Shouldering my canteen and grabbing the two vials, I followed him over to the sampling site. He'd been working to fix the machine for the past two days. We needed viable samples from the bottom of the lake – comparative samples necessary today or he stood to lose the overall results of the last week's worth of findings.

Stiff shoulders crept towards my ears, matching the tension in my fists; they throbbed as my nails dug deeper into my palms. *Calm down. Back away. Don't do anything you'll regret.*

Moments of his persistent griping about my organizational

habits slammed into my mind, his constant complaining about my age, his lack of trust toward me. Regardless of my own agenda, I would never endanger anyone or anything as important as this project. My title alone demanded respect, and he hadn't shown a nanite of confidence in me or my training. My jaw clenched as the anger of the past three weeks mingled with the return of frustrations I hadn't faced in nearly eight months.

Denali hunched over the verrin-sampling device to watch as the latest trial sample rose out of the pond. The seal appeared intact and the vial pristine. It worked. My breathing technique forgotten, my patience training now battled with a high-strung will.

Logic nipped at my neural pathways, but something deeper in my soul clawed to the surface and broke through the carefully-mortared bricks of my wall of calm. I leaned over and snatched the vial with the latest sample from the machine. This was the only way for him to listen to me. Denali bolted up and slipped on the mucky bank, temporarily submerging his left foot.

"What are you–?" he sputtered, shaking his leg.

"Now, you listen, Professor." I twirled the tube through the fingers of my free hand. "I can understand and even sympathise with your nervousness about the need for complete accuracy on this project. It doesn't surprise me that you're anxious about someone ruining your work again, but I am a Contractor."

And even though I plan to leak this information, it won't be done in a damaging way. I had to believe that – it had to be true. I gripped the oh-so-important vial in my fist. My mouth went on autopilot.

"My meticulous training to be a knowledgeable and efficient assistant and to uphold moral guidelines most commoners don't even know exist should always remain paramount in your mind. That report…" I pointed with the vial to the pocket of his lab coat, "… has extensive information about new life forms in its detailed, highlighted subheadings."

I stared the old Shimug down. The professor's breathing betrayed his waning years. He stared back at me with dark-blue coliths scrunched around haughty black eyes, stark against his grey skin. He looked like a fool. Now that the beast was free, I stopped fighting and gave over fully.

"The point of a summary is to be brief and give an overview

of the main report. I clearly mention the evidence of new life at the end of the last paragraph on page three."

"They give me a *child* to work with," he said. "They restrict me to dealing only with the CTF, and only with one assistant, and expect me to maintain perfect records for their eyes only – impossible! If I hadn't checked up on you, my notes would be a mess. Am I to believe that you are actually capable of handling the positions you're here for? The Kronik is delusional if it thinks I can make progress by triple checking a teenager's work while completing my own studies. This is preposterous."

Heat flared up the skin of my neck, warming my cheeks.

In a low voice I said, "And you never found a single error in all that time, did you *Professor*?" I spat his title at him and tossed all three verrin samples at his chest. He fumbled the catch but ended up holding the vials tight. Safe. I turned, chin up, and walked away.

Knowing my voice would carry, I didn't bother to turn around as I said, "Don't forget to text 'position legitimately terminated' when you submit my last credit statement to the Facility."

I now had a couple of miles to trek before I could catch public transport back to Darzeth-Prime. It was a dry, dusty, dirt road that meandered its way back to Vrazeth's borders, the last town before the Expanse. The breeze cooled my cheeks and my temper. *Where did that come from?* I rubbed a hand over my face as if to scrub away the memory. This wasn't how a job was supposed to end, and I certainly didn't need my superiors at the Facility judging my work ethics again.

Lately, I'd found it difficult to complete an assignment to its official contracted date. Sure, the shorter tasks were easier to finalise, but on the longer projects, something always happened.

Over twelve months ago, I worked with a local architect as Liaison and Design Interpreter with the construction crew for a new public recreation centre; he blamed me for misreading the specs, and costing the company extra in materials and supplies that hadn't been budgeted. An Ethics Committee representative agreed that I had not been mistaken but still removed me from the project because the architect claimed I was too green to realise the error between the accounted budget and the required materials.

And then, nearly eight months ago, I was *fired* from the Platinum

Hall Contract when the Site Manager refused to use me to string the lights, even though they were short-staffed and I'd been hired to fill that position. As the CTF's first graduate under the age of twenty-one, and a teenager looking younger than I actually was, these kinds of issues had never really cropped up with the Facility before. I was ready for anything, but the world, it seemed, wasn't ready for me.

The Gamma sun, smallest and palest of the three, crept above the horizon as Alpha, more commonly known by its spiritual name, Zola, squatted mid-sky, halfway through its daily cycle. I straightened the canteen around my neck, and removed my cap to let the breeze dry my sweat.

My watch-com beeped. It was the Training Facility's tone. Denali wouldn't have reported me yet and, since it was just a text, I flipped up the face of the watch-communicator.

'*New Possible Assignment*' flashed across the small grey screen. Clicking to accept the one-liner, a concise synopsis of the available work appeared. Jobs only came through my request portfolio if they didn't conflict with a current contract. I rarely got updates since my selection parameters were a little out of the ordinary – but then, so was this new job.

'*Position for a guide into the Deserts.*' The trip date and duration were listed as '*TBA*'.

"This is insane, even for me," I said, and hit the delete button. Nobody went into the Deserts voluntarily. Nobody was that irresponsible; it had to be a joke.

I tapped the screen for voice recognition. "Zaith Beji."

Since I now had the rest of the day off, I had to get a hold of Zaith. We had a lot to discuss. Tossing my cap up in the air with my other hand, I caught it on my head, jammed the bill down to shade my eyes, and kicked at a rock on the road. After the third buzz, Zaith answered.

Chapter Two
The Rally

I should have stayed in bed. Well, that's not entirely true. I'd never overslept a day in my life, so lying in bed would have been redundant. I never should have left the house. If I had just stayed home, I would have still had a contract and been working far away from here.

Shaking my head at the futility of my intensions, I scanned the mounting crowd. *I shouldn't have agreed to meet her here. We'll never be able to talk.* A steady throng of citizens streamed past, pulsing with a fever for the Cause. Moving from the parking lot to the far side of Klax Square I listened to incoherent, excited chatter bleat from the livestock of Spoken Truth followers.

Every one of these Rallies drew in from the masses a dizzying array of delusional cause-seekers. The Kronik may not be perfect, but since the New Renaissance nearly a quarter of a century ago, progress on Xannia had grown exponentially. Someone was always at odds with the status quo. Usually the rabble-rousers disbanded as quickly as they emerged – logic consistently triumphed over illusion and these people were seriously deluded. Fortunately Zaith had an excuse: she's a reporter.

Standing under a broad-leafed korelin tree a few feet from

the paved path, I tapped a finger on my folded arms. Absently, I traced the thin black outline around the colith on my forearm. Small leccers, a type of gliding rodent, scurried in the distance – a far preferable sight to watching grown Xannians do the same for the best view of the Rally stage. I glanced at my watch-com a third time – *late again. Why did I agree to come? I should've said I was busy and I'd see her after the Rally.* But I'd been the one to call her.

I clenched my teeth. This morning's events still rankled. *I have to talk to Zaith.* The Ethics Committee was bound to hold me accountable for the dismissal if Denali didn't adhere to the amendment in our contract. If the professor had just let me do my job I'd still be on the inside gathering information – I'd still have a chance to verify the truth – *but no, I'm here instead, waiting to break inconclusive data to a reporter focused on a wholly different story.*

The deliberate click of heels against the path cleared my mind. A grin tugged at my lips; I turned to face my friend, Zaith, the one person attending this Rally unprepared to walk on soft grass.

"What's with the shoes and the hair," I asked, tugging on Zaith's bright-red locks. "If I wanted to blind myself I'd stare directly at the suns."

"Ha, ha." Zaith pushed my hand away and pointed. "You're just jealous." She winked. "The heels are an important fashion statement to help emphasise the hair. It's the latest in treatments, the first 'Vivid-Shimmer Red' this side of the Prime," she said, running her fingers through the mass of curls highlighting her ebony face, mischievous eyes, and jade coliths.

Grabbing my arm, Zaith led me across the lawn toward the Rally stage, mindful to walk on her toes. Her black utility bag was the only sign that she meant business.

We couldn't have been more opposite. My own thick black hair, natural to all Xannians, was plaited and coiled up on my head to keep it out of the way. Though it was often a hindrance with my work, I couldn't bear to part with it. Zaith imbued fashion's essence, and as a lead reporter for *National News Now*, hers was a presence never forgotten – even at the risk of sinking her expensive heels into soft turf.

Zaith's firm grip on my arm matched her determined tip-toe walk. I needed to talk to her about the professor, but the size of the crowd gave us no privacy. I had to push thoughts of that morning aside.

Zaith asked me here for another reason; now was obviously not the time for revelations or distractions.

"Your meeting with Toufin was short. I thought you didn't have time to cover this Rally," I said.

Zaith's eyes narrowed. "He rescheduled for tomorrow; something about needing to stay at the workshop an extra day. Extended analysis. This is more important. I would've found a way to be here, no matter what."

"*Extended analysis?* I might have believed that if it he hadn't said it—"

"That's ancient history, Taya. He's been nothing but professional – at least toward me," she said, laughing.

Zaith pulled a View-X, a portable recording device, from her shoulder bag and flipped through a small book of notes. We approached the rear of the mass of people crowding the stage, the vast majority clumped in the natural amphitheatre bowl of the terrain. Someone in tan fatigues walked up to the microphone and removed his jacket. The suns were unusually warm for late spring. The top of my head burned slightly in want of my usual CTF work cap. I'd left it at home, when I'd changed before meeting Zaith.

I'd watched my new friend get herself hooked on the whole Spoken Truth concept over the past few months. The notion that history repeated itself was not inventive, but the Speakers took specific documents from the past to theoretically show their relevance and impact on the present. Most of the documents were centuries old. All of the Speakers stretched the smallest similarities so grossly out of proportion; it was obvious that they were drawing irrelevant connections. *Obvious to me anyway.*

Zaith got so caught up in the idea that our past could have a direct influence on our future that she managed to convince the Assignment Department at her Network to produce a month-long special on the topic. Today would be fodder for her second report. I'd gone to a few of the Rallies with Zaith before her legitimization. She liked to drag me to them because of the questions I dared to ask.

The crowd was always the same, even if the people were different. They would gawk at someone pretending to know more than us, relying on evidence that should have stayed between the pages of history books. People will always disagree with the advancements made since the inception of the New Renaissance, but these Speakers were clearly extremists. If I didn't point out the flaws in their reasoning and the illogical comparisons, innocent people would blindly follow nothing but pomp and circumstance.

At all the Rallies Zaith brought me to, she deemed the reps unreliable. Anyone could poke holes in their theories; I just happened to be the only one who would.

"So, why are we here to see this one? I thought you were convinced the Speaker at the last Rally knew exactly what she was talking about. How could anyone else compare?" I asked, as Zaith put a fresh chip into her View-X.

"That Speaker did, for a Metek." One of the nine races of Xannia, the Metek Speaker had touted dark-green skin and bold gold coliths when I'd watched the excerpt on the news two weeks earlier. "But anyone who is anyone knows that only Talians could ever know the real truth. They are our society's founders after all," Zaith said.

"And that makes them better than the rest of us?"

"Not better, Ms Cynical. Just more likely to know."

"Superstitious nonsense." I kicked at a fallen nut. It didn't get far. The grass here was tall, thick and luxurious. The invigorating scent of nature wafted from crushed and broken blades as more people arrived. I couldn't believe how busy the Square was.

"Who is this guy? He's important, right? Or is he just some idiot banking on the status of his race?"

Zaith narrowed her eyes at me, irked. "He's the son of the seventh Council Advisor."

No wonder Zaith had said she wouldn't have missed today's Rally. She must have gotten an insider tip.

So, he was a potential candidate for Kronik after his father retired; a big-shot's kid, most likely with an overdeveloped sense of self-importance. *The Kronik cannot be happy about this.* The numbers continued to double every few minutes. There were close to five-hundred people waiting to listen to his version of the Truth; Zaith attributed the influx of attendees to the Speaker. I concurred with her assessment, but for different reasons.

The Talians founded all known civilization and instituted an elite hierarchy, leading to the current governmental structure. However, this fact alone did not elevate them, as it did according to Zaith's theory, to be more 'likely to know' the future, and therefore to attract a greater crowd. If anything, the influx of people in the Square was due to the Speaker's instant celebrity status. Talians were rarely seen in public if at all by the common citizens. *People are inherently curious.*

Zaith and I stood at the back of the crowd on the crest of the natural amphitheatre. It gave her the room she needed to record the event without the fear of being jostled, or having to edit out unwanted chatter. The space between the heads in front of us left ample room to watch the spectacle. With my general sight being tested by the Facility as 'beyond exceptional', watching from this distance didn't bother me one bit. I could see several bystanders squinting and caught mumbled complaints about 'not having arrived early enough'.

I blocked out the noise of the collective hum of voices and concentrated on the Talian in front of the microphone. His back faced the crowd as he spoke with a technician. Standing tall, his hands moved with purpose. So many of the past Speakers would close in on themselves, and try to disappear behind the microphone. People like that were afraid. Anyone attending these Rallies should be afraid.

The Kronik had a history of dealing with rabble-rousers. I was surprised this Cause was still active. *Maybe it's so farfetched it's not even showing up on the radar.* Twenty-two years ago, a group of rebels were sentenced to sail the Nine Seas of Darius. It was only a matter of time before these Truth Seekers met a similar fate, if there was any credence to their ravings. *They do say history repeats itself.*

"Are you ready?" I asked.

"Yeah," Zaith said. "Just a couple more adjustments, then I'll be able to zoom in for the best frame."

I waited for the Speaker to face the crowd. Like everyone there, I had never seen a Talian before, except on the wire. All Talians lived behind a massive stone wall in the Compound. They were a society of recluses.

Slowly turning, the Talian addressed the crowd. The motor on Zaith's View-X whispered as she zoomed in for the shot of a lifetime. A Talian hadn't been seen in public since the Kronik's brief appearance at the docks when he sentenced the rebels all those years ago. Before that, it was at the Transfer of Succession after the death of the previous Kronik. I glanced around. No other news crews were in the area. *One of her sources definitely leaked the information.*

Those parts of his body that could be seen, around his blue short- sleeve shirt and tan pants, glistened silvery-white. His wavy coliths, not more than a bold black outline, mirrored his equally wavy hair. As my eyes adjusted and worked similarly to Zaith's zoom button, what I found most surprising were his grey eyes – a clear genetic anomaly. Every other race on Xannia touted coal-black eyes from birth.

Zaith's breath rasped. Her hormones were likely in overdrive again. I didn't respond. Instead, I focused on the sound of his voice, slowly tuning in to the words he spoke.

"The signs are everywhere. We have to act fast. The legends of old are key to understanding how we, the people of Xannia, can stop the destruction of our planet. The increased occurrences and severity of the quakes are evidence of the degradation our already-fragile planet faces.

"Think about the simplicity of life. Ask yourself why crime is at an all-time low and question the plausibility behind how there is a job for everyone, and everyone has a job. Consider the ill events of days past, for they will unlock the knowledge that lies dormant within you. The Kronik cannot be trusted, and they are using the New Renaissance to blind you to the Truth." He paced the stage with the microphone, holding eye contact with the crowd.

"What do you remember of the seasons when you were a child, or the state of the ground that we walk upon? A ground that has continued to shake and rumble with increasing unrest at the lack of attention the Kronik has given this pertinent issue.

"Within the folds of time and passing of our culture as outlined by the Ancients…"

I hummed to distract my brain. Clenching and unclenching my fists, I tried to focus on the sting of my nails digging into the palm of my hands. *Walk away. Just walk away. Better yet – bite your tongue and leave well enough alone.* But his words overpowered my physical deterrents. I knew where he was going with this – but then again my schooling was more thorough than most.

I gave in to my voice, "The Chronicles you allude to were supposedly lost in the Deserts long ago."

Zaith stabbed a heel into my shoe.

They were reinforced with steel; all my shoes were, but she didn't need to know that. I could see him, but the mass of bodies between us made it difficult for him to spot me. He searched the crowd, looking for my voice.

Approaching the edge of the stage, he squinted. Shrugging, he continued, "The Ancient Tablets will illuminate the path to the Chronicles. After studying the Sacred Scrolls, the Journal of Migration, and…"

Oh no. The Job Alert I received that morning had not been a mistake. *I need to show these people his insanity before he seduces them with his theories and promises.*

"How do you propose retrieving the Chronicles, supposing they are not merely rumour? And once you find them, how do you intend to read them?"

Hushed comments spilled forth and then dissipated. The spectators cleared a long, thin path from the platform to the back of the crowd where I stood, giving the Talian a better view of me.

"What in Zita's name are you doing?" Zaith hardly moved her lips, never once taking her eye from the View-X.

He said nothing as I stood there, staring right at him. I was not afraid to confront a Talian; not ashamed to meet one eye-to-eye as the crowd kept their heads bowed slightly in reverence. I respected the Kronik, not because they were Talian, but because they ruled for the betterment of the people. I could separate my commitment to my government from the worship of a false prophet.

Zaith bit her lower lip. We had an arrangement: I was never an official source for her stories. But I couldn't keep my mouth shut. The theories Professor Denali was so close to proving kept ricocheting around in my head. History and some ancient supposed chronicles were not going to solve this problem.

The Talian countered with a fierce passion lacing his every word.

"Clues were left behind on the Ancient Tablets preserved in the Museum of Darius. We need to study them, analyse them, and form a band of Kahn-lea. With the information we gather, we'll take to the Deserts and retrieve the Chronicles. Legend states that the 'pure one' upon finding them, will be granted the sight of old."

Something clicked in the back of my mind: *Legends – not facts. There is no substance here.* "Bedtime stories, dreams and fantasies are all that's left of the truth behind the Ancient Tablets and Chronicles. No one could ever know if what they risked their lives for was real, or if they were even looking in the right area of the Deserts.

There's no need for all this blather about your Spoken Truth." Chatter rose among the audience.

"Who is she?"

"Why is she challenging the Talian?"

"Is she right?"

"Why doesn't she believe?"

The Talian held up his hand for silence, never once breaking eye contact with me.

"We will never know when we'll face the end of our existence. We'd be fools if we did nothing and died because of it. The Kronik, the supposed men of my race, continue to flounder, hide, and avoid the problem. It's our turn now. This is a time for believers and doers."

The crowd agreed with him, dismissing me entirely. They refilled the space between us. My skin pricked cold. My spine tingled and itched.

This was not over.

The Kronik may not be handling this problem publicly, but they have been dealing with life and death issues since the Great Migration over two thousand years ago.

He has no idea of the damage he'll cause – the death sentence for anyone involved. And they believe him! Didn't they hear him? He said 'take to the Deserts!' He has to be stopped.

My body vibrated with fury. His disregard for the sanctity of life shattered my common sense. I couldn't let these people be led to the slaughter.

As he spoke about the forming of a legion of Kahn-lea, the ancient term coined for a band of citizens dubbed *'Explorers of Fate'*, I opened my belt-pack and retrieved my Clinex. The small, round, reflective weapon emitted plasma bursts to a range of three hundred yards. It would get the job done. Though it was a CTF-issued weapon, it was compact and discrete. No one would see it coming, no one but Zaith would know it was mine.

Zaith, oblivious to my actions, continued to carefully record the first sighting of a Talian in public since before the two of us were born.

Grasping the Clinex in my left hand, I closed my eyes. I took a deep breath to steady my nerves. Then, stepping back, I opened my eyes again and took aim.

Chapter Three
CTF

The door closed on the public hover transport as I dropped onto the plush bench by the window. Leaning back, I looked outside as the lulling whirr of the fans gracefully lifted the long vehicle. Greasy forehead impressions smeared across the pane prevented me from being distracted by the flowering wall of bushes along the far side of Klax Square.

Rummaging through my belt-pack around my waist, I pushed the Clinex to the bottom. As I searched, my mind tumbled back to the Rally.

Shaking my head to dislodge the brilliant flash of light from my mind's eye, I dug past a compact magnifying glass, clear bags of landscape samples I forgot to leave with the professor, and the vivid red lip-colour Zaith gave me last Ageing Day. Not that I ever wore it.

Jammed under the Clinex at the bottom, my fingers found a wad of tissues and a package of anti-bacterial wipes. Tearing open the package, I furiously rubbed the grimy windowpane, oblivious to the other passengers. But the task only proved mundane enough to bring me back again to that moment at the stage...

A blast of round blue-white flame arched from the small spherical weapon, incinerating the tree limb next to the Talian's head.

The crowd dropped. Only the twitter of birds and the murmur of Zaith's View-X persisted.

The Talian remained standing, unfazed.

I slowly lowered my arm and raised my voice, "That could have been one of many things: an assassination attempt, an electrical storm, or the end of the world. Any way you look at it, you could have been killed and there was nothing you could have done to save yourself.

The same goes for this hopeless mission you're trying to conduct. Why waste valuable time, when all these people could be enjoying life; be it for the next ten minutes or the next ten millennia." I slipped the Clinex away and turned, quickly leaving Zaith and an astonished crowd to recover…

Sighing, I lifted the latch of the small receptacle in the floor and discarded my wipes. Finally able to see out the window, I crossed my legs, folded my arms and leaned my shoulder against the glass.

I visualised the stage and mentally scanned the perimeter – no Justices, no bodyguards, and no one I knew. Except Zaith. I could only hope for a miracle with her editing skills to avoid incarceration. Idiot! *What were you thinking? You weren't and that's the problem.*

Building after building flashed by, a dizzying array of coloured glass, tinted concrete, and reflective metal alloys. The industrial regions of Darzeth-Prime were anything but bland. I tried to lose myself in the blur of metallic hues as the transport brought me closer to the central core of the city. I caught sight of the time on my watch-com in the window's reflection.

Time – I'd become impatient with the professor this morning, acted totally irrationally at the Rally – I couldn't understand it. I was failing my training. *I'll have to risk going to the CTF instead of home.* Jadis, my pet lynx, wouldn't expect me until later anyway – then I could take her for a run along the trails. I shifted, crossing my legs in the opposite direction. I could only hope word had not yet reached the Facility about my day.

The transport inched to a stop at the city's most famed depot. The green-tinted, glass-encased structure was a landmark: one of the oldest surviving buildings from before the quakes. The public transport's automatic double doors whisked closed as the last passenger boarded.

An older Shimug bumped into several people before tapping the back of his pale-grey hand. A blue fan-like beam splayed out from the top of his wrist echoing the deep-navy of his coliths. Waving it slightly to and fro, he walked with greater confidence. I noticed the opaque, white film clouding his eyes. Astounded at the advancements in technology for the blind, I couldn't help but study him for the rest of the ride.

At my stop, the transport rolled away as I walked toward the Contractor Training Facility. The structure stood out as an absence of light, a black hole surrounded by *pretty things*; trees flourished on the corner where it stood, and brilliantly-coloured buildings surrounded it across all lanes of traffic. The charcoal-grey mirrored glass of the inverted pyramid-like structure sat framed in chrome and black polished granite. The walls of the Facility angled away from the standard design. It was done gradually and gracefully as the architect planned each floor with a hundred square feet more space than the one below it.

The public was not permitted past the high, broad, main entrance without a rarely granted appointment, or the intention of remaining for several years.

Walking past the fifteen-foot high, black wrought-iron emblem symbolic of the Facility, my eyes followed the flow of the metal. Pride swelled in my heart. I had sacrificed my childhood to get this far on my own, to finally be in control of my destiny and my life.

From a young age, all Xannians knew to revere and respect the CTF emblem and the company's slogan of *'Strength, Power, and Unity.'* For me, at fifteen years old, it brought stasis and power. Now, at nineteen, it simply meant home.

Climbing the sweeping steps of the walkway, I veered away from the main entrance and had my irises scanned at the decoder screen next to the employee access. The door was made of the same material as the rest of the building, and blended into the façade as it slid into the wall.

The inner corridor surrounded me with two-way mirrors. The ones on my left looked in at the main reception area; the ones on my right reflected my furrowed brows and staring eyes. That mirror watched the corridor.

Turning at the end of the hall, I headed toward the central bank of elevators. Three sets of large chrome doors stood silent as sentinels near the centre of the building. I approached the closest pair and placed my palm on the reader. In the accept/admit column, floors one through eight lit up, 'R' for the roof access to track and field, and the ground floor blinked 'L' for Lobby. I smiled, remembering how important it was to make that last climb between the seventh and eighth floors. To have that symbol appear on my access grid meant I had endured – I was among the elite. *But only the Facility recognises it. Everyone else just sees some kid playing dress-up.*

I should check in with Niless in the Contracts Department, tell her... tell her what? No, not right now. There'd be plenty of time for that later. Besides, Niless' desk sat opposite the Master Keeper's office – no sense in being the metal rod for his lightening strike. I pressed the smooth screen for the first floor.

Each level focused on a particular theme to guide learning. One side of each level was devoted to the gymnasium and the other half was split to support scholastic studies and the dorms. The first floor gym, Focus, was dedicated to maintaining concentration for extended periods of time during physical duress for complete mental readiness. This was exactly what I needed to reinstate calm and patience, and to clear my mind.

During class, learning about math and science and using their algorithms for consistency, helped me find my mental zone of calm far better than reading and analyzing poetry. Don't get me wrong, I enjoyed all aspects of my learning, but I couldn't always find a practical use for everything in my daily life. Math and physics had clear variables, answers were right or wrong. Those were outcomes I could readily understand, anticipate, and control.

The chrome doors wisped open and I exited into an anti-chamber with three black doors, one on each wall. The centre door was the Observation Room, for building staff and special visitors. Families often felt detached from their children during the course of training. Though I had taken only two and half years to progress, the average stint lasted between three and five.

The Facility found that parents and guardians needed to keep in contact with their children – to observe them. Mind you, the reverse was never permitted until seventh-level graduation. It was a rule that served more often as a breaking point for new trainees than the physical and mental challenges of the levels; a problem that never once occurred with me, having no family to hold me back. Abandoned at the age of eight, I learned overnight who I could trust and how to survive.

I walked through the door marked 'women,' found my locker, and changed to work out. As I removed my watch-com, it beeped. I flipped up the display screen – *Zaith*. I left the call unanswered.

Explanations would have to wait, I needed to straighten myself out that much was obvious. I snapped the face shut.

Eyeing the room where I'd spent the least number of months training, I considered the relevance to my current predicament. Maybe that's why I had become so impatient today. After all, it had been four years since my instruction on this level, and that two-month stint seemed so insignificant now. Meditative stretching accompanied me every day thorough every level of my training but no one tested me on it after Level 1.

I stepped onto the dark-blue warm-up mats, the two-way observation mirrors, locker, study, and bunk rooms behind me, the two-story gymnasium ahead. I stretched my arms over my head, pressing on first one elbow then the other as I rocked from side-to-side in a deep knee bend. Gently leaning to the right then the left, I held the stretch. Standing, I arched slowly backwards into a bridge and touched the floor with my hands.

I saw the attachments, weights, counter weights, knotted rope ends and connections that littered the ceiling and upper walls. Floor space was crucial when training, so most of the extensive work was done suspended in the air. Sparse sections of loose netting were available to catch those trainees who were thrown off guard.

I flipped my feet over my head, landing in an upright position. My earlier frustrations bled into the floor with the firm landing.

Being there felt right. I needed to focus on a physical activity first. Jogging over to the far side of the room, I climbed about ten feet into the air on a ladder of rounded metal bars, similar to those found on a child's outdoor play set. The skin on my palms tightened over the cool steel. These climbing bars were not for children. This course was intended to teach personal pacing and awareness of the needs of the body. My only concern would be finishing. It would force me to judge the passage of time based on the internal rhythms of my own body.

I looked at my hands. The calluses and creases attested to the rough work I had endured. At fifteen, working in the mines had hardened the flesh along my index finger and thumb but that had been repetitive, mindless labour. While my hands had been anything but soft, they were inarticulate and unresponsive. The vocabulary of labour now written across my palms was far more intelligent and capable. Still, it had been years since I'd practiced. I was taller and heavier. The outcome was an unknown – assuming anything at this point could be disastrous.

I peppered my palms with the chalk pouch. Scanning my thumb, I launched into the gruelling task, hauling my body through the air hand-over-hand. Immediately, the rotator cuffs in my shoulders tensed against the weight of my suspended form. Launching my torso forward and up with every swing of my arm, I calculated my approach for the sharp twist ahead. Knowing the bars would level out after the incline, I maintained a rigorous pace.

At the levelling, I dropped my speed by half and loped one arm after the other, extending my reach for every second bar. A loose damp hair niggled the side of my nose. I brushed at it with my passing bicep, but it continued to fall back in my way. It was too moist to blow off my face and besides, I needed to keep my breathing focused and even – I had to ignore the damn thing to finish on time. More hairs joined the first. Briefly closing my eyes, the next three stages of the course appeared in my mind.

As I reached the halfway marker on a steep downturn, my sweaty palms slipped on the metal bars. Stopping, suspended in mid-air, I wiped one hand and then the other on the legs of my shorts. Twice more I nearly lost my grip. *Blast it!* The strength in my hands was not a factor to my possible demise; it was the stress of my body weight on my shoulder joints. One-hundred and thirty pounds was getting harder and harder to haul around these days.

Too often, I stopped to wipe my hands. I couldn't afford to rest, though. If I did, I wouldn't be permitted to leave without first perfecting the task. I had to be within one minute of my previous score. My internal clock was at odds with reality as the seconds dragged into minutes. The joints in my fingers burned even as they slipped with increasing moisture. The only good thing was that the professor, the Rally, the Talian dropped from my mind with each bead of sweat. I set my focus to the next bend, the next curve, and the next incline.

As my left hand gripped the last bar, I swung my right arm under, punching the finishing pad with my thumb. A single bell jingled briefly. I clung to the vertical ladder, wrapping my arms and legs around the cool rungs. Still ten feet above the floor, I slid down the rails and sat at the base with my back against the bars. I took a moment to massage my neck before looking up.

One of the instructors pointed at me as he spoke with a group of trainees. The mixed crowd of new recruits stared at me, open-mouthed. I smiled wanly. A small chuckle escaped. Wiping my forehead with the back of my hand, still frozen in a claw grip, I brushed damp hair away from my face and stood up. Walking over to the time- meter, I checked my score. I'd heard the bell. If I hadn't, I'd be worried; it meant I scored within the top ten.

Second place – sixth was my previous record. But it felt like forever since I started the climb.

"One below the Master Keeper," I whispered. I held a place of honour now. No one ever placed better than the Master Keeper, which meant that I ranked first among my peers. I couldn't believe it. Rumour had it the Master Keeper had perfected every challenge, on all levels, without even breaking a sweat. *There must be a glitch in the system.*

I took a long drink from the fountain beside the time-meter. The light-orange liquid soothed my dry lips; verrin never tasted so good. I thought back to Vitexid's Lakes by the Expanse. The professor's work on the quality of the verrin outside civilization showed just how weak this life-sustaining liquid was becoming.

Maybe I should have said something to Zaith at the Rally... No. I made the right call. My information was vital, but the Square had been too exposed. Besides, Zaith needed to concentrate on her current assignment. I shook my head, unable to keep the morning's events at bay. Wiping my face on an available towel, I contemplated how best to use my remaining time.

Stepping from the elevator after my workout, I walked down the mirrored employee-hall toward the door. I had to return Zaith's call from earlier. The mess at the Rally needed addressing – fixing. Too bad there wasn't a training level that specifically focused on eliminating stupidity. *Zola knows, I need it.* Emotional restraint was touched on during my time on Level 7, but I never considered it an issue until after graduation. I fingered the edge of my watch- com, waiting until I got outside to make the call. I didn't want to be seen lingering by any ranking officials.

A flash of red caught my eye. I turned to look through the two-way mirror lining the employee access hall into the foyer beyond.

"What are you doing here?"

Chapter Four
Tides Turn

Backtracking up the hall to the elevators, I rounded the corner to the civilian entrance. Zaith leaned against the side of the front desk, her curly red hair falling close to Levin's face. He did his best to keep her occupied. This was unprecedented. Reporters were not granted access to the building – and for good reason.

"What in Zerameteth's name are you doing? Attempting to cause a major breech flirting with the office staff?"

"As a matter of fact…" Zaith stood tall, holding a visitor's badge encircling her neck. "I was just returning this." Drawing the badge over her head, she swung her lavish curls past Levin one last time before returning the ID.

"Here you go, Honey." She kissed the plastic laminated holder with her deep-purple lips, leaving a perfect impression behind. Tossing the badge to the desk, she wiggled her fingers at him then looped arms with me.

"I was just saying my goodbyes to that unfortunate soul," she said wistfully, straightening her revealing lavender business suit with a free hand.

"Oh? And why's that?"

"He'll never be able to taste Bullooberry Passion personally."

"Zaith, Levin's engaged with a Life Bond. You didn't stand a chance." I turned and aimed her at the doors to leave.

"Why must you always interfere with any attempt I make to spice up life? I saw the cherry tattoo in the crook of his thumb. It was so small anyone could have missed it; anyway, I thought I'd test his willpower a little."

"Someone ought to test the amount of Thyafeen in your veins."

We exited CTF through the main entrance. Zaith snatched back her arm and gave me a shove. I stumbled sideways. I was not in the mood. Bending to steady myself, I scowled at my knee, took a breath and forced a laugh before joining her again. *She doesn't know about this morning. Relax.*

Six months after graduation, I grew tired of the boring mandatory probationary assignments. The moment I could flex my muscles a little, I did. My first adventurous assignment took me to Network News Now as a Max-X technician for Zaith. With Zaith's more portable View-X in for repairs, she had needed a grunt to handle her equipment. She'd never once mentioned how young I looked, though there were easily five years between us. The way she spoke to me made me feel like we'd known each other forever. News about the professor and the incident at the Rally would have to wait, again.

Why I'd found her loitering in the lobby was a more pressing matter at the moment.

"So, what's with the access badge?" I asked.

"Let's talk on the way to the Solar Plex. A lot has happened since lunch."

"All right." I changed the subject, still mulling over how Zaith could have gotten inside the building. "What are you driving this month?" I scanned the street parking.

"The blue rider – over there." Zaith pointed.

"You don't know the make of the rider you're driving, yet you can identify any shade of lip-colour on the market."

"As long as it's new and it runs, I'm perfectly happy." We reached the rider.

I ran my fingertips over the glittering metallic-blue fibreglass hood and up along the frame by the windshield. "It's a Zaphernnin Seven, these are just as current as your hair-do," I said.

Zaith unlocked the doors with her remote. The hydraulics lifted the body another foot from the ground for easier accessibility. This rider was built for two passengers and sat approximately three inches from the road when in neutral-hover.

I slid into the formfitting seat, recalling the wire-commercial about it; there was a built-in sensor that scanned the way ahead, compensating for the transport's height according to the lay of the land. I found it particularly interesting that the spokesman claimed it rarely adjusted itself in the city, due to quality road surfaces. Shutting the doors, it dropped back down, resuming neutral. Zaith placed her thumb on the ID panel, starting the electric motors with a quiet hum.

"We should figure out what to watch at the theatre, what we haven't seen in a while. Maybe a nice thriller or war flick with a lot of guns and shooting," she growled, pulling away from the curb.

"Let me guess," I said, trying to make light of my earlier irresponsibility. "You're still mad at me for trying to kill your Talian, and you're going to make me pay for ruining your report?"

"I know how much you love to be on the wire, Taya," Zaith teased. "But I edited that part out. Well, I edited you out of that part. No, when I went back to the station to finalise my material for tonight's program, Toufin showed up."

"Oh, really? A repeat of past scandalous behaviour?"

Zaith nodded. "Let's just say it started with Tazarian orchids and ended with a bloody nose – not mine."

"Hey, speaking of being caught, why were you returning a visitor's badge at CTF? There's a strict policy and you're not part of it." I turned to face her as she drove.

"I'd been in the viewing room on Level 1. By the way…" Zaith hit auto-drive and flashed me her 'aren't I charming' smile. "What were you doing in the last ten minutes of your workout in there? You looked like a statue. Not nearly as challenging as the android duel with the big sticks was after that climb you did."

I blinked rapidly. *Today's Workout? The Light Image Loading exercise – What? How did Zaith get into a viewing room?*

Zaith absorbed the change in my eyes and stiffening posture.

"Don't freak!" She held up her hands in surrender. I sat up and folded my arms across my chest. A visitor's badge was bad enough but access to a viewing room was unheard of.

"It's all good," Zaith tried again. "You know I've been hounding the Training Facility for years to let me document their recruitment practices, training procedures and what not – I finally worked things out with the Higher-Ups." She brushed the curls from her eyes, letting them widen and soften. I had seen her use this technique on unsuspecting interviewees. I wasn't buying it.

Zaith tilted her head and smiled, trying to judge my response. She continued, "When Touf arrived at the station, early or late or what have you, without any of his papers and carrying a bundle of orchids behind his back, I shut the door in his face and took the extra time to finalise things with Niless, my liaison at the CTF. So you see, part of my privileges allows me to view new recruits, supervised at all times of course. I thought I'd take a quick peek at Level 1. I tried to call you to see if you wanted to meet me there – so you could apologise over the Rally incident and all but your com went straight to voicemail."

I pictured the openly astonished faces of the trainees as I broke my record on the bars. It was an incredible step for the Facility to allow an outsider, let alone a reporter, to enter the premises so nonchalantly. The last time Zaith mentioned this was right after we met. True, it was a project she'd been working on for years without success but Zaith hadn't mentioned it since. I looked her in the eyes. Blue contacts stared back. It felt wrong.

"Huh, that's quite the feat," I said. We rode in silence for a few minutes, neither of us looking at the other.

"So then, how is standing stark still supposed to be challenging?" Zaith asked at last.

"I'll only talk off the record, until I see that agreement of yours. You being in the Facility is beyond huge."

Zaith feigned shock and dramatically pointed to herself, mouthing 'me?' "Of course, Taya. Have no fears, the *contract* of our friendship means more to me than any other."

"I'll hold you to that." I tried to shrug off my concern. There was no one I trusted more than Zaith. "I don't know if you had a chance to take a good look around or not, but I was standing on a rubberised platform. The bottom is covered in tiny sensors that detect the smallest shift in weight." I dropped my voice low.

"Directly above, a leather sac hung suspended over my head. Filled with sand, it weighed half my body mass." I leaned closer to Zaith, enjoying the ability to speak freely about the Facility.

"If I'd shifted, twitched, or moved an inch within my time limit, that sand bag would have squashed me before I took a breath. The trick is sustaining absolute immobility."

I sat back in my seat. Zaith stared wide-eyed at the road ahead. "You're certifiably insane, you know that?" She flashed a mischievous grin, and pulled into the parking bay at the Plexis, the local name for the Solar Plex Theatre.

The Plexis was a long, low, many-winged modern structure in the entertainment district, just beyond the industrial complex. From above, it looked like a child's drawing of half a sun. The warped blue mirrors covering the building created a distorted sky effect. No discernible breaks or creases marred the glass.

A large plaque mounted on a crystalline water fountain boasted that a famous architect had won an award for its construction a decade earlier. The walkway leading up to, and surrounding, the Plexis was made from crushed quartz and amethysts set in concrete, creating large, wave- like swirls on the ground. It held a soft glitter most of the day and on clear evenings.

Zaith stepped from the rider to join me in the lot. "So, you left work early today to meet me at the Rally."

"At your insistent request, as I recall."

"Yes, and I also remember we didn't get a chance to discuss *why* you left work. Was this another unforeseen extended leave of absence?"

"Yeah, that would be an appropriate summation."

"Oh, Taya. Not again? What's going on?" She paused. "Does the Facility know?"

"I don't think so, not yet. This isn't a trend I like either. I feel bad about walking away from this one. Niless kept it on the back burner for me for two days while I finished my last position." I hesitated. Somehow Zaith's sudden appearance at the Facility made my urgency to share disappear.

"And?"

"Give me a minute to sort out my thoughts. There's only so much I can tell you without getting myself into trouble."

"I know," she sighed, as the automated doors swept silently to one side.

Early in our friendship, I found a loophole in my contract with the Facility that allowed me to talk to a therapist or close family member to relieve stress. Since I don't have a family, I argued Zaith was like a sister to me. I had to be careful, though. The Senior Council's Board of Ethics showed considerable concern for my 'loose' interpretation of the rules.

We approached an automated teller machine. Zaith moved in front of the sensor and the small screen lifted up from an access panel on the floor. It flashed blue with a number of icons.

"Over the last three weeks, I've managed to piece together an approximation of Professor Denali's theory, among other things." Zaith dropped her hands from the screen. She stared at me.

I pointed to the monitor.

"Keep talking," Zaith said, scanning her credit chip.

"I've got details about his research, and I managed to rifle through his files."

"Are you telling me you got a position working with the *professor*? And you walked away? You're insane, Taya!"

Two small, green micro- disks fell from a metal tube into a plastic catch basin. Snatching them up, Zaith grabbed my arm and dragged me down one of the wings of the Plexis, away from the open circular games room and Skylight Buffet food atrium.

Zaith found a secluded corner. Scanning the area, she pulled me into an alcove.

"Now," she whispered. "Tell me everything you can."

Heat bit at my cheeks. My heartbeat doubled. I lowered my voice. "Over the last three weeks, Professor Denali and I spent the majority of our time in the outer regions of the Expanse, analysing and collecting verrin and plant samples."

I glanced over my shoulder. This was tantamount to top-secret information. I had to be careful. "He's concerned about the water saturation of the verrin and its resulting desalination – how this is affecting life in the nearby ecosystems. He's extremely nervous about the whole project."

"How long has he been working on this?"

"Maybe a couple of weeks alone in the field and then a few more with me. It's the same research he went to trial for."

"Sister Zita! What did you see?"

"Well, the equipment he has is of better quality than he used with the Institute. That, coupled with his jittery behaviour, made me wonder who was backing his research, since it was reported that the trial left him bankrupt, and no one would associate with him."

"Did you find out who was supporting him?"

"Yes. He slipped up. But you can't rely on anything I say here." Zaith waved at me to continue. "The Kronik told him to hire one Contractor for three skilled technicians – not that he believed I was capable of anything without a chaperone," I grumbled.

"The fewer people involved the better," she mused. "It makes sense if they don't want to alert anyone about his suspicions. You mentioned something about his theory."

"Yes. I couldn't get much about the conspiracy he claimed destroyed his previous work, but I understand why no one wanted to believe him, why it was all hushed up." *Why what some Talian says about the past has no relevance on our future.*

"And…" Zaith held her breath.

A door opened. I stopped breathing. A theatre patroller walked past us into the next room.

I exhaled. "We shouldn't be doing this here. Not now. I know it's important but we're supposed to be relaxing – getting our minds off work and what happened this morning. I can tell you late–"

"Taya!" Zaith grabbed my shoulders.

Time for the end of the world.

"Okay. The verrin samples show a minute increase in temperature.

Also, the molecular density of the verrin is markedly altered. There's definitely a lot more water or a lot less verrin in the outer lakes compared to the standard chemical balance and fortified swill they give us here.

"I heard Denali muttering to himself about the increase in

seismic activity over the last five years. I think, he thinks there's a crack widening in the outer crust. He's working to prove this fault line is close enough to the lakes to cause the verrin to warm gradually, slowly altering its chemical makeup. The early results are staggering."

Zaith remained quiet for a moment, her eyes wide and calculating.

"Meaning?"

Chapter Five

What Began As A Pebble...

Meaning–" I broke off. The patroller left our wing of the building. We were too public here. I exhaled deeply, grabbed Zaith's arm and pulled her into our theatre.

Eyes quickly adjusting to the dim light, I rapidly calculated the best place to sit; based on the number of people, the number of seats, and the general grouping patterns of the patrons – the far back corner would work. The overstuffed high-backed armchairs would help muffle our conversation.

We shimmied down the aisle closest to the door and turned our bodies to sit facing each other. Leaning forward, we touched foreheads. Now we wouldn't be overheard.

"Meaning," I whispered, "if his geological calculations are correct, the heated fissures near the natural sources of verrin are destabilizing it. The stronger and more frequent the quakes, the more the crust widens and eventually it will become irreversible – soon there may be no natural sources of verrin."

"No, that's not possible." Zaith shook her head, unable to fathom the very near reality of doomsday. "We need... our survival depends–"

Zaith choked. Her face blanched, making her black skin a dark ghost-grey. She grabbed my arms and opened her mouth – no sound. She shut it sharply. A group of teens entered the theatre.

"*You* think, *he* thinks–" Zaith began. I nodded.

"So you don't know for sure?"

I shook my head. "I wasn't about to come out and interrogate the man. As it is, he nearly caught me rifling through his files. His preliminarily findings are astounding. A couple more weeks and I'm certain he'll have the proof he needs to convince the Kronik he's not a crackpot." I sighed and sat back, sinking into the cushion of the chair. Having shared the weight, it seemed less daunting.

"Come on, Zaith. Shelve it for a while. You're not going to save the world today. There's a lot of footwork to do yet."

Zaith nodded, her eyes unfocused. She held out a green scan-chip for me. We activated the touch-screens on the backs of the seats in front of us and waited for the voting options to display.

"You're not going to watch, are you?" I said.

Zaith looked at me. Refocusing, she flipped her scan-chip into the air. "I think I'll give this to some poor sot on his way in as we leave. I've got too much to think about."

"How are you going to get a headset if you don't use the chip? The patrollers'll toss you out if you're not jacked-in – and I wouldn't want to miss seeing you hauled off by brawny men."

"Ha, Ha," Zaith said. "I've got a system."

"A system?"

"Yes. Trust me. As long as I'm wearing a headset, the patrollers will ignore me and I don't have to go into virtual space. I can sit here and pretend to laugh, and ooh and ahh at the comedy as I figure out how to handle your news."

"How did you ever–?"

"Last year, when I broke down and went on a date with Touf."

"Ahh, yes." That was a familiar story.

The final voting selections flashed on the touch-screen giving us six different planets to choose from. Decades ago, the Kronik had launched a number of small probe-like satellites to see what life lay beyond our own small solar system. Originally used as a kind of 'spy com', the satellites were eventually deemed obsolete and the Entertainment District bought the rights for a yearly fee.

When virtual reality finally linked up with the system, immersing viewers in the show, the theatre business hit its peak.

I felt almost light-headed, intoxicated. The heavy burden of knowing a forbidden secret lifted with the sharing of it. Zaith would know what to do, where to look for information without alerting the wrong people. I'd done my part. My services were no longer required.

I slid my chip into the slot at the top of the panel and voted for the planet I wanted to see. Zaith did an interesting double-select trick then scrunched up her nose and gave me a wink. The headsets released from below the monitors. We put the devices on, waiting for the votes from the rest of the theatre patrons to tally. 'Pentenet' flashed briefly on the screen. A song I'd heard on the top twenty that morning played, while the headset accessed my audio memories, personalizing the experience. The planet came into view.

I liked the high-jinks the ornate natives always found themselves in and the species itself was uniquely comical. I'd figured it out once – I would be almost twenty-eight years old if I'd been born on Pentenet. A single year on Xannia equalled one and a half years there, and most other single star systems. I liked the idea of having my level of maturity match my age. I settled into a view from under the main character's desk as oblivion descended around me.

I shifted to an aerial view as the procession for the mass wedding began. Chuckling at the outlandish and bizarre costume pieces, I had succeeded in forgetting about my bad day. The wedding party had their long thick hair fanned out, supporting large colourful stones along the outer edge.

A piercing screech ricocheted through my head. The wedding blurred. I squeezed my eyes shut.

"Taya!" Zaith shouted, tearing my headset off the rest of the way.

I opened my eyes. Patrollers yanked hardware off viewers in the front rows. I looked at Zaith, confused. Our headsets hit the floor. Zaith hauled me to my feet. A long rumbling quake shook the ground.

"Zaith! What in Sister Zita's name–?"

Pushing me down the aisle, Zaith moved us forward. The rumbling grew in volume and intensity.

"It started maybe five minutes ago. It hasn't stopped. You know, if you're jacked-in you're oblivious." Zaith shouted as the quake roared over the buzzing in my ears from the fast-break.

The building shuddered. A deafening crack resounded. Several people shrieked – others cried out, but many were still oblivious to the danger. The floor dropped a foot, and Zaith and I grabbed the armchairs for support. Exploding glass from the lights and tinted sky-windows ricocheted off the metal support beams. Fragments sliced down, stinging and pock-marking our skin.

More screams.

I shook glass from my hair and slipped on the skewed floor, smashing my knee. I winced, cursing.

The patrollers scrambled from the theatre to alert other patrons. Cries and shouts bounced off the walls, muffled every few seconds by more shattering and heavy crashes coming from down the hallway.

En-mass, the theatre group surged toward the exit. The ground dropped another foot. Bodies tumbled, littering the aisle with twisted arms and legs. A hand grabbed the loose braids on my head, yanking my neck back. I pulled off the offending grip and hauled the woman onto her feet. The roof shuddered. It crashed to the floor and I threw my arms up to shield my face, letting go of the woman behind me. Yells and screams pulsed from the people behind us, muting the sounds of collapse.

Massive concrete chunks crashed down in front of the door. Thick dust coated the air like an empty verrin glass. I coughed. The powder wafted in clouds around our heads.

Zaith and I linked arms to stop the wake of bodies behind us from tumbling into, and under, the falling debris. I ran my tongue around the inside of my mouth and spat. A wall crumbled somewhere at the back of the theatre, spraying more glass fragments over the crowd.

A few young girls shrieked, crying uncontrollably. I actively worked to tune out the voices in order to focus and remain calm. The instinct worked fine now. *Why not earlier?*

"Zaith!" I shouted. With a look, my eyes told her I was staying.

Zaith nodded. I helped patrons over the rubble of concrete and glass through the partially-obscured door. Dirty, glass-marked and tear dampened hands grasped mine. I stood on the rubble, partly blocking the exit, guiding terrified souls out of the shattered room.

I noticed Zaith open a small purse-like compartment on her belt. She removed a Mini-V, one of the smallest video recorders ever developed. Turning it on, she wore it like a headband and clipped a small microphone receiver to her ear. Once situated, she reached for the patron closest to her and helped the older man scramble over the broken ceiling.

The hall was in shambles. A clear path to the outer washroom exit allowed our group to escape from the sunburst-shaped building. Fewer and fewer people came from the theatres down our wing. Staying inside the crippled building, Zaith and I checked each room as we passed, searching for others who might be trapped. The quaking ground signalled constant reminders of aftershocks yet to come.

The Skylight Buffet and Atrium was obliterated. Water sprayed from the sprinkler systems by the game areas, falling just short of the fire that burned in the central kitchen. The scent of charred meat and fried plastic wrap singed my nostrils. Pools of useless water glistened with a deadly electrical charge.

I looked up.

The Beta sun shone in a perfect blue sky through the jagged opening in the skylight. The ground around me, however, was littered with glass and still churned. Overhead sprinklers at the buffet had been disconnected when the glass ceiling shattered.

The fire flared. Orange and blue whips of flame cracked and licked at the decimated kitchen.

Openings to two of the other wings were sealed. Gouged and red- streaked limbs pushing through piles of rubble, grasping at the air, swam in my peripheral vision – *survivors*. I deked around live electrical wires by the gaming machines as they twitched and sparked near the pools of sprinkler water. Shimmying by dense patches of glass and rubble on the floor, this ballet of the macabre etched itself onto my subconscious.

The ground dropped a third time. Desperate hands disappeared.

I climbed a mass of fallen concrete and reinforcement girding to a spot just above the rubble-clogged hall. Clutching a protruding piece of grid-work above my head, I jumped up and kicked out.

Meshwork dug into my palms and fingers. Gritting my teeth, I swallowed the dull throb of pain. Streams of blood mixed with water ran down my arms. I kicked and smashed the loose upper rubble with my heels – jarring my molars with every connection. On each back swing after impact, I drew my knees up and struck out again. A portion of the debris gave way. Hooking my legs over the bottom of the widened hole, I pulled myself into the darkness beyond.

Two small dusty children huddled next to a woman trapped by large chunks of debris, covered with streaks of blood. Two adolescents held onto a boy with a gash across his forehead. The kid was suspended between his friends on shaky legs, his eyes were not focusing. *Probably concussed.*

The passage behind them had vomited debris from the collapsed ceiling, blocking the way with a mass of concrete and metal. I pointed to the opening. The boys nodded. I picked up the kid with the concussion. The juniors scrambled and crawled up the rubble towards the gap and waited for my help. I lifted the injured boy just as Zaith's face appeared.

A look passed between us. She was just as aware as I was of the lack of structural integrity in the walls surrounding us. Zaith lifted the boy from my arms. Two swaths of blood stained his clothes where I'd held him. I couldn't look at my hands. I couldn't let my own pain get in the way of what needed to be done. Using my arms as a lift, I heaved the other boys up and out of the chamber.

I turned and tucked the two remaining smaller children up under my arms. They flailed about, first clutching at my clothes and hair and then pulling away to reach back for their mother. Finally, they clung to each other and wailed. I glanced at the mother. Her eyes were closed but tears leaked from under her lashes as she pressed her lips together. *Save who you can, then go back if there's time.*

Until now, I'd never had to use my emergency training. *At least they won't ever feel abandoned. As long as they're alive, they can hate me all they want.*

"Hush, now. You have to let go of me and reach for the other lady." I sent the children through the opening to Zaith one at a time.

The building shook. I chanced one last glance at the woman on the floor lying beneath large chunks of concrete rubble. Turning, I scrambled back through the opening and perched on the ruins.

I inhaled a deep breath. Salty sweat coated my lips. I wiped my face on my bare forearm, forgetting about the blood. My eyes refused to clear completely – hazy, watery. A second breath shuddered through my body. *You are the master of your destiny – you are in control.*

Dropping down, I landed beside Zaith and the five kids. We each picked up a small child. The juniors supported their friend with the head wound. I motioned for everyone to douse themselves in the water from the sprinklers.

With a sharp jerk of my head, I signalled the plan. Zaith and the others ran with me for the main entrance. The earth gave a final vicious shudder. The walls collapsed inward.

Chapter Six

...Rolls Into a Boulder

Chaos ruled the scene outside. A large ring of emergency vehicles surrounded the Solar Plex. Parking lots were transformed into first aid stations and barricades were positioned to keep the public out of harm's way. Zaith and I brought the sobbing children to a public collection area. The names of all those attending the theatre were being double-checked against the admission list.

Zaith spied her Network setting up just behind a mass of concerned citizens, and went to join them. I searched the crowd for the Head Justice on site. The roar of the onlookers replaced the rumble of the ground. But the quake had finally subsided. I pushed the image of the trapped mother back deep into a pocket of my mind. Now was not the time to succumb to weak, paltry emotions.

"Jezetek!" I identified the commanding Justice from his black fatigues and equally black buzzed hair. A gold shoulder insignia marked his rank.

"Jutaya. Saw you exit the building. Gimme an update." The broad-shouldered Metek demanded gruffly, immediately assigning me to his duty roster with the use of my formal identification.

His dark-green skin gave him the appearance of deep

camouflage, but what always caught my eye was the naturally appealing placement of his gold coliths. During training, we often verbally sparred by tossing military tactics around like lovers whispering sweet-nothings. That and communicating in code was the closest I ever came to having a boyfriend. I wished we were back in training; anywhere but here.

"It's a mess in there. If you can get in past the collapsed foyer, there's a fire in the kitchen and rubble strewn about from the ceiling and walls." I wiped my drenched hair away from my face.

Jezetek handed me his field cloth from one of a half-dozen pockets on his pants. Good thing it was black. After wiping the smeared blood from my face and arms, I staunched the remaining flow from my palms, wincing.

I fell back on tactical talk. "Quadrant one is secure but two to five are unknown. However, the building only had six theatres open in various quadrants. Patrons should be utilised and questioned about an approximate number of bodies noticed in each of the screening rooms as they exited. Employees should be questioned about staffing numbers and open quadrants. There were approximately twenty-five to thirty citizens in theatre four, first quadrant. Tek." I sighed, returning his cloth and resting my hands on my thighs. "There are still people in there." Falling back on protocol was the only way to keep my mind clear and focused.

"We've already begun our investigation. I need you to—"

"I'm not getting paid for this," I cut him short. I couldn't go back in there, but I could help out here. "This is my time. I'll be at the medical tent." I flexed my hands slightly before jamming them under opposite arms. "If you need me for tactical planning, let me know."

I nodded my respect to him as the superior officer on scene. Tek clapped me on the shoulder with a squeeze, and then barked out orders to a Justice on payroll. I wove my way through the crowd. I would never have been so presumptuous if Tek was just a random Contractor. He'd enrolled a year ahead of me, and was four years my senior, but we'd graduated at the same ceremony after a year of friendly competition. I knew he understood my restlessness.

A hand shot out of the crowd. It locked around my bicep. Stumbling back, I was pulled to face a distraught Matin-Glaaon man. Swinging up my free arm, poised to strike, I caught a glimpse of something other than malice in the man's eyes. Bodies bustled, pushing us closer together.

"Where's my wife!" he demanded, his bronzed jaw set with determination.

"I don't know what you're talking about." I glowered, lowering my poised arm. He shook me. My teeth rattled.

"Where is she? I know you know where she is!" he shouted, tightening his grip. In a split second, my hand struck out and gripped his oesophagus. He gasped; his hold loosened but did not fail. The silver coliths on his cheeks rippled. His eyes widened in fear.

"I don't know who you are or who your wife is. So back off, or you'll need a machine to help you breathe." I didn't need this right now. Not with the meeka I was dealing with.

He jerked his other arm forward.

I tensed.

Two small children clinging to his hand emerged from behind. I let him go. He dropped my arm to massage his blood-printed throat.

"Macheik and Taika said you left their mother behind. Where is she?" he repeated.

I looked him in the eye, weary and drained. "You need to talk to the Extraction Team. Tell them that CTF Contractor three-nine-two-five reports that your wife was partially buried under heavy rubble at the base of Quadrant five just before the building collapsed. Sir, she was trapped; there was nothing I could do."

He nodded and looked around, mystified. I tapped his arm and pointed to an area behind us. He stalked off without a word, pulling along his tear-stained children. I shook out my arm to get the circulation running again, and resumed my path to the Medical Tent.

The crowd grew every few minutes. An emergency update on the wire was most likely the cause of it. Zola knew Zaith hadn't wasted any time handing over her first-hand footage of the disaster. *She'll probably get an award for it, too.*

Bodies packed what were once empty parking spaces, flowing to the rhythm of their sorrow. People sobbed, waving red kerchiefs in the air, praying for the ruby-coloured Alpha Sun, Mother Zola, to shed light on this tragedy. Wives, husbands, family members, temp-mates and friends consoled one another on every side of me.

Always it was someone else's hand wiping tears from a loved one's eyes or clutching tight to a heart-mate or lover. A woman gripped her kerchief near her chin, eyes unfocused and clouded as her grief spilled out over her cheeks. I could not pass without disturbing her.

So, I stopped and stood, becoming one with the crowd.

I swayed as murmured chants weaved through the air: his heartache, her wail, their sobs. The suffocating atmosphere of despair seeped into my skin, latching itself onto my bones. I absorbed the pain and frustration of the people; the ache in my soul doubled me over. I groaned at the earth – the sadness jarring me, spiking my stomach.

The ache penetrated my senses like a needle, shooting in and out, weaving and tightening threads around my bruised and vulnerable heart.

Blinking rapidly, I stood and shook myself, pulling away from the despair – throwing up the mental barriers carefully honed since childhood. Rubbing my temples, I gingerly walked the few remaining yards to the Medical Tent. The steady rhythm of dozens of footfalls announced the mobilizing efforts of the Extraction Team.

Entering the cordoned off emergency medical area, I stepped inside the tent. A doctor, clad in light blue scrubs and a lab coat approached.

"Do you need assistance?" he asked, eyeing my marred, blood-stained palms and red smeared cheeks.

"No, I've come to offer you my assistance as a trained Emergency Medic with the CTF."

"My staff and I have everything under control here, thank you."

"You won't for long. The Extraction Team is entering the building. Severely injured citizens will arrive any minute; the team is fast and thorough. You'll have new patients streaming through your door before you have time to examine the ones you've already got."

He hesitated.

I pulled my ID from my belt-pack and flashed it at him. "I'm volunteering my services. I was in there helping people as the building buckled around us. I'm not going to harm any of your patients."

He nodded, waving over an Attending Medic to show me the ropes. The doctor returned to supervise a man having his arm cast.

"I'm Niterrii. I'll help familiarise you with the layout and the supply locations. Come, let me wrap your hands before we get started."

"Jutaya," I replied with my full name. Moving to shake hands with Niterrii I stopped short. We both chuckled. I was kind of a mess.

"It's nice to know that someone around here isn't afraid of me."

"It's not you personally," Terri explained. "It's who you work for, and the fact that you could call rank on him in a crisis – leaving Dr. Gretotik with a mark on his record."

"That's not my intent, but it could be arranged." Terri was being kind.

I knew the doctor was just like the professor, just like the architect, the site manager and everyone else who laid eyes on me. Terri chuckled as she bathed my hands in an alkaline base, then lightly wrapped them in gauze to help clot the blood but keep their manoeuvrability as I tended the wounded.

The tent space was ample and could hold four hundred cots with ease, not that I thought we'd need them. Supplies were basic but plentiful. We'd be able to improvise whatever was lacking when the time came.

Terri brought me around to see the two dozen or so patrons already admitted for a variety of ailments from concussions, to sprains, to broken bones. We knelt beside the adolescent I'd helped rescue in Quadrant five. He had ten fresh stitches above his right eyebrow and drifted between sleep and consciousness. Terri gently placed the back of her hand to his cheek.

"After a quick monitored nap, he'll be ready to join his friends again."

"He might not get all the rest he needs," I mused as four Justices walked into the tent carrying limp bodies. We rose quickly and showed them where to lay the patrons. Just as we started diagnosing ailments, another three enforcers entered with more casualties.

* * *

I flopped down on the living room couch, my long hair knotted and tangled from being wet, tied and retied all afternoon and evening. My muscles ached. Sitting there, it felt like my body drew itself down into the couch and through to the floor. Jadis, my lynx, jumped up on the couch and lay her head on my lap. While she settled, I fumbled for the remote and clicked on the wire. Flipping through the channels, I absently patted the large cat. Nearly every station gave updates on the outcome of the 'super quake' that afternoon.

"Twice as large, and five times more destructive than a quake of average proportion – Hundreds of citizens still gather in the hopes that loved ones will be found alive in the remaining rubble – Dump trucks have been carting away full loads every half hour for the last three hours – Fourteen of the two-hundred and fifty-seven attending patrons died – Images can't describe the horror of those frantic moments. If this young lady hadn't been here today, thirty or forty lives would have found it near impossible to make their way to safety. The young woman denied us an interview but continued with efforts to help in the Medical Tent where much of today's devastation could be seen firsthand."

I left the station on Network News Now as Zaith wrapped up an exceptionally long day of reporting. Her face streaked with soot and the particles of debris in her hair, gave a dishevelled authenticity no one else could claim. Her firsthand images from the belly of the Plexis were being broadcast on all stations, but key pictures were saved for her own station.

It was odd for me to watch myself doing what I'd only really felt as a driving impulse. I had no time for rational thought, just reaction and instinct. What had been a blur of faces at the time became a clearly-plotted rescue story with me as the heroine of the day. I leaned back and scratched Jadis between the ears. At least nothing had aired about the Rally.

"I'd hoped to avoid having the Facility Officials publicly aware that I'm out of work already," I said to Jadis.

Perhaps they'd overlook my potential misconduct with the professor in light of all the positive publicity. Zaith had never come right out and said I was a Contractor with the CTF, but citizens would know anyway. Only so many people in the world were capable of dangling from a ceiling in the midst of a super-quake.

I flexed my itchy, grooved palms beneath matted but fresh gauze then turned off the wire, and rose to take a shower before going to bed. A flashing light caught my attention in the semi-dark. I clicked open my watch-com.

"Messages," I said, leaning against the banister on my way upstairs. A blue screen flashed on the monitor. It was voice only.

"Play messages."

The numbers 'one of one' flashed briefly before Zaith's voice filled the room.

"Hey, it's me. Thanks for all your help today. Get some rest and sleep in for a change. Don't worry about the Rally footage; it's been buried for a while. Catch ya later."

A hot shower called to me. Closing my watch-com, I climbed to my room with Jadis trailing behind me.

Chapter Seven
Ultimatum

R*escue teams completed a final sweep of the Solar Plex early this morning. All patrons have been accounted for, and all rubble removed from the site of this former landmark.*

"In other news, the Kronik has given the affirmative for taking precautionary measures toward the use of ground-penetrating sonar to aid in the charting of plate tectonics," blasted a news broadcast revealing the latest developments. I clicked off the wire's audio output.

Nothing has changed. The professor is certain the world is coming to an end and, once everyone knows, it'll be the same split as always: half the citizens will trust in the Kronik and the other half will follow doomsday soothsayers like that crazy Talian.

I was still tired after yesterday's unusual events, but I was restless. The wire had nothing new to say – the Kronik was still hedging around the issue of the quakes, making it look like they were doing something while not actually doing anything of any significance.

The house was clean, because I never let it get dirty, and there was nothing to read and nowhere to go. No matter that this was actually one of my scheduled days off, I needed to move to feel productive.

By mid-morning, I found myself on the elevator to the eighth floor of the CTF. I hoped desperately that my actions at the Plexis yesterday would overshadow any rumours floating around about the Rally. Having had significant prior dealings with the Ethics Committee, I was walking a fine line with company policy and the professor. But, if they found out about the Rally – I couldn't even think about it. I couldn't afford to be cast out. I'd been reckless and irresponsible. It was only by Zola's graces that no one had recognised me.

The doors slid open to the reception area of the Assignment Room on the eighth floor. Niless was in the middle of a call on her desktop view monitor. She was surrounded by a bank of ten other screens and the office vis-u-fax. I walked over to her large oblong desk and sat on it, waiting for her to finish. I debated whether or not to ask Ni about Zaith's contract. I decided not.

Niless eyed me perched there as she wrapped up her conversation. She'd worked with the company for nearly a century, but she didn't look a day over sixty.

"Taya," Ni said, turning away from her monitor. "You were born trouble."

"Oh?" I feigned innocence in the face of her deep-green complexion.

"I've been trying all day to find someone to replace you with Professor Denali."

"Oh."

"Don't even start. I held that spot–"

"Two days for me. Yes Ni, I screwed up. But it wasn't entirely my fault."

"Oh?" Her gold coliths sparkled with her heightened sense of responsibility. I laughed.

"The short answer is he thought I was too young."

"Taya…"

"It's true. He didn't trust me. Didn't hold up his end of the contract. Denali consistently stopped my work, judging my capabilities inaccurately. It was the Platinum Hall debacle all over again – I just covered my ass better this time. He wouldn't let me complete my assigned duties, thus disengaging the contract's validity and releasing me from all subsequent entitlements. It's all legitimate and clearly printed on the revised copy we sent by vis-u-fax."

"My dear, how often you seem to entangle yourself in these predicaments is beyond counting. You need to be careful."

"Don't worry, Ni. I always cover myself." I tapped each of the three knuckles on the back of the centre finger on my right hand, top – middle – bottom – a discrete prayer to each of the sun gods, should they actually exist. *There shouldn't be a problem.*

"Have you got any mail for me?"

Niless nodded, and handed me a black envelope with a red CTF seal on the back. It was labelled *'Ethics Committee Board of Governors.'*

They know.

I leaned over Ni's desk, grabbed a trans-ink pen and scrawled my name across the front of the envelope in white.

Lying on my stomach across the desk, feet in the air, I found the trash can and tossed out the letter.

The door to the Master Keeper's Office swung open. I glanced at the black spherical camera affixed to the upper corner of the room. I looked at the desk I lay across and the unopened envelope in the garbage. *Oh no. This can't be good.* Two sets of firm hands grabbed my arms and lifted me to my feet. I didn't recognise either face.

They were older and wore deep crimson gowns akin to the colour of drying blood. They turned me to face the office door. My feet never touched the floor. The Master Keeper, dressed in a navy business suit and black shirt, crossed his arms. His eyes bored into mine – I couldn't look away. A shiver ran the course of my spine. *Zerameteth, give me strength!*

With a curt nod, he stepped back and closed the door.

"Come with us, Ms Fyce," the muscular man to my right said.

He and his equally-strong partner did not let go of my arms, but they did set my feet on the floor. I nodded. What else could I do?

After escorting me to the bank of elevators, the man on my left scanned his thumb. Three additional floors lit up beyond the ten available on my own access grid. As the doors slid shut, I saw Niless rest her head in one hand and mouth my name in dismay. She hadn't seen this coming either. My guards didn't let go. The three new floors were highlighted: BL 1, 2, and 3. *Base Level? No one ever mentioned there was a Base Level.*

"Where are we going?"

"Didn't you read your summons?" Lefty said.

"This is where the Committee meets?"

"This is where the Committee assesses," Righty said.

The doors opened on BL 3 – the lowest level. Dim, blue-white baseboard lighting illuminated the slate floor and not much else. It was cool and damp, like a sub-basement in one of the outer territories where I'd done a couple weeks' work with a handyman. I couldn't tell if the walls here were moist or not, but the ceiling was at least fifteen feet high and the corridor was wide enough to accommodate the three of us side-by-side.

The symbol on the first door we passed glowed phosphorescent. I'd never seen an emblem like it before. It looked like code. We stopped at the second door, nearly thirty paces farther along than the first. My brain temporarily kicked back into gear.

If they wanted me out, I'd be out – right? But I'm not. I'm here, whatever that means. Last time a Committee rep talked to me, we were in the meeting room on Level 8 – nothing freaky happened then. Why now?

I ran a coarse tongue around an equally-dry mouth. My bladder threatened to overflow – I crossed my legs. I couldn't shake the nerves. *How did they find out?*

Righty knocked on the solid wood door. *Why is there no tech down here?* The door swung in and, for some reason an image of wrist and ankle chains flashed in my mind, but there was nothing there.

Our footsteps echoed in the small chamber. On my right, five Board of Governor Committee representatives in dark crimson gowns and matching skullcaps sat at an elevated arced table. A large, phosphorescent light hung suspended from the centre of the ceiling, casting dark angular shadows on the faces of the male and female Governors of the EC, Ethics Committee.

Only one face looked familiar, *Governor Felnir*, and he wasn't smiling. *Taya, Taya, Taya – what in the world have you done this time?* Righty and Lefty released me in the middle of the room, and disappeared into the shadows behind. It took a moment to straighten my legs having to compensate for the full weight of my body again. The hair on my neck prickled as I chewed on the inside of my lower lip. This had to be some kind of nightmare. *How am I going to survive this?*

"Jutaya Tannya Fyce," a male voice said.

I jumped at the sound of my own name.

"Yes?"

"The members of this Committee are to be addressed as *Sir* or *Honoured One*," a woman said.

"Yes, sir?" I tried again, not sure where to look or who to look at.

The slight echo threw off my usually acute hearing. I couldn't tell which voice came from whom. The shadows here distorted features, making angles move at odd times.

"Do you know why you're here?" Male Governor.

Do I?

"Yes, sir."

"What have you to say in your defence?" Different male.

Why didn't I read the letter? I can't admit my stupidity. Do I just come clean? They must know everything or I wouldn't be here. So what's worse – my loose interpretation of contract fundamentals or...

"I fully admit to discharging my weapon in public, but I did so under duress and with the utmost concern for the safety of all those present – including the Rally Speaker."

"Explain." Female Governor.

From the general shifting of bodies in chairs, my answer surprised them. They must have seen me discard the summons – figured I was ignorant. That may well be the case but my ability to deduce and reason under pressure had only strengthened with my training.

"Yes, sir. Thank you for this opportunity." Another round of nervous shifting. They really didn't know what to make of me – nor I them.

However, democracy still appeared to be in play. I couldn't afford to make a wrong move. I had to show them I could still be trusted. No lies.

"The Speaker intends to convince innocent civilians to follow him into the Deserts, a veritable death sentence as we all know. He chose to rely on unproven sources and his own theories to sway the hearts and minds of naïve curiosity seekers – people who do not have all the facts about the current situation."

"And what situation would that be?"

What do I say?

"The end of the world, sir." More shuffling, mixed with head shaking and some muttering this time. *All or nothing, right?*

"What makes you believe your insight into the situation is any better than those attending the Rally?" Different male Governor.

My back ached. I tried to release the tension in my shoulder blades by pressing my shoulders forward, but I didn't want to draw any undue attention to myself. I'd done a fantastic job of that already, so I stopped and stood still.

"Due to the delicate nature of my work with Facility clients, I have gained unquestionable foreknowledge regarding the geological disturbances we are facing and their effect on our natural verrin supplies. The Speaker is not a geologist, he is the son of a Council member who, disregarding the cultural norms of his race, blasphemed against the Kronik. Since it is not within my power to publicise what I learn under contract, I utilised the resources available to me to help make my point. Innocent lives should not be sacrificed for the whim of a Truth Seeker – even if one of those lives is his own." *Maybe there's a chance I'll get through this.*

"We will take your position with the Facility, your expertise, and your perspective under advisement as we determine how best to proceed," said Governor Felnir.

The small group of Committee Members wheeled their chairs into a tight circle above the crest of the table. I didn't dare look at my watch-com, so I kept track of the time using the beat of my heart and my fingertips.

Ten minutes. This did not look good.

Twenty minutes. A hand flailed above the bowed heads.

I'm not going to get out of here. My breathing quickened.

Thirty-three minutes. The bowed heads lifted and the circle broke. The Committee Members rolled back to their positions behind the table. The man in the centre, my previous liaison, stood up.

"Jutaya Tannya Fyce." I cringed at hearing my last name spoken aloud with such frequency. "The Ethics Committee Board of Governors with the Contractor Training Facility finds you at fault for discharging a Facility-issued weapon in a place of public attendance."

My life is over. My knees wobbled. I gripped the sides of my pants, balling the fabric up into my fists.

"However, because no harm came from the event, we deem that your intentions were honourable and you strove to work within the parameters of the Facility's Best Practices Act. Therefore, we have decided not to incarcerate you. Instead you will be placed under Observation. Should you decide to blur the lines you have been contracted to uphold on any project, or even during personal time, within the next six months, you will be stripped of your status with the Facility and sentenced to work the mines. Do you understand this verdict as I have presented it to you?"

Do I?

"Yes, sir. On my honour, I won't let the Committee down."

"Dismissed." He sat down.

Lefty and Righty resumed their previous positions and escorted me out of chambers.

I sat on the steps outside the Facility building with my elbows on my knees, my forehead cradled in my aggravated palms. The hum, whirr, and rush of passing riders cocooned around me, trapping me with my ignorance and shattered pride. Had my actions at the Solar Plex helped me? I couldn't tell.

I'm on a leash with a choker collar. I can't afford to screw up again. What am I going to do?

My watch-com beeped. I ignored it. It beeped again with a tell-tale thrill at the end. The Facility had sent me a message. My heart squeezed tight trying to hide, to disappear. The com beeped again. I let my aching and bruised arms fall across my lap. I flipped up the watch face. It was a text message.

"View," I said, my voice flat.

'Contractor Requested' it read.

"Review."

And there it was again, taunting me – 'A *Guide into the Deserts*'. That maniac was going through with it, and now he'd specifically asked for my services.

"He can't be serious."

I read the synopsis and general description. The chart detailed a standard request for a Bodyguard, a Justice, and a Guide with varying rates of pay just slightly above normal.

The contact information said to call ahead for an appointment with Diaz Mindexid Lisle at the Chalklin Pond Restaurant.

I snapped the face of the com shut and stood up. I hailed a personal-rider. *He wants to work with me, does he? We'll just see about that.*

* * *

I pushed open the inlaid cherry rose-vine wooden doors of the restaurant. The aromatic scent of roast ganoo hung in the air like a fog.

Grabbing the closest waiter by his collar I growled, "Where's Mr. Lisle, kid."

The quivering idiot wobbled an arm toward a dark-red velvet tapestry masking the rear of the dining area. I let him go, straightened his black satin jacket and tweaked his scarlet neck scarf. Giving him a sharp nod, I walked to the back.

Pulling down my navy suit jacket at the hem, I smoothed my grey pants and hit the buzzer to the left of the drapery.

I walked in.

He sat at a desk on the far side of the room with his back to a large picture window, working with his head down. He wore a formal black business suit today, playing yet another role in the saga of his one-man show. I stood in the middle of the room, arms crossed. My lips parted to speak–

"I've been waiting for you," he said.

"Excuse me?"

"I said…" He looked up at me, his grey eyes frosted nearly white around pin-head pupils. "I've been waiting for you. Please, have a seat." He motioned to the deep-red velvet chair opposite him.

I remained standing.

"What I need to know is if you're up for the position? Can you handle the contract?" That was a slap in the face I didn't need. "I can handle the contract just fine, Mr. Lisle." I was tired of everyone questioning my experience. "If you doubted my abilities, you shouldn't have requested me. You insult me."

"That isn't very reassuring."

"Neither is traipsing around a death zone with a host of unprepared and unqualified commoners. I'm not here to accept this Contract. I'm here to set you straight." *I'm not going to risk my job or my freedom for this farce.*

An eyebrow rose. "What makes you think I need to be set straight… that I haven't considered the dangers of this mission, hmm?"

I unfolded my arms and leaned forward against the chair-back. "Like I said at the Rally, you're playing with innocent lives to validate your own endgame. The citizens following your Cause have placed their common sense on the shelf. Someone with an ounce of intellect has to speak on their behalf. This is a suicide mission. Don't make me regret not killing you."

Okay, I shouldn't have said that. Calm down, rationalise it out and convince him to drop the request. I cannot be held accountable for the actions of this idiot.

He tilted his head. The light made his pale eyes shine. Then it struck me – he was Talian, the Society Founders developed the CTF and gave regulation to all weaponry. That's how the Facility knew about the incident at the Rally. All he had to do was look up the public personnel files and he could match me to my photo. *What's he up to?*

Mr. Lisle sat back in his chair. He drummed the fingers of one hand on the wooden arm-claw.

"Why do you assume that I haven't thought this through? That I believe the lives of the Kahn-lea are expendable?"

I pushed away from the chair and walked to the door. I'd get Niless to help me out of this. She'd know what to do.

"Wait." He stood up.

I stopped, hand extended to the curtain.

"Not all Talians are alike."

I grabbed the edge of the tapestry. He slid around the edge of his desk.

"I'm going – no matter what. And I'm taking the Kahn-lea with me."

I whipped around, releasing the drape. My eyes flashed, matching the anger screaming in my heart. *Are you insane?*

With each word, I stepped closer to him, "You – are – going – to – kill – them."

"Not if you help me."

We stood inches apart. The cocky smirk on his face was gone. I couldn't identify the emotion that had replaced it. Innocent lives were on the line – including my own.

"No one has survived the Deserts. I don't want to die. Drop this foolishness or remove me from your request. I want nothing to do with you or this insanity." *And I don't want to go back to the mines and lose my freedom.*

"The Ancients survived. If anyone can find a way, it's you." *So he has read my dossier. If I take this job, I'm dead. If I don't take this job and he complains, I'm as good as dead. Niless can't help me. Dammit!*

"If I do it, I'll be doing it for the flock. Not for you." He returned to his desk. "Present your terms, Ms Fyce."

He knew my last name; a carefully-guarded fact that only a privileged few were told. My public files only gave my last initial, no personal details. Shaking off my unease, I walked up to the desk, leaned forward and gave him the company policy.

"First and foremost, I do not perform any duty beyond those specified in my contract. Under any circumstance. So make damn sure you've requested every service you need. The CTF receives payment in full for Contracts lasting between one and twenty days. This ensures that the credit is not counterfeit and that my sources are paid in the event that anything should happen to me, under said contract. Any days extra that are paid for will be reimbursed or cost tallied, depending on what side of the prepaid date the contract is completed.

"*You* do not give *me* orders. Any order I give will fall only within the purview of the contract. Respect and cooperation are pivotal.

This should not be a boss-employee relationship; we are equals until the contract is terminated." I shuddered at the thought.

"The minute you say it's over, there's no turning back. I cannot quit, but if there's sufficient evidence that I'm being prevented from performing my duties, our agreement will be considered null and void." *At least I hope that's still true.*

I stood up straight, trying to figure out why I felt I had to justify myself to this man. There were maybe half-a-dozen or so years between us, so it wasn't social-seniority kicking in. Still, he put me on the defensive.

"Where do I sign?" he asked, looking for a physical document. "Don't be a fool. Your name means nothing to the CTF. We have to shake on it. My contract documentation is accessible in the Facility's mainframe. If you feel the need to test my memory, I'll call it up for you on your access screen. Otherwise, supply a witness and I'll notify the Contracts Department." My words were braver than my nerves. My hands shook slightly as I waited for his response.

He pressed a button under the rim of his desk. The waiter I encountered earlier entered. Removing my portable vis-u-fax from the large interior pocket of my jacket, I set it on the desk and called up headquarters.

Niless' face filled the screen. "Sealing a contract?"

"Just make sure you're watching and receive the hardcopy image."

She nodded. This wasn't time for chitchat.

The Talian and I locked eyes, extended our arms and firmly shook hands.

"Got it Taya." Niless logged out.

The vis-u-fax powered down. The waiter left. Our hands remained clasped. He gingerly rotated my wrist, sweeping a thumb across the thin layer of gauze. I snatched my hand away.

"Never call me Ms Fyce again, Mr. Lisle. My name is Jutaya."

"The feeling's mutual. Call me Dezmind."

We sat down to review his plans for saving the world – something we spent all of three days preparing for; not the end of the world just the end of my sanity.

Chapter Eight
To the Expanse

My crossed arm was jostled. Dezmind pulled his hand away from my elbow and cleared his throat. I snapped out of my musings back into the moment, picked up a sheet of tracing paper and shook out the creases.

"This is the last piece, right?" I asked, passing it back to him, scanning the small vaulted room of the museum.

"Yes."

I looked back to the group. His followers. Most of them were standing again. A few of the men were pacing, others spoke in near- normal tones. Kriteclif, the curator of the Museum of Darius, returned to his post by the main door, caught my eye, looked at his watch and left for the third time in ten minutes.

"It's time to go." I turned to face Dezmind inside the cordoned off area where he'd traced the images of the Ancient Tablets. "I can't believe you left this 'till tonight. Come on. We've overstayed our welcome, and the group's restless."

"So, take them outside. I need a moment to gather my things and speak with Kriteclif."

"I cannot leave you unattended." My voice came out stiff, like a recording, ready to launch into a recitation of the contract I still couldn't believe I'd accepted.

"Then figure something out. This won't take much longer." Scowling, I glanced at the pile of papers at his feet. Faded blue words and diagrams scrawled across each piece, written in a script so ancient it was now only studied by boring scholars wanting yet another series of letters to add to their names.

Closing my eyes, I inhaled slowly through my nose, releasing the breath past my teeth, and out of imperceptibly parted lips. Turning, somewhat composed, I approached the group. I just couldn't bring myself to recognise them as a Kahn-lea. That would be admitting too much.

"Who here is strong in both mind and body?"

Stealing glances at one another, shoulders shrugged and the heads of the ten assembled citizens shook warily. A Matin man from the back stepped forward. I hadn't had enough time to do a thorough background check on everyone, but I knew enough about this man to make a determination. "I believe I meet those requirements."

"I need to elect an Acting Commander for situations when the group is separated from Dezmind or me. Are you up for the task?"

"Yes."

"What's your name?" I had to ask, to make it look good. These people didn't need to know I'd done cursory background checks on them. I couldn't give away all my secrets.

"Syvis Plicket."

I addressed the group, "Syvis will be Acting Commander in any situation where his presence is required. Are there any objections?"

No one moved.

I spoke directly to Syvis, "Take them outside, single file, and make sure everyone is prepared to travel the Deserts. Here's the master list of items. Make sure only the necessities are brought. Dezmind and I will be quick to follow. At that time, he will conduct a brief meeting concerning his preliminary findings. Understand?"

He nodded, a bit confused as I handed him the list of required travel items. I sighed and clarified, "This will save us time so that we can be on our way faster. At the current rate, the Gamma Sun will be dominant before we're ready to leave." He nodded, more confident, and swiftly orchestrated the group's departure from the building.

The room, sparse with antiquated relics, opened up in the group's absence. I took off my cap and ran my fingers through my bangs and over layers of plaited hair, then I jammed it back on again. *This is ridiculous. He should have waited another week.* I walked up to Dezmind as he hailed Kritecliff.

"A moment of your time, sir, before we depart."

Dezmind motioned for me to step beyond hearing distance. I complied. I wanted to leave as soon as possible and this was an argument I didn't feel like fighting.

After Dezmind's discussion with the curator, I escorted him back through the strangely-labyrinthine building. Approaching the main doors exiting the museum, I swayed to my curiosity.

"What was that all about?"

"Just making sure I know more than he does," he muttered, burying his face in the tracings.

Outside, Syvis dumped out one of the teenager's backpacks. He pulled out a solar hair dryer, and half a dozen other items not on the list, loading her arms as he went. I could just make out the argument between them. Syvis stood his ground. The petite blonde Glaaon, of pink skin and silver coliths, emptied her stash on the reject pile in the middle of the circle of bodies. Syvis addressed the girl's friend.

The old man, one of the married couples, the new arts graduate, and now the blonde sat idle. I stopped Dezmind's blind walk near the edge of the group, allowing Syvis to complete his task. No red flags had arisen when I'd searched his profile in the master-database, unlike some of the others here. Hopefully, we wouldn't get separated again.

When all was said and done, I tossed Syvis a burlap sack with ties. He gathered together the discarded items. I removed a parcel-post tag for the CTF from my belt-pack and attached it to the ties. Syvis left the bag in front of the museum's parcel pick-up. Returning to the group, he nodded to me.

My elbow pierced Dezmind from his musings. He narrowed his eyes at me and raised a brow. I jerked my head toward the group. I found that the less I actually said to him, the more civil I remained.

His eyes cleared. He faced his followers.

"The Tablets are written in a dialect from a time not long after the first arrival of the immigrants from the Ancient City. They tell of a sacred gathering place which I have chosen to interpret as the Pit of Chance. Those who enter it are faced with three trials before reaching Understanding. The trials have been labelled *Fate*, *Destiny*, and *Truth*, with no further details. To reach the Pit of Chance, we must cross the Deserts beyond the three *Life Pools* on the edge of civilization. There is more I have yet to decipher, but this much shows us where we begin. We go southeast at Vitextid's Lakes on the outer edge of the Expanse. Everyone still with me?"

Silence permeated the evening air. Eyes darted this way and that, avoiding contact and unspoken decisions.

A horn blasted, breaking the settling unease. I signalled to the driver of the transport to give us another minute.

"I am ready to aid in Xannia's salvation," Syvis stepped toward Dezmind.

Gradually the others joined him, convinced of the role they would play in the planet's future. It was all for the greater good, but there was no good to be had exploring the wasteland beyond the Expanse.

Limited though it was, my research over the past three days verified that much at least. I opened my watch-com and texted the head Engineer at the CTF the co-ordinates for the large supply package I'd prepared in anticipation of this insanity. *What is it about those lakes? I can't seem to get away from them.*

Dezmind led his followers across the street to the public transport he'd arranged. It was little more than the four-wheeled junker that made regular runs out to the last town, close to where I'd worked with the professor. It was clearly two trans-points away from the scrap heap and had no hover capabilities. It coughed and heaved as if preparing for death.

I had offered to arrange for suitable transportation through my CTF connections, but Dezmind had stubbornly refused – probably because he didn't want them knowing more about his plans than necessary. I got the distinct feeling that he was playing a game he didn't know the rules to by being out of the Compound. Still, this mobile piece of garbage was costing him twenty credits more than standard rental rates.

I fumed.

We weren't ready. *I wish Zaith could've come. At least her zany attitude was normal.* These people were a mass of contradictions I wanted nothing to do with. If everything I had worked so hard to achieve didn't hang in the balance, I'd have told that Talian where to shove his false prophesying ideals.

Arguing voices drifted from behind the transport – a man and a woman. I slipped toward the rear of the vehicle to investigate as the rest of the group climbed to their seats at the front. Dezmind stepped down from the landing, a scowl searing his usually even brow. I waved him back. I didn't need him sticking his nose into every little thing – I didn't need to deal with another *professor.*

"Find out what's wrong and fix it," he griped, pointing to his watch-com. Now that we were so close to leaving, his impatience to depart was obvious.

Against my better judgment, I slid back toward the front of the transport. "What part of my contract does being treated like *meeka* fall under?"

"You're my bodyguard; you figure it out." He turned and boarded.

I clenched and unclenched my fists rapidly. The jolts of pain firing through my nerve-endings were meant to distract me but I found myself grinding my molars as well. *I shouldn't be here. These people shouldn't be here.* But here we were. I returned to my previous position and listened carefully to the couple's dispute.

"You have to trust me," the man said. "I don't want you getting injured. For the last time, you're not coming."

"No, Morrtice," she replied. "I refuse to be a widow. I won't miss this. I want to be part of it just as much as you do. I know the risks."

Family differences of opinions. There was no time for this; not now, not later. The matter was easily rectified.

As I sat down beside Dezmind on the antiquated transport, he asked, "Was that necessary?" The vehicle pulled away leaving two bodies standing in the dust.

"You're questioning my abilities again."

"And you're being evasive. This has nothing to do with your abilities."

It was phenomenal how he could penetrate my calm. We sat at the rear of the vehicle en route to the edge of the Expanse.

Shifting left to look at him, his piercing grey eyes threw me off again. I blinked, re-adjusting my composure. "There are at least ten different reasons, rules, regulations and areas of fine-print that I could pull from not to answer you. But I will anyway since it's trivial now that we've left them."

He waited.

I took a breath, struggling not to scowl. "They were squabbling over the situation. The guy wanted the woman to go home; she didn't want to leave. With their differences of opinion, and a highly volatile situation on our hands, their inability to completely focus on the trials ahead would have numbed their senses, making them less likely to survive in an emergency. The fewer people I have to worry about, the better; the less these people have to worry about, the better. Clear?"

"Perfectly. Thank you." That was unexpected.

I was sure he'd push the matter, but I dismissed the thought and leaned back, tilting slightly towards the aisle – watching. As much as I now regretted it, I had a job to do.

Seventy-five minutes later, I sat down beside an older gentleman of Nirian decent. His dark-grey skin emphasised a shock of white hair. The jade-green of his coliths helped to accentuate rounded cheeks, a prominent jaw, and keen eyes   eyes that glowed at my arrival and a smile that welcomed.

"It's Werks, right?"

"Yep, that's me. What can I do for you, Little Lady?"

"Perhaps you need optic enhancers, I'm not Tamaine." I waved in the girl's general direction. Tamaine was hard not to miss.

"I have perfect vision and excellent hearing, my dear. While you are both taller and more solidly built than that young woman, you do not match me in height or girth," he laughed, and pulled out a scarlet kerchief to wipe laughter tears from his eyes. I smiled.

"You know, I've been watching Dezmind at the restaurant for some time now. He's a good lad. Was steadily working away in that back room of his for months before he invited me to the Rally."

"You work at the Chalklin Pond?" I knew that kerchief looked familiar.

"Head Chef for forty years." He patted my hand. "Don't you worry so much. We know the dangers. We accept them. My wife, may Sister Zita warm her soul, would have given our house away if it meant she could be here. Mitina ran at things head on. But don't fret your heart, Love; I'm not ready to join her any time soon. I'm only seventy- five. I've got at least another fifty years ahead of me before the clockworks start to run down."

I listened to him chatter on. I'd already spoken with Deltek and Lutrice, the remaining married couple who shared a passion for making a difference. It took the better part of thirty minutes to learn anything of significance about them – kind, soft spoken, but reserved and guarded.

The teens, Tamaine and Jantice, talked alternately about the Cause and graduation, but never actually 'said' anything. Syvis, while reserved, spoke with me briefly about his expectations for the expedition, but nothing of himself.

A few minutes later, I patted Werks on the shoulder. "I'd love to stay and chat, but–"

"You've got work to do. Yes, certainly – a lot of work to do." Giving him one last smile, I slipped into the aisle. Then I paused. The man at the front by the doors sat with a rigid back, his arms folded high across his broad chest. Raylan. The negative aura surrounding him made me more cautious than usual. I had to be careful with that one. I turned back and sat next to the poet, Merik, instead.

Chapter Nine
Ready or Not

"Just wait a minute, will you?" I said.

The driver of the heap in which we'd arrived at Vitexid's Lakes snarled at me, neither agreeing nor disagreeing to my request. I jumped down the short flight of steps and jogged over to the lower cargo hold of the transport. The derelict spun the wheels kicking up sand and rocks, leaving me in a dust cloud. *So much for double-checking that we got everything off that hunk of junk. So unprofessional.* Still, I was glad to see it gone. Where we were headed there was no place for new or old electronic-based technology.

I brushed the worst of the dirt from my tan long-sleeve, light-weave shirt and brown pants. At least the remaining particles weren't noticeable. The CTF Transport Officer waved me over from high in the cab of his flatbed rider. Thanks to my text sent before boarding the antiquated rental outside the museum, our supply package arrived right on time. I ran over to speak with the driver of the now empty supply-rider.

"What's the word, Mac?" I asked over the hum of his air intake. Somewhere in the back of my mind, I wondered at the efficiency of the air filter keeping the flat-bed rider aloft with all this sand around.

"It's all good to go. The gang helped me unload. I've got another run to make for the Facility. You mind if I take off?"

I knew I didn't have to double-check the flat-bed, he was Facility after all.

"Sure thing. Thanks for your help." He gave me a sharp salute with two fingers touching the bridge of his nose, honked the horn, and left for the city. In the transport's wake stood a mound of materials to be re-compiled.

I scanned the area. The three lakes on my right glowed a shimmering- orange with the setting of the Alpha sun. Beta held just north of mid-sky as Gamma sat slightly east. We would track our journey according to the Gamma Sun, spiritually known as Zerameteth – the Child of Light, since it would be visible during the late night hours leading up to the darkness of twilight.

Syvis held the schematics I devised for the altered wagon dubbed 'the hauler' as he delegated tasks to various receptive members of the group. Nothing existed for travel through the Deserts. No one was foolish enough to try. I'd had to design and build a vehicle to haul kegs of verrin over a variety of sand-based terrains.

Working with the CTF's onsite Engineer, we researched the old tech the Ancient Journeymen used during the Great Migration, and any new tech free of electrical properties. Our resulting hybrid was the only good thing to come out of this fiasco. It was all about balance.

Engineer Hevec and I found a way to reduce the weight of the hauler by half, and eliminate the weight of our cargo. By magnetizing sheets of Zerillitite, a lightweight transformative metal, Vec and I matched the polarity on a second layer of magnets and got it to hover above the first by nearly two inches. Similar technology existed on a smaller scale using traditional, dense magnets, but we pushed the boundaries and our experiments paid off. Coupled with a lightweight synthetic rubber for the oversized tires installed with automatic release valves, to compensate for air expansion in the heat, three people could pull the hauler with ease. Getting to work with Vec made prepping for this contract almost bearable.

Dezmind crouched off to my left, reviewing his tracings of

the Tablets and looking over his notes; a pastime with which he'd absorbed himself for the majority of the trip. Flipping open a small, worn, red-leather book, I studied my own notes. The book had been a necessity since it was common knowledge that large technological dead-zones littered the Deserts. Between that and the drifting pockets of charged magnetism, any information stored on an electronic device would be useless.

In the chaotic three days since sealing our contract, Dezmind had held two more Rallies, looking for recruits and volunteers 'spreading the word'. Zaith had attended each one, since Dezmind also brought other speakers with him. *Interesting that none of the other speakers are out here with us.*

I, on the other hand, had spent much of my time in public libraries and bookstores, researching the Deserts and organizing supplies based on my findings. Of the five major libraries and all known bookstores in Darzeth-Prime, I'd found only four non-fiction source publications on the Deserts. The Kronik had published one more than forty years ago, which had subsequently been updated and revised to allow for new information, about ten years ago.

The other three sources were small, pocket-sized books that read more like journals than reports. They were the detailed experiences of one man's journeys as far into the Deserts as he dared go. He was known only as M. Doire. I'd first suspected his gender when reading a particularly descriptive passage about the hazards of relieving yourself at night in foreign territory. His books, being the most in-depth and honest, not to mention unbiased compared to the text developed by the Kronik, were my sole resources.

He'd described four different types of Deserts, speculating others beyond his reach, and included rough maps of each area he covered. More important though, were his detailed descriptions of each Desert habitat, with side notes on how he'd survived without food rations. Some of my handwriting was difficult to read, since my palms were still healing, but I could make out enough words to trigger the right memory.

I had taken it for granted that Zaith would find a way to come with us – for her story. I always assumed she would be here to help me keep my sanity with this rag-tag bunch, but Touf was being vengeful. He'd denied her request, on the grounds that if she didn't make it back, the Network would lose a 'valuable asset'. *Therefore, I remain the only sane person here.*

I looked over to see if Dezmind was ready, but he continued to scribble furiously. I checked on the group: the three women seemed to have bonded quickly as they fitted the sheets of magnetised Zerillitite to the substructure of the hauler. The men, however, even while working together, kept apart, all except for Werks and Deltek. But then Werks seemed to get along with everyone.

I glanced at the setting sun, Beta, closed my notebook and approached Dezmind.

"We need to leave within the hour if we're to minimised heat exposure during our allotted trek times. The sooner we leave the better. The hauler's nearly ready."

"I just need a few more minutes. Once I have a vague map outlined, we can go."

"Good. I'll check the group for concealed weapons."

"I don't think that's necessary."

"I do."

I walked over to a gentleman with pale blue skin and gold coliths, gnawing on the end of his pencil while watching the other four men lift the upper bed of the hauler into place.

"I don't mean to disturb your train of thought, Merik, but I need to check you for possible weaponry."

"No problem, I wasn't composing."

"Could you turn your pockets inside out," I asked firmly. He obliged, his teeth continuing to reduce his pencil to pulp.

He was a poet, I'd learned and very focused on his art. He'd readily spoken with me on the transport about his need to write something of consequence; that this was as worthy a cause as any, and why he'd chosen to experience the adventure personally.

He didn't think we'd find anything out here, but had thought the experience might be inspiring. He wasn't even sure if he believed Xannia was in any great danger to begin with. I could understand his hesitation when faced with the Kronik saying one thing and this rogue Talian saying another. Dezmind had no idea just how serious a game he was playing, and I couldn't afford to set him straight if I wanted to keep my freedom.

I patted down Merik's beige dungarees, finding only a supply of pencils and a small pad of paper. His belt-pack contained basic medical supplies, dried foodstuffs, and a small vial of synthetic verrin as recommended. Should the worst happen and the group be separated, I had to be certain everyone stood half a chance of surviving until I found them again. More than three days without verrin and death was a slow stretch of your shadow away. One small drop of the concentrated synthetic every few days would be enough to live on.

"Just wait over there with Dezmind until I've checked the others." He nodded, nearly oblivious.

Syvis finished his inspection of the hauler, and met me as I approached.

"It won't be long now. Not more than ten minutes," I said. He nodded, then turned out his pockets before I could ask.

"I just need to conduct a quick search," I clarified.

When I'd spoken with him earlier, he'd responded mainly with a nod or shake of his tanned head. He was not a naturally verbal man.

As I stood from checking his shoes, he pointed at Dezmind and Merik. I nodded, and he went to join them.

The women, finished with their task for the hauler, stopped talking as I neared. I still caught the end of their conversation.

"The Kronik *say* they've been researching the problem for more than a decade," Lutrice said. "Yet they've still 'formally reached no concrete resolution' on the source of the quakes."

"Either they have no clue whatsoever, or they're hiding something," said Tamaine. "They're actually saying more than they realise. I can't believe this business with the ground sonar "

"She's coming," shushed Jantice.

I made no effort to dissuade them, and allowed them to believe I hadn't heard their slight against the Kronik.

"Hello, ladies. I just need to make a last check of everyone before we head out. Stand at arm's length please."

I started with Tamaine. Her soft features and pink skin lent her an air of unfettered innocence. She and Jantice, a tall Nirian-Balanis cross of dark-grey skin and deep-purple coliths, had been best friends since early childhood. Certain there was nothing but fluff between their ears, especially Tamaine's, I was surprised at the poignancy of the previous conversation.

"Jutaya? All set now," Dezmind called.

"Right. I'm almost done too," I replied.

Raylan brushed by my left shoulder as the women joined the rest of the group. I snagged the back of his brown canvas jacket, pulling him around to face me. What I had read of his dossier made me shudder, but attitude like his needed to be dealt with immediately or it would only get worse.

"You haven't been checked yet."

I stared into his dark-green face. His light-silver coliths gave him a tempered look, but I knew better. His dark-green skin, inherited from his Metek father, had absorbed the man's aggressive genes.

Likely he saw his silver coliths as a mark of weakness from his mother's Glaaon heritage. The man was a walking time bomb.

"I don't need to be checked by you," he sneered.

I leaned in to his ear, yanking him a step closer and down a few inches, "Toss out whatever prejudiced baggage you came with, or I'll drop you right here and leave you to rot." I let him go, and stepped back with my hands on my hips. "Now, you can turn out your pockets and extend your arms, or I can do it for you."

He scowled, but complied. It would've been impossible to speak with him earlier about his behaviour, but this was not how I wanted our first contact to go. I should have left him behind. I would have, too, if Dezmind hadn't made me feel guilty about the couple. There's no way he was as indifferent to my decision as he claimed to be. I would just have to keep a close eye on Raylan. He seemed loyal, but only to Dezmind.

"Move it," I said.

His eyes flashed defiance, but again he complied.

Dezmind handed me his open notebook before addressing the group. I scanned it as he spoke.

"Friends, after deciphering the ancient inscriptions on the Tablets, I've been successful in plotting a course to the Pit of Chance. The road ahead is long and wearisome.

The weather will come in extremes and we'll face unknown

dangers. But together, we're stronger. If we persist and maintain a steady pace, I see us back again in just over a week. Together, we'll retrieve the Chronicles and save our home."

A cheer went up. I shook my head, unconvinced. The mark of a good speaker was to believably tell people exactly what they needed to hear. I had to admit, Dezmind could do just that, but it was a dangerous weapon to wield.

I finished tracing his map over mine, detailed by the explorer Doire. Dezmind's map led us straight through large areas of unknown territory. As the group dispersed to gather their belongings and load the verrin onto the hauler, I quizzed Dezmind.

"Are you in a great hurry?"

"The sooner we get there the better. As you so deftly pointed out at the Rally, we really have no notion of time, and the delays we've experienced so far need to be the last."

I opened my mouth to retort but shut it again. Now was not the time. The less I said on the subject, the better, so I showed him my map and returned him his notebook.

"Look, it would be safer to go around these unexplored areas. However, it would save time if we just ploughed right through. It would also be dangerous."

"What do you suggest then?"

"Ask your subjects," I snapped. He had to realise that he couldn't force these people to blindly follow him.

"Jutaya—"

I left before he could finish his sentence. I opened the map as I neared the group assembly-lining the kegs of verrin onto the hovering hauler bed. The wheels of the wagon reached my lower ribs. It was a behemoth but still half the size of what it would have been had Hevec and I not modified the design.

Doire's notes showed few sources of verrin throughout the Deserts, and I didn't want to rely solely on prefabricated concentrated slop. I had been fed enough of the stuff while working deep in the mines as a child. Sure, it had kept me alive, but I never felt right after using it for long periods of time.

I stood tall and spoke, "You have a choice to make. Time is of the essence." I pointed to the map. "There are two routes here, both are dangerous. The longer route will allow us to prepare for possible obstacles, the other won't. You have five minutes to decide."

I walked back to Dezmind and knelt down as he reviewed his calculations. Taking out a pencil, I erased the longer route from the map.

"They haven't decided yet," he said.

"That was simply a necessary formality. From what I know of them, the majority will choose to take the risk and the others will follow. It's all about pleasing you." *Even though you want to kill them.*

"Jutaya—"

"Now," I cut him off, "where exactly is this Pit, and once we get there, what do we do?"

Dezmind heaved a long sigh of resignation. "Just about here…" He pointed. "Or within about a half mile radius as best I can tell. Here's what I've managed to sketch of the actual chambers leading up to the Chronicles. The Tablets gave no indication of an inner map, but I did decipher vague descriptions of what we'll be facing with the three trials."

He showed me the sketches, fairly detailed and not so vague as he implied, consisting of five rooms: an entryway, each of the three challenges, and the final holding cell.

Syvis approached. "We've decided to go with the shorter route. Also, we're having some difficulty setting up the Anti-Heat Tent over the kegs of verrin. We could use your help."

"Jutaya will assist you," Dezmind said absently.

"Actually, we'll both assist you, Syvis. We've studied our options thoroughly and are well prepared for the excursion."

Dezmind glared at me, but there was no chance I was backing down. And he knew it. If he wanted to lead the people effectively, he had to do more than string together a bunch of fancy words.

The group had done a fantastic job constructing the hauler. The men placed the last of the kegs onto the levitating platform.

The AHT lay partially unfolded and set up. The group's only mistake was trying to construct it on top of a loaded hauler.

"Okay, first off we only need to raise half of the tent on the ground. We can place the other half of the tent poles, the extra rope and the securing clips down the middle of the wagon between the kegs. Next, we'll raise it up as a group and then place it over the hauler and secure it firmly."

For two hours, we walked east as Gamma crept lower into the evening sky. The heat gradually dissipated. With night blossoming, the temperature dropped dramatically with the setting of our smallest sun.

I wore a bandana over my nose and mouth, to keep from breathing in the finer particles of sand kicked up by our feet and the occasional breeze. My socks rode high over my pant legs and I had triple-wrapped my long hiking boot laces to create a seal against the sand. The goggles firmly affixed to my face with diver's gel were the only ones currently in use by the group.

I had fibre-mailed a small attachment to everyone yesterday detailing what equipment they needed to bring to survive this journey. Included with the attachment was a list of clothing and items that would aid them as they travelled. I hadn't highlighted it as mandatory though, so most people were improperly prepared. Until they suffered through a night's walk, there was nothing more I could do. They were all old enough to be on this quest, which meant they were also old enough to ignore my advice.

A dry gravelly plain that sported scattered sprigs of vegetation repeated itself endlessly as we trudged along. Our formation looked like a giant pendulum with the hauler bringing up the rear, its three towers linked to the front equidistant apart, and the remaining individuals linked by lengths of rope from the central tower. Dezmind and I led, our safety line dragging behind and between us as we walked. Forsaken howls of the large wild dogs, Kitotee as Doire named them, echoed in the early evening.

It was time for the second shift to pull the hauler. I disconnected my line and slowed down to match the speed of those who would relieve the towers. I lightly tapped Werks, Syvis, and Jantice on their elbows, a signal we had all agreed on for switching fluidly. They unlatched their safety lines one at a time from the person in front and behind. Then, they slowed their pace to match steps with the hauler at the back of the string of bodies.

Three ropes with T-shaped handles were attached to the wagon, equally spaced to allow for ease of movement. Deltek, Lutrice, and Merik unhooked and exchanged places with their replacements one at a time. The wagon slowed slightly, but that was to be expected during the first active switch. Group one gradually joined the ranks, connecting themselves to the safety line attached to the middle tower. I saw several more scarves and bandanas emerge during the transition, but no goggles yet.

I'd read about silk-sand and sand-eaters during my research of the Deserts. I didn't want to lose anyone out here because they had nothing to hold on to. The ropes linking our bodies to each other, and ultimately the hauler, were a necessary safety precaution in my eyes. Only Dezmind and I were able to move beyond or among the line for extended periods of time. Even Syvis would remain attached to the life-line until his services were required.

To the majority of the group, this was a gross over-calculation of a highly paranoid mind. They chose not to listen when I gave my reasoning for these measures as we rode the antiquated transport from the museum to the edge of the Expanse. Silk-sand was imperceptible when compared to regular sand and could suck a person beneath the ground in less than sixty seconds. Doire speculated that crevices in the dry earth had been filled with magnetised sand. Held together only by static electricity, the unsupported 'filler sand' became the trap known as silk-sand.

Sand-eaters, on the other hand, lived beneath the surface and burrowed underground. If someone were to stand still for too long, the eaters could tunnel the sand out from under them. Limbs would be lost instantaneously, whole bodies even, if no one was close enough to help. Both dangers were more likely to occur in or around the Powder-Sands Desert, located on the far side of three other zones beyond our projected course, but there was no sense in risking something similar happening before then. Being prepared meant being in control.

The Beta sun lightly kissed the ground as Gamma glowed an ominous, faint yellow, in the eastern sky. A mild breeze caressed my warm cheeks as I outpaced the group to join Dezmind in the lead.

Tamaine shrieked.

Everyone stopped. About to attach myself to the safety line, I paused, puzzled by the outburst.

"March side-to-side," I commanded. Tamaine stood rigidly in

place, staring with wide furtive eyes, squeezing the circulation from already-pale hands.

"What is it?" I demanded. She was too naive to be out here – another unpredictable element I didn't need to deal with.

"Listen," she forced out through clenched teeth.

"The animals have been howling off and on for some time now," I said.

"No. Different. Otherworldly," she insisted, trembling. I quieted the group, except for the soft shuffle of their feet.

It started low at first, a piercing whine or whistle. As it mounted in volume, its pitch altered, giving a sense of motion, rising and falling. The sound had registered in my mind as we walked, but instinct had told me to dismiss it. Deltek, Lutrice, and Merik searched frantically, quickening their steps as they looked around.

Now that we were quiet, the sound pulsed from all around us. It faded to nothing here and there, but always returned. Echoing hollow as it increased in volume, it never grew louder than a voice speaking, but seemed to come from a greater distance.

Why can't things ever be simple? I rubbed a hand over my covered nose and mouth, mentally flipping through the pages of notes I had written. There had to be a logical explanation. Nothing in Doire's journals…

A memory triggered. I took my notebook from my belt-pack, flipping through it to the sub-heading 'Desert Sounds'. Scanning the page, my shoulders relaxed and the nagging pain at the base of my neck subsided. "Don't worry. It's just the sand. Carry on and I'll explain."

"The sand?" Lutrice asked.

"Is she crazy?" Tamaine chimed in.

"Let's move, people," Syvis barked.

"I'm sure she knows what she's talking about," said Werks.

"Let's go, let's go, let's go! We shouldn't be immobile for so long," I blasted. All eyes trained on me as the procession moved forward once again. "It's clearly described in my notes. The strange whistling sound comes from sand avalanches."

Gasps erupted from a few individuals.

"Don't worry, we're only surrounded by small, raised areas.

It's more a case of wind erosion than anything else. When certain grains of sand rub they can emit a sound. The more the sand moves, the more the pitch changes."

As long as it's just the wind shifting the sand, we'll be fine.

Small sounds erupted from Tamaine every now and again, little squeaks actually. She alternately gripped and released the safety line attached to her waist and repeated something wordless over and over again. Likely some old prayer to the Trinity – the ancient Sun Gods.

A soft, delicate melody slipped into the air. I looked over my shoulder. In his hands, Merik held a small, reed-like cylinder, punctured with a double set of holes in various sizes. It appeared to be made of a pale, blond wood and looked hand-carved. It vaguely resembled a child's pipe instrument.

Merik's device played notes from the major scale, and though it sounded hollow, it came across as forlorn rather than eerie. Its simple, full-throated tune floated as if on the delicate wings of a merimec, a small, round-bellied song bird, into the vast Desert night. The sand-whistle abated under the dreamy consistency of Merik's tune.

Soon, Tamaine stopped squeaking and wringing her hands. We forged ahead in the settling cool of the night. I took my sweater out of my pack in anticipation of the bone-deep chill to come. One hour until Beta slept, six hours until Gamma, and thirteen hours until bed.

Chapter Ten

Barren Beginnings

"Make sure each peg is staked the full two feet into the ground. We don't want a gust of wind to ruin our rest," I instructed. I walked the perimeter of the AHT, advising and coordinating the raising of the tent.

Jantice spit. "Euahh," she muttered. "I can't get rid of the sand in my mouth."

Tamaine nodded. "I've got granules rubbing places even my betrothed hasn't seen."

"Jantice," I said, "swallow the sand. Don't waste your saliva. And don't talk. The more you open your mouth, the more sand will get in."

She gave me a dirty look, wiped her mouth on her sleeve and finished tying off the tent to the stake.

"Tamaine, after you wipe away most of the sand trapped where it shouldn't be, tuck your pants into your socks and tie your boots tighter. It'll happen no matter what, but closing off places where it can get under your clothes will make it more manageable."

I finished my circuit and caught up to Dezmind talking with Syvis and Raylan. "My eyes are sore too. I think it's from the finer particles of sand we kicked up when we were walking," Dezmind was saying.

"That's right," I added. "Next time, wear your goggles and don't forget the diver's glue." I motioned for everyone to remove their backpacks and follow me into the tent. There was no stopping the sand from following us in, we'd just have to get used to it. I was not taking my boots off unless absolutely necessary. There were too many crawly-things out here to risk it.

"Lay your packs around the inner perimeter of the tent. On their backs now, people, we need to disperse the weight evenly. Lutrice, don't worry about the side against the wagon, it has enough stable pressure," I directed.

The refractive nature of the navy fabric was widely used in smaller applications in the city as a way of keeping riders cool during the hotter summer months. I'd contacted the manufacturer and put a rush order on this larger tent design. I made sure Dezmind paid extra for fuse-thread to ensure that the holes punctured by the sewing needles in the fabric sealed immediately after penetration. There were a lot of weird things out here you did not want to wake up to.

Alpha was ready to ooze over the sand on the south-west horizon when we arrived here, the only semi-sheltered area since leaving the Expanse. It was nothing significant really, but the relief the shade would offer would be tremendous. The heat of the suns during the day was triple what we were used to. Any shade would be at least ten degrees cooler than the air temperature. The AHT would detract another ten or so degrees, making our extended daylight rest and sleep periods that much more comfortable. Besides, the less sweat we lost, the less verrin we needed to consume to avoid dehydration.

I left the AHT to check the surroundings one last time. I'd seen evidence of a snake hole on the other side of the hill and I wanted to zap it again. Deltek sat at the base of the mound in the first pooling of shade. The hill rose about a storey-and-a-half from the ground to a rounded ceiling, but its circumference was relatively small, maybe a hundred paces.

When we first arrived, I had everyone keep back from the hill as I inspected the site. I circled it, threw large stones at it, and finally gave it a small blast with my Clinex. It turned out to be just a pile of compressed rocky sand. I was still being chided for expressing undue caution. Many were still only doing cursory sweeps before sitting down, and nearly no one bothered to check themselves for strange bugs when standing up again.

The fools have no idea how lucky they've been so far.

In the last thirteen hours, we'd managed to trek close to fifty miles. The average Xannian walks about six miles per hour but this lot was working more around the four marker. While the ground was relatively flat and compact, these people were neither trained hikers nor avid recreational walkers. In the last hour before sunrise, our speed had been cut in half. Exhaustion had set in and the chill of night stiffened overworked muscles.

Deltek found a pointed rock, no farther than an arm's length from where he'd planted himself. His canteen hung open around his neck. Raising the rock, he proceeded to carve something in the crater left behind by my Clinex.

"Deltek, cap your canteen," I said.

"In a minute. I'm using the verrin to keep my work from breaking apart." He poured a few drops of his daily reserve onto the rock in his hand. I stormed over and crouched down beside him.

"What in Zola's graces do you think you're doing?" I couldn't believe he was wasting resources.

He laid his arm to rest across his lap, rock free. "That," he said, and closed his eyes a moment, the night's exhaustion pulling at his black and yellow Jeridan features.

In the centre of the crater he'd carved the word 'Latrine' in large letters. Below, was an arrow pointing left, beneath which the rock was stabbed.

Deltek opened his eyes, capped his canteen and lurched to his feet. With a cursory brush of his clothes, he snatched the rock and wandered to the back of the hill for privacy.

I frowned. He needn't have wasted his verrin. A simple rock for 'available' and nothing for 'occupied' would have sufficed.

Raylan and Syvis helped Dezmind remove the centre planks from the hauler for a place to sit during our meal. The magnetised Zerillitite was strong even though it was thin. He placed the laminated boards wood-side down over a few rounded rocks.

Werks offered his cooking expertise. "Jutaya, I know you prefer that everyone eat small meals from their own supplies, but with this being our first full night on our quest, I thought something a little more traditional would lighten the mood and give us more of a celebratory atmosphere."

"What do you have in mind? We only have personal food packs to work with."

"I slipped a little something extra into my pack after Syvis checked us over at the museum."

"Oh? And what exactly have you smuggled out here?"

"It's a surprise."

I frowned. His wide, hopeful eyes and playful smile won me over.

"All right, but make it quick. I want everyone in the tent within the hour." He gave me a quick salute and bustled off to make his preparations. I went to check on the others.

"Close the panel; we're trying to rest," said a groggy voice from the back of the tent. I let the flap fall back into place as I caught sight of Jantice's hand falling from her brow to her stomach. Lutrice, Tamaine, and Jantice each lay parallel to a tent wall and line of packs as advised. The more they combined their mass with something or someone else, the more they extended their surface area and the less interested sand-eaters would be.

"We already donated rations for dinner, does Werks not have enough yet?" Tamaine asked drowsily.

"I'm sure Werks has what he needs," I said. Raylan and Merik remained silent, but I could tell they were still awake.

"Mmm, 'kay," she mumbled before dozing again. I left the tent.

A bright red flame licked into the air.

"Werks! What are you doing? No fires." I shouted, running over to the source. I kicked sand over the flames.

"Jutaya, no!" He stepped between me and the small burning mass. "I only need it for twenty minutes. That's it. I promise."

"Fire attracts bugs and snakes and other deadly creatures you won't see coming."

Dezmind and Syvis trudged over with a hauler floorboard stabilised on their shoulders.

"Why don't we use the boards to block the light while he cooks?" Dezmind suggested. The worry lines and fear mingling on Werks' usually jolly face swayed me.

"Keep the fire small. No more than twenty minutes."

Deltek returned from his 'occupation' and stabbed the rock back in the crater, then joined the men as they helped block the fire.

With the flame under control and everyone in the group accounted for, I decided it was a good time to 'occupy' myself before dinner. *This better be worth it.*

Tamaine shifted positions for the fourth time before finally choosing a spot on my portion of the plank. That girl really bothered me.

The fire was extinguished using sand, and then two planks were placed side-by-side over the stone ring to make a table. A place setting with a black snap-flex plate, a dull knife, and a fork sat neatly before each person. The flex plates were ideal for this trip as they could be rolled to take up less storage space, but snapped flat to make a plate with slightly raised edges. Werks had brought them along, since the rest of us carried only dried fruit and meal packets.

The kindly grandfather remained true to his promise, and the meal had only taken twenty minutes to prepare. Roasted meat and fresh herbs wafted past dry noses and chapped lips – a familiar scent from my hours spent planning with Dezmind in his rented office at the back of the restaurant. The Alpha sun lazily stretched its rays over the horizon as our gathering rested nicely in the growing shade of the hill.

Werks turned around, carrying an arm full of steaming flex-cups filled with young root-vegetables sautéed in a spiced amber liquid. Over each cup sat a piece of flat bread.

"Werks," I broached cautiously, "this looks delicious, but how much verrin did you use?"

"One cup for the entire meal," he stated proudly before turning from the table again.

"Do you mean to say there's more?" I asked incredulously.

"Plenty more. Now, let your bread warm slightly before using it to eat your vegetables." With that, he returned to his preparation board. Hot food was not advisable out here in the Deserts. Doire had noted that his body required more water and more verrin to acclimate his internal temperature. *But it's only this once – remember? He wants to celebrate; they all do.*

"I wonder what he used for spices," Lutrice said.

"I'm famished. I need substantial sustenance to keep me going," Raylan said around mouthfuls. The other men agreed and nodded as they dug into their vegetables. But before I could lift my fork, Werks returned.

"Oh my," Jantice declared. She'd certainly chosen the expression forming in everyone's mind. Werks set down a full-sized ganoo, a farmed bird stuffed with dressing, on the middle of the table.

"How… how…" Syvis muttered, astonished. All eyes were fixated on the succulent bird glistening before us. Werks sat down. Syvis' cheeks grew bright when I made eye contact with him. He really hadn't known about Werks' little surprise.

"And there's dessert too. Come on then, let's dig in," Werks said. Merik was the first to find his voice. "How? How did you do it? There's so much–"

Werks smiled from ear to ear and clapped his hands twice.

"I wanted to surprise everyone. I knew our first day, or night if you will, would be draining and long, and hopefully uneventful as far as bizarre dangers were concerned. So, I cooked this ganoo back at the restaurant a couple days ago. I froze it with all its juices in a vacuum-sealed bag and packed it for the trip. From the stop at the museum until twenty minutes ago, it's been gradually defrosting in my pack. A campfire, some veggies, one cup of verrin later – and presto," he said opening his arms wide. "My gift to you in celebration of our important quest. Now, let's eat."

And we ate.

The vegetables had been sautéed in the bird's juices, masking the slight metallic flavour of condensed-anything, doing far greater justice to the contents than I ever thought possible. The ganoo fell from the bone and melted in my mouth as the spices tingled the sides and roof.

By the time dessert was served, two slices of canned rehydrated fruit lightly coated in a mixture of juices, even Raylan and Syvis wore contented smiles and joined the conversation. The air fairly shimmered with good humour, and not a scrap but the bones remained. Werks gathered them into a sealable bag with promises of soup for another meal.

Full bellies and tired muscles sent many a glance at the AHT. Before retiring to the tent for the next sixteen hours, as the Alpha and Beta suns dominated the sky, I demonstrated to the group the best way to rinse their dishes with a bit of verrin and catch the drips in their cups so as not to waste a drop.

Gradually, one-by-one, the group returned their dishes and utensils back to Werks then chose a nice piece of covered ground in the tent and someone to sleep beside. They would be dividing their sleep in half with a four-hour window of wakeful inactivity to keep energy levels high and perspiration low during the intense heat of the day.

Dezmind wandered off around the side of the hill as the last person disappeared into the tent. I returned to the fire pit. Using the toe of my boot and a wiry branch from a nearby loose shrub, I shifted the coarse sand and fine ash from side-to-side, walking full-circle around the ring of stones.

We'd managed to make it through night one of this crazy ordeal. I looked up into the brightening, clear blue sky. A large bird glided and careened in the distance. I squinted to see if I could make out its type, but it was too far away. The heat rising from the sand would create waves of mirages as it met the heat of the suns, making it difficult to judge distance by sight alone. But usually at dawn and dusk those waves could be avoided. The bird must have been well over five-hundred yards away if I couldn't make it out — that and the ineffectiveness of my long-range sight in the half-light of dusk or dawn made me unable to determine much with any kind of accuracy.

I sighed, not from weariness, but from the release of constant anticipation. Yawning, I rubbed my full stomach.

A distant muffled cry drifted, barely perceptible to my ears. I stopped to listen. I checked the hill's shadow; it had lengthened considerably since everyone dispersed. Perhaps I imagined the sound. It was more like the echo of a memory.

No, there it was again.

I moved quickly to the left of the hill, circling around it cautiously. If the sound was muffled, it was only because something large was blocking it.

"Is everything all right?" I called.

No response.

A dense 'thump.' My body went on high-alert. I raced the remaining steps to the halfway point behind the hill. Dezmind lay face down in the sand, unmoving. A trace of dark blue clothing disappeared around the hill. I knelt to check Dezmind's pulse.

Jumping up, I threw myself at the wall of sand, thrusting one booted toe after another into the compact dirt. At the top, another flash of dark blue whisked by below and slightly right. I crouched and launched myself into the air. Arms and legs spread wide, I plummeted toward nothing, humid air rushing around me. I slammed hard into someone.

"Get off me witch, or I'll kill you too!"

"I highly doubt that," I grunted, slightly winded as I tried to pin down the perpetrator.

"Go to hell," he growled, easily overpowering me. He scrambled to his feet. I rolled to one side, pulling my Whipstaff from the pocket of my left leg. I took a wild shot. Strings of energy ions sprung from the short wand, looping painfully around his neck.

"You first," I said.

I released the link. His body dropped. It lay on the ground at an odd angle. I crawled over, heaving to catch my breath.

Dead.

Picking myself up, I ran back to Dezmind. He'd had a pulse; I only hoped he still did. As I rounded the hill, he lay on his side with his back to me, holding his neck and moaning. I dropped down beside him, my heart clawing to get out of my chest as fear drove the adrenaline like lightning through my veins. Placing a tentative hand on his back and then on his side, I tried to assess his condition.

"Dezmind... Dezmind, sit up."

He took his hands away from his neck and placed them on the ground. A large, nasty purple mark pigmented his silvery-white neck, just above his collarbone.

The Perggle Hold.

Nothing else looked quite like it. Luckily, not enough pressure had been enforced to do much more than knock him out.

He struggled to sit up. "Could you turn away a minute?"

"Excuse me?"

"I was in the middle of occupying this space when I was so rudely interrupted."

"Oh. Right," I muttered and turned away. He scuffed the ground with his knees and feet, struggling to get up.

"Are you sure you don't require my assistance?" I asked, trying to make light of the situation. Knowing things were well in hand now – I wanted to ease the tension if possible, distract him so that he wouldn't fire me. That had been too close.

"And just what aspect of your contract would that fall under?" He took the bait.

"Perhaps it can fit in somewhere under bodyguard. But, if you're sufficiently capable of looking after yourself, I have a corpse to dispose of." I turned and left before he could reply.

"Gone," I spat the word like a curse. I rested one hand on my hip as the other massaged my temples. He was dead. I hadn't intended to kill him, but I did nonetheless. A vicious shudder tore through my body. I swung my head between my knees and breathed. Now was not the time to vomit. When my pulse steadied and the nausea ebbed, I slowly walked around the spot where the body had lain.

Oh, no. Where is it? I couldn't have... I'm supposed to be saving lives, not taking them. Dammit!

I shook my hands vigorously beside my legs as I walked. There were no footprints, drag marks, or foreign indentations of any kind – other than an impressed outline where he'd fallen. It wasn't silk-sand, he'd lain there immobile before I'd left, and the sand here was of the wrong consistency.

The ground beneath where the body lay was definitely not

consistent with the rough, pebbled surface we'd been surrounded by for the last ten or more hours. The remaining sand was finer, though not as pale as Doire had described powder sand. It seemed to be made of the same compound as the rest of the ground, just smoother, more fluid. Minute traces of a dark-blue crystal mingled with the fine particles.

I picked up a rock from the base of the hill and tossed it onto the outline in the sand. It landed with a soft thud, nothing more. I tried a few more, one where the head was, one mid-section to join the first, and a couple where the legs had been.

Still nothing.

Snagging a thin branch from nearby brush, I poked it into the ground around the rocks. I hit a solid base under the finer sand. Kneeling down beside the impression I snapped the branch and dragged its tip over and through the dirt. Pale particles glistened in the sunlight. Inspired, I grabbed a handful of the coarse brittle dirt surrounding me and crushed it between two rocks. It wasn't the same.

Something happened here, but what, I don't think I'll ever know. If it was a sand-eater, the fine particles would have extended deeper into the ground. If an accomplice had dragged the body or taken it away, there would be marks or tracks left.

Angry and concerned voices erupted from the opposite side of the hill. Dezmind must have hauled himself back to the tent site. I stood and wearily retraced the attacker's steps back to where Dezmind had lain, looking for anything that seemed remotely out of place or odd. I found nothing.

As I materialised around the front of the hill, Dezmind submitted to being coddled by the women as the men paced about arguing.

"Are you daft?" Raylan shouted. "I thought you were supposed to be protecting him! What good are you? Did you even manage to catch the attacker? My word woman—"

"Shut your mouth or I'll give you something to complain about. He'd be carrion fodder right now if I hadn't been here, so back off."

"Don't remind me," Dezmind muttered, rubbing his neck as he gave me a tired smile. "I apparently hired the right woman."

But his attempt at praise didn't even register as I continued in spite of myself, "In fact, I don't recall any of you coming to the rescue or even acknowledging that anything was wrong until it was over. So don't be giving me grief. I'm handling my job just fine." I locked eyes with Raylan. He didn't say anything more.

"Who was it?" Syvis demanded.

I ran a hand over my face. Pulling off my goggles and bandana, I said, "Werks."

Eyes flitted from face to face and heads turned to assess the truth of my words.

Jantice spoke first, "Werks? Impossible! It couldn't be him."

"No, not impossible," I corrected, "just improbable. But the fun doesn't stop there."

"What do you mean?" Syvis asked.

"His body's gone."

Chapter Eleven
Question or Observation

No one got much sleep that day. It had been mild inside the tent, and dim. Very little light pierced the AHT. Still, those sixteen hours were marred with tossing and turning, coughing and sighing, shifting and fidgeting.

Those who slept managed only a few hours here and there. Tamaine dreaded falling asleep, even though it was unlikely she was in any danger. When she did drift off, she woke screaming, elevating the tension near to breaking.

I napped when Dezmind was awake, but remained alert most of the time. I could manage without sleep for three days, under normal circumstances, but I had been trained to. These people wouldn't even last the next several hours in their current condition.

We had to repack the tent twice before getting it into a semi-transferable state. Even then, the hauler's centre floorboards were still loose. The group was eager to carry on: anywhere but this campsite seemed preferable. I stayed behind once they'd gone, to examine the impression in the sand one last time.

When I caught up with them, I noticed a double set of tracks in the sand and discovered they'd lost fifteen minutes by heading west instead of east as instructed, even though Dezmind was leading them. I hadn't noticed the manoeuvre at the time since I was behind the dune and their general walking noise carried easily over these vast planes whether they were near or far.

Night arrived like a shadow taking watch. The group had been quiet for the past half hour. It had taken them an age to calm down and steady their pace, and now they lagged with fatigue.

It was a cool, beautiful evening. The stars shone like white crystal orbs. I squinted and the black night disappeared as the sky washed in pure light. Unfortunately, I appeared to be the only one enjoying the evening trek into oblivion.

Deltek and Lutrice huddled close, crimping the safety line, trying to keep each other warm. The girls temporarily latched onto Merik, but Raylan and Syvis walked solitarily on. Those who bothered to bring goggles or sunglasses wore them and either bandanas or scarves to cover their noses, mouths, and necks. No one talked, keeping the intake of sand in the mouth to a minimum.

I nudged Dezmind in the arm with my elbow. He erased a scribble from his book and looked up.

"Yes?"

"I've got an odd feeling about those two," I said, jerking my head.

"Is that so?"

I looked at him, unimpressed.

"Why did you nominate one of them as group commander then?" He egged me on.

"He volunteered. It would have caused a scene if I'd denied him. Besides, his dossier reads well, but I can't gauge his emotions. Raylan on the other hand, keeps me on edge. I think he does it on purpose. He's got issues."

A long silence stretched between us. These quiet times were becoming more comfortable. However, the weight of this one told me Dezmind was thinking about something. I angled the map into the faint glow of the Gamma sun, a glow much like the moons I'd seen orbiting other planets in other systems. The memory of my first day attending Level 7 at the CTF flashed through my mind.

Yes, Gamma was like a moon but I believed more in the theory of it being a rogue star caught by Xannia's gravitational pull before the pair of them were sucked in by the twins – Alpha and Beta.

He spoke, "You don't talk much, do you?"

"Is that a question or an observation?"

"Question."

"No." He laughed, heartily and full, letting his voice carry out into the vast Deserts. He rubbed his bruised neck.

"Did I say something amusing?"

"Rather, it was what you didn't say that was so inspiring." He was awfully chipper, considering.

"Well, if you like to talk so much, you can be the one to chew on sand for a while. Just don't overdo it or you'll dehydrate yourself."

"Will you respond if I do?"

"No promises." This time I looked directly at him. Bad move. He was smiling that cocky smile of his, though this time there was a softer look in his eyes like he'd suddenly stopped trying to be someone else. *Interesting.*

"Ask me a question. Get something off your mind." He broke the spell.

"Why are you keeping things from me?"

"Like what?"

"Oh, don't play coy. You know exactly what I'm talking about. This whole nonsense concerning the Tablets and the Chronicles and your information – it's difficult enough to manage a contract without people keeping things from me; all the facts haven't been laid out from the start. And *three days* preparation time! What was that? I'm supposed to become an expert on the Deserts in three days? *And* you couldn't even get yourself to the museum to figure out the map before we set out with everyone. That was an organizational nightmare.

"A rendezvous point separate from your last minute research would have at least afforded us time to discuss your findings without an audience or the clock counting down the minutes to this insanity."

I snapped, crushing any residual trace of friendliness between us. His unprofessionalism and the ultimatum, set by the Ethics

Committee Governors, floating over my head, finally broke my restraint.

"Is that why you're so aggressive toward me? Because I don't tell you *everything?*" His unbreakable calm irked me even more.

"You missed my point entirely, or rather I think you'd like to have me think that, and that's exactly what I'm getting at." A wild animal wailed in the distance.

He stared ahead into the vast Barren Plains, eyes vacant.

"I don't know all the answers, but I have to appear as if I do. The answers I do have, need to be kept secret, for now." I couldn't fight a man who refused to rise to my ire. His soft words quenched the heat of my anger.

"More mystery," I muttered. Again we were quiet.

I rubbed my arms to warm them before swinging my pack over to one shoulder. I pulled out the sweater the CTF gave me for successfully completing my first contract. It was faded from black to charcoal- grey; the once red lightening flash on the company logo was now a muted orange. I slipped it on as we walked, manoeuvring my pack as required.

"Tell me something about you," Dezmind asked.

"You're the one who wanted to talk."

"Okay. All this time you've been spending analyzing the Kahn-lea's behaviour patterns and individual personalities, I've been doing something similar with you. Would you like to hear my findings?"

"And if I don't?"

"I'll tell you anyway."

"Then why ask?"

"Simply a formality."

I looked at him sharply. Actually, it would be interesting to hear his misconceptions. Surely he didn't believe he had me pegged.

"Shoot," I said.

"Right then. You're an only child, both parents deceased. A close family member chose to place you into Contractor Training rather than a Foster Home or an Orphanage. You have relatively few friends, and only one friend you can truly rely on — but then, one can only truly rely on oneself, right? You thrive on adventure and block out any external interaction that threatens to ruffle your life routine. You hide in your work behind carefully laid out contracts." He paused. "So, what do you think?"

How did he get all that from forty hours of contact? Sure, he'd read my public file with the CTF but that was just a listing of jobs accepted/completed or otherwise.

"Close," I said. "My parents didn't die, they gave me up. I had no relative to put me anywhere, least of all Contractor Training. That was my own choice, my way of saying *I'm better than you ever thought I was.* I have plenty of friends at the Facility, and those I've met through jobs, I keep in contact by cyber-mail, though my best friend and I see each other often."

"What about all the other stuff?" he queried.

"No comment."

"You're parents gave you up? So you were a foster kid after all?"

"I managed to stay out of the system."

"What happened?"

"I'm not a fan of reliving my abandonment. After eight years I would've thought I meant more to them. I was their first child after all. Not that it mattered."

"So what did you do if you weren't in the system?"

I didn't say anything. Living on the street was not something I was proud of, neither was giving up my freedom for five years to work in the Government-run Mines. I pushed the unwanted memories back into the pit where they belonged. Talking was overrated.

"Do you have me figured out yet?"

"Haven't even tried."

"Why not?"

"Don't want to."

Four hours later, the group continued to move at a slug's pace. I raised my right hand into the air and the procession halted.

Stepping away from the head of the train, I stood before them. Dezmind shot me a confused look as I detached from the safety line. I walked the length of the rope until I reached the middle.

"We'll rest here for the next hour. Remain attached to the safety line and find a place to sit somewhere on the hauler. Sleep, snooze or stare at the stars for all I care. When this excursion continues, I expect everyone to keep pace until dawn."

A collective sigh rose from the group as they planted themselves around the hauler. Dezmind and I would take the next shift with Merik. I'd give Syvis a chance to demonstrate his commitment to the Cause by leading the group for a two-hour trek. I spent much of the silence between Dezmind and me crafting a detailed map for Syvis to use. It was everything I'd learned from Doire's Journals – I didn't want him getting us lost.

Dezmind sat to my right, and took out his book and pencil again. Tamaine sat to my left. She moved her back against the kegs of verrin, half-rubbing and half-scratching warmth into her arms and torso. Dezmind drifted between writing in his book and meditation just as Tamaine fell into a deep sleep. Both she and Jantice lay against Merik with their head on his shoulders. He didn't seem to mind the extra body heat as he chewed on yet another pencil.

I wonder how many he brought?

The group slept soundly. Taking my own advice, I watched the sky. Dezmind sighed deeply, relaxing more into his meditative state.

The heat of his body pulsed into mine as we sat with legs and shoulders touching. The limited space available on the outer edge of the hauler meant getting cosy was a necessity. Strangely, I didn't mind. I couldn't remember the last time I sat amicably next to a guy. I had to admit to myself, that despite his ambitious faults, he was a nice guy – for a Talian.

An astounding number of stars clustered in the heavens. The light pollution from the city and the measly six hours of twilight each evening prevented all but the brightest stars from being seen back home.

I recognised a red dwarf in the southern hemisphere, the trio of blue stars called 'Betiny' after the first mother-settler of Darzeth-Prime, and many others I hadn't bothered to look for since the early days of my training. Astronomy had been one of a few delights I experienced in my studies. Mythology had helped explain why the stars were granted certain names – Zola the Great Mother, Zita her supportive Sister, and Zerameteth the wayward

Child of the Light. Science had shown me what they were made of, catalogued them as Alpha, Beta, and Gamma, and revealed to me how to find them during each seasonal shift.

If I closed my eyes and remained perfectly still, I felt alone in this vast arid wasteland. The only one who could cross it – and live.

Tamaine shrieked.

Will that girl never relent?

I opened my eyes and grabbed the blonde's flailing limbs. Tamaine poked a shaking forefinger between my arms to a spot by a sand bush. The earth at the base rippled and moved as if alive. One tendril, then another pushed its way forward as it pulled itself up out of the ground. It didn't move like any animal I'd ever seen before, though its main body mass resembled something the size of a small leecer.

"Oh no, oh no, oh no! It's coming!" Tamaine hyperventilated. I let her go. She rocked in place as I reached for my Clinex.

"Don't be such a baby. It looks harmless, Tam," Jantice said as she jumped down from the hauler.

"Jantice, don't touch it! Let me handle it," I said, following close.

"No. You're just going to kill it."

"It's safer that way. It might kill you. It's probably poisonous or has a lethal bite. Don't be foolish. Nothing out here's safe."

"Nonsense. It might be the tamest creature since the domesticated mountain lynx. Don't prejudge." Jantice crouched down and held out her hand to it. Doire's notes for sucking out poison and detoxifying bites flashed through my head. Delicately it crawled onto her palm employing the use of twice as many legs as my pet lynx. It was fuzzy. I could see the individual hairs on its back as it crawled around on Jantice's palm. *This can't be happening.*

It rested in her hand for some time, Tamaine fretting all the while. Everyone watched from a distance with an intense fixation.

Jantice daubed a few drops of verrin into the cap of her canteen using only her right hand, moving slowly and methodically. She placed the cap beside her palm, where she supposed the beast's head must be. Its entire body was covered in light and dark spots, but at one end of its double-fisted body the darker spots glistened. *I'm going to regret this, I just know it.*

The little creature crept forward and crouched low, partially covering the verrin. When it resumed its stance in the middle of Jantice's hand, the cap was empty. She closed her canteen and slowly stood up, holding the creature.

It moved again, all eight appendages travelling independently over her palm and onto her wrist, crawling up the length of her arm. I held my breath and ran my forefinger over the Clinex's charge sensor.

Jantice giggled, "It tickles."

Crawling over her elbow, up her bicep, and over her shoulder, it finally settled onto her head – perching there a moment, unmoving. I slowly released the air burning my lungs. The little beast then continued its jaunt down to Jantice's right shoulder, onto her arm and finally settled on her other palm.

Once again, it waited, motionless.

She brought her left hand over to it, and slowly stroked its back. One by one, each of its hairy spindly legs crouched to a squat, or it lay down perhaps, but either way it appeared content to be held and petted by Jantice. For now.

I followed her back to the hauler, and powered down the Clinex. Jantice sat between Merik and Raylan, both of whom appeared interested in her new pet.

"If that thing bites you, don't expect me to save you. That goes for all of you," I warned. But the men held out a finger to pet the strange Desert creature just the same.

"What will you name him?" Merik asked.

"How do you know it's a him?" Jantice countered.

"It, then. What will you name it?"

"Tamaine? What do you think?" she asked softly.

"I don't know," Tamaine said, quietly sobbing. "It has no personality, it's just all hairy and spotty."

"Spot then. I'll call it Spot. I found it in a spot, it looked like a spot of something at the time we noticed it, and it's covered in spots," she declared.

"Oh, what a fabulous batch of deductions that was," I muttered. Dezmind chuckled beside me.

"Loosen up a bit, Jutaya. It probably would have done something by now if it was inherently vicious."

"Perhaps, but the last thing we need is the group getting overly confident with one nice creature in the midst of Deserts full of killing machines," I argued.

He patted my shoulder before resuming his meditation. I felt a smile tug at the corners of my mouth but I flattened it before the sentiment could reach my heart.

He was not my friend. At best, he's the man who'll destroy my career. Despair flickered in its absence as negative thoughts pushed around my mind. *You can only depend on yourself. Do the job and do it right, or you'll wish you were the one who'd died out here.* I suddenly felt more isolated among these people than I had in a very long time.

Zaith, why didn't you come? Nothing holds you back. Where are you? I sat down and thought of my first trip to the local animal shelter; the first time I met Jadis – trying to latch on to a different memory. But reality dragged me back to the present. There was still half-an-hour for the group to rest if they could. Whether they would or not, was now a dilemma.

Chapter Twelve
Plain of Spheres

The next night, I watched as the Beta sun sank into the eastern sands close behind Alpha. I'd never bothered before to just sit and look at the suns as they rose and fell. I never really had the time to waste.

I rested my head against the back of the AHT. *What am I doing here?* I knew the answer to that question even as I tried to find a scapegoat. Dezmind picked me because of my dossier – I hadn't exactly been quiet around the office about how working in the Expanse didn't faze me. And if I'd reigned in my own fear of letting the innocent come to harm, I wouldn't have shot my weapon in public like that.

As much as I tried to stay angry with Dezmind, the logical part of my brain screamed that it was my own fault. But being here during my ethics probation just made everything that much worse.

I stared out across the vast Desert plain, letting the empty space fill my equally empty heart. The horizon glowed deep red, capped with an orange slice that faded into the yawning blue of the evening's sky. Though the Gamma sun shone a fierce pale yellow, its light didn't carry the same intensity as the others. Some scientists still worked under the archaic theory that it was a new kind of moon, but that was ridiculous – moons didn't produce heat.

Waiting for the group to rouse, I sat in the diminishing shade of the tent and drew my thoughts back to the task at hand. I needed to set a certain pace to be able to match our progress with Dezmind's original timeline. Our supplies mandated nine days: one week.

Doire had been very specific with the maps in his journals: the speed at which one should travel, key landmarks and formations to watch for, and a coded legend identifying vegetation, type of Desert, and danger zones. All of this, combined with Dezmind's expectations, sliced grooves in my mind with the repetition of it all.

Today we'd pass though an uncharted zone, just beyond the borders of the second Desert; the Plain of Spheres. I needed these people awake and alert, so I let them sleep for now.

Figuring in the hour's rest the night before, this extra time, and our march at half-speed yester-night, we were behind schedule nearly half a night. Perhaps we'd gain an hour today, but no matter, it still threw off the calculations.

If the damn Pit is even out here. We could canvass miles of ground, expend energy and supplies, and still end up with nothing. *By the time we get home again, Professor Denali will have confirmed his theory about the cracks in the earth's crust and be working toward solidifying for report to the Kronik.*

The ground-penetrating sonar surveys the girls mentioned back at the Lakes were a clear sign that the Kronik was taking Denali's work seriously. Studying the active fault-lines might provide a clue as to why the quakes were increasing.

The tent flap shifted. Someone exited. The distinct smack of liquid hitting the ground broke the still of the approaching evening. Those same feet scuffed the earth, burying waste remnants. A minute later, the flap fluttered again. *Sleep while you can, you're going to need it.*

Taking off my cap, I ran my fingers through my bangs, wanting to shake out the rest of my hair as well. However, it had taken a long time to pin it in place; I didn't want to let it out yet – sandy and filmy as it was. Instead, I fanned my face with the brim of my hat, resting my forearms on raised knees.

I tugged at the dirt-stained gauze wrapped around each of my palms. I hadn't had time to change the bandage since the morning before we left the Prime. Zaith's story of heroism had apparently done nothing to save me from this place.

Someone rounded the tent and sat down beside me. I put my hat back on.

"It's getting late," he said.

"Yes it is, but we must wait," I turned to face Dezmind. He stared straight ahead, out into the sprawling Deserts. The mark on his neck, now black and yellow, peeked above his blue shirt collar. His travel scarf hung loose around his shoulders. *That mark shouldn't be there. We shouldn't be here. I shouldn't have had to kill a man.*

"How much longer, do you suppose?" he asked.

"A night or two, if your map is accurate." I picked up a stone and chucked it out at the horizon. He turned to me and held up a roll of fresh gauze. I reached for it but he nabbed my wrist and gave me a stern look.

My self-preservation instinct flared. *I'm perfectly capable of tending my own wounds.* However, this was not a battle I needed to fight. I let him play medic. He was good at that – he played the businessman and the prophet, so why not try on another title. I felt an inexplicable need to shore up the wall between us.

"You still don't believe it, do you?" he asked quietly, being rather rhetorical as he gingerly unwrapped my scabbed palm. It was as if he'd heard my thoughts before joining me. I answered with a question of my own.

"Why do you believe? What is it that you know that makes you so sure the Chronicles are out here? That the answers are out here?"

He massaged a healing ointment from his belt-pack onto my hand, tracing the knotted flesh that was once a girder trench. He had a firm grip but a tender touch. I hadn't expected the old, smooth calluses that peppered his palms. *I wonder what other roles he's played?*

"Ah, you still want your mystery solved," he mused. "I don't suppose you'd believe me if I told you it was my destiny."

I snorted and chucked another rock with my free hand. "We make our own destiny. The suns are not Gods, they're just suns."

"No, I didn't think you'd understand." A hint of laughter laced his deep voice. He carefully wrapped my hand, keeping it mobile but protected. "My father is one of the top ten advisors to the Kronik; he made sure I was taught well and that I studied all of my lessons, history especially because *'our past has much to tell us about our future'*, or so he would say. My life has been laid out for me pretty much since I was born; the status I would have as a Talian, my place in the Kronik's Council after my father retired, even who I was to marry."

"So what?"

He paused in his ministrations to look at me. I didn't need to hear about his perfect life. I wanted to hurt him with my pain.

"My parents left me to die when I was eight years old. That's not fate, it's cruel. Why should they love my younger brother more than me? Your *fate* would say it's my own damn fault. There's no such thing as destiny and there are some truths we're never meant to learn."

His fingers twitched slightly as they supported mine. A worry-line creased his brow and he lowered his eyes. For a moment we said nothing. My flash of anger disappeared almost as fast as it had hit me. He continued to wrap my hand.

"My life didn't stay perfect," he said. "It all came crashing down with a simple twist of fate. Yes, *fate* Jutaya – my fate. From that moment on, I could hear the words spoken between the lines, saw deeper into meaning, and distrusted the whole foundation of my culture and upbringing – in a way, I did die. Who I was no longer existed. I could see the lies and deception teeming around me, even though I didn't understand it at first."

"What did you tell your parents? Your father?"

He allowed himself a sad smile. "I left them a note. They wouldn't have understood. My father would've put me into a mental health treatment centre. Don't get me wrong, I love them – him – but they're too close to the Kronik to see what I've seen. It wasn't until later that I learned the full extent of those lies, when I left the Compound. A hidden people I wasn't supposed to meet taught me the other side of the story, taught me how to live again. There's a whole world most citizens know nothing about, and that's not a good thing."

It seemed like there were things neither of us could fully reveal.

He held his hand out for my other palm. I gave it to him. Sure, he was being evasive, but listening to his story erased at least one suspicion from my mind – Dezmind had not ratted me out about the Rally. He really wasn't *one of them*. He was here, right?

Not hidden behind some compound wall like all the other Talians.

"A woman I was never supposed to meet found me lurking in her bushes when I was nearly eighteen. At the time, she was the only one I could trust to tell me the truth. As she sat there in her green prison, she gave me hope; the answer to the one question that had plagued me for nearly six years – what I needed to break away and leave the Society and join civilization... to become who I was meant to be. It's because of that, I know what we are looking for is out here, somewhere. I don't believe in coincidences, Jutaya. Things happen for a reason."

His eyes were unfocused, as though seeing something inside his mind – maybe he wondered what the Gods were doing abandoning me as a child. I almost felt bad for throwing my past at him like that. Maybe he was flesh and blood after all and not just some puppet pulling strings or an actor playing his part.

He ran his thumb lightly over the thin black tracing around a red colith by my wrist. It gave me the shivers. I slipped my hand out of his – part of me wished I hadn't. He tucked the remaining gauze in his belt-pack. I tossed another rock as Beta dipped beneath the horizon. He'd given me an answer, to be sure, but broadened the mystery nonetheless.

I flipped up and checked my watch-com, scattered waves jumped, broke apart, and rejoined. The vast electrical fields out here blocked the signals from the communication satellites above.

I snapped it shut.

Technology was useless out here, as useless as believing in fate and destiny. But I agreed with him about needing to know the truth. The problem was its elusiveness. Dezmind was a dreamer, and that would only get us killed out here.

Rustling sounds and awakening yawns announced it was time to rally the troops. I jumped up and turned to look at Dezmind over my shoulder. "I'll figure you out yet. No, I'll figure *this* out," I corrected myself. I rounded the corner and entered the tent. "Rise and shine campers, it's the setting of another day. Let's pack up and keep moving." I spared no time for luxury as the group collected and packed for that evening's march.

* * *

Another night and another day passed without incident. Tonight we ate as we travelled and I pushed them hard while they were fresh. Few complaints were voiced since most realised we were still making up for lost time.

Part of the group's willingness to accept physical punishment like this had to do with Dezmind's early evening pep-talk, telling them that it was about a night's walk to our destination – bad idea in my mind. *What happens if it takes longer?* I hoped he planned that far ahead.

As we walked, subtle changes appeared in the physical make up of the Desert. The consistency of the ground gradually altered: squat patches of leafy vegetation sprouted where the waist-high spindly bushes used to sit, and slowly, ever so imperceptibly, the ground became uneven, loose, and difficult to walk on.

"Oh!" Tamaine exclaimed. The group's rapid progress ground to a halt.

"It's okay!" Jantice called out from the back of the line. "She tripped on a crack," Jantice helped dust off Tamaine. I disconnected from the safety line to check out the situation anyway. Tamaine squeaked again when she caught sight of Spot sitting on Jantice's shoulder.

"Must you carry that thing about with you? Put it on a leash or something, I don't want it coming anywhere near me." The back of her shirt rose as she fended off Jantice's good intentions.

"Funny, you didn't protest last sleep when Spot rested a couple of hours on your stomach," Jantice cracked.

"What!" Tamaine shrieked.

"I'm joking. Spot stayed in my pack the entire time. It likes dark cool places." She stepped back and looked Tamaine over. "You've still got some sand in your hair."

"I'll get it," I interceded as Tamaine struggled to finger-comb the dirt from her blonde mane. The group continued east, a notch slower than before. I glanced at Tamaine's back and caught sight of scratch marks and gouges in her skin.

This girl is going to be the death of me. I hooked into the line between the girls and helped Tamaine with her hair as we walked. Not sure if what I saw was a pre-existing condition or something relevant to the Deserts, I casually asked her, "What happened to your back?"

She gave me the *don't pry* look. "There's nothing wrong."

I swallowed a sigh and stopped an eye-roll before it got the better of me. If anything, Dezmind had shown me that being subtle sometimes was better than my direct approach for dealing with these people.

"You're bleeding."

She blew her messy hair out of her eyes and crossed her arms. "It's nothing, Jutaya. That thing…" She motioned with her chin to Spot sitting on Jantice's shoulder, "makes my skin crawl. I can't help it." She attacked her arm through her sweater with her nails.

Getting the heebie-jeebies was one thing, but this looked like something else. I held out my hand, a silent request to see her arm. She gave it to me and I pushed up the sleeve to see red welts and criss-crossed scratches.

"It feels like your skin is crawling?" I double-checked. I felt a shudder run from her shoulder down her arm. "Relax, Tamaine. Just let me take a closer look, okay?" She bit her lower lip and nodded.

Releasing her hand, I rifled through my belt-pack and pulled out a magnifying glass from my time with Professor Denali. Manoeuvring beside her, I linked arms with her allowing her forearm to rest on top of mine. I scanned her skin with the glass.

"I don't see anything."

She turned her ankle in another crack and jostled the glass up to her sweater. Then I did see something, something that made *me* shudder.

"What?"

I looked at her directly. "Let's just say it's not *nothing.*" She looked ready to squeak. I held her arm firmly. "There's no need to make a scene. If you feel itchy, don't scratch – rub. When I find a spot with some cover, I'll nod at you and you can ask to relieve yourself. When you're out of sight, take your sweater off, bury it, and put on a clean shirt. Oh, and rub some of your verrin over your torso and arms like moisturiser. At the next official stop, I'll check you again."

"What is it?"

"Nothing that'll hurt you. You're doing a bang-up job of that on your own."

Dammit. It slipped out.

She frowned at me.

"Trust me," I said and released her arm. Tucking my magnifying glass away, I disconnected the safety line to join Dezmind at the lead.

Soon after, Tamaine saw her moment and took it. There were few complaints as she left to relieve herself behind some sparse shrubs it was Tamaine after all and everyone had come to expect such things of her. As it was, I never did tell her about the sand mites devouring her sweater. No wonder it felt like her skin was crawling she'd ground some of them into her scratches. I'd look for the healing plants Doire used in similar instances, between here and our next stop. I didn't want to think what her body would've looked like had I not seen it in time.

Two hours later, our progress slowed by half. So skewed and rutted was the ground that anyone could twist an ankle if they weren't cautious. Patches of tall, brittle grasses dotted the landscape and I got Dezmind and Syvis to collect the healing-plant samples with me along the way. Catching sight of a round, knee-high object about twenty yards out, I raised my hand to stop the group. I moved to a central position to talk to them.

"As you might have noticed, the landscape's been changing for the last couple of hours. We're well into the second Desert now. The shrubbery is low and you'll find clumps of dry grasses. The land will eventually even out a bit, but not much, and we'll have to avoid even larger cracks in the ground. We're just coming up on the sand spheres. Don't worry about them. They're harmless, but there'll be a lot of them to avoid. If you fall on one, the worst that'll happen is it'll crack or crumble. Try not to trip. The fewer times we need to stop, the better."

I waved my arm forward twice and the procession picked up again. The spheres were scattered about randomly at first, but after a while the ground was littered, making navigating the hauler a virtual impossibility. We ran over what spheres we could, but not all of them crushed under the weight of our load. A number of times, we had to stop, right the hauler, and reload fallen kegs. This slowed our progress drastically. There was no way we'd reach the Pit tonight.

"Look! Over there! There's someone out there," Merik yelled.

The group stopped.

Someone out there? My mind flipped through all the possibilities. *Zaith? No, she'd be behind us, not in front. Doire? Perhaps – but why not call out? Another Assassin? Damn – I hope not.* I moved away from the chain of bodies.

"Who could it be?" said Lutrice from the hauler. She, Deltek and Merik had been manoeuvring the large device for the last while and couldn't see very far ahead.

"They're not moving, whoever they are," Merik said.

"Stay here. I'll go check it out."

The form remained still. It was difficult to judge the distance but it couldn't be more than a couple of hundred yards away. I dug out my Clinex from my belt-pack. I didn't know who had hired Werks to kill Dezmind. The Kronik, the Council, or anyone affiliated with the Government could easily have an agenda. Dezmind was rogue – he admitted that much – and it was obvious someone wanted him dead. He understood his situation better than I thought. He knew he was in trouble, and that put all of us at risk.

As I walked towards the staid form, the ground levelled out considerably. It was still uneven, but had fewer ruts and spheres. The figure still hadn't moved. Since night neared the full darkness of twilight, my eyes had difficulty adjusting. This was the one rare time of day that I couldn't trust them. Blinking repeatedly, I tried to push against the haze that clouded my vision.

My breathing quickened, my pulse followed. How could they have known my vulnerability? I had told no one, not even Zaith. Reaching down, I picked up a stone and whipped it at the figure; its two arms remained elevated – frozen.

Nothing.

No response.

I walked closer.

A faint aromatic scent teased my nostrils. I stood before the supposed seven-foot tall person and laughed. The over-active imaginations of the group saw a man where a plant stood. As my muscles relaxed, relief and anxiety fled with the sound of my voice. This plant was flowering; a good sign. I turned and jogged back to a now clustered group of travellers, whispering furtively.

"It's not alive. Well, at least in the sense that you mistook it for. Come on, there's something I need to show you." I reattached my safety link.

Dezmind lifted an eyebrow at me. I just shook my head, bemused. He shrugged.

"Bring the hauler," I said, as they resumed their positions.

Walking past the looming figure, the group realised their mistake, many laughing at their own insecurity. The next few plants flowered as well, but I stopped when I spotted one with oval, fist-sized objects clinging to it.

"Gather around. I want you all to see this," I called.

The group assembled in a circle around me and the plant.

"This large plant is called a cactus or cacti. These ones in particular are called Mercy cacti. They bear a fruit, the prickly pear. As you can see the stalk grows green." I pointed to a new fruit pod, "And the fruit is two shades of red when ripe, barely discernible in this light. One type is far more acidic than the other. So acidic in fact, that if ingested it will eat you alive from the inside out." There was a collective groan.

"One organ after another would slowly fail, like the deadly Bolantio Poison. The other type though, is sweet. Its flesh is slightly dry, but underground verrin reservoirs give the plant just enough sustenance to allow positive nutrients to flourish. Though it will never quench your thirst, it will make a fine meal substitute for pre-packaged cuisine."

"So which one can we eat?" Raylan demanded, arms folded high on his chest.

"I'm getting to that." I continued, "What I am about to impart must never be forgotten. Each cactus is unique. The colour code for edible fruit changes with the plant."

"How are we supposed to know which one is safe then? We'll

be taking a chance with our lives if we just blindly choose," Raylan scoffed. He was really trying my patience. I'd lost the group again.

"I won't go anywhere near that stuff," Jantice said.

"It's a death trap," Deltek muttered. "Why even bother telling us about it."

"There must be a logical explanation," said Merik.

"Why are you taking her side?" said Tamaine. "She's tempting us with what we can't have."

I couldn't believe the hostility coming from these people. I lost my resolve to be more like Dezmind and scowled at them, the ungrateful mites. No one realised the amount of planning and the pressure to know enough about everything possible to keep them alive. No one believed me, again. Contractor status be damned. I should just quit and be rid of it all – except that would mean living out the rest of my life in the mines. I had to find a way to get through this fiasco.

Dezmind raised his hands. The group quieted.

"Patience, friends. The long road is testing us, but we have to continue to keep faith and trust one another. We're standing on the precipice of history, truly exemplifying all that the Kahn-lea represents. Take a moment, listen to Jutaya and give her your complete attention. She's the only one who can get us to the Chronicles and safely home again." *Does he really believe that or is he just saying that because he needs to hide his own incompetence for bringing us out here in the first place?*

"There's a way to test the fruit," I stated, and carefully plucked one from the large limb by my head. I unsheathed a tiny dagger from beneath my belt-pack and cut the pear in half. Holding both halves in my left hand, I used the blade to cut away a patch of spikes from the side of the cacti.

"Slice the pear and clear a spot on one of the plant's limbs. Hold the face of the fruit to the cleared area for a few seconds, let's say thirty." I removed the pear from the plant. There was no change. "The darker red fruit is edible on this particular cactus," I stated, and tossed a piece each to Syvis and Raylan.

They turned the fruit round and round a number of times, squeezing it and poking at it. Raylan even sniffed its fleshy centre.

"Show us what will happen with a poisonous one," Syvis said.

I nodded and reached for a pale red pear, plucking it carefully from the cacti. I sliced it, let half fall to the ground and placed the face of the other half against the same spot on the plant. Thirty seconds later I let it too, fall to the ground.

"Oh, my word," gasped Lutrice. Around the edge of where the pear had been, the plant's skin had severely wrinkled, creating deep grooves. The very centre though, was the cause for her outburst. The green of the plant had blackened considerably and, as we watched, small holes connected until there was nothing but a shallow crater the size of the pear. A trace of burnt sweetness alighted on the breeze.

"How do we know this one won't make us sick? Why should we trust you?" Raylan shoved his piece under my nose.

My certainty would never be enough.

I had my doubts about the pear at first too, but believed the author's authenticity after the poisoned pear reacted just as Doire described. The Desert Voyager had proven his commitment to science and truth. I'd never again second-guess his writings. *Too bad I can't say the same for everyone here.*

I plucked another deep-red pear from the cactus, sliced a chunk of the skin off and ate it without hesitation. The group dispersed and, using the dinner knives I'd salvaged from Werks' pack, began testing the fruit on other cacti.

"Don't eat more than a couple or you'll find yourself needing to stop for personal time more than you'd like." A few snickers and shoulder glances at Tamaine lightened the mood. "This is still fruit after all, and very fresh fruit at that. Collect as many as your packs will carry, they'll last a good couple of weeks before they start to rot."

That would keep them busy for the next quarter-hour. Time well spent for a change.

After the picking session, everyone regrouped from gathering provisions and moved to take up their previous positions.

"Wait, Deltek," I called. "We're going to switch up on the hauler now."

He nodded and found a position in line instead.

"Raylan, Jantice, Tamaine – take the next shift. When you're ready, give me a shout," I delegated.

Raylan frowned. Disengaging his line, he walked up to tower over me. "That's not smart. I'll end up with most of the strain. This is a rough road and they're just city girls."

I smiled. "City girls? Are you implying that they won't be able to complete the task I assigned to your satisfaction?" I raised my eyebrows.

He glared at me.

"You know their abilities as well as I do," he said. "We'll have more spills and waste more time if you pair them up," he growled. I took a step closer to him and rose onto the toes of my boots, our noses barely an inch apart.

"I've noted your concern, but I feel it's unwarranted. Take up your position, middle pull."

He exhaled heavily, the sweet scent of pear mingled with three-day- old mouth bacteria soured in my nostrils. I remained perfectly still until he broke eye contact and strode over to the hauler. The girls, already hooked up on either side, acknowledged his arrival.

He grunted, "You'd better keep up," before yanking on his hold, starting our walk without warning. It was a small sacrifice to let it pass; I'd had enough of Raylan's attitude for one night. Perhaps walking with the girls would do him a bit of good.

We progressed at a careful pace, the hauler only toppled once before we reached steadier ground. I glanced over my shoulder from the front of the line. Between the bob and sway of heads, I could make out a deep scowl etched on Raylan's face. He'd been hoping the match up would fail miserably. The one thing he kept forgetting was my map tucked away securely in my little notebook.

It was true I had known we would be travelling in uncharted territory, but the cactus field was clearly marked with a vast plain on the other side of it, littered with few obstacles for about an hour, probably more. Doire had turned back at this point and explored in another direction but one thing I'd learned so far being out here was that the landscape changed very little. I figured the girls would have no major trouble with their burden. I was also pleased to see that the strenuous task kept Tamaine from scratching.

Dezmind bumped elbows with me as he hooked onto the line. "You look awfully smug. What's up?"

I shrugged my shoulders. "I just might be getting through to Raylan on some level."

"I noticed you stuck him with the girls. I have to admit, I was going to let him off the hook. I was thinking the same thing he was."

"And how do you know what he was thinking?" I challenged.

"I asked him before I joined you."

I felt the anger flash up my neck, across my cheeks and into my eyes. *How dare you.*

"Whoa, don't get upset. I have to make sure they *all* feel like they're the most important link in this chain. All I did was hear him out, let him blow off a little steam – let the girls overhear his concerns and maybe have them realise the importance of being part of a team."

"You should leave well enough alone, or I just might abandon you here with this band of misfits."

"That's an empty threat and you know it," he said. Before I could retort, the sorrowful song of Merik's wooden instrument wafted through the night air.

I turned my head forward and held up my chin. If he second-guessed me one more time, I'd prove to him just how serious I was. I may not be able to quit this contract, but I would leave him and his disillusioned followers long enough for them to realise just how much they needed me.

My resolve to push everyone away melted a couple hours later as muffled sobs reached my ears. Maybe one of the girls had strained themselves and didn't want to admit it. No one else seemed to notice. I walked toward the hauler and found Jantice clutching something near her stomach, crying. It looked like she was getting ready to release her travel pet. *It's about time she gave that thing up.*

I approached and walked beside her. Spot lay in her cupped hands. Something wasn't right.

"Jan–"

"It's dead, Jutaya."

"Do you think it was foul play?" I asked. Tamaine and I might not have been the only ones to harbour a grudge against the furry beast. "I never thought – no. No, I don't think so. It's been quieter and drinking less today. I thought maybe it was home sick but then I probably haven't been feeding it properly. It's deflated, so much smaller now."

"Could it be hibernating? In some kind of stasis?" I asked. I knew it was dead. I don't know how I knew, but I did. As much as I hated having it around, I had to be mindful of Jantice's feelings – something I was lousy at to say the least.

She sighed. "No. It's dead."

"Let's bury it then." Jantice looked at me, confused and yet relieved. *I'm not that horrible, am I?* I halted the line and waved everyone over.

"What now?" Raylan said. Dezmind placed a hand on his shoulder. I bit back a retort.

"Oh." Lutrice sighed, catching site of Spot.

Crouching in the centre of the circle of bodies, I used my hands and dug a hole. As Jantice whispered to the small creature lying across her fingers, I searched for a couple of rocks to mark its burial ground. Deltek and Merik handed me a few from nearby. When I knelt beside Jantice again, the hole was filled and she held her palms to the small mound. I passed her the rocks and she made a ring around the grave.

Chapter Thirteen

Once Upon a Story

Muffled footsteps scuffed loose sand. Chilled air made breathing sharp and lungs frosty. Everyone kept to themselves, even Deltek and Lutrice who normally huddled against the cold. I thought about Jantice and her strange attachment to that creature. Sure, I had Jadis, but I'd known her nearly all her life and it would make sense to mourn her passing. But this was a matter of days, not years. I know I was a part of it but I couldn't understand it, no matter how I looked at the situation.

The wind picked up at one point, causing a sand whistle that accompanied us for the remainder of our night's walk. Merik played his pipe to sooth frayed nerves. It sounded like a funeral piece. They were all affected by the creature's death. Perhaps they finally felt their own mortality out here. Syvis walked, with his map, beside Dezmind. I followed just behind the pair; not because I felt Syvis needed the leadership reassurance, I just wasn't in the mood to talk.

Dezmind, Dezmind, Dezmind. Why did you drag all these people into the middle of nowhere? Witnesses – it's the only thing that makes sense. It rubbed my soul raw.

It would have been so much easier with just the two of us. No assassination attempts, no foreign pet creatures, no jittery group members, and no jerks.

I'd tried to talk him out of it during our initial planning session back at the restaurant, but he'd said something along the lines of *not keeping this from the people*. The political reality was that, in order for his plan to work, he'd need survivors to be praised and to spread the *Truth* in his name. In the end, he really wasn't very different from any other politician. They all managed to twist the truth enough to sell their wares, and by the sounds of things, his basket was half-empty.

Every time he spoke with me, I got mixed messages. His compassion and empathy for the people travelling with us knew no bounds. His patience was limitless and he always knew exactly what to say to soothe frayed nerves and calm hysterics. But his faith blinded him. In order to show the Kronik, and the known civilization, that his research into the past revealed glimpses of a forgotten truth, he was willing to risk innocent lives – had we met under different circumstances, I never would have thought him capable of it.

Dezmind looked over his shoulder, trying to spot me in the line. I looked toward him, but through him more than at him. I felt a deep line crease my brow. Every time I thought about it, I relaxed, but invariably it crept back again. Dezmind shifted as if to leave Syvis and join me, but I made it clear I didn't want company from anyone least of all him.

I'd been on a warpath since he mentioned speaking to Raylan in front of the girls. Sure, I could see his point but he never thought to include me in his plans. If Dezmind sided with the man it would have destroyed everything I'd been trying to do to bring some semblance of equality between Raylan and me – a woman in authority.

Dezmind didn't get it, didn't know how close he'd come to annihilating the strange but evolving trust between me and that man. The contract clearly stated that we were partners out here. He never bothered to realise how his simple acts of reaching out could undermine my authority; and not just with Raylan, with the entire group. These people looked first to him, not me, and in that split-second of doubt we could lose another life.

We stopped an hour early that night, long before the rays of the Alpha sun eked out over the horizon. I knew we were nearing our destination and figured that stopping now would be better than searching for the Pit in the pitch black of twilight.

Camp was set with the planks from the hauler as benches in a circle. A two-foot hole had been dug and lined with rocks. Everyone tossed their light-tubes in for a pretend camp fire. The hole shielded the glow from night creatures and our tightly-packed bodies screened the limited upper glow.

There were many strange and wild things out here I knew nothing about. Doire's simple warning of 'always be prepared' never left my thoughts. I double-checked the security of the area before joining the group sitting around the fake fire.

We had lucked-out actually, finding a collection of small dunes near a crossover to the next Desert – Valley of the Dunes. By the end of our night's walk, significant patches of soft sand had appeared, giving rise to small dunes and fewer cacti. This was the first area that was significant enough to shelter us from the hot winds that came and went during the day.

Tamaine moved to my right, guiding a still weepy Jantice to a seat beside Merik, before settling down. Jantice's canteen was open and a stream of verrin discoloured the tan casing. I frowned. *It was a two day attachment to a strange creature. This is ridiculous.*

Lutrice asked what was on everyone's mind. "Are you okay, dear? Are you feeling any better?" Though she couldn't have been more than forty, Lutrice had unofficially become 'Mom' to the group.

Jantice nodded across the glow. Dezmind cracked the warming pouch on the base of his travel rations before choosing the seat to my left.

He whispered in my ear, "Someone left the stopper off the active verrin keg." I nodded. I was pretty sure I knew who it was but I'd address it after a day's rest. Right now Spot's death was foremost on everyone's minds. Well, Jantice's inability to hold it together was the real issue.

"Much better, thank you. I'm sorry, I just can't explain the tears."

"It was a cute little thing. Death affects us all differently," said Deltek, his yellow coliths crinkling around the edges of his eyes, beacons on his dark face in this last hour of black twilight.

"What's on the menu besides warm travel rations?" Raylan asked Dezmind.

"Whatever you can find in your pack, I suppose," he said. "I don't have a feast for you and it's probably better that you don't overeat. You use up more verrin as you digest."

"Is that really true?" Deltek asked.

Dezmind gave me the nod, acknowledging that I was the factual source. I nodded to confirm, sucking back my own quantity of meal rations.

"I never feel full anymore," Raylan complained.

"Here's to breakfast," Merik joked, raising his ration pack into the air. Raylan glared at him.

"I have some bread in my bag we can share," Syvis offered, rising to retrieve it.

"The packs should be sufficient," Dezmind replied so I wouldn't have to. He was trying harder to support me. *I wonder if he finally realises why I'm pissed at him.*

Syvis returned. He passed the hard crusted bread around the circle. Everyone tore off a chunk to be polite, even me. This learning thing had to go both ways. The bread looked as though it had been baked especially for the trip. The crust was difficult to bite, but the centre was fabulously fresh.

We sat and ate, listening to the night sounds. The mini sand avalanches didn't bother Tamaine anymore. The soft whisper of wind across loose sand provided a white-noise that hid many of the rustles and creaks of the night. The stars slowly disappeared, the sun inching toward the horizon, as a faint, dark-red lined the distance.

After everyone had eaten, it felt too early to bunk down for the day, so Merik took out his wooden pipe and played a light tune as we relaxed. Finishing his third piece, he set the instrument aside.

Lutrice broke the silence. "You play so well. I've never seen or heard an instrument like it. What's its story?"

"Funny you should say *story*, for there are two; one about the origin of the piece, and the other about the making of it. But, I'll combine them into one tale if you'd honestly like to know," he said.

"Oh, yes please," said Tamaine, curious about the source of the soothing music.

"Writing poetry is much like any other profession, though it's rarely entered into anymore. After basic literature training in a senior institution, most students tend to enter the business world. Very few continue on in the arts. If you do continue, you must find a mentor to apprentice with. I was one of three apprentices to the only Arts mentor residing in Darzeth Prime.

"In my last year of study, when I finally got to focus and choose a particular artistic strain, I was also instructed to select an instrument that I felt exemplified the music I wished to make with my words. During the course of my studies, I had to research my chosen instrument and learn about its origins: how it was created, its main function, and so on.

"At the point my mentor felt I'd consumed all there was to know about my choice, I was then challenged to improve upon it in some way – just as I strove to improve upon my chosen field of study in the Literary Arts.

"I spent the better part of a year trying to perfect my musical art: metal shop, carving, bending, puncturing, twisting, moulding – until finally, I realised that it couldn't be done. The sound I was trying so desperately to achieve was being dulled by tricks and ornamentation. All I could really hope to attain was something suitable and close to my ideal.

"So, I took a branch from the neeta tree beneath which my mother had been buried. I carved a simple recorder in place of the elaborate clarinet I began with. From there, I added the extra holes – a process I had discovered during my earlier attempts – and altered the hollow of the shaft in such a way that the inner chamber curves slightly.

"When I finally brought the completed piece to my mentor, he congratulated me on finding the 'simplicity of beauty.' It never plays as well as I imagine it should, but every now and then, I come close to that perfect moment." He picked it up and twirled it nonchalantly before putting it away.

"I had no idea poets studied to such depths," Lutrice said, leaning against Deltek who wrapped an arm around her shoulders. "I've been studying cultural and social interaction since my first streaming year at the institution and have never once been challenged with such depth and passion. You must be quite the poet," she said.

"Actually, no. Had you ever heard of me before now? Seen my name advertised? A collection of my works published?" he asked.

Lutrice thought a moment, then shook her head.

"The problem with simple beauty is that it's been done before. Nothing I could write would be an original thought, unless something new happened. I haven't written anything in the five years since I left my mentor. In all that time, not one idea entered my mind that hasn't already been thought of. It's sad to think that my greatest achievement has been to create a bizarre nameless pipe-instrument out of a material that will biodegrade into nothing."

"Is that why you're journeying with us? For inspiration?" Jantice asked.

Merik nodded.

"Anything so far?" she tried again.

"Bits and pieces, about the Deserts mostly," he said.

"Could we hear some of it?" Tamaine asked.

He shook his head with a faint smile. "Perhaps it would be better to wait for my publication."

Dezmind broke the awkward silence that followed. "Lutrice, you mentioned being a student of society. What sort of work does that entail?"

"Oh, nothing grand really."

"Surely your work must be rewarding if it has brought you to us," he asked.

"I'm not a cause-seeker if that's what you mean."

"I think he just wants to know a little more about what we do, that's all," Deltek reassured her, kissing her temple and rubbing her arm. "We work for a branch of big business that links back to the Kronik. We're statisticians mainly, except our office is the city and not some room with four walls and a roof," he explained.

Lutrice picked up after him, "We study society, the way doctors study disease looking for cures, or the way scientists study atoms and look for ways to blow things up," she said referring to the tragic accident twenty years ago when a research lab exploded, killing helpless children in a nearby day-care centre. Most citizens were still unwilling to forgive the advent of the New Renaissance because of that incident.

"We don't canvas homes or ask silly questions about your preferred breakfast cereal," Deltek said. "We study behaviour within society, its causes and functions. We blend in with our surroundings and observe basic interaction in various forms, in various places, for various reasons."

"We actually met during a study of the same situation," Lutrice smiled warmly. "We were focusing so hard on blending in that we wound up relating to each other on another level."

Deltek clarified after blank stares flashed around the fire, "There are certain tactics we utilise to be able to observe without interfering. It was the use of those tactics on each other that triggered the recognition of another Situation Analyser.

"We'd never met before, and being assigned to different departments, we really tested our abilities that day. We were actually able to flirt with each other as we tried to remain inconspicuous to everyone else around us. It was because of that, we bonded on another level and have been inseparable ever since."

Lutrice smiled at him, continuing, "It was during one of our more recent studies that we happened to hear a Speaker talk at a Rally about the Spoken Truth. Since then, we've been interested in really making a difference, rather than simply reporting on how others can make a difference."

"That's so romantic," Tamaine gushed. "I just love happy endings."

"You were terrified about your own, when you learned your parents made a life-pact for you," Jantice teased.

"I've never met anyone who has a cherry. What's he like?" Lutrice asked cheerfully.

Tamaine tilted her head at the slang reference to her fiancée, but didn't say anything about it.

"At first, I really was terrified to find out. Life bonds happen so rarely anymore that I was afraid we wouldn't be compatible and would be stuck with each other," Tamaine confessed.

Jantice jumped in, "She was supposed to meet him when she turned of age, but she ran away the morning the meeting was set. Her parents, luckily, understood her hesitation and realised it was still too soon for her to feel committed to someone."

"They tried twice more after that," said Tamaine, "but every time I found an excuse not to meet him. Finally, my mom took me aside one day and said she would do everything within her power to break the bond if that's what I wanted. I just had to meet him once before I made my decision."

"So," Jantice continued, "his parents found out his plans one evening and relayed to Tamaine's mom that he and his friends would be at the Plexis. Her mom then pulled me aside and convinced me to get a bunch of our friends together to head over there too – to check out her cherry."

"My betrothed," Tamaine corrected lightly that time.

"Your *betrothed*. Anyhow, when we got there, we couldn't tell which one he was, so Tam had the girls and I go over and flirt with them – whoever declined our advances would be her guy."

"The problem was no one did," Tamaine said. "All of my girlfriends walked away with a guy, even Jantice. I was so frustrated I stormed out the front doors to catch a transport home."

"But, as she stood outside the Plexis trying to remember where the closest stop was, this gorgeous Balanis-cross with pale blue skin and rich black coliths walks out from behind the crystal fountain, holding a single red mika-flower."

"He walked right up to me. I was dumbfounded. Speechless. Frozen in place. He bowed deeply and held out the flower for me – I could just make out the cherry at the base of his thumb and–"

"And you know what she did?" Jantice asked the group. Wide eyes and head shakes answered. "She fainted."

"He rode with me to the hospital and sat by my gurney holding my hand, waiting for me to open my eyes. Really though, I don't think I've woken up yet," she confessed.

"So your parents were pleased?" Merik asked.

"Oh, yes. The wedding is set for next month," Tamaine squeaked, gripping her hands and shrugging her shoulders up to her ears.

"How long has it been since you first met?" Lutrice asked.

"Just a few months. I know how this must look, but I'm not running away again. I told Bazdin I had one last thing I needed to do before I could settle down. I've been following the Cause for months now and I knew at once that this quest was something I had to be a part of. I was lucky enough to be able to convince Jantice to come with me. I really didn't know what to expect when we got here, but I'll be pleased when I get home." She absently rubbed a spot on her shoulder.

Dezmind, Merik, Jantice, Deltek and Lutrice laughed at her declaration.

"What about you, Dezmind?" Jantice asked.

"What about me?"

"I've heard a few things about the Talian culture; don't you have something similar to life bonds?"

"Ah, yes. You could say that, Jantice. Only, ours is a little more guaranteed. We rarely experience the trepidation that Tamaine felt. What else have you heard? The Society tends to keep things quiet about our customs, it's interesting to learn about the misconceptions the general public have about my race. Maybe I can set a few things straight for you, clear up some minor detail you've always wondered about," he offered.

"I've heard you use magic," Tamaine whispered.

"Magic! Not quite," he chuckled. "Although we are a bit different in other ways. We have heightened abilities that lay dormant in most of the general public. Abilities that you could single out as being extraordinary, but really they're quite commonplace for us."

"Like what?" asked Merik.

"Well, some people can retain glimpses of others' thoughts, though even they are rare for us, and both people need to have the ability for it to work right. Some can move objects with their minds, other have heightened natural attributes: they can run faster, lift incredibly heavy objects, or hear nearly indistinguishable sounds. Sometimes more than one trait can manifest."

"I've heard that you look different because you're less-evolved," Raylan said. "Since the days of the first public records, Talians have been in powerful positions, allowing them to bypass physical labour, overexertion, and exposure to sunlight."

The whole group had been thinking it. Even I wondered about that particular rumour. The grey eyes, pale skin, wavy hair – what Raylan said made a great deal of sense, which surprisingly echoed many of my own opinions.

"A very common misconception," Dezmind said. "As far as we can tell, our silvery-white skin is just another colour representing another race: Tamaine's is pink, yours is grey, and Jutaya's is bronze. The only real difference is that we don't mix cultures; or rather it's stated that we can't without help from our doctors – and that is only permitted in very rare circumstances. You see, we have evolved a bit differently in that sense.

"As for our hair and eyes, I couldn't say for certain. It's true that we bureaucrats involved with the Kronik don't stay outside for long periods of time, but not because we can't or because it'll affect us in a negative way.

Besides, inside the Compound is a microcosm of the rest of Xannia: farmers, doctors, florists, you name it. We live as you live."

"Rumour has it that Talians deem themselves better than the rest of us, which is why we so rarely get the opportunity to see any of you," I accused, touting the one bit of trivia that was never really trivial to me.

"Jutaya, really!" exclaimed Lutrice.

"No, I'd like to know," I said. "Why do your people keep themselves locked away in a Compound behind tall walls and Society buildings? Why are you the first one to mingle with the commoners?"

"It's all right, Lutrice. Jutaya has a point. I'll answer as best I can."

Everyone leaned in a little closer as he prepared his thoughts. Even astounded Lutrice moved in for the big reveal.

"You're right of course," he admitted.

Astonished faces looked around the glow-fire at one another.

"But only partially," he amended. "The Kronik and his entourage of Councillors, Advisors, and Attendants, my father included, don't leave the Compound for exactly that reason. They've grown pompous and arrogant over the years and continue to pass that prejudice on to their families.

"The Kronik makes wire appearances only when he's afraid his ruling might be challenged, or he'll make an appearance during extreme times of crisis. I've heard my own father speak condescendingly about the masses, it's very unfortunate. He is a great and kind man who's believed the rhetoric for so long that he's now deaf and blind to the truth." His eyes misted over for a moment before he blinked away traces of the memory.

"But, the Compound is just another city. The difference is jobs tend to be passed on within the family. Since I'm the son of an Advisor, one day I too would have been an Advisor when my father retired. My schooling revolved around what I would need to know to be competent in the position and my family have been grooming me for the job since I learned to count and spell. Children are taught to delight in and respect their position, no job goes without reward. Occasionally families have apprenticed neighbour children, but it's always a trade off of skills.

"These people know as little about you, as you do about them. You are a mere curiosity at best, but are treated as an historical statistic or myth more than anything else."

"But why?" Deltek asked.

"The Kronik and his governing body like to keep it that way. All Talians live by a strict code, especially when it comes to mating. When the Kronik learned thousands of years ago that we couldn't naturally breed with any other race, a program was set up for matching families. This would allow our population to increase without the fear of deformed children or inbreeding.

"Later, with the help of a Seer, a telepath of sorts, this process mingled science with emotion and Soul Mates were paired up instead of simply matching genomes. Since no Soul Mate can be found outside our own community, people are content to live as they do and have regarded the 'Law of Interaction' as more of a redundancy than anything else. The people are happy."

"So you have a Soul Mate?" Tamaine asked.

Dezmind went quiet for a moment, as if unsure how to respond. His eyes shadowed as he dipped his head, mulling over his thoughts. "Every Talian has a Soul Mate, but I'm afraid you might not want to hear about mine. There is no happy ending."

Chapter Fourteen

Beneath the Mystery

Tamaine looked crestfallen, her eyes unfocused as she gazed into the glow, obviously sensing a deep wound in the man before her. I watched as the girl absently rubbed the cherry in the crook of her thumb.

"Perhaps there's still hope," she said wistfully. "Tell us about her."

Dezmind smiled ruefully. "There's little to say about someone I've never met and may never meet."

"But she's out there, right? There's a Soul Mate for everyone. You said so yourself."

"Yes, but sometimes things happen that even the Seer cannot foretell."

"Like what?" Merik asked.

Dezmind smiled at the group's curiosity and indulged them. I watched his face take on a new vibrancy as he spoke to *his people*, endearing them even more to his plight. This was his arena now and I couldn't help but feel drawn in, too. There was something magnetic about him.

"The story of Thomas and Lynnia should help you understand. It's the first of only two such instances where something has gone awry with a pairing. It's a fairly recent story, only maybe fifty-odd years old, which just goes to show how bizarre and unfortunate a situation it was.

"Every Talian child is brought before the Seer at the age of twelve; it's thought that by then both Soul Mates will be born. No couple is separated by more than twelve years to allow their fertility phases to coincide.

"So, at the age of twelve, young Thomas of Applex Mar, the village by the orchard, was brought before the Seer and given his Reading. He was to be a great tender of bounty whose warmth and compassion would shine through all that he produced. His Soul Mate was the seven-year-old daughter of a Shoemaker, two villages south in Ninben Mar.

"Now, it is unknown whether the Seer said more to the boy that day or not. For when little Lynnia of Ninben Mar was brought before the Seer five years later, she was told her beau of Applex Mar 'would never see her smiling face.' When Lynnia told her parents she thought her Soul Mate was blind, they questioned the Seer. News surely would have spread if a child had been born blind or had befallen a terrible accident. The Seer replied only with 'accident yes, very tragic – by the end of the day you will know.'

"Lynnia and her family felt helpless and confused. Was it something they could prevent? Or had the tragedy already happened and there was nothing left to do but sit and wait?

"Before dinner had fully begun that night, word reached them of a tragic act of heroism. The seventeen-year-old son of an Apple Harvester, two villages north, had rescued his younger brother from drowning. Though the young boy was saved from the undertow of the river, the older boy had been lost. His body, never recovered, was probably swept out to sea.

"And so, at age twelve, little Lynnia was without a Soul Mate. It was thought that perhaps the younger boy would take his brother's place, but every Talian has a different destiny. Even those whose fates have changed."

"Oh, that's terrible," Tamaine said. "What ever happened to little Lynnia? Was she really destined to be alone forever?"

"She had her family of course and her friends, but a Soul Mate she would supposedly never have again."

"What became of her then if this was only half a century ago?" Lutrice wondered.

"Unfortunately the main tale ends there, and most children never think to ask further about Lynnia," he said.

"Most children?" Merik highlighted.

Dezmind laughed a short burst. "You caught that, did you? Yes, most. But if I continue, we'll be getting into my story, which is a tale and a half in and of itself, and Alpha has already begun to rise."

"You can't stop now. We'll never get you to tell us later," Jantice pointed out. "Jutaya, let him continue."

I shrugged my shoulders. "It's up to Dezmind. Zola knows I haven't anything to offer the circle but two sentences about my Lynx, Jadis. By all means continue."

If I was to build trust with these people they had to feel comfortable around me. It would be suicide to march them to bed now.

Dezmind cast an odd look at me when I mentioned my lynx, but continued without pause. "My story and that of Lynnia's are not so surprisingly intertwined. A disturbance like hers is bound to have repercussions."

He took a deep breath and ran his right hand through the hair at his temple, shaking the waves as his fingers came free. "At age twelve when I was brought before the Seer, I was given the great news that I would strike my own path in this world and help make Xannia a better place to live. Of course, at that age I figured my best chance of that would be by becoming Kronik after taking my father's place as Senior Advisor when he retired. I would then be one of the ten considered for the position.

"But then, she gave me the bad news. She told me that my Soul Mate was the unborn child of an ill-fated union." He paused briefly to let that fact sink in. "Later, my parents explained to me that my Soul Mate would have been Lynnia's daughter. I was devastated. I couldn't bring myself to believe even the possibility of it.

"I spent the next year in denial, bottling up my anger and confusion. How could a boy destined to be Kronik not have all that life could offer? That's when it finally hit me. I couldn't be a great man with only half a soul. I'd been fooling myself into thinking I was just like everyone else. I went through my junior scholastic days brooding, verging on collapse into depression. My friends went their separate ways. I refused to go out anymore or even speak with my parents.

"Then, one day a thought occurred to me in the midst of a history lesson in my seventeenth year. The Seer had been wrong once, what if she'd done it again, without even realizing it? Thomas wasn't supposed to die. If the Seer had truly known his future path, he wouldn't have been considered a valid mate and been joined to Lynnia. The idea that I still had a chance – that all hope wasn't lost – gave me new purpose. I had to find Lynnia. She was the only one who could help me.

"After months of searching housing and town directories and enquiring into her current whereabouts, I was nowhere closer to finding her. People only remembered her story. Representatives I asked only responded with more questions about my enquiries. I was stumped. Someone didn't want her to be found. There had to be another story out there that explained it all. So, I went to see my Grandmother.

"She'd been a Story Collector in her youth and knew more about Talian myth and prophesies than most people did about math and science. I spent the better part of a month visiting her after classes, letting her tell me whatever story she wanted. My family was happy that I'd finally come back around, so they didn't interfere with my visits.

"Finally, one day, she asked me if there was anything in particular that I wanted to hear. I gave her one word: *disappearances*. She was thrilled that I'd picked such a difficult topic, for very few cases had ever been recorded and even fewer had been passed on by word of mouth.

"She began her tales well back into the ancient times, but it took only two visits for her to reach a tale that took place only seven or eight years earlier. Even though it was recent, most of the details were sketchy.

"A woman had been found sneaking out of the Compound late at night for months on end. For her crimes, she was forbidden to leave her family's estate. One night, a commoner snuck into the Compound in search of his Lost Lady. With a sketchy map to guide him, he located her family's estate where she'd waited in the gardens by the shore-cliffs at midnight since her imprisonment.

"This common man scaled the cliff face high above the sea to be able to rescue his Lady. "That night they escaped and disappeared for nearly four years. Her family and the Kronik were relentless. When the Justices failed to find them, they recruited Special Agents to locate the fugitives.

"She was eventually found by one of these Agents, and both she and her husband were brought before the High-Court of the Kronik, where he and he alone has total rule.

"The forbidden union was deleted from all civilian records and judgment was passed without trial. Her husband, known only as Matheson, was banished to the Deserts – branded with the family's house crest across his right cheek; forever marked as an outcast and a disgrace to all Society. He was helioed as far into the Deserts as the craft could safely fly, and left with nothing but the clothes on his back.

"His wife, being Talian, was given grace, but she too was branded a betrayer with the house mark. However, her sentence was to be continued on her family's estate. The sea-wall gardens were forever her home and prison. Construction workers blasted away the rock face her husband had scaled to save her, sealing her within its leafy catacombs. The Lost Lady had truly disappeared from Society."

"That's horrible! How could anyone be so cruel?" Tamaine sobbed, as Jantice comforted her after wiping her own moist eyes.

"But how does that connect to you?" Deltek asked.

"Yes, how?" chimed in Lutrice and Merik. Syvis and Raylan nodded, also caught up in Dezmind's suspense story. I cocked my head to one side and raised an eyebrow, waiting for him to continue, as I knew he would.

"My Grandmother had given me a very big clue without even realizing it. She'd said that all record of the Lost Lady was erased from civilization."

"So, how does that help if you don't have a name to go by?" Deltek queried.

"Oh, but I did."

"Of course!" cried Tamaine. "Little Lynnia from Ninben Mar."

Dezmind smiled. "My new task was to search for her name in birth records, death records, scholastic records, town records, you name it. I went to Ninben Mar and Applex Mar, and the Compound's Hall of Records and found – nothing. The child never existed. Now, I know what you're thinking; it's a myth, maybe she never really did exist. Not true. All myth has some basis in reality, and besides, I was working on pure faith at this point.

"If there was no record of this girl, she had to be the Lost Lady, and I needed to find her. I scouted all the sea-cliff estates and tracked each family's lineage, until I found one that connected a boy's name back to the town of Ninben Mar.

"All the records showed was that the son of a Shoemaker had been matched with the daughter of an Advisor. Housing records showed that this boy took his family with him to live at his new wife's estate. I'd found her, even though her name was never mentioned. All I had to do was get to the gardens of that estate and pray to the third sun, Zerameteth, that Lynnia the Lost Lady still lived.

"I canvassed the area for over a month. I studied the rock face, the blast zones, and the seabed. If I was going to get in, it would be following in her husband's footsteps. I spent the next three months leading up to my eighteenth birthday, preparing my body for its coming trials: honing and toning, building up stamina.

"Finally, it was time. The cliff was sheer with little to hold, let alone climb. So I started at the back of their neighbour's gardens, where security was a virtual joke. I sat on the cliff and let my legs dangle over the seabed far below, turned around and slid over the edge. I held onto the trunks of small nezza bushes and, hand- over-hand, inched my way along the edge of the cliff. When I reached the centre of the ridge between the two blast zones, I fought to lift myself up onto the tiny lip of ground behind the bushes before crawling into them – exhausted.

"Once I'd caught my breath, I rolled onto my side to get a better look at the gardens. And there she sat, in a chrome wheelchair covered in braided flowers and trails of ivy. Her long wavy black hair fell in ripples down either side of her pale, pale face. A lost, forlorn look etched her very skin; the hint of a shadow that wasn't, burned on her right cheek. She turned her face, so gracefully, and looked right at me through the bushes.

"'You've come at last,' she whispered, barely moving her pale lips. She didn't look like a woman about to enter her fifties. In the faint light of the fading Gamma sun, she looked no more than twenty.

"'Please',"I whispered. "'I'm not who you think I am. I've come to ask you—'"

"'Shhh,' she said, cutting me short. 'I know who you are.' She sat there, very quiet and still for a long time. Then, without a word, she turned her chair and wheeled away into the gardens beyond. In her place, a piece of paper rested in the tall, thick grass.

"I knew she wouldn't come back, so I crawled into the clearing on my hands and knees. I was weak and tired, yes, but this was no ordinary garden. I pretended to be a night animal. I crawled in circles until I reached the note, and continued until I was hidden in the undergrowth.

"I didn't look at the note. Instead, I placed it in my pocket and mentally prepared myself to leave. Even as I knelt in the neighbour's gardens again, I didn't look at the note. I left the Cliff-Side Estates, and quickly exited the town of Shoris Mar, taking only back streets home.

"I lay awake on my bed as Alpha crept to brighten the night's sky. Finally, I rolled onto my stomach, away from my bedroom door, and raised my arms as if to cradle my head while I slept. Instead of sleep though, I had the note by me as I lay there resting. A small ink-smudged date had been printed in the bottom right corner. I frowned and turned over the letter. Staring back at me in the early morning sunshine was a bleached photo of Lynnia holding a beautiful little girl," Dezmind whispered.

"So there's hope after all," Tamaine whispered back.

Raylan spoke directly. "How's that possible? I thought you said Talians couldn't mate with other races."

"Quite right," Dezmind responded, blinking back to the present. "Or so we've been told. The best and brightest common citizens are not catalogued and recorded with the CTF just for posterity's sake.

Every once in a while the Talian gene pool stops or drastically slows in growth; when that happens DNA is *borrowed* from other sources. I never said it was impossible for us to mate with other races; just that medical assistance was required. Not all Talians know this. I only know because of a business conversation I overhead my father having.

"My theory is that we've borrowed enough DNA over the years that even though Lynnia and Matheson were not traditional Soul Mates, they were able to reproduce. And, it is for that reason alone that they were banished without a trial. To keep as dark a secret as this hidden would require some drastic steps. The Kronik, as much as he loves Xannia, loves his pride even more. He'd be the last one to admit that his genetic superiority was dwindling.

"I couldn't say this at the Rallies for fear of being incarcerated, but I did my best to hint that this perfect society is actually full of flaws. The New Renaissance happened only as a deterrent – the Kronik couldn't have a revolt on their hands, so the noisy were silenced and the innocent were kept blind by innovation and invention. Zola, I wish I could tell you everything."

I sat back, stunned. I'd never heard of a genetic conspiracy before, and while his claims against the New Renaissance were not new, I hadn't expected them to come out of his mouth. Zaith would've had a field day if she were here. Luckily, most of the others didn't seem to comprehend the significance of what Dezmind was saying.

Tamaine's next innocent questions drew all thought away from the blatant announcement. "And you've been searching for the little girl in that picture ever since? How old was she? Do you think she falls within your twelve-year framework?"

Dezmind gave a small laugh at her unfailing ability to grasp onto any ray of hope. "That's why I like you, Tamaine, you keep the faith. I was able to make out part of the smudged date on the photograph, which set it to be about ten years earlier. The child herself couldn't have been much more than two. But I've stopped looking for her."

"What?" Tamaine gasped.

"There are only so many leads I can follow, and the Kronik had a hand in the disappearance of the child, I'm sure of it. I'm now content with knowing of her existence – it means I at least have a remote chance of being with her some day.

"In the last seven years, I focused instead on Xannia and its entire people. I left the Compound a year after my discovery, when my schooling was complete. In that year, I made a lot of important connections during my search for Lynnia's daughter – learned a great deal about the disquiet of the people and where the desperate go to find help. But my queries only took me so far. It's a matter now for the fates to decide.

"I've since turned my energies toward the growing quake crisis and other humanitarian efforts. That led me on the path to defining the Truth behind the Kronik's claims about the source of the quakes. I had to inform the people about my discoveries – even if that meant getting caught, and being locked away in a garden of my own.

"And here we are, achieving great things together in the name of truth, for Xannia. But now, we really must get some rest. The new day has dawned, and the temperature is steadily rising. Come now, the Pit of Chance awaits us when we wake."

A satisfied group headed for the AHT, content with the knowledge that Dezmind would indeed lead them to greatness.

I slipped a piece of the healing-plant Syvis and I found earlier into Tamaine's hand and whispered, "Rub the juices into the worst scratches and save the rest for later." Then I watched as the number of travellers around our fake blaze dwindled to zero. I turned my attention to stacking the seating planks and gathering the light-tubes to line up for solar regeneration as we slept.

Dezmind stuck his head out of the tent, turned, said a few words to its occupants then materialised fully. He walked right over to me. His normally straight posture looked rigid and tense. Something bothered him. Standing across the stone ring from me, he folded his arms across his chest. This was new. His body language was never defensive.

"Do you need any help?" he asked, as I reached for another handful of light-tubes. I nodded. He released his arms and crouched low to reach for some of the deeper tubes.

"What's on your mind, Dezmind?"

I could feel his eyes on me even though he faced the small pit. None of us had bathed in several days but the musky scent of his body did not repulse me as Raylan's nearness had. It mingled with whatever soap he'd used to launder his shirt.

"You mentioned the name Jadis earlier. Odd name for a cat, don't you think?" he said casually.

I wiped my nose with the back of my hand and placed the last of the light-tubes out for regeneration. *He wants to talk about my lynx?* "Mountain Lynx," I corrected.

"Yes, of course. Is that a common name for a pet?"

I sighed at his relentlessness. "No, just a name from my childhood. Why?"

"No reason, really. It just caught my interest. An old name like that usually has some history." He paused a moment. "Do you know its meaning?"

"It's just some name from a fairy story I was told as a child, back when my parents still loved me." *Why did I say that out loud?* "I never thought to look it up. I just liked the sound of it."

"Do you want to know what it means?"

Actually, I kind of did. "I guess."

"Mountain Lynxes are rare pets, are they not? Naturally wild and protected by animal rights?"

"Yes," I said, as he helped me stack the last of the hauler boards to one side for evening prep. "Mine came from one of the few abandoned litters the Animal Protection Agency cares for each year. Being raised in captivity, I'd heard they couldn't be returned to the wild, so I submitted my name to adopt one." I brushed a stray strand of hair out of my face. "Are you going to tell me what Jadis means or will that be all? I'm due for a date with my pillow," I said, turning to leave.

"You're not very good at this conversation stuff, are you?"

I turned back. "Excuse me?"

"I'm just saying," he smiled. "You haven't had a lot of practice interacting with people."

"Dezmind, I know how to talk to people just fine. Contractors are trained to handle *any* situation." His eyebrows rose when I said *trained.*

"I'm going to sleep now." I turned and walked to the tent. Before I entered, he said one word:

"Illuminate."

Chapter Fifteen
Valley of the Dunes

I rested on my back, lying perfectly still, eyes closed. *Illuminate.*
*That made sense. The fairytale revolved around a princess who controlled
the stars.* The tent had been opened half a dozen times already, but
I didn't move. For the first time in a long time I actually didn't
want to get up. *What do princesses and stars have to do with Dezmind's
interest in an ancient name? What does it matter?* I was far from being
tired physically but he – no – this group had a way of sapping the
energy right out of me. As long as Dezmind remained in the tent,
so would I. I was guarding him after all.

The sounds of shifting boards and the collection of light-
tubes by the others floated through the thin material of the tent.
Everyone was seeing to the official clean-up and reorganization
of the hauler. Either they felt bad about leaving us to tidy up this
morning or they were afraid I'd make them eat on the run again.

Dezmind hadn't stirred in a while; very unlike his morning
habits. "Dezmind," I whispered.

"I'm awake. Just thought I'd let you get a little extra rest for a
change. I wasn't planning on getting up until we were called to go."

I sat up slightly, resting on my elbows. "I really shouldn't have stayed. I'd better get up."

"I say we let them show us how 'competent' they are by remaining right here until we're called. It's about time we were the last ones to saunter out." He was right, but it irked me to admit it. I shifted to my side in order to get up.

"I think I've wasted enough time for one day."

"Jutaya, lie down."

Something in the sound of his voice, weariness maybe, stopped me. "What's up?" I asked, resting my head in the palm of my hand as my arm completed the triangle of support. He lay on his back with both hands behind his head, staring at the ceiling.

"I know I hired you to take care of us but you don't need to, you know, *always* take care of us."

I snorted a laugh. "Dezmind, there's no one else out here to do it. None of you know what I know about these Deserts and even that's a second-hand stretch of the truth. You of all people know why I'm here."

"You don't want me to get these people killed." That about summed it up but I didn't say it out loud. "Our forefathers in the great migration—"

"Stuff it Dez," I said. He turned to look at me. "I know you're here because of the Cause and your noble search for the truth. But I didn't just shoot at you at the Rally just because you were threatening to put people's lives on the line – I did it because you were being a pompous know-it-all."

"What?"

"You made it sound like you had all the answers, but our first night out here you admitted to me that you didn't. I don't like being lied to. You claim the Kronik is lying to us but really, how are you any better? Because you're a nice guy?"

"Are there no shades of grey in your world, Taya?"

"Excuse me?"

"You tend to see things in black and white, good and bad. I don't think I've lied to anyone – because I believe in what I'm doing. Do you understand that?"

I laid back and looked away from him. "You're making my head hurt."

"Look at it this way; you believe in right and wrong but you still chose to fire your Clinex at me. For you that was a justifiable action, an action for the greater good and I'm sure it's not the first choice you made that blurred the lines."

Zaith's face plastered itself in my mind as I heard myself telling her about my time with Professor Denali – what I'd learned – bending the CTF code of ethics to work in my favour – to help people. Yeah, I guess I was familiar with that grey area.

"I'll make you a deal," I said.

"What's that?"

"I'll reserve further judgement on this fiasco..." I coughed and sat up. "This quest, until we find the Pit of Chance. If it exists I'll support you and this Cause one-hundred percent. But if we never find it, you have to promise me you won't risk any more innocent lives on a hunch."

I rummaged around in my pack until I found my hairbrush. Holding it and my hat firmly in one hand, I left the tent without another word. I located a secluded spot near the back of the hauler where I could still hear the group working and talking, and Dezmind muttering.

Taking out my clips two and three at a time, I finally let my hair down. I had to stand to bush it, otherwise I'd get sand swept up in the ends. I looked at it as I threaded handfuls through the fine bristles. *The more time I spend with Dezmind, the more he reminds me of Zaith. They have this zest for life and an inner drive for truth that's just baffling.* I shook my head to clear it. The stark blackness of my hair feathered in front of my eyes. I'd never bothered to colour it, not like Zaith.

Zola, how I wished she were here. She'd help me figure this out and keep my sanity. I let her voice echo in my mind and take me away from the madness. *Taya, it infuses the follicles with special moisturizing vitamins. You would look ravishing in deep blue highlights.* I smiled to myself. Zaith never failed to have a bad case of the frizzies after getting her hair done. So few people bothered to leave it natural anymore that I felt a silly pride I'd kept mine black. Granted, it was now sandy and grimy after four days of travelling. *A nice refreshing shower would do wonders right about now.*

"All hands!" Lutrice called.

I quickly twisted ropes of hair into place, clipped it tight, and planted my hat on just as I heard Dezmind exit the tent. I walked around to join him with the others. He looked awfully well-groomed for someone who had just crawled out of bed. Even his dungarees looked clean and crisp. *How many extra pairs of pants did he bring?*

Packing up was a well-practiced skill now. Everyone accepted a particular job and we were able to get the task done in record time. As the group fell into position heading east into the setting sun, I took out my map to judge our timing. Tonight was the night, after all. If the grey existed we were going to find it.

"We've entered the zone you've circled here," I said to Dezmind two hours later. "We should find it any time now. Is there something in particular we should be looking for?"

"No, not really. Other than its name, no other physical description identified it. That sketch I showed you at the Lakes was purely conjectural. Just keep your eyes open. It's out here somewhere."

Oh yeah, that's reassuring. I put away my notebook and scanned the horizon. Tall hills of pinky sand partially blocked my sightline.

The further we walked, the less direct our path became. While trying to stay on the hard, packed ground and skirt around the base of the mini-dunes that lay in our path, we veered off course. The dunes themselves were not much bigger than a couple of bungalows, but their soft sand was not ideal for walking or climbing.

No longer in line with Gamma, I looked behind me, twice – we continued to drift off course. We'd have to go over the next dune. Approaching it, I halted the group. "This time, we go over. It won't be easy, but try to maintain your balance. Crawl if you have to.

We'll take the pace down until we've crossed it. Once we start, we can't stop."

The first few steps weren't so bad, but the sand gave way and sliding became an option of how far and how fast. For every two feet gained, another was lost in backslide. Jantice and Tamaine fell regularly, but since they were near the front of the safety line there was no direct impact on the hauler. On the whole, everyone found a rhythm and made it over.

It was gruelling lugging the hauler along with us. We couldn't stop for fear of having it slide right back down to the bottom again. Sand in my mouth was nothing new, but the amount of powdery stuff kicked up during the crawl made me wonder if I'd ever swallow grit-free again. On the other side we switched up who was hauling. I checked our position; we had to climb one more.

"Okay," I called. "Last one. On the count of three. One – two – three."

Deltek had the middle position on the hauler while Jantice and I took the outer ropes. Having wrapped the length around our stomachs, we had our hands free for balance. My bandana slipped down from my nose over my mouth from the excess sweat. It dropped down my neck and landed on my chest which just happened to be in line with the hill as we climbed. I blew the powder away from my mouth but it didn't help – only fogged up my goggles.

Jantice suddenly dropped out of sight. The hauler dragged left. "Deltek!" I yelled.

"She's gone!" He stopped pulling.

The weight of the hauler yanked us back. The others crested the peak. I turned around to face the hauler so I wouldn't be dragged backwards. Deltek followed my lead. I searched underneath. *Where are you! Dammit.*

I crouched low, sliding behind the hauler as it slowly returned to the bottom of the dune. I caught sight of Jantice. She was suspended face-up by the safety line underneath the bed. Her right arm disappeared under the closest wheel. Yells rang out from above.

"Can you grab her other arm and pull her to you?" I shouted to Deltek. The rush of the sand and the noise of the others made it hard to hear.

"I think so."

He mimicked my crouch and shortened up his lead-line even more. He grabbed for the girl's lifeless arm. He missed.

Why isn't she moving? "Get her – come on, get her before this behemoth stops."

Deltek swung under the hauler suspended by the safety cord. I grabbed his hand. He grabbed her arm. We pulled Jantice free of the wheel just as the hauler stopped moving. Deltek and I scrambled to unravel ourselves from the ropes, and disconnect from the line. Deltek dove under the hauler as I attacked the taut cord still attached to Jantice. Together, Deltek and I dragged her out. I dropped down next to her head. She was breathing, but barely.

"Taya!" Dezmind called above the cacophony of voices.

"Deltek—" I said gesturing over my shoulder with my head.

"On it." He moved to keep the others away from Jantice as I worked.

I blew loose particles of sand from her face, and cleared her nose of debris before drizzling verrin into her mouth and massaging her throat to encourage the swallow reflex.

"Taya." Dezmind dropped down beside me, breathless. I passed him my canteen.

"Keep her hydrated. It's part of the problem." I checked her face, neck, chest and stomach – all fine on the surface. I picked up her hand. "Dammit."

"What?" Dez asked.

I lifted Jantice's hand and pulled up her sleeve. Round pale welts the size of a watch-com face pushed against her grey and purple skin. Dez sucked in a noisy breath.

"Lean her torso against your chest," I said.

He pulled her up, hugging Jantice under her ribcage. I removed her sweater.

"What is it?" he asked.

Tamaine didn't look like this. It was something else. "I don't know."

Eight large bumps, spaced somewhat evenly, led from the back of Jantice's hand up to the inner elbow on her left arm. I searched the rest of her upper body under her tank top before running my hands over her legs. *Just these eight.*

The largest lump, the one on her hand, twitched.

I am so not ready for this.

Forcing myself to act, I pulled the knife from my belt-pack and sliced open the lump. Dez shuddered. A filmy white sac wriggled in the open wound. A thin line of blood snaked between her knuckles and down two of her fingers. I pushed the sac with the flat of the blade. It fell onto a stained knuckle but remained attached by a single white thread.

"Syvis!" I called.

He skidded around the side of the hauler, his bronze face ashen in the pale light. "Grab a collapsible cup from my pack."

He opened the bag still on my back, and then crouched next to me.

"Catch the white thing as I cut." He shoved it under the sac by Jantice's thumb. I severed the link and it fell into the cup. A black line crept toward the muscle lining Jantice's hand.

Poison.

Doire said most creatures are poisonous out here. I put my lips to the open wound and sucked. *Rotten fruit.* I spat it out and sucked again. Twice more and the wound was clean.

After the fourth incision and removal I was lightheaded and woozy. I couldn't risk my health with another. I looked up.

"Dez–" He met my eyes and nodded. Somehow I knew I could count on him. We swapped places.

When the last of the parasitic sacs were removed, Syvis jogged a good distance away to bury the cup and its contents. Jantice looked like an industrial accident victim. The eight gaping wounds needed to be treated.

Dez and I had no strength. A clear head and a steady hand were needed. I instructed Syvis on the finer points of sewing up battle wounds – that's what I'd been trained for, not this mess. When he'd sutured Jantice's cuts, Syvis helped Dez and I lift her onto the bed of the hauler. *First one teen, then the other. This is not the track record I signed up for.*

"Get Tamaine and bring her here. Explain in general terms what we did to Jantice and tell her to sit with her friend on the hauler. She needs constant supervision right now. Dezmind and I will speak to the others."

Syvis nodded.

When he returned with Tamaine, Dezmind and I went around the opposite side of the hauler to make what explanations we could.

Neither of us was particularly steady on our feet so we laced arms across each other's backs and clutched a shoulder.

I just wanted to curl up in his arms and sleep. I don't think it mattered who I was currently using as a crutch, I would have taken any of them at this point – even Raylan if he kept his mouth shut.

"What are we going to say, Jutaya?"

"Whatever we need to, Dezmind." Now that the immediate threat was over, we returned to using our full names; business-like, orderly, and predictable – exactly what I needed to focus my thoughts.

When we stopped, I leaned my forehead against the back of his sweat- soaked shirt, made icy with the night's frigid air. I wasn't hiding exactly, everyone knew I stood behind him, they just didn't know why – I hadn't the strength to stand on my own.

He calmed the voices. "Jantice is alive, but she's dehydrated and suffering from a lack of…" he paused, "nutrients."

Yes, that made sense.

"Tamaine will stay with her on the hauler and take care of her as we travel."

Neither of us was in any fit state to travel far. There was a longer pause.

Oh, it's my turn now. I'm in no mood to pander to these people any more. What do I care if they hate me so long as they listen to me? I leaned away from Dezmind and moved to stand beside him.

"Spot poisoned her."

Dezmind stiffened. I hadn't shared my deductions.

"Turns out it was a female. She lay what I can only assume were egg pouches just under Jantice's skin in eight different locations." I rubbed a hand over my face, popping the dive goggles up onto my forehead and letting my eyes breathe in the fresh night air.

"These pouches were parasitic and have severely drained her. My advice to you remains the same as when we started: if you don't listen to me, you'll die. Syvis?" He stepped up beside me. "Take out your map, head east. Find a place for us to rest. I don't want to be anywhere near here in case some other creature wants to dig up the sacs and eat them. We'll regroup then. You're in charge."

He turned to the group and delegated tasks. Dezmind and I

hooked onto the back of the hauler to talk privately while Syvis led the others. He linked arms with me to keep me steady.

"Dezmind, are you sure your map is accurate?"

"Is that what you really want to talk about right now? You were more than a little blunt back there."

"Look, Tamaine is watching Jantice, there's nothing more to discuss about it. I'm tired of being ignored and treated like some freak. This is serious."

I took a breath and lowered my voice – sound travelled easily in the Deserts, that's why I put the hauler between us and the others, but Tamaine was still close. "We should be there by now."

"I know." He shook his head and scanned a few of his notes. "I don't get it," he mumbled. "I've followed everything to the letter, deciphered every symbol, every word. I know it now like the back of my hand. It should be here."

"Keep your voice down," I said. "We don't want a riot on our hands just because your plans went awry. Think of a way to let them down easy when we set up camp. We can head home tomorrow night."

He stared at me, but his gaze looked through me. Dealing with Jantice had drained both of us, but a spark of defiance flashed in his eyes.

"It's here. It's out here. I know it is. I can feel it calling. This isn't the end, Jutaya. We've just missed something."

"*We've* missed something? Whatever gave you that idea? It's *your* map in question here. Mine is perfectly accurate. We've hit every Desert and vegetation field exactly when we were supposed to."

I lost my footing and staggered. Dezmind gripped me tighter to keep me upright, squashing some of the papers he was desperately double- checking in the process.

"Are you saying we're lost?"

"No. I know exactly where we are on the map and I know exactly where we aren't. Face it Dezmind, the Tablets were wrong."

"I don't believe that."

"Then you didn't translate them properly. Either way, you promised me at dusk tonight that we'd turn back if we couldn't find the Pit."

His mouth pursed into a tight line, stuffing mangled sheets of notes and drawings into the top of his backpack as it hung against his chest while we walked.

"Admit it. It's time for me to take these people home."

Syvis called a stop.

"It's out here." Dezmind said.

I threw my hands up in the air. "Fine. You've got one hour to go back over those notes before I turn this farce of yours around." I shook off his arm and detached from the rear of the hauler.

"I'll figure it out – and you promised to keep an open mind," he said, then sat on the rim of the nearest hauler wheel, using the hollow around him to block the random gusts of wind and sand as he painstakingly reviewed his original tracings of the Tablets. The others climbed onto the edge of the hauler.

I paced. I knew if I sat down I wouldn't be able to stand up again. I had to push through the fatigue and hope the minute traces of poison in me would be dealt with by my immune system. Sure, Doire had mentioned the possibility of poison, and I had looked into how to handle a snakebite, but this left me shaking inside.

We shouldn't be here. I was right at the Rally and I was right in my defence against the Ethics Committee. His beliefs are going to get us killed.

After a few too many circles, Syvis and Lutrice looked on the verge of asking questions, so I left. I wandered away, analysing the landscape and pretending to look for a spot to relieve myself.

It was inevitable. Dezmind would have to admit defeat. If either map was wrong, it had to be his; my map had proven its worth and reliability again and again. Yet, something about all this pulled at the back of my mind. My thoughts jumbled from Spot and Jantice, to Tamaine and the mites, Werks' frozen stare after I'd killed him, and then back to the maps.

I flipped through my notes again, scanning page by page. I had information on plants, animals, water and verrin resources, travel zones, landscapes, illnesses and cures – everything a guide would need. It was useless; there was nothing here that could solve this. I briefly ducked behind a dune to maintain my charade of looking to relieve myself before backtracking and returning to the group.

They'd begun whispering amongst themselves, debating about when we might find the Pit, what the Chronicles might consist of, and wondering how proud their relatives and families would be when they returned home. They avoided mentioning Jantice, but I saw the concern in tight lips, wrinkled brows, and furtive glances.

"It's actually quite astounding," Lutrice said. "Given the age of the Tablets and their relevance on life today. Dezmind's ability to interpret the importance of artefacts like those and bring to light lost information is the epitome of the Spoken Truth."

"I read on one of the museum plaques that they were over two-thousand years old," Deltek added. "It's amazing how well they've been preserved. It was like being in the presence of a lost relic."

"Yeah, lost at the back of that museum," Raylan said. "They probably only kept them around because of their age, not realizing their significance. That museum wasn't much more than a shack with poor lighting and ragged carpeting. I'll bet it's like Dezmind says – the Kronik and his Advisors are hiding things from us in plain sight."

They fell quiet again as Tamaine's words filtered through the tent. She spoke quietly to Jantice, offering comfort with the sound of her voice, though I doubted it mattered much at this point. It would be a while before Jantice was in any condition to wake up, let alone reply.

Something niggled in the back of my mind. *Why is time important? What had I read or written down from my research that dealt with this? It had to do with the Great Migration, yes, but not the first- hand accounts that the Kronik put in their text book. But it's the text book that was the source, which is why I can't quite place the reference. Did I discredit it too fast? Have I missed a vital clue to unlocking the secret of his map?* I pulled at my hat and shook my head rapidly from side to side. *Stop making a scene.*

I needed to clear my mind, let the image surface on its own. I sat down in the rim of one of the hauler's tires and rested my head in my hands. I pictured the text book on the dull metal surface of the library work table. Then, I focused in on the cover and watched my hand open the book to the table of contents: Introduction, Natural Resources, Plant Life, Animal Insect & Other Life, History of the Migration. I saw my fingers flipping forward to follow a vague curiosity I had about our past, blaming the Talian and his nonsense for even making me wonder – then it hit me.

Should I tell him? He'd never think of it himself, he's too absorbed in his notes. But if I don't tell him, we could turn back. Go home. End the insanity. On the other hand, I've been hired to guide and protect. If the Council find out I withheld pertinent information from a client, a Talian no less, they'd – Zola, I don't know what they'd do – toss me in the mines for saving lives. What's wrong with these people!

I sat there debating with myself for what seemed a lifetime. Still, if I gave Dezmind this information, the lives of these people would weigh even more heavily on my shoulders. Werks, Tamaine, Jantice – no more.

No more.

I was forced to take this job by an unrelenting idealist, and I was being forced to keep it or forfeit everything I'd ever worked for. *If I tell him, I'll be just as much to blame should anything else go wrong – no more scapegoats – no more white lies and half-truths working in the realm of the grey. It would be black and white again, but this time I would be one-hundred percent accountable.*

Not wanting to draw undue attention, I got up and casually walked down the length of the hauler to Dezmind. He sat buried under tracings in the wheel-well. Leaning over one particular sheet, his nose nearly rubbed the page. I let my faint shadow fall over his hunched form.

He didn't move.

I must have watched him for a good ten minutes as the war continued to wage inside me. I had the power to end this but my mind kept asking, *what if?* What if he really uncovered a secret buried by the Kronik a thousand or more years ago? I dropped to my knees beside him, splaying sand particles over his papers.

"What the–?" he muttered, and shook his page clear. "It's only been thirty minutes, Jutaya."

"Oh, stop with your 'Brooding King' routine and look at me," I said, resigned. *I'll never forgive myself – I know it. But I can't avoid the truth.* "I figured it out."

"What?" He sat up, stunned.

"I just overheard Deltek talking about the age of the Tablets."

"Yeah, so? They're old. You knew that."

"Yes, but I didn't realise just how old they were until he said it out loud." Dezmind didn't understand my conviction about this simple revelation. "But my map is recent, only maybe twenty or thirty years old," I said.

"Okay, I'm gleaning that there's some great significance looming here. What is it?"

"Of course you wouldn't get it," I snapped. "I'm the one who studied the Deserts. I'm the only one of us who bothered to research the death trap we're in," I just had to say it out loud one last time.

"I can't believe it took me this long to realise what's happened. It relates to a simple historical statistic I read in a text published by the Kronik. The problem is, I skipped over it. I didn't read the numbers just got the sense that the Deserts expand something like a twentieth of a mile a year. Now, in the course of twenty years this doesn't change the landscape much, but in two-thousand years, you can imagine the impact."

He considered it but that fevered spark remained absent from his eyes.

"So, what you're saying is, I just have to recalculate my map to include two-thousand years of growth onto the beginning of the ancient Deserts, then re-align it with your map?"

"Exactly."

"Wait." He slid to the back of the deep rim and leaned against the wheel-well, tapping his knee. "The Tablets clearly mark the Lakes as a significant landmark, and that's where we began…" His voice trailed off and he shook his head.

"Read me the exact lines you're using to decipher the coordinates."

He shuffled through his notes. I caught a glimpse of a few images mixed in, but nothing identifiable. He pulled out two tracings.

"This is where it gets past the rhetoric and details the instructions." He pointed to a few symbols on the tracing before quoting, "Walk the path of the one that leads to night. Use its sight from the triple lakes' light."

"Okay, what else?"

He shifted to the next tracing. "From last touch of dust you must waver nary, monument of stone where death lies buried.

Track carefully these pacings of sacred script, leading to the lowering of the crypt."

I looked at him sharply. "Crypt?"

He smiled grimly. "It's not what you're thinking. The term was coined in the ancient language to mean 'deep hole in the ground' – our Pit of Chance. Shall I continue?"

"No. Give me a minute." I stared, unwavering, at the two tracings running Dezmind's words over and over again in my mind. *Yes, the Tablets mention Vitexid's Lakes, but they don't say to start there – they are giving the bearing east as they describe the Gamma sun.* "What do you make of the passage about the monument of stone?"

"I assume they mean the Ancient City – that the Pit will be located nearby."

"That doesn't sound right." I shook my head to clear the way for a new thought. "What if you're wrong? What if they refer to something else? It mentions burying their dead. They must have travelled an extremely long way to leave the Deserts behind.

"If my theory is correct, maybe they erected a monument from the last dredges of sand before reaching fertile ground. You know, it would be symbolic of leaving the past, their fallen friends and family, at that point between the old and the new." I ran the coarse sand through my fingers, thinking.

"We passed nothing on our way here to verify what you're saying. There was nothing out here until we reached the Valley of the Dunes and you can't tell me one of these..." He pointed to a nearby mammoth of a dune. "... is hiding an ancient monument."

The gears turned faster in my mind.

"No, Dezmind. Not one of these dunes. The dune. That one lonely dune at the edge of the Barren Plains. The small one no bigger than a house where—"

"Yes," he quickly cut me off, "I remember it."

I squinted at him, trying to read his response. He'd never been terse with me before. Sure, I didn't have the exact figures but this was important. He went back to scouring his notes.

"That was the monument. I'm sure of it." I pushed his papers down, away from his face and waited for him to look me in the eyes. "Covered with two thousand years of wind and sand."

I paused.

He was quiet.

He went back to shuffling the tracings. What was wrong with him? I was giving him the answer he needed and yet...

"You speak in metaphor; you read in metaphor; if this is truly the path you seek, would that not also lie in metaphor? My map is correct. This is where you asked me to bring you. You know where I stand on the issue and yet for some inexplicable reason, I think I finally understand what you really believe, what you're spouting to these people." I paused. "I didn't have to come to you with this. I could have let your time run out."

The night was quiet. Tamaine fell silent, and so had the rest of the group. It was as if we were all waiting to hear this monumental decision. I don't know how long we sat there, looking. Thinking. Wondering.

I glanced up at the sun. "You've got twenty minutes." I shifted to leave.

"Approximately a twentieth of a mile a year? That's an odd number." I rested my arms on my knees. I didn't think I had the strength to stand anyway. A particularly vicious gust of sand-laden wind nearly pushed me over.

"I know. It was the Kronik, what can I say?" I paused, "But it was close to that, I'd stake my life on it." *I am staking my life on it.*

"I only glanced at the page. So, a twentieth of a mile would roughly translate into one-hundred miles over two-thousand years. That means we would get to the Pit in about two nights. We've been averaging maybe fifty miles a night."

Dezmind took my map, erased the lines I'd drawn on his original map. As he entered the new information, his movements took on a deft and sure air. He had no proof of the strength of my mental recall, so this was just as much a leap of faith as any he'd taken so far. But was it trust in me or his destiny?

Something told me he wouldn't risk finding the Pit on some whim of his guide's – there was belief, in me. He held up his map. The new course put the Pit in the heart of the Powder Sands Desert, where most of Doire's known dangers lay. I knew Dezmind's conviction. With or without me, he would stay to search the Deserts.

"What are you going to tell them?" I asked.

He gathered his papers together, made all the more difficult by the wind. "Exactly what you told me."

The mounting airstream whipped my hat off my head. I caught it with both hands before responding, "They won't be amused. They'll lose faith. This isn't some simple misunderstanding; you'll be demanding that they remain out here four days longer than they've signed up for. It's not just two days less rations to get there; it's another two days on the way back. And I can tell you now, with tending to Jantice and the extra time we've already lost, we don't have the necessary supplies for it."

"You'll think of something. In the meantime, try to have a little more faith in my rhetoric."

He stood and moved to face the group. I followed, curious to see how he would dig himself out of this one.

"Listen up, everyone. It has been discovered that—"

"Sand Storm!" I yelled, grabbing his arm and pointing off to the left of the horizon. A swirling dark frenzy loomed, spanning what distance we could see.

"Syvis, Raylan, Deltek get on the hauler ropes. Everyone else push from the back or sides. Tamaine, get down here! We're rounding this dune in less than five minutes. Go! Go! Go!" I cried, pulling Dezmind with me to the lead.

"What are you doing? It's just sand," he said, as we attached our lines to the front of the hauler pulling forward to help the others.

"That is not only a suffocation chamber," I grunted, pulling, "but a meat grinder as well. Those particles of sand may feel soft to step on, but they'll rip you to shreds in seconds. We have to find as much protection as possible. Out here, I only have the dunes to work with."

We jogged the hauler to the opposite side of the dune in less than four minutes. The wild winds buffeted my senses as the storm neared. The gusts whistled and roared, flapping the sides of the AHT. We only had a few minutes to prepare.

"Right here!" I ordered, pointing to a deep crescent in the side of the dune. "Place the hauler between us and the storm, at the very centre of the crescent's base. Get Jantice. Collapse the tent over the verrin and tie it down. Link your packs across the length of the wheels. Now, people! Move it!"

Particles of sand sliced down as we worked, penetrating our skin like a million tiny knives. Syvis carried Jantice's limp body over his shoulder. Tamaine and Lutrice connected packs with Dezmind. I helped the others collapse the tent. Wide eyes and blank faces occupied bodies performing tasks at record speeds.

Hurtling sand blasted overhead – its roar deafening. I shouted, "Face the dune!" Then dove and covered my head with my arms. Others joined me within seconds, crowding tightly together, giving added weight and mass to our wall of protection.

But something wasn't right.

The sand wasn't supporting my weight. Pushed farther and farther into the dune face, I struggled to free myself. It swallowed my legs and half my torso. Gasping, I sucked in one final breath of air before the wall consumed me whole.

Chapter Sixteen
Buried Alive

My heart leaped into my throat. It was like being suspended between the outer atmosphere and the stars, where the oxygen dissipated into the vacuum of space. The sand, loose and fluid, sucked my body in farther and farther until–

Dropping to my knees on solid ground, I gasped for air. Stale air. Two more bodies fell in, knocking me to my hands. Before a complete thought formed, I grabbed an arm belonging to each and dragged them further into the dark cavernous space. More people landed. I ran to the wall of sand pulling them from harm's way. When all eight group members were accounted for, I caught my breath and looked around.

What new torture is this? A solid rock chamber of sorts – no, not so much a chamber as a cave, outlined in the gloom. A dim natural glow, that I could only guess came from the sand, gave me just enough light to see by.

The winds and sand must have worked to cover the opening over a long period of time. I thought, for sure, we'd somehow fallen into silk- sand. Whimpers and whispers wafted past my ears. Thick, dense web- work, like saturated strands of gauze, tracked over the ceiling, part-way down the walls, and into the maw of the cave. I shuddered. Nothing advanced, but something lived here.

Oh, Zita, why grant me sight if only to see this? I strained my eyes, searching for the monster or monsters that had created the tangled masses above.

"Dark," came a muffled cry from one of the women. Though my eyes had adjusted quickly, it was difficult to discern who belonged to which huddled shape. The low, natural lighting gave the interior the feel of dusk at the cusp of twilight, and that didn't bode well for me: clarity was lost and with it certainty about my surroundings.

Come on eyes, why won't you work properly! The largest mass was likely Syvis, still holding Jantice. By voice, I could hear Dezmind consoling Tamaine as Lutrice whispered to Deltek. Everyone else was silent. At least they were still huddled in the middle.

Keeping my voice low and even, I said, "Don't talk. Don't move. And whatever you do, don't activate a tube-light. I'll be right back."

A hand grabbed my arm as a body detached from the dark mass – Dezmind – his grip and stature unmistakable at this close proximity. I pulled him a couple of feet away from the group. His free hand traced up my arm to my face. I didn't think my heart could race any faster, but it did. The dark hid my scowl.

Holding my neck, he pulled me closer, resting his forehead just above my ear.

"Can't this wait? We need to talk about what just happened, where we potentially are and how to deal with the situation," he said. "The Kahn-lea don't know what to think and to have you, their guide, abandon them right now will only make matters worse."

I turned my head so we were cheek-to-cheek, mouth-to-ear. His skin was rough with sand particles.

"I didn't say anything you wouldn't have said yourself. What did you expect? Some polite, 'Oops, this'll be a tough one to get out of?' And no, this can't wait."

"What are you thinking? That was the worst possible way to talk to them. They're vulnerable."

"It's the simple truth. We don't have time for anything else."

His stance changed, maybe it was the tone of my voice but he asked, "What do you see that we don't?" Perhaps even in my personal blindness I still saw better than any of them. His grip changed from rough to tentative, holding me so loosely it was almost as if he wasn't.

"A nest. A very large, very intricate web designed to trap prey. A dense web-work right above our heads."

"Then let's get out of here."

"It might be abandoned. If it is, we'll be safer in here than out there. Keep them calm while I check it out."

I grabbed his shoulders and turned him to face the huddled mass. Slipping the Clinex out of my belt-pack, I inched toward the back of the cave.

Walking upright for nearly twenty yards, I forced my eyes to see more than they were capable of. The strain caused the muscles in my sockets to throb. Doire's notes only mentioned smaller cave creatures in passing: snakes, many-legged insects, and beasts similar to Spot. The noticeably stale air could indicate abandonment. The fact that there was any air at all, pointed at a way for things to get in and out to whatever degree.

I looked directly above me. *What's on the other side of all this webbing?* Nothing attacked, so I could only assume nothing was there. The moisture of my breath, the beat of my heart, and the blood flowing in my veins should instantly attract any predator. The cave narrowed.

Sticky filaments clung to my hair, nose, and cheeks. I knelt, pushing them off my face. My hands shook. I dropped the Clinex. Hugging myself, I rocked back and forth. *What am I doing here?* I knelt before an opening only a small child would successfully slip through, untouched by the trap. I had to go in. I couldn't possibly return to the group without completing a full survey of the cavern. We couldn't stay otherwise; yet the dangers of the razor-sand outside nearly equalled the unknown horrors of this den.

I picked up the Clinex and traced the activation sensor. *I could blast it – run the settings up to incinerate and destroy anything alive in there.* I shook my head. *What if the source of our air originates from back there? What if I cause a collapse?* I bit my lower lip and forced myself to crawl in.

It was pitch black beyond the opening, but the sub-cave felt expansive – it had height but not depth, and was big enough to stand in – not that I would. The sand was denser here. The natural glow reduced by half.

Squinting into the charcoal depths, I reached for a rock with my free hand. Finding one embedded in the soft sand by the wall, I tried to budge it. I turned to dig it out. Brushing away clumps of dirt and rubble, my hand hit other larger rocks protruding from the ground as well. I had to risk it – I cracked open the face of my watch-com for some light and gasped.

There, at the back of the cave rested a man. I couldn't say for sure that it wasn't a woman, but the jaw line and build of the torso were definitely larger than the average woman. Even in death, much of his hair remained intact. I'd never seen anything like this half-buried figure before. A skeleton wouldn't have fazed me, but this was well out of the realm of my comprehension. It looked like every drop of moisture had been sucked from him.

I flashed the dim light around the small chamber. The webs and cording hung low and heavy. It was a good thing I chose not to stand. But still, I heard nothing, and nothing moved.

A thick leather strap near the body's torso caught my eye. Whoever this was might have important resources with him.

Absently, I ground fine particles of sand between my teeth. *I wonder what happened to the poor guy?* If it had been dehydration, lack of verrin, those would have been three horrible last days. I couldn't imagine feeling my strength and vitality slipping away, knowing I could do nothing to save myself. But there was always the possibility he'd been something's dinner. I couldn't imagine dying like that, all alone in such a desolate and harsh place.

As I worked to dislodge the leather pack, I touched the stiff clothing moulded onto his body. A hand protruded. Apparently, what I had mistaken for a rock earlier had actually been his wrist. What I had thought was sand coming off in my hands were fragments of dry skin.

I want to scream!

Instead, I swallowed a bit more sand as I leaned forward to shift the pack from side-to-side.

My eyes involuntarily settled on his face. A dark, slightly open, toothless mouth froze in laughter, taunting me with his fate if we continued with this quest.

Something about the deceased's face drew my eye. The shadow of an image seemed impressed on the weathered skin of his cheek. Wondering if this was perhaps something more than decaying skin cells, I leaned closer. Yes, the skin was darker there, but I couldn't tell why.

I was ready to give up on the pack when a particularly fierce jostle knocked a couple of items loose: a wallet and a small tin box. I stuffed the box back into the leather bag then picked up the wallet. It opened at an employee ID badge for an Architect named M. Doire.

What! The author of my research books? This withered husk is Doire, the man who trekked the Deserts?

I sat there, staring at his badge. It was true that the last publication of his work was printed nearly ten years ago, but somehow with all the knowledge he'd gathered, I'd assumed he'd still be out there somewhere, alive.

I shoved the wallet back into the pack and yanked. That bag was coming with me. If he had any notes in there about his more recent travels, I needed the insight.

Muffled voices slipped through the small opening behind me. That didn't bode well. The pack popped free.

M. Doire. He'd become my saviour during the course of this journey. I'd hoped to meet him one day, but not like this. I slid around on my knees, and crawled back through the opening – eying the webbed ceiling.

Shouldering the pack, which was more of a satchel with a single, wide strap that rested against my chest, I hurried back to the main chamber. I shut my com in the lighter area, walking with my eyes trained on the woven layers above.

I think we can safely ride out the storm in here.

Stepping out of the narrower passage into the vaulted room, I manoeuvred around the noisy group. Raylan dug furiously at the wall of sand.

"No!" I screamed, and fired my weapon.

Chapter Seventeen

Desert Tricks

The giant web-crawler dropped from the ceiling on a thick strand about to cover Raylan's huddled form. I slid up the setting on the Clinex with my thumb, and shot again. The hovering creature incinerated. Fine particles of ash exploded into the air.

The plasma flash blinded me, but not before I saw the shift of smaller bodies through the dense strands above. *Can we get out before the others attack? What if we can't? What if we can and they follow?*

"Dammit."

I lunged forward to where Raylan should be, luckily he hadn't moved. Hauling him back to the group, I pulled the Whipstaff from the leg of my boot and pushed into the centre of the bodies.

"Heads down and huddle tight!" I ordered. A ripple moved across the webbing. We were out of time. *I hope this doesn't kill us.*

Charging the staff, I jammed it against the Clinex, super-boosting the energy. Raising the weapons over our heads, I blasted the ceiling above us, around us. After the fifth pulse, they shorted out.

Stuffing them into Doire's shoulder pack, I ducked down for cover, straddling Jantice's middle. Her head rested in Tamaine's lap as her legs curled under several other pairs of feet. Everyone crowded together tighter. Thick ash fell in a steady rain. I heard the occasional thump around our perimeter. Peering when I could, I verified that nothing else moved. I hadn't killed them all, but I'd got the bold ones.

"Scarves and bandanas up," I said. "Syvis, you take Jantice. Everyone, we're gonna run at the wall as one large wrecking ball – shoulders and backs to take the brunt of the impact. Ready?" I looked at Syvis. He nodded. "On my three – one, two, three!"

I slipped on a couple of smaller half-incinerated corpses, but managed to keep upright as we crashed into the wall of sand. I held my breath. Our bodies smashed into each other. *It's not going to work.* Then, the sand engulfed me as we barrelled through.

Tiny crystals speared the skin of my upper cheek. The torrent of wind and dirt nearly ripped off my hat and bandana. Choosing not to fight the howl of the storm, I climbed the half-covered hauler.

Everyone watched for my next move. *Good.* I took my gloves out of my belt-pack and put them on. The group followed suit. This was just the outer edge of the storm. We had no time left. The rolling body of the mass hovered only minutes away.

Dezmind helped Syvis hold Jantice as Lutrice worked with Tamaine on gearing up her friend with a set of bandanas to cover her mouth and neck, and gloves for her hands. Jumping down, I tapped various people on the shoulder and motioned for them to dig. The wheels of the hauler, open to the tempest, needed to be dislodged.

Lutrice broke away to help the others as I herded Tamaine and Syvis, still carrying Jantice, through the small opening at one end of the hauler. Underneath the verrin transport, Syvis and I placed Jantice's limp form on the ground, with her shoulders and head in Tamaine's lap. They would be shielded for the time being. I motioned to Tamaine instructions for when the hauler was freed. Syvis and I joined the rest of the group battling the storm.

The granules battered our bodies as we fought the wind to shift the hauler. With the bulk of the sand removed, three men pushed and two men pulled. The teens now rode the hauler, which remained wrapped in the AHT.

Lutrice and I dug at the remaining lumps of sand as necessary. Even with my eyes mostly closed, tears streamed down my face trying to wash out the sand. My dive goggles were in my pack after our earlier stop. If we didn't get moving fast, we'd lose too much internal water to the elements. Our bodies digested verrin in such a way that the compound associated with H_2O was broken down and absorbed by various internal organs. The remaining water then flushed through our system via sweat, tears, saliva, and urine – vital moisture for preventing dehydration. It was just too bad straight water didn't hold the necessary nutrients to keep us alive without the verrin compound. Maybe then we wouldn't be in this mess.

It budged.

The men rocked the hauler like a baby in his mother's arms. The massive wheels broke free and rolled several feet. I motioned to Lutrice to join Deltek and Raylan at the rear and relay for the others to keep pushing.

I ran to the front. The faster we put distance between us and that cave, the better. What nested in there knew we were out here, and it was only a matter of time before they grew bold again. I knew we couldn't walk for long. The storm had only just started and we'd be torn to shreds in no time. I paced out five minutes as we trudged through zero visibility. Sand grated in every crevice of my body, rubbing it raw.

I gave the signal to Dezmind and Syvis to stop, and raced to the rear to relay the message. Through one-on-one contact with everyone, I managed to convey my next instructions. Within another two minutes, the kegs were removed and the AHT was strapped around the hauler and under the heavy canisters now resting around the perimeter. Nine of us huddled shoulder-to-cheek-to-knee under the transport, exhausted, sore, sand-blind and bleeding, but alive.

Trapped for over two hours, the group slept a little but mainly sat with their thoughts. The howl of the wind made our skin crawl, or maybe that was the sand mites. No one complained of feeling 'buggy' but there was a lot of arm and leg rubbing in a hot and stuffy environment. Our air supply was constantly on my mind and when the intensity of the storm dulled before fading altogether, my brain stopped coming up with bad contingency plans.

After all this, Dezmind still faced telling the group about the map fiasco. He knew to wait, so as not to make the burden of being trapped even worse. But now was the time. The storm had passed, and with the absence of violent winds or the whip of razor-sand against the sides of the AHT, wounds were being tended and whispered words shared. He had to bring it up before they remembered on their own.

I placed my lips next to his ear. The nearness to him urged me to do more than speak and that startled me. I swallowed past a dry mouth and said, "Dezmind. You have to tell them."

"I'm not feeling so confident about my speech anymore. It was so much more compelling before the storm – the cave. You sure you don't have any other desert tricks up your sleeve to divert attention again?" he asked lightly. His eyes remained as dark as the night, belying his true feelings.

"Do you want me to say something?"

"No, I'll do it. Are you able to – do you mind?" He inclined his head over his shoulder. I frowned, not understanding why he wanted me to leave. "The Kahn-lea and I need to have a heart-to-heart on this one. I want them to feel like this is my decision. There are still too many hostile feelings aimed at you, and they're really on edge. I need them calm."

"I have to stay close. If one of them is another assassin, or has simply had enough of all this, I won't be able to get to you fast enough."

"I don't think there's anyone here who would do that. Besides those who still follow me will step in – if necessary."

Heat radiated from the hand he placed on my shoulder. "Don't worry; I take full responsibility for anything that might happen."

I folded my arms. *That's not what the contract states.*

He looked back at me. His eyes locked with mine and said more in a split-second than any of the pretty words he used in his speeches. "Fine. I'll go."

So much for turning back. 'Do you mind' he says. If he thinks the group is restless and on edge, he has no idea how sending me away affects my nerves. I don't trust any of them and neither should he. I wriggled out from under the hauler, punching my way through the accumulated sand. No one said anything. They likely figured I'd left to check on the storm.

Outside the air was clear. Gamma rested on the horizon. I

focused on widening the breach I made as my thoughts swirled.

Werks had portrayed the epitome of goodness, fooling all of us. Who knew what lay at the back of these people's minds? Raylan never hid the fact that he had a suspicious nature. His ravenous dislike for female authoritarian figures made me fear more for my own life than Dezmind's, but it could be a façade. Ray had serious problems he needed to deal with. I was not convinced by our morning of stories that nothing sinister lay in these people's hearts. I would not be caught unaware a second time.

As I dug around the outside of the hauler, I caught snatches of the conversation, but Dezmind spoke in hushed tones, so I couldn't make out much.

"– delicate mission... moment of truth... decision is yours to make. I will not... mistake... new information... great help, I did think to ask her..." His voice wafted in and out. At least he seemed to be doing exactly what he said he would. *It's about time he learned to let them decide.*

Back at that first Rally, he'd focused on 'the responsibility of the citizens for the health of Xannia' with no mention of the horrors awaiting them in the Deserts. Granted, we all grew up with the stories, but people take for granted what's right in front of them and need to be reminded. Not that it mattered now.

No one made a sound. I could only assume he explained the situation: no comments, no groans, just a group of adults finally acting their age.

Raylan was the first with a question, "And how do we know that it won't be buried or hidden like that cave? We'll be risking twice as many days out here than we thought. Much as I dislike what life's given me, I'm not ready to leave it behind."

He'd made no effort to lower his voice. Even Dezmind didn't answer right away.

"Think of the greater good... place your trust in Jutaya's..." The soft words came through the fabric of the tent. "Take all the time you need. Let us know your decision when you're ready."

Dezmind crawled out through the widened hole. His jaw was set and he looked through me rather than at me. It chilled my blood.

"You're going on without them, aren't you?" I said.

He stopped, with his hands on his hips. Looking right at me, a deep frown creased his brow. Analysing me, his eyes bore right into my soul, searching for something not within himself – maybe an answer – but something I wasn't sure I could give either. His gaze raked like razor-sand, leaving me exposed and raw on the inside.

Unable to stand the tension, I answered my own question. "Of course you are; and you want me to take them home. Well, I'll tell you what – Syvis is perfectly capable of following his map. He can take them home. I'm not going to leave you here and risk dealing with a dead employer. The Facility would agree with me."

"What if they encounter one of those creatures you've been telling us about? What if the cave beasts follow them? How will they defend themselves? Who will protect them?"

"Dezmind, what you don't understand is that where you're going is far more dangerous than anywhere we've been so far. There are no records of those large creatures anywhere but in the Powder Sands Desert."

I stomped the ground with my feet. "This is packed dirt; only the dunes around here are soft. I've been cautious of anything and everything well before it was necessary, in an attempt to teach these people caution and preparedness. And somehow, I don't think you believe me, or at least you don't think any harm will come to you out here.

"Don't you see? Doire was an expert – or at least as expert as an architect in the Deserts can be – and he's dead!"

"What?"

"I found him, shrivelled and half-buried at the back of that cave, no better than any other prey out here. You're a Speaker, the son of a Council Advisor. You come from a life of luxury, and you think what some woman said about you when you were a sheltered twelve- year-old will see you through this safely. You are the one that needs protecting–"

From yourself.

Staring at me, a smile touched his lips then disappeared just as fast.

"You're full of contradictions, Jutaya. I'm sorry to hear about Doire, but I think you only want to believe that no harm will come to these people. They've already been through so much more than

I – well, I guess you were right about that, anyway. We both know you're not here for the money. Though I pay well, I don't pay nearly enough for what I've asked of you. You will remain with the Kahn-lea. You will keep them safe, just as you've been trying to do since the Rally."

What if I don't want to? It was a horrible thought. They were the whole reason I was out here. *Nothing has changed – has it?*

I watched Dezmind as we dug at the sand around the wheels of the hauler. So much had happened in four days. Everything was different but, at the same time, everything remained the same. If anything, the respect we now shared only strengthened my resolve to keep him alive. *Keep them alive.*

When had that changed?

Maybe nothing was as it seemed any more. The grey areas in my life were overtaking my sense of right and wrong. My head swam with the implications.

Opening my mouth to respond, I shut it again as Syvis wiggled his way out from under the hauler. I stood up, wiping my gloves on my pants. Dezmind turned to stand beside me, our shoulders touching. Odd how it took four days and four catastrophes for us to become equals.

Syvis rose slowly and deliberately, mentally choosing his words with each step. He nodded to Dezmind.

"Although the group is divided, those who want to go home don't want to do so without everyone else. Therefore, the Kahn-lea will remain as a single unit, for together we believe we're stronger."

Dezmind placed a hand on Syvis' shoulder. "It warms my heart to hear of everyone's dedication. Let's inform the others that it's time to dig ourselves out of this mess."

Everyone's dedicated to themselves, Dezmind. I bit back the words from being vocalised. He would believe what he wanted to, regardless of the truth.

Cold nibbled at the upper edge of my ears. I slid my hands up the insides of my sleeves and cupped the cuffs over my frosted appendages. Stepping higher as I walked helped generate more heat, too.

Continuing our trek through the Valley of the Dunes, I did my best to guide us around large obstacles rather than tire the group with surmounting them. Only when we strayed more than a few degrees, did I give the command for a dune-crawl.

Dezmind travelled within the group for more than two hours. Speaking with everyone individually, he worked to satisfy curiosity and stave off fear of the unknown. He spoke of my notes, resources available for our survival out here, like the Mercy Cactus. His ability to diffuse tension and lift even the lowest of spirits boggled my mind. With all my training, I could just barely keep myself together.

Keeping even strides with Merik, he and Dezmind currently spoke in riddles about the meaning of life. Jantice, now awake, still rode on the hauler with Tamaine. I don't think the news about Spot sat well with her. *Teenagers.* I never experienced that phase of the mind where my internal logic was greater than my external resources. *The benefits of having to grow up too fast, I guess.*

With no one to talk to, I kept pace and rifled through Doire's travel pack. My knuckles grazed the metal box. I pulled that out first. It was the size of a two-fisted sandwich. *What I wouldn't give to sink my teeth into one right now.*

The dull metal grew dark around the corners and near the hinges. I popped the simple latch and opened the domed lid. Inside were several jagged spears of a dark-orange crystal. I sniffed them. The hint of something familiar, from my early childhood, teased the recesses of my mind. I picked one up and tried to snap it in my palm. A few shards crumbled from the ends but the crystal remained intact. *I'll look at these more closely later.*

I shoved the larger items in the pack to the bottom: frying pan, rope, clean shirt, and placed the box with them. My gloved hand was blind. There didn't seem to be anything harmful in the pack, so I stripped it off and stuffed it under my belt. Now I didn't have to look at everything with my eyes.

Moving a large piece of flint, a folded knife and casing, and a couple of bandanas, my fingers curled over leather – his wallet. I pulled it out. One thought returned to me – *Why, in Sister Zita's name, was an Architect wandering around in the Deserts?* I flipped it open to his personal ID. I found Doire, the same man who authored my resource books. *But why?*

As an architect, he would've been taught to think logically and work with facts, numbers, and countless other elements dealing with design. *So why was he lying preserved in a hidden Desert cavern guarded by a nest of vicious creatures? He should be creating some new masterpiece.*

The edge of something white, stuffed where his credit chip should've been, caught my eye. Tugging on it, two folded pieces of paper slid out of the pouch. Holding them against the flat of the wallet, I opened them.

Photographs?

He had a family; a beautiful wife and little girl smiling in one picture and an image of the little girl around three or four years old in the other. The portrait of the girl looked posed and formal. She smiled, but it didn't reach her eyes. Both photos were well-worn and bleached of colour, likely from sun exposure.

Did something terrible happen that caused him to leave the city and his job? Maybe the child died and the mother went insane with grief and he left the horror of it all behind? It must have been something like that; something bad, for him to abandon his family to go out exploring the death trap that was the Deserts.

And yet, I felt close to this family somehow. *I don't think I know them.* Even nine years ago, I worked for the government. Before that, I'd come in contact with so few people. Perhaps, it was only that they reminded me of 'family,' of my lost childhood. My parents had loved me once, but then everything changed. After leaving home to look for food, I'd spent many summer nights huddled at the base of large trees in various city parks. *Maybe that's where I've seen this family, or one like them.*

I tucked the photos into a zippered slot at the back of my belt-pack and dropped the wallet into the bag. I let my eyes absorb the dark. If we made it home again, I wanted to find that girl, her mother. If by some remote miracle other relatives were still alive, they would indeed like to have the mysterious disappearance of Doire solved.

Closure meant a lot to people. There were too many loose ends in my own life. Doire's family had a right to know that his time in the Deserts hadn't been in vain.

Letting my hand rifle over and around various objects in Doire's pack, I scanned our surroundings. The soft dunes loomed ominous in the faint starlight. My fingers slid along a particularly heavy seam in the pack. I absently flicked and pinched it as my eyes tracked the position of the stars. In the absence of Gamma's light, my knowledge of the constellations was all that kept us on course. The seam in the pack relaxed. My fingers slipped into a hidden compartment. I nearly stopped. Looking at the pack I felt the edges of a book.

Another Journal? His last work?

I looked up.

Something dark and shimmery caught my eye. Bringing my hand and mind out of the contents of the bag, I focused more acutely on what I was seeing. Slowing my pace, I matched steps with Syvis.

"What do you see just up and to the left, over there, sheltered by that divot in the crescent of the dune?" I asked.

He squinted, trying to catch a glimpse of the *something*. "I'm not sure. It almost seems like the dune is casting a shadow. I can't make out much more than that, and even then I'm not sure if I really see it."

"No, it's there. But you don't see a glimmer? A strange ripple or inconsistency with the sand?"

"Why? Do you think it's serious? Something we need to avoid?"

"No. I'm just trying to make sure I'm not imagining things. Prolonged exposure to heat causes hallucinations – mirages."

"But it's night." He stated the obvious. It was just what I needed.

"You're right. Well then, I believe we've stumbled upon a ground- spring." Syvis looked at me with puckered eyebrows. I reworded our discovery. "Water, Syvis. I think it's water."

Holding up my right arm, I motioned for the group to head left, slightly off trajectory. Dezmind joined me.

"What's going on?"

"I would like to have a bath," I said, and pointed to the small oval-shaped patch of water no bigger than a shallow swimming pool. It probably wasn't very deep.

Doire had written that the deepest ground-spring he'd come across was knee high, but this one was also slightly larger than any he'd made note of. Professor Denali theorised that the gradual warming of our climate was desalinating our natural sources of verrin over long periods of time. The random springs Doire took care to note down during his travels likely used to be lakes of verrin, very much like the ones in the Expanse. In contrast, he'd only noted two small sources of verrin.

"Look! Water!" Lutrice called from behind Syvis. Detaching myself from the lead, I stood between the group and the pool.

"We're in luck. We've found a ground-spring. We still have to be careful though. If I determine that it's safe and uninhabited, there'll be a few rules to follow."

"Will we stop here for our day's rest?" Deltek asked.

"I wish I could say yes, but we are not the only living creatures out here who'll want to use this water. We'll walk another five or ten minutes to make sure we're clear of any direct path leading to the pool, and then we'll rest."

The groans were not as full-throated and elongated as I expected. Water was a good thing, even if it wasn't verrin.

"First, we'll fill our empty verrin kegs; second, the men will retreat behind this dune while the women bathe; third, the men can bathe when we're done; fourth, don't use soap in the water – if you need to, scrub and rinse on the sand. We don't want to pollute it; we just want to use it. We're to leave this resource pretty much as we found it."

Deltek, Merik, Raylan and Syvis each picked up an empty keg as the women set their packs down by the edge of the pool. Taking one of the boards from the hauler, I used it to prod, stir, and penetrate the water in various places. I wanted to use one of my weapons to zap it, but neither worked since the overload in the cave.

I hoped the Whipstaff just needed time to recharge but I may have scattered the ion pattern beyond recognition. The Clinex was spent and I didn't have a spare plasma cartridge. The Facility didn't permit more than one active cartridge at a time. Still, if I hadn't used my weapons, we'd be burying our dead right now. I poked the middle of the pool again. Nothing surfaced, so I gave the 'go-ahead' to the men to collect the water.

When Dezmind finally led the men around the side of the dune, the women rummaged through their packs for cleansing items. Lutrice helped ease Jantice into the cool liquid. Tamaine, however, stayed somewhat apart. I took off my sweatshirt. Tamaine cast her eyes down, turning to walk away. I jogged over.

"What's up Tamaine? A nice bath will help clean out your wounds."

She muttered something indistinguishable.

"What's that?" I asked.

Tamaine lifted her head, but still did not make eye contact. "I don't want to pollute the water. I don't want them to see what I did to myself."

"Now you're just being ridiculous. It's dark. No one but Jantice might notice and she's still recovering from her own battle with the Deserts." I gripped her shoulders and guided her toward the water. "The plant extract I gave you is all natural; it'll dissolve without any harm to the environment. Now come join us. Stop being so paranoid."

Nodding, Tamaine allowed me to bring her back to the pool and the bathing women. She gingerly removed her sweater and undershirt. Her torso was riddled with scratch marks but most of them were bright pink and healing nicely.

Jantice kept her newly-wrapped arm above the water as she bathed, borrowing Tamaine's sponge to help wash around it. The friends didn't say much but they communicated plenty.

Lutrice was almost finished. She walked into the middle of the pool in her under-garments, and dunked her whole body. *That looks so refreshing.* I spared no time and cut into the crisp water with a shallow dive, surfacing on the opposite bank with a shiver. Resting my head on the sand, I let my body float under the surface, adjusting to the cool temperature. Lutrice dressed and then helped Tamaine rinse her back.

Washing my hair, I dressed and retrieved another segment of the healing-plant for Jantice and Tamaine.

"Another five minutes ladies, then I'll be sending the men around," I said. Picking up my two packs, I walked toward the other side of the dune. The tone of the voices made me stop. Leaning against the sand piled beside me, I listened to the conversation.

"– no more land for development. If we keep growing at this

rate, we may not be the only ones who'll have to cross into this wasteland," growled Raylan.

"The Kronik refuses to acknowledge that there's even a problem," said Syvis. *We are looking into the people's concerns.* I doubt it. Just like they are with the quakes and the food supply and the verrin situation."

"Verrin situation?" asked Deltek.

"I wouldn't be surprised with everything else that's gone on lately, if the whole trial around that scientist last year wasn't just a fabrication or farce to shut down his findings and satisfy the Press," Syvis remarked.

"I'd advise you to keep sentiments regarding Kronik conspiracies out here in the Deserts," Merik said. "The last time there was a rebellion, the Kronik sent the dissenters to their deaths on some foolhardy exploration – the Nine Seas Massacre.

"Those in power have always been there and do not take kindly to disruption. I've no doubt they're keeping even more from us than that. During my studies, I found large gaps in our heritage records. I made a comment to my Professor about it and was told, ever so casually, that there are some mysteries better left unsolved."

So, Zaith and I weren't the only ones noticing bizarre inconsistencies when it came to the Kronik and its practices. The difference here was that the distrust of these men went beyond the occasional policy. I always firmly believed that the Kronik knew what it was doing; those involved were just being covert about it. Ultimately, the Kronik's decisions were made for the good of the people. *I wonder what Dezmind thinks about all of this talk – the scepticism over the rights of our forefathers? But then, if he cared about such faults, he never would have risked looking for one of its buried secrets.*

This stuff was far too heavy to be discussing in the middle of a Desert in the dead of the blessed night. Approaching laughter and snippets of chatter from the women helped me resolve to break in on the conversation. "Okay guys, your turn. Try not to take more than twenty minutes. Remember, we still need to find a place to bunk down for the day. Enjoy your baths. I don't plan on stopping for a leisurely swim until we're headed home."

I slid down the side of the dune and settled on my pack as Tamaine, Jantice and Lutrice arrived. This would be as good a time as any to check out Doire's secret compartment. I got comfortable, but kept one eye and one ear on alert.

Chapter Eighteen

Trapped

The next night, squeaks from the softening sand needled the silence as I scuffed my feet. The impenetrable sense of isolation worsened whenever I was left to my own thoughts.

The nearness of our goal drove Dezmind to leave me. He never spent more than a few minutes checking in on our progress before dissolving into the night again. At least, when he was beside me, I found the need to concentrate on the job. But with the absence of his unspoken questions buzzing silently around me, my thoughts waned; a younger Dezmind straining biceps and quadriceps as he trained for his mission to find the Lost Lady. Wet wavy hair plastering his forehead – his hands chaffed, riddled with bloody slices from gripping the bark of the nezza bush. I sighed at the unwanted images.

My eyes swept over the sea of sand before me, beside me, and beneath me. I rubbed my nose, breathing into my palm to warm my face. It was bad enough that I wasn't focusing on my duties, but now it was all too often I daydreamed about things that required a personal mental smack. Besides, a pure-blood Matin was not a viable candidate for Soul Mate of the year.

Stay sharp.

Stay focused.

Jantice laughed out loud. Dezmind walked with her. The sound caused me to draw images of the pair of them; foreheads close, noses touching, lips... Stop it. I was glad she felt better, but she could feel a little less better as she walked next to Dezmind.

The group neared the end of a long night, whether we were on the verge of finding the Chronicles or not. *I just want to curl up on the couch with Jadis and watch the wire. We've never been separated this long before.* Even weekly-based contracts had let me go home in the evenings or on weekends.

Pulling out Doire's unfinished manuscript from the secret compartment, I rifled around in my pouch for the pencil Merik lent me. Flipping past the dozen or so pages I'd already shaded in, I lightly rubbed a new one. Luckily, Doire wrote with a heavy hand. Most of the writing was partly visible and I'd been able to make out a thought or idea here and there initially. But by sweeping the pencil tip back and forth across the surface of the page, it made the rest of the words appear.

I didn't have the opportunity to read much of what I uncovered, but the few phrases I did focus on were riddled with descriptions of the landscape. The idea of rock-like spikes protruding from the ground ignited my imagination in a different way; I envisioned Raylan begging for his life, suspended by his belt over a large stretch of spear-sharp landscape.

Shaking my head to clear the image, I allowed myself a small smile. It wasn't right to think like that about the people entrusted to my care, but sometimes – well, sometimes it was thoughts such as those that kept me sane.

Dunes lengthened and grew as I placed one foot in front of the other. The soft, fine sand beneath my feet made the simple act of walking feel like wading through deep water. Progress had slowed since the bath break the night before. We started out with renewed vigour tonight, but when the rigid ground lost consistency, spirits faded along with our speed.

This time, both teens burst out laughing. The skin on the back of my neck crawled with each juvenile giggle. Keeping these people light of spirit was one thing, but tickling their fancy was quite another. Snapping the book closed, I tucked it into my belt-pack and unhooked from the line. I gave Syvis the nod as I walked past. Relieving Merik from pulling the hauler, I watched as Syvis positioned himself at the lead with his map.

"I'm still okay, really," Merik said.

I waved him on. "I need to exert a little excess energy right now. Why don't you go and keep the girls company. I'm sure Deltek and Raylan won't mind."

Both men nodded, focused on the job. Merik shrugged and joined the line where Dezmind had been, having already moved on to chat with Lutrice.

The dense air weighed on my skin like bad breath in your hand after a mouth check. Alpha hovered just below the horizon, warming the air in anticipation of its arrival. I hadn't spoken to Dezmind all night and refused to be included in his conversation with the men to either side of me when their turn came due – not that he tried to include me anyway. Since I'd called him out on possibly abandoning the group, he'd kept his distance.

I plodded on, tuning out the chit-chat, diving into the physical labour. Having wrapped the centre pull of the hauler around my waist, I walked closer to it than Deltek or Raylan. Though I hadn't worn a layer of gauze over my palms in several nights, the pale tenderness of new flesh would not survive rope burn. The modified pull we used for the earlier dune crawls saved my hands.

A small group of dune-peaks rose up ahead of us. I looked to the west, registering a significant lack of starlight at its horizon.

"We'll stop up here to rest for the day. The Pit shouldn't be far now. We'd best enter it on full stomachs and be well rested," I announced.

As we entered the ring of dunes, the group collapsed and found places to rest around the hauler. Everyone needed a few minutes before setting up. My calves ached as I rubbed spikes of pain from my shins.

The malleability of the powder sand sapped the stamina from my soul. The air out here lacked scent. Even bringing a handful of soft pinky-sand to my nose, I couldn't detect an odour – it was unnerving. I was used to relying on my senses to interpret my surroundings. I didn't like these Deserts – I felt stripped, exposed.

Deltek and Lutrice were the first to rise and prepare the glow pit. Dezmind and the girls gradually followed to arrange the AHT. I crawled over and plunked down beside Merik near one of the dunes. He shifted at my arrival; questions floated around his large pupils.

Choosing to ignore what couldn't be answered, I contented myself. "Receive any monumental inspiration yet?" I asked, taking off my cap and wiping my forehead. Several of my clips had loosened; my hair fell lopsided on my head. Removing the rest of the clips, I shook it out over the front of my shoulders to keep it from trailing in the sand. He stared at me, transfixed by its length.

"A bit, but nothing truly fulfilling." He paused, cautious. "Shouldn't you be overseeing something?" He leaned back on his elbows, resting his head on his satchel, confident that his reminder would prompt me to go.

"There's nothing I need to do right now except relax. The glow-fire is well under way and the tent is clearly being taken care of."

I also leaned back on my elbows. Jantice looked at us quizzically as she staked a peg for the tent. She nudged Tamaine in the side with her elbow and nodded at us.

"So, you've never been published," I said. Merik got a far-off look in his eyes before half-closing them. "I'd like to hear a piece. Would you consider reciting one for me?"

He turned his head and looked at me, straight on, no pretences. "I didn't think you'd be interested in poetry."

"My best friend took me to a few private readings of her favourite authors. Some were good, others I won't comment on," I explained. He narrowed his eyes again and looked down at the pale pink sand. He ran it between his fingers making spirals between them. He shook his head, no.

"Come on, I promise I won't bite. I'd really like to hear how you've been able to create in this stark place," I coaxed, channelling Zaith's ability for using humour to set others at ease.

"All right, but no feedback. I'm not finished yet, it's still rough."

"Perhaps saying it out loud will help you refine it."

Tilting my head to one side, I looked for Dezmind. He and the girls had finished with the tent, and were walking in and out arranging back packs. I caught his eye and managed an unanswered grin before returning my attention to Merik.

He didn't clear his throat, or take time to contemplate life. Speaking with a steady, calm voice, he stared at the sand through his half-closed eyes. His words like cotton candy, melted in the rising Desert heat.

"Blazing suns align with bitter winds tire petrified bones;
trudging, trudging, trudging
along.

Daylight sleeps,
the Evil word scars cracked skin scraping away the man
no longer walking alone.

Deep restlessness grinds the soul coarse as the sands of time;
drifting, blowing, falling
as oblivion trudges on."

His hand stilled. We two strangers linked for a moment. Tamaine's laughter broke the calm.

"May I ask one question?" I checked.

"Just don't criticise," he said.

I nodded. "You don't set up any particular pattern throughout the piece and yet, you chose to repeat the imagery of the first verse again in the last stanza."

He sighed, slightly resigned but not entirely deflated. "It was a message I hoped the listener would understand, without explanation," he blocked.

"Then let me see if I got it, okay?"

Pushing his pack away, he fell back onto the sand, using his arms as a headrest. He motioned with his head for me to give it a shot.

I continued, "The inconsistency of each line and verse leads the listener into an expectation of difference that in and of itself never changes, acting as a constant – telling us, secretly, what we already know."

I thought for a moment. "When you closed with your opening,

it was like the renewing of a bizarre cycle that suggested something more, but a 'more' that is completed by the listener – to reveal and bring to the surface something that perhaps we might not want to see in the pattern of our own lives."

He remained motionless for a time, and then sat bolt upright.

"I think…" he said, pausing, "that there's more to you than meets the eye." Rising swiftly, he grabbed his pack and jogged over to the girls who were exiting the tent.

I guess I wasn't wrong.

I located Dezmind again as he gathered the last of the light-tubes.

"Let's eat!" Lutrice called, passing out the night's variety of insta-food. I rolled over and lay on my stomach, my hair splayed out over my back. From that vantage point, I saw the first pale-red resonance of Alpha peek lazily over the low dunes.

Hopping to my feet, I stretched and walked over to join the others. I tossed my light-tube into the hole. Finding a place to sit across the circle from Dezmind, I casually asked Tamaine about her betrothed.

Light, non-committal chatter dominated the circle. I grabbed the last food pack, and snapped the base. The pouch heated instantly. I sucked back the mush.

My throat closed as I desperately tried to swallow. I just managed to stop my gag-reflex. I'd been playing spoiled since we arrived, choosing not to help, so I had no right to criticise someone else's choice in shared rations. It tasted rotten. I looked at the label. The mix of fruit and game did not work.

Multiple times throughout the meal, I tried to catch Dezmind's eye. He refused to look at me. When he wasn't eating, he spoke with Syvis or Deltek, who sat closest to him – no one else.

I half-heartedly listened to Tamaine carry on about Bazdin and his studies in Medical Business Administration; what alternate courses he'd taken, his interest in languages, chemistry. But I couldn't sit still. Shifting this way and that, I became more unsettled with every sentence. With only the occasional nod now and then, eventually Tamaine figured out that I wasn't listening. Turning, she spoke with Jantice instead.

Still, he refused to look at me.

"Dezmind," I said. "Why don't you explain to everyone a bit more about what to expect when we arrive at the Pit? You know, prepare them for what might lie ahead," I suggested, knowing full well that he didn't have a clue as I hinted at the likelihood that it didn't exist.

He looked at me. A strange light flashed behind his eyes. He cocked his chin, ever so slightly, to the right. Feeling his gaze cascade from the crown of my head to a point just below my hairline, I shivered.

My heart jumped. My fingers twitched incessantly, now painfully aware of my casual appearance. Mortified with my childish behaviour, I bit my lip and dropped my eyes. A steady heat crept from the back of my neck up across my cheeks.

Just what are you trying to prove, Taya?

Looking up the next moment, I heard Dezmind reiterating the possible challenges.

"As I mentioned before, there's very little that the Tablets said about the interior of the Pit, except that we have to first pass through it to reach the Chronicles. There are no descriptions about the intricacies of the challenges; they'll likely be physical, but from what I understand, our wits will be employed to solve a puzzle or read a piece of text. What are Fate, Destiny, and Truth really?

"Our ancestors wouldn't have made the Chronicles impossible to locate, just difficult. They weren't meant to be kept from us, but preserved *for* us until the time would come for their wisdom to be revealed. Common lore labels the Chronicles as lost. They are far from it. The Ancients knew we'd need this wisdom in future days and made sure it wouldn't vanish."

I stood up and left. Walking to the side of the furthest dune, acting as though I intended to relieve myself, I paced in small circles.

Pulling at the hair near my scalp, I grimaced – needing to feel something, something real, something true. I couldn't understand what was happening. *I'm not Zaith! I'm not some mindless teenager. This is ridiculous.*

Dropping to a squat, I rested my backside on the dune with my legs at a ninety-degree angle. Taking a few deep breaths, I retied my hair. The repetitive nature of lifting, twisting and clipping helped relax me and worked to clear my mind.

Placing my CTF cap securely on my head, I flopped back against the dune, punching the sand with my elbows. *What's wrong with me? This is insane. Get a grip, Taya.*

A scream pierced the air.

Chapter Nineteen
Powder Sands Desert

I jolted upright. A cacophony of voices rose like fireworks. *Dammit.* I looked into the brightening sky. *Peace, that's all I ask!*

Pushing myself off the dune, I ran back to camp. Merik stood frozen behind Jantice, reaching for her empty food pack.

Tamaine shook, curled in a ball behind the bench, but everyone's eyes remained fixated on the three, yard-long dark-grey spikes sticking up through the middle of the glow-fire.

"Don't move!" I rasped, fear choking the strength from my voice.

Whatever it is, it's probably blind.

No one got hit.

No one got hurt.

The Creature likely aimed for the centre of the disturbance. Below. It definitely came from somewhere below.

No, no, no, no. Not a Sand Eater.

Definitely not.

New creature – new danger –

No one moved, obeying with little effort. Wisps of haggard

breathing filled the humid air. My eyes tracked swiftly over the region surrounding the camp, then searched amid the light-tubes.

I spotted it; a dense moist film and a dark shadow under the tubes – the only living thing still moving. I checked everyone's faces. I had to be sure they wouldn't bolt.

"Listen carefully," I whispered. "It's under the glow-fire. Don't move if it touches you. Think rock." I couldn't afford the loss of another person, another soul.

Hours passed, or rather, what felt like hours. Call it intuition, job experience, whatever – I knew the thing had left. I straightened up.

"I'm pretty sure it's gone, but still, no one move. If someone's going to have an encounter with it, it might as well be me."

The light-tubes flickered and died. I looked closer – they had dissolved, melted where the ooze touched them. I drew my Whipstaff, praying it still worked. Touching the tip of the staff, to the widest spike, I engaged the ion beam. It lit up and snaked out, grabbing the anomaly.

I yanked.

The spike flew fast. I disengaged the beam. The spike planted into the side of the closest dune. I repeated the tactic with the other two spines.

I scanned the area surrounding our campsite. Jantice and Lutrice gathered to comfort Tamaine. The others tentatively cleaned up – making sure to avoid the dark, molten spot in the sand.

Three significantly large dunes flanked us. Each appeared to be equidistant. We'd set up camp in the centre, where the spikes came from—

Oh, how can I be so stupid! Why wasn't I watching more carefully?

"Pack, fast," I said. "It'll be back. We have to keep moving. We're not safe here." Blank faces stared at me. "Come on, people! We're losing precious time; Alpha's rising. Let's get to it."

"What do you mean it's coming back?!" Tamaine shrieked. "Is it going to follow us?" Jantice asked.

"Are we still in danger?" Merik chimed in.

"What exactly is going on?" said Dezmind.

"Hurry and pack," Raylan urged.

"Don't forget the hauler boards." Lutrice reminded.

"Does everyone have their pack?" Deltek asked.

Merik and Deltek handed out packs from inside the tent. Lutrice and Dezmind fixed the hauler as Raylan and Syvis collapsed the AHT around the other men. Tamaine hovered by the women. I helped collapse part of the tent and load the wagon. Flitting from one task to the next, I kept a steady lookout over the surface of the sand for any sign that the beast had returned – to its nest.

Trudging through the sand was the last thing I wanted to do at that late morning hour with the heat baking us from the inside and the sun burning us on the outside. Fear kept the group mobile, though lack of sleep took its toll with the pace. Exposed skin grew angry- hot, the higher Alpha rose. With Beta soon to follow, dry mouths and cracked lips would be among the least of our problems.

I could only hope that if there was a Pit to find, we could get to it before the extreme heat hit, but not knowing an exact location didn't help. Our radius of possibility was just too large. I imagined wandering in circles covering the same ground time and again, looking for a landmark that likely no longer existed – if it ever had.

I would have turned us around after the sand storm if I knew this waited. I should've left Dezmind to fend for himself back at Doire's cave. He probably would have turned around after a day or so and given up of his own accord.

Then again, maybe not.

Glancing over my shoulder, weary, tired and deflated eyes hung low. These people were rapidly losing any sense of why they were here.

Dezmind's last speech had been almost two hours ago. Already they needed moral support.

Facing forward again, I slowed until I kept pace with Dezmind. "The gang is seriously disheartened. I hope you have something good saved up in that speech reservoir of yours because they need it. It's likely some of them are wondering if it's worth the trouble, being chased by monsters they can't see. Find a way to reassure them."

"Are you even leading us in the right direction?" he snapped.

Another trio of close-set dunes materialised. Those damn burrows were everywhere.

"I'll ignore that," I said.

Focusing on putting one foot in front of the other, I led the haphazard troop further into the desolate landscape. We had to get past this nesting ground, and the only way to do that was to keep moving.

Nothing surrounded us but fields upon hilly fields of soft, sandy dunes rippled and wrinkled by the dry Desert winds. As Alpha dominated the sky, its light reflected off the fine pink particles in the sand. Goggles remained a permanent fixture on the faces of everyone who'd brought them; they automatically tinted with the intensity of the light.

A slight breeze stirred. Single dunes ranged the span of city blocks, so when we spotted a smaller grouping of three, we avoided the area. *I don't know, maybe we're avoiding the Pit too.* If we lost our footing and slipped into one of the many gullies or valleys of this Desert, we'd suffocate in no time. Our odds of finding Dezmind's treasure were getting smaller and smaller.

I don't know how many times I decided to turn us around, yet I still found my feet dragging this sorry bunch of misfits further into the quagmire. If we could just get clear of these underground dens, I would rest everyone up and head home at nightfall.

Dezmind's voice broke through my thoughts as it carried back to the struggling group.

"I know we've travelled a long way, and that you're feeling the destabilizing nature of the Deserts. But we have to keep reminding ourselves that we have an objective; a very real, very impending goal. We're Xannia's last chance. The Kronik can't help us, and those who don't believe in our cause are barriers and roadblocks in a necessary quest for survival. We have a higher sense of purpose – we're going to save our homes and those of our neighbours – and we'll live to see that day."

Interesting – the very person guiding them to 'salvation' is the barrier keeping them from being saved. No wonder he hasn't talked to me lately.

Alpha and Beta climbed higher. Blisters and heat rashes formed on a variety of body parts. Verrin rations for the 'day' were gone, and the water reserves we now relied on did half the job of verrin. The chemically-generated verrin we added to the water helped, but for how much longer? We couldn't skimp on our supplies for fear of heatstroke and severe muscle cramps.

Travelling by day was killing us slowly. We had to find another resource and this time it had to be verrin. So far, no one had tried to siphon any they hadn't already been assigned, but I didn't know how long that peace would last.

Seventy hours – nearly three days since the map correction and we still weren't any closer to anything. Shielding my eyes, I looked toward Gamma peeking above the horizon. A small wispy cloud crossed in front of Beta. The sky below it shimmered. The breeze returned, dancing across my hot skin, teasing my need for cool air and shade.

More clouds joined the passing of the first, bringing a diminished heat with the light wind. Something invisible tapped my arm, slightly moist. I double-checked to make sure my canteen was closed. The cap hadn't budged.

The shimmering sky drew above us. Colours danced in the heavens – great curved bands of light.

"Look up!" I called back to the group. Appreciative sounds erupted from the girls. Merik's eyes watered or was it something else? He touched his face then opened his arms to the sky. Shimmering particles delicately showered us.

"Rain!" he cried, his face shining with child-like wonder.

The procession stopped. Everyone held their arms and faces up to the sky. A misting of water floated down and caressed scorched and angry skin. I looked at the sand. It remained warm and dry. I crouched a little and the droplets reduced. I sat down entirely and not a one reached my up-turned face. *They're evaporating before they can reach the ground – astounding.*

A deep rumble echoed. It didn't appear to be thunder. The clouds were too sparse and had nearly passed.

The ground shook – an all-too-familiar sensation. I jerked around to shout a warning–

The earth heaved.

Mid-turn, the others tumbled to the ground before a word escaped my mouth.

A scream, yells – the sand shifted and rolled down the side of the dune. I scrambled to my feet to warn the hauler crew, but it was too late.

The back end of the transport shifted with the cascading sand. As it slid down the incline of the dune, the safety line pulled taut dragging the others down with it. Scrambling over the shuddering ground, I hauled Dezmind to his feet.

"If we don't run with it, we'll be dragged like the others," I shouted, sliding with the sand.

He nodded.

Supporting each other we dashed down the hill, close on the heels of the churning Kahn-lea. At the base, no one tried to stand, they just crawled over to the hauler; which surprisingly remained upright on a slight angle at the bottom. Dezmind and I collapsed as the earth gave a final vicious tremor.

The beautiful rain was gone; the air surrounding us now was hot and heavy with a humid silence. Breathing was difficult and would only get worse the longer we stayed at the bottom of the valley. We gathered beneath the hauler for shade. Dezmind and I sat uncomfortably half-in half-out of the suns' light.

Raylan spoke, "What now? What was that? I don't want another strange beast rising from the depths of this sandy crypt."

"Stay calm," I advised, slightly out of breath. "That wasn't a Desert creature. It was a quake; not quite as bad as the last one in the Prime, but a quake just the same. Is everyone all right? Any sand burns from the fall?" I asked.

Whispered "no's" and shaking heads answered.

"All right, we need to rest but we really should get this thing back up on top of the dune. These dunes are nearly five times bigger than the ones we crawled in the Valley but the air is too stagnant to remain down here. We're more likely to encounter strange things in the bowels of this place than if we keep to the high ground. I haven't seen a nest in a while, so when we get back to the top, we should rest for the day." I looked to Dezmind to gage his reaction.

"We can straddle the hauler across the top of the dune, get some sleep and look for the Pit tonight," he added.

I nodded, resigned to leaving us exposed while we slept.

"This is the plan then," I said. "We'll need the men pulling the hauler using their safety lines and we'll have the women pushing. Let's attach our lines to the back and shorten the lead between so as not to trip on our cords. When we start, we won't be able to stop until we get to the top. Ready?" I asked.

There were several sighs, but the entire group voiced a resounding "yes." Perhaps the thought of temperature-protected sleep was enough to rouse their last ounces of strength.

I supervised the connecting of the men's safety cords before returning to the rear of the hauler to check on the women. They had tied large knots in the lines to reduce the length and elevate the cords as they pushed. I snapped my line onto Lutrice's and took a step back to see the full scope of the task. Dezmind came around to the back and clipped on between us.

"Are you sure this will work?" he asked, following my gaze up the side of the long dune.

"It might. The incline isn't too steep; it's just being able to maintain momentum as we climb that will be the challenge."

An after-quake rumbled aggressively. Sand shifted and scattered around us. It lifted one worry from my mind. We wouldn't have to deal with it as we climbed.

But something wasn't right.

I moved even though the ground stopped shaking. I looked down. I was up to my shins in silk-sand.

"Dez!" I shrieked, yanking at my right leg to free it. Turning from Lutrice, he rushed toward me.

"Taya!"

"Back! Back – stay back. Try to pull me out by the cord."

I held my arms parallel to the ground, as I was now engulfed up to my waist. The circumference of the falling sand expanded rapidly, pushing him further back. Dezmind shouted out a warning, calling for the pulling to commence laterally instead of vertically. Syvis peeked his head around the side of the hauler then disappeared again.

Up to my torso in sand, I threw my packs onto the bank then dug down for the knife in my belt-pack. I pulled the blade up out of the sand. Neck deep, I sawed at the connection now dragging Dezmind and Lutrice in after me.

"Taya! Don't do it! This'll work!" he cried.

"I'm pulling you in too fast. It's too late. We can't afford to lose anyone else."

I cut the cord.

I sank to my chin.

Suddenly, Dezmind came soaring over the disintegrating edge of the vortex that devoured me. The teens and Lutrice braced at the top of the conical, holding tight to Dezmind's cord.

He grabbed my wrist.

"Let go! It's no use. Finish what you came for." Sinking further, I tilted my head up to catch a final breath.

Dezmind's grip tightened. My hand went numb.

"You might be able to live with death, but that's something I don't want to get in the habit of," he grunted, suspended between me and the ridge of sand.

"W-what's... one life when... when you're trying to save... to save millions. D-De-Dez," I sputtered, forced to shut my mouth.

"If I let you go – no. No. I know what I have to do–"

His cord went limp. He dropped toward me.

I shut my eyes.

The extra weight exploded into the centre of the sand funnel as the earth consumed us.

Chapter Twenty
What Lay Beneath

Sliding amongst the fine particles of silk-sand, my instinct to survive kicked in. I fought to swim to the surface, flailing my arms, but the excess energy expended my oxygen reserves. Fire seared my lungs.

Making contact with something suspended in the sand, my hope surged. *An old root? The remnants of a small bush?* Clutching at it, I still descended. My lungs heaved internally for air that was not there.

I lost consciousness.

Black.

Everything was black. I couldn't open my eyes.

Lying on my back, I felt a cold, hard, rough surface beneath me. My head ached and throbbed. A heavy weight pushed me down. Sand – it infiltrated every inch of my clothing, my body.

I tried to sit up, my limbs stiff and sore. I must have been lying there for a while. Releasing the root I'd grabbed during the fall, I let my hand trace the ground, searching for a sign of where I was.

I kept my eyes shut. I tried opening them, but they were caked with sand. Coughing, I clutched my dry throat. Three extra days suddenly felt like three weeks. *We should've turned back. How long have I been lying here?*

"Ohhwhoo," I groaned, struggling to roll onto my stomach.

I licked cracked and sore lips. Wincing, I thought twice before attempting it again. Forcing myself to swallow, I slowly brushed the sand off my face, unclogging my ears and nose.

Luckily, the particles were dry and with a few dull shakes of my head, the majority dislodged. Carefully, I wiped particles from around my eyes, lifting first one dry lid then the other, attempting to blink without pain. I couldn't see anyway so I stayed still, closed them tight and let them water.

A sound.

Jerking my head to the left, I strained my ears and cocked my head sideways – listening.

There it was again.

Blinded by grainy particles I kept my eyes shut as I painstakingly crawled toward the faint sound. I felt the contours of the ground: a dip, a crack. I searched, searched for something – anything. My hand bumped into an object. I traced over it with my fingers. It was semi-cylindrical and rubbery beneath a coarse coating. "Humputh."

I yanked my hand back. Coughing erupted.

It was Dez – spitting sand out of his mouth, choking on his dry throat.

"Dez–" my voice scraped. I replaced my hand on his arm.

"Hummoh," he sputtered incoherently.

"Don't talk. I'll help the best I can."

Crawling, with slightly more ease, I slid beside him and followed the length of his body up to his face. Meticulously, and as gently as possible, I brushed off the sand. Tiny particles covered his face like a mask; rough and ridged, they distorted his familiar features. Leaning against his chest, I blew lightly across his face.

The fall must have been hard on him, descending headfirst. With care, my fingers traced his eyes and then his ears. My eyes still closed, I managed to locate his right hand and brought it to his face to let him work out the rest.

I felt his eyes water. Removing my hand, I let his tears flow freely. My fingers brushed the delicate waves of his hair.

I snatched my hand back.

What are you doing! Open your eyes and figure out where you are!

Rolling away from him, I lay momentarily on my back again. My hands fell to the ground. My eyes remained shut.

Something wasn't right – I had come to dread this basic inkling. Tracing the ground again, this time I found an edge to cup my hands around. I rolled onto my stomach and dragged myself closer to the edge. From there, I methodically followed it – round and round and round.

We were on a circular platform, maybe five yards wide – no extending walkways.

"Taya?"

"Yeah?"

"Do you know where we are?"

"Not yet, but I think I can open my eyes now."

Cautiously, one eyelid rose, then another. I looked over the edge. We were in a dimly-lit chamber, ten feet or so from the next level down.

What's lighting up this place? It reminds me of the creature cave.

My hand bumped something.

Lousy root.

I grabbed at it to chuck it into the expanse.

"Eh!" I dropped it.

The root was the bone of some large, long-dead animal. I pushed it over the edge with my foot, and rolled onto my back.

I gasped.

My throat burned. A coughing fit shook my body. Still, I stared wide-eyed. My heartbeat tripled. I gasped for air my lungs refused to provide.

Not five feet above us, the rounded tip of a huge funnel suspended down from a ceiling of sand. It extended up about fifty yards, expanding to almost half that. It looked like a large graduated spiral resting like half of an hourglass frozen in time.

The sand looked grey in the low light of the cavernous chamber. The tip of the gigantic stalactite pointed to the centre of the platform supporting me and Dez.

"How is this possible?" I rasped.

"Incredible," he said, opening his eyes. "Likely some sort of natural occurrence. You did say that one of the major causes behind the Deserts 'dead-zones' was increased magnetism, right?"

"But on a scale this large? We're in an underground cavern and it's suspended from the ceiling," I said, looking further into the chamber. "But I have a sneaking suspicion this is what we've been looking for."

"My sentiments exactly."

"What now? I have no experience in terrain like this, for a situation like this."

I shifted around to look at him, the cavern surrounding us a blur. My lower lip trembled as my heart beat erratically. The space collapsed in on my mind, closing off my senses from the environment.

Everything lost shape and texture, swimming before my eyes. The space covered me like a wet blanket: heavy, moist, and suffocating. I gasped for air. A haze shrouded my brain. I stood, stumbled. Small flecks of light flashed behind my eyes as greyness glazed over their surface.

Breathe!

Breathe!

I stumbled again, closer to the edge of the dais.

Control.

Control.

I need control.

Pressure on my left arm made my head wobble. It came again, harder, stronger – more demanding!

What

"What?" I shouted.

A pair of hands gripped my arms. I couldn't regain control of my neck muscles. A voice filtered into my mind, distant, faint but constant – like the unwanted whisper of trees in the night.

"Jutaya!"

I snapped to. The fog dissipated.

"What? Dezmind stop. What?"

He held me in his arms. I clung to his embrace. The haze thinned to nothingness.

"You tell me. Are you all right? You almost walked off the edge. Is something wrong?"

I rested my forehead against his chest, and then gave myself a cerebral slap. I pulled away.

"I'm in perfect mental and physical health. I have to be. It's my job." I fell back on the standard training response and threw off his arms. My voice resounded like thunder, but I felt no bigger than a sand mite.

Space was space again, and I could breathe and see just fine, but the expanse surrounding us held a deafening silence. There was too much of nothing.

"Then tell me what's wrong." Soft words, gentle, calming – everything I needed to lose hold of my sanity. I flung them back in his face.

"You've got a mission to complete." I took a step back. "I've got a contract to uphold," I stated, clear-headed. I glanced up at the ceiling.

They'll be lucky if they make it back in one piece. I turned away from him.

"Taya, we can't help them now. You'll have to trust that Syvis will do the right thing. You were right in appointing him as liaison."

"Whether I was right or not isn't the point. How am I supposed to keep them safe if I'm trapped down here?"

"I thought Syvis was your contingency plan," he pushed. *One that I hoped never to need.*

"Get your map. Let's go." I picked up my canteen and stalked to the edge of the platform. I was solid, stable, back in control. If he wanted me to focus on getting him through this, then that's what I'd do.

Jumping down to the next level, cat-like, my body barely registered the distance. In fact, it felt like training: comfortable, familiar. "Blood, sweat and tears," I whispered.

I'm fine.

Dezmind landed behind me. A heavy thud echoed throughout the cavern. He moved to stand beside me, large enough to diminish some of the space. Holding his map, he scanned the expansive chamber, squinting, brows furrowed in concentration. He grumbled something under his breath and crumpled his notes.

"It's useless. This is beyond anything I ever imagined. We're blind." His voice echoed empty and hollow.

"Then I guess we need to rely on our other senses to get to the Chronicles. Let's go." It was a command, not a request. I knew polite behaviour would be of no use.

We crossed the vaulted stadium-like chamber toward a framed hole the size of a tractor tire in the side of the tiered wall. I maintained the awkward silence. Feelings would only get in the way. Every soldier had to be alert, absent of emotion to survive. Not that I had ever fought in a war, but my military training at the CTF was all I had to fall back on now.

The other side of the hole was no more helpful in its barren state. The ceiling above was just as high as the previous chamber, but the rounded walls appeared to be made of a tiered molten rock, not sand. I traced a hand along the wall beside the formed opening: cold, damp and rough with many dips and crevices attesting to its imperfection. The entire cavity was dark brown. I couldn't quite make out the smell though. It wasn't bad, or pleasant – just there, like something familiar – like Doire's crystals.

Shaking my head to clear the thought, I turned back to look at the room. Coarse, clumping sand lay under our feet, stretching out for nearly twenty yards. Halfway to the opposite side sat a large pool – possibly verrin. It radiated a warm pink-orange glow, far richer than the three surface lakes of Vitexid's.

"Look." I pointed. "There's something inscribed on the flat of the wall – just above the surface of the pool."

Dezmind walked to the edge of the liquid and knelt down on the bank. He leaned his body over the surface to get a better look, though he was still a good distance away. His body froze there as the fingertips of his right hand touched the ground for balance; he studied the characters.

I shifted from foot-to-foot, put my hands in my pockets and then took them back out again. Finally, I walked over to him.

"What does it say?"

No response.

"Can you read it?"

Silence.

"I need an update over here!"

Turning his head he said, "Weren't you ever taught that patience is a virtue?"

"No," I lied.

He frowned at me again. "No, I can't read it, but the script is familiar. It's similar to a couple of the scrolls I researched when learning about the Chronicles. I get the feeling that it's telling us something about this pond – this place. Look here," he waved to a symbol on the left, "that one and the next two are similar to the ancient inscriptions on the Tablet for fate, destiny, and truth. That one on the right is similar to the idea of community or gathering but that's all I can make out."

"Is it verrin?" I asked, moving toward the pool, but the closer I got, the more intensely an itch developed just behind my ears. I backed off. The feeling subsided.

"Do you feel that?" I asked.

"Feel what?"

"Never mind."

I tried again, getting closer this time, my nose an inch away from the surface of the pond as I sniffed the liquid. Jerking back, I raising my hands to my ears.

Oww – That's like fire!

"What the–?" I gulped air noisily and sat back on my haunches. Losing my balance, I wound up sitting instead.

"What?" Dezmind's voice strained as he turned to lean over me. I traced the skin behind my ears.

"It's my ear-marks," I whispered. "They're expanding." My voice was too shaky for my liking.

This isn't supposed to be happening!

"Let me see."

He gently tilted my head. I uncovered the mark. He pushed loose hairs back up under my hat and leaned in closer.

Even through my shaking and growing wariness, the feeling of his breath on the side of my neck made me close my eyes. It was light, warm and comforting – soothing really. I gave in to these primal senses, leaning against him as he inspected me.

Fingers traced over my skin. The mark under my other hand receded and returned to normal – the fire gone. Once again they were merely two thin, black, jagged marks, like tattoos on the surface of my skin.

Dezmind backed away and stood up, deep in thought. I righted my head, looking down at the sand. I couldn't look at him. He knew I was weak.

Snapping his fingers, he sent a jolt through me. I stared past him, confused.

"Nadian's Theory," he said.

"What? What about it?" I rose, waiting for an explanation.

"His theory attempts to explain our origins. It's based on autopsy reports, examinations of skeletal remains, and historical findings from ancient archaeological dig sites."

"Didn't he die well over two centuries ago? Wouldn't his findings be just as ancient, and likely as unreliable?" The nervous tension that resurfaced with the effects of my marks amplified.

"No, there are still those in the scientific community working to prove his theory. As a matter of fact, there was a special about it on the wire just last month. Anyway, I think he's right."

"That we originate from amphibians? And when did you come to this conclusion?" I asked.

"Just now."

We stood there – staring – trying to read the other's mind. Mine raced, thinking about the consequences of believing Nadian's Theory. Reaching up, I touched the skin just behind my ears, and looked at the pond.

"Gills that have been lying dormant since our ancestors took to the land – it's so farfetched, so base."

"All along, our path to the truth lay in the past," Dezmind said, rubbing his own marks, contemplating. "Here we are, in a place created by the first known citizens of Xannia. You know…" He pointed to the pond. "We may have to swim through this stuff in order to get to the Chronicles. Perhaps this is the physical manifestation of the three trials."

"It burned. It ached and itched like crazy. Besides, what if it's a trap? What if there's a hidden door or passageway to the next chamber? We haven't even looked at the whole room yet."

I jogged over to the nearest wall, agitated and flushed,

searching for a hidden niche: feeling, pushing, and then pounding on the rock. Panic swelled in my chest. I fell to my knees; my hands absently searched the wall.

Everything I'd ignored, refused to believe in, hung out to dry on cynicism, came crashing down. I smacked my forehead into the wall, digging into its imperfections with my hands. Bright red blood drizzled from broken fingernails, pooling in the lines of my palms.

It's true.

NO–

Yes.

It's all true. The Ancient Tablets, the Chronicles, the stories, the Rallies– The end of the world?

'Believe in nothing and survive, believe in something and suffer its consequences – the half truths and the lies' – The immortal words of the first instructor. The words carved by a laser into the beam above every training level door; words I live by–

"I can't believe it. I can't. I won't," I repeated, banging my forehead against the cold, rigid stone.

"Taya," Dezmind paused, waiting for a response I couldn't give. "I'm going in."

I heard him turn. I spun around.

"No!"

He dove.

I froze.

A cold sweat beaded my forehead. I trembled uncontrollably. Scrambling to my feet, I tore across the ground to the edge of the pool.

"Dez!"

I twisted away – pacing, holding my wet crimson hands to the sides of my temple. My feet skirted swiftly over the sand; back and forth, back and forth.

I have a contract to uphold. I'm supposed to be the guide. I'm supposed to be the bodyguard. I'm supposed to know!

Back and forth.

Back and forth.

There's no question then. I have to follow him – but I don't want to die!

"Think!" I shouted.

Every fibre of my being pulled against the unknown, the impossible truths, the loss of control.

Find a way to survive.

Turing back to the pond, I took a long look at the inscription carved into the wall.

Running forward, I leapt into the air.

Chapter Twenty-one
Fate and Destiny... But Truth?

Eyes closed, I swam under the surface of the liquid toward the wall. But there was no wall. The dense substance dragged me down, saturating my clothes. The fire blazing behind my ears burned into my brain with piercing fingers of flame. Holding my hands on either side of my head, I swam on, kicking fiercely.

The skin beneath my hands rubbed and peeled away. Two jagged slits the length of my marks broke open.

They vibrated.

My lungs burned. Wrenching my hands up above my head, I scrambled to reach the surface. *I can't do this.* I had to get out.

My palms hit something hard seconds before my head smashed into it. I sunk a little, reeling. Opening my eyes, nothing but pale orange- pink swirled around me. The darkness above loomed and closed in. The thick liquid distorted everything. Hands wavered unintelligibly before me.

What have I done?

My lungs contracted, searing with the lack of air. Forcing my way up to the surface, I found the obstruction. Placing my hands on its slimy ceiling, kicking my feet, I brought the side of my face against it and pushed. My heart reverberated in my ears. Kicking my feet again, I hit the obstruction repeatedly, scratching its rough surface with my torn fingers. There was no way out. No turning back. No control.

Throwing my head back, I screamed.

Maybe twenty seconds went by, maybe twenty minutes or two hours. It felt like no time and forever all at once. As the liquid filled my lungs it sluiced through the paper-thin filaments on my neck. Images of my childhood hijacked my mind as the burning behind my ears kept me paralyzed while the current of the underground lake drew me on...

My mother's face smiling in the sunshine as she pulled the curtains open on a new day – my heart wrung itself at the memory. My father holding my baby brother, Blain, and laughing, before turning to me and scowling a curse; Blain sleeping on my bed as a toddler and me on the cold floor in the next room; lying on the floor of my barren room, listening through the ductwork as my family walked out on me; scavenging for food in trash cans at age eight; learning to avoid concerned adults and curious Justices; working the mines at age ten; leaving them at fifteen to join the CTF...

I fought against the barrage of images, of the life I didn't want to remember. Punching and kicking out at nothing and no one, twisting and tying myself into physical and mental knots sapped my energy until the world went black and the voices in my head repeated themselves unimpeded.

My body drifted slowly upward. There was no ceiling now to stop me from rising. My eyes snapped open. I grabbed at the rock in front of me. With effort, I dragged myself up along an embankment, gills flexing wildly in the open air – air that acted like sandpaper against my throat.

I gasped, but nothing happened.

Hauling my body onto a solid shore of rock, I lifted my torso with shaking arms. My head hung limp. I heaved and coughed.

Orange-pink liquid splashed against the rocks and back up into my face. Gagging, I brought up the last of what was in my system. My left arm collapsed and I fell to the ground.

Through the matted strands of hair plastered to my face, I looked out at another enormous cavern. The walls here were smooth but the same odd, low light as before magnified in the space.

Coughing one last time, I lay semi-conscious. The burning sensation dissipated as my gills closed, returning to an inactive state before the world went dark again.

My head throbbed with an achy resonance. Gingerly, I pulled myself into a sitting position. I had no idea how long I'd been out for. "Zola, Zita, and Zerameteth." I cursed out the suns' ancient names. Raising my hands to massage my temple, stiff clothing restricted me. Much of it clung to my skin.

I'm still alive. Is Dez?

"Dezmind! Dez, are you here!" My throat felt raw with the shout. *Where is he?*

I pried matted hair from my face, shuddering with disgust. I didn't have time to fidget with it now. I left it as it lay, and searched for Dezmind and a way out.

Wavering on unsteady legs, I stood to analyse my surroundings. I felt safe but Dezmind's absence threatened to unnerve me. I looked around. I was on a rough shore made of the same material as the cavern walls. In front of me, across from the pond, the ground sloped drastically up to the base of a steep plateau. What started as a forty-five degree incline escalated rapidly halfway. It ended in an outcropping of rock forty feet above, but close to the outer cavern wall.

There was no place to go but up. My muscles protested at the thought, forcing me to sit down. I ran my hands over my face, anchoring my elbows on my crossed legs. *What was all that – the trials? Were the ancients laughing at my life or was that just my mind anticipating death?* I sighed with frustration and pushed my fists into the hollows of my eyes. I tried to stand again and managed to walk over to the angled wall.

None of my gear came with me except for my belt-pack. It

held the essentials: my verrin drops, a pack of protein pills, an energy bar, safety pins, flint, folding travel blade, magnifying glass, spare bandanas, the two small note books and a pencil. Digging out my knife, I chipped away at the rock. Only fine, thin shards broke off. It was dense.

I gazed up at the rough surface. Eyes flitting here and there, I mapped a mental path to the top, my survival instincts revving into high gear. *I'll have to stretch in a few places, but there seem to be enough crevices and chunks to warrant the risk.*

I crunched and pounded the stiff material covering my body, then limbered up for the climb. There was no sense in waiting. In fact, the longer I put this off, the more likely I would talk myself out of it. This was going to take a miracle or one really stubborn woman luckily I had the second option covered. Gripping a small protrusion of rock, I slowly, awkwardly, ascended.

Dezmind must have found another way out.

"He'd better be alive." I said aloud, forcing back dark thoughts of his body trapped somewhere under the ceiling of rock in the lake below.

I used my anger and frustration to spur myself on. I had more than a thing or two to say to that man. Tender finger tips, some missing nails, searched crevices and tested holds. I absorbed the pain in my hands, burying it deep in my psyche.

The swim had rejuvenated my slight dehydration, lending my muscles the strength and energy needed for this climb. I had soaked my bandana in the reservoir and stuffed it in a small zippered compartment. With my canteen gone, I would need something to keep me going until I found Dezmind.

At the halfway point, things got tricky; a tad too steep as my battered fingers threatened to go numb from repeated abuse. I was thankful this wasn't a sheer cliff but that didn't make climbing it any easier. Still able to use the slight angle to my advantage, I held my breath. Inhaling in short bursts meant reduced oxygen to my muscles, but I couldn't help myself. Aiming my sights on the next hold, I forced my body on.

Nearing the overhang, my muscles shrieked at the impossibility of my task. From the ground, I hadn't understood just how long the plateau was at the top of the cliff.

I had three things going for me though: the first was the fact that I was an accomplished climber, the second was that the length of the plateau was almost as long as I was tall, and the third was a handy outcropping of rock just below the base. The problem remaining, and it was a big one; I was now severely drained and losing energy fast. I either had to chance it and risk breaking my neck, or find a nice hovel somewhere to die – like Doire.

I wasn't going to give up.

Taking hold of the small outcropping, I found a solid, comfortable grip. Slowly, incrementally, I walked my legs up the side of the cliff, holding my torso in place. I searched for significant toeholds. My arms trembled as I suspended myself, parallel to the ground.

I couldn't stop. Not now.

Methodically rotating my torso inch by searing inch, I brought my legs in close to my body, knees to forehead. The knitted flesh on my left palm broke open against the jagged rock I clung to. *No! Dammit. I need traction!* I was scrunched up as though I might spring into the air upside-down. I didn't jump. Instead, I rotated my legs above my head, moulding my body into an arch, the same shape as the overhang above.

Holding my frame in this outward-facing handstand, my arms shook violently. Step-by-needling-step, I extended my legs until my feet reached the outer edge of the cliff.

I gulped mouthfuls of air. A streak of blood trickled down my arm. The skin on my other palm split. In one fluid motion, I stretched my arms and pushed.

My legs slipped past the edge of the plateau. I curled them around the rim. Using my legs to support me, I swung my body away from the cliff. Crunching my stomach muscles, I grabbed onto the lip with my damaged hands.

Body frozen in anguish, my stubborn righteousness won out. I mentally called upon the sun guardians for every ounce of strength remaining.

Holy Trinity – Help me! If they existed, I needed them now more than ever.

I hauled my body over the edge of the cliff. Crawling a few feet from the perimeter, I collapsed. Every muscle vibrated in agony. I lay there, breathing in fits and gasps. My body twitched sporadically and I broke out in a cold sweat.

I knew my muscles would seize if I left them alone for too long. After a rest, not nearly long enough, I flexed each muscle in turn as I lay there. Eventually, they protested only mildly.

Rolling over, I sat up on my knees without using my torn hands. The cuts weren't as severe as the originals, but they throbbed nonetheless. Fresh and dried tracts of blood trailed under my sweater from my wrists to my elbows. Between my battered fingertips and abused palms, I managed to zip open my belt-pack. I grabbed a spare bandana, slightly moist, ripped it lengthwise and tightly wrapped my hands. Jantice had used the last of my gauze. I re-zipped the pack.

Resting my hands on my thighs, palms up, I sat up straight and worked the kinks out of my neck. During one particularly lingering half-head revolution, a dark object caught my eye. Slowly turning my head forward again, I focused on the sculpted piece.

Not ten paces away, perched on a black granite pillar the shape of an inverted isosceles triangle, was a black spherical object. It was somewhat larger than the circumference of an old public transport tire.

I stood. My head spun and my legs wobbled. Steadying myself on the cavern wall, I waited for the nausea to pass. I couldn't risk staggering into that thing – whatever it was.

I took a few tentative steps forward. My head stayed clear, and my legs, thankfully, supported me. Covering the rest of the distance to the object, I reached out to touch it. But I didn't.

What if something's wrong with it? What's it doing here anyway?

Surveying the platform for a way to identify what it was and why it was there, I analysed my surroundings – the ledge extended from the corner of the upper chamber.

"What the–?" I said out loud, staring at the wall beside me.

I walked over to the corner where the two walls met. There, in the rock face, was a ladder – no – steps chiselled right into the stone. They were carefully shaped and detailed. Across the front of each step were glyphs – symbols eerily similar to Dezmind's rubbings and the writing above the pool of verrin.

Taking a step back, I looked directly up at the ceiling. A

rectangular outline, meticulously carved, had more writing at its centre.

No, not writing.

I looked closer. It was a picture – a picture of a simple table and a basin with rays of light shining out of it.

Something round and tubular caught my eye, tucked up in the crevice where the back wall met the ceiling. I went up a couple of steps for a closer look. A rounded rock-tube of sorts cut into the stone. It extended out and down, across the back wall to the edge of the platform and into the cavern below. But it stopped a few feet below the edge.

That's strange.

Jumping back down to the platform, I looked over the sphere. It didn't appear to be made of rock; actually it looked a bit like the metal girders of most modern structures. It also had writing inscribed over its surface, but nothing I'd ever laid eyes on.

Oh heck, why not? I've come this far.

Reaching out my hand for a second time, I grazed its surface with my fingertips.

Nothing happened.

Cool to the touch, I found it was not a true sphere after all. It wasn't perfectly smooth. Three-inch square plates, perfect in their simple complexity, spanned the entire orb. They were raised and lowered about a quarter inch, alternating. Each square had markings. I circled the orb. Every inch was exactly replicated. I looked again at the pedestal it rested on. Its striking resemblance to the CTF convinced me this was what Dezmind searched for. The writing on it could be an earlier form of the ancient writings.

Instead of searching for rock tablets or preserved parchment, we should have been looking for this. It makes sense that the Elders inscribed something as important as the solution to a prophesy in something as stable as metal.

But would they have known how to make metal back then? Well why else would it be here?

Stop being so paranoid, Taya!

Fine then, I'll bring it with me.

Removing the sweater from around my waist, I laid it temporarily over the orb as I rummaged through my belt-pack for the bundle of large safety clips I'd packed.

I just hope this thing's hollow.

Working to seal up the neck of my sweater, I then ripped off the arms and pinned them back on closer to the waist.

Now came the moment of truth. I picked up the orb, heavy but not solid, and worked it into the cradle of my sweater. It stretched considerably, but fit. Heaving it up onto my back, I wrapped one sleeve over my left shoulder and the other under my right, securing them with a tight knot.

I bounced on the balls of my feet. It held. Up the rock ladder I climbed. At the top, I raised my hands, pushing up.

My muscles flared red-hot – the stone shifted. Pushing up until my arms fully extended, I slid the cover over on the floor above. A faint yellow-white light lit the swirling dust overhead. I climbed sideways, up through the opening to allow for the orb to fit.

I sat down on a pale stone floor covered with an age of dust and wisps of loose sand. Directly in front of me stood a large stone table with a solid base – I couldn't see much of the rest of the room.

Behind me rested an equally large stone chair, maybe a throne. On either side of the throne, two slightly smaller chairs stood guard, with square pedestals set next to them. Just behind, a stone wall rose up to meet a high ceiling of the same material. Remnants of webbing littered the upper walls and floor. Something had cleaned the place out recently.

Standing up, I took better stock of my surroundings. I'd had a feeling I would come out into *somewhere* from the Pit. Then it dawned on me.

"Of course. The Ancient City."

On the other side of an old stone fountain, a few steps down from the raised stage, lay the ruin of a cityscape.

The suns played off the dust in the room like glitter floating in children's tales. It was late in the day, whatever day it happened to be.

Between the fountain and the opposite wall sat rows upon rows of benches, heavy and solid in their construction. I set the orb of the Chronicles down on the throne, and took the liberty of exploring this archaeological masterpiece. *Has Dez already come through here? Where are the creatures that used to live in the webs? Dead? Hunting? Better not stick around too long.*

The carving of the fountain drew me toward it: a large, round basin with the three suns and their rays shining out extended up from the centre. The spout was made of three spheres, likely also representations of the suns. They ranged in size from largest to smallest in ascending order. The smallest was punctured at the very top to allow liquid to flow over and into the basin below.

My mind linked back to the stone tube in the underground chamber. *Why didn't I see it sooner? It's a pipe – and that liquid I swam through used to flow right up to the edge of the platform.*

"It is verrin," I muttered. "Pure verrin."

But it's so different. And yet–

I thought back to the lake sites I'd analysed with the professor. Even then, I'd noticed subtle differences compared to the city's supply. As a child, my parents indulged in drinking imported, pure verrin from ground springs near the outer territories.

Catching sight of a chunk of orange, part-way out of the spout made me curious. I climbed into the basin and reached down the tube with my fingers. They were too big. Rifling through my belt-pack, I searched for the pencil Merik loaned me. I slipped the point of the pencil and my knife into the spout and wiggled free a wedge of orange rock. I folded the knife and put both items away.

It looks identical to Doire's stash in the metal box.

Sniffing it, I rolled it around in the palm of my good hand. Shrugging my shoulders, I licked it.

Yep. Tastes just like that stuff in the cavern. Pure verrin, has to be–

I jumped.

A scratching noise came from the windows at the end of the room. Hopping out of the basin, I pocketed my find, scurrying to hide behind the table. I slid the stone slab back in place using two grips I hadn't noticed before. Crawling, I crouched just under the lip of the table – waiting, listening.

Footsteps–

Dezmind? Another creature?

I peered cautiously around the side of the table. Someone stood framed in the doorway.

Chapter Twenty-two
Ghost from Another Life

An outline was the only thing discernible, backlit by the setting suns. It was a slighter form than Dezmind's, with something broad perched on its head.

Jantice? Tamaine?

"This is the only one," the stranger spoke.

I jumped and hit my head on the lip of the table. Something dislodged, clattering to the floor. Snatching it up, I stuffed it into my belt-pack, not really knowing what it was.

"Who's there?" The woman's voice demanded, stronger, edgier, than her first pronouncement.

It can't be. I must be hallucinating.

"Show yourself, now!" she demanded.

I stood up.

We stared at each other.

"I found you!" Zaith cried, scrambling between the rows of benches toward me. I stepped out from behind the table. We embraced.

"You're real," I said, touching her face, squeezing her arms.

"Of course I'm real," she laughed, pulling me into another fierce hug.

"No, I mean…" I held her at arm's length. "How is it possible? How did you get here? Why are you here?"

"Relax," Zaith said, gently prying my damaged hands from her arms. "Sit down and we'll talk."

Zaith led me to the closest bench. The suns sat low, sinking into the horizon.

"No, I've got to keep moving. I'm wasting valuable time. Dezmind and I were separated. I have to find him."

"Where are you planning to go? What kind of tracks do you expect to see at night? I know your sight is exceptional but Taya, come on, you're not invincible. Look at you. You're a mess. You need a wash, a change of clothes, and a good night's sleep. But, not before you tell me how you wound up like this," she said, motioning from my matted hair, to my bloodied hands, to my crusted boots.

I really didn't know where to go, so I stayed. It didn't take much convincing on my part – safe with Zaith or set out blind into the unknown. Besides, there was no guarantee that Dezmind had travelled through the Ancient City. *Too many loose ends and not enough answers.*

I eyed the bundle resting on the throne.

Maybe some answers lie there. I gave in to my fatigue.

Looking Zaith in the eyes, I said, "I'd rather get cleaned up and settled before I launch into any of my adventures. I'm not saying anything until you've explained what in Zola's name you're doing here."

Zaith laughed and hugged me again. "Atta girl."

"And we leave after a nap. I'm not walking during the day if I don't have to."

Zaith smiled. "I'll get my stuff and we can set up camp here. It's the only building I've found that still has a roof."

I pointed at the shredded webbing throughout the structure. "How did you do that, and how do you know they won't come back?"

She patted me on the shoulder. "Trust me," she said, and hurried out the door. A moment later, Zaith returned pulling a cart sporting a folded umbrella made of the same material as the

AHT. It was a small cart with large tires, well packed and perfect for personal travel. I'd never seen anything quite like it.

I watched Zaith set up camp. Unloading first her main pack, she then emptied another, slightly smaller canvas bag. Placing a large metal bowl between the two front benches, she then removed a cup and small collapsible bowl from her pack. There was even a bar of soap, a washcloth, and fresh gauze. Passing the latter two of the items to me, she filled the cup and bowl with water from one of the two small kegs on the cart.

Removing her wide-brimmed sun hat, piles of straight, shiny plum- colour hair tumbled down over Zaith's shoulders.

I smiled.

Only Zaith would take the time to streak her purple hair with bleached highlights before setting out on this journey.

As I washed, she set up a long, low-burning alcohol-based flame in the large metal bowl between us and explained her arrival.

"As you know, Touf wouldn't let me take a leave of absence to come out here. He freaked out and claimed my research on Professor Denali was top priority. It took me until the day you left to cut through the bureaucracy at the Network before I could bypass him. Besides, I hit a dead end with Denali – for the moment. I have eyes and ears on him while I'm out here though.

"Anyway, Touf needed extreme reassurance that my contract regarding coverage of the Rallies included a clause allowing me to compile information over the course of a number of different weeks."

I wiped my face and neck with the clean water first. The gentle fall of water from the wash cloth back into the bowl accompanied Zaith's tale.

"That's what finally allowed me to follow you. Touf couldn't believe the possible connection between Dezmind's quest and the Professor's findings. He didn't know whether to be ecstatic or angry. You know very well that he didn't want to lose his star reporter on such a dangerous assignment, but at the same time, who better to cover such a controversial piece? I followed your group's tracks until a sand- storm hit–"

"How did you survive it? It lasted for hours," I said from around the soft cloth.

"I hid behind a dune and covered myself with the cart and the umbrella. Actually, it only lasted maybe thirty minutes. Remember, I'm still a day behind you at this point, likely it was winding down by then."

I nodded then cautiously submerged one bloody hand then the other into the bowl.

"Of course, after that, your tracks were gone. But, I wasn't so foolish as to rely on cart tracks in the sand. I figured you had a way of mapping your progress. So, without the use of a compass, I started marking my way by the only other reliable thing out here – the suns. I figured out long before the storm hit that you'd been travelling southeast with Gamma at night. Eventually, I saw signs of your tracks again. I was mindful not to linger at one site in particular. Large spikes spearing a dune do not bode well, no matter where you're from."

"That wasn't one of my finer moments," I said, easing the bandana pieces from my hands. "Sorry, go on." Zaith shook her head at the sight of my palms, shredded yet again.

"I figured I must have gained about half a day on you by that point. There was very little track disturbance from the weather."

"Yeah, we lost a lot of time between there and when the storm hit." I gingerly rinsed my wounds and the exposed parts of my arms before letting my hands just soak in the now brown water.

"But when I saw a frenzy of tracks at the base of a valley, I realised something big must have happened. There were large wagon tracks leading northwest along the valley floor and I thought I could hear something in the distance. Twenty minutes later, I saw your campsite."

She took my hands from the dirty water, dried them and wrapped the fresh gauze around my damaged skin. It made me think of Dezmind, his touch – the smooth calluses. I shook my head to clear it as Zaith continued.

"There was a lot going on, but I never caught sight of you or Dezmind. So, I back-tracked to the disturbed area and carried on the original path until I arrived here, a day later, hoping to find you."

"And here I am," I said, carrying the bowl to the open door

and tossing out the water. "What about the room?" I pointed to various trailing webs around us as I sat back down.

Zaith frowned.

I know that look — she's debating telling me the whole truth.

"I didn't want to come out here without some way of protecting myself." She opened a large pocket on the leg of her pants.

"A Clinex!" I shouted.

Zaith whipped up a finger to my lips. "Yes, I asked the Facility. No, they didn't give me this." She paused. "It's black market and that's all I'm telling you."

Silence. My mind whirled at the implications. *Black market? How could she — Where would they — Who has access to —*

"It's your turn, Taya."

"Do you know how to use it?"

She pointed around the room. "Stop worrying. I'll give it to you when we get back home. Now, I have a story to write. Talk."

"Right." I sighed.

I hated not knowing things and she knew it. I focused on the journey instead.

"The Kahn-lea were exhausted by the time the tremors hit. We slid down the dune. I imagine Syvis took charge and got everyone well away from the spot where Dezmind and I disappeared. They needed to rest before heading home. Probably gave us up for dead."

"How did you and Dezmind get separated?" Zaith asked. I changed out of my stiff clothes and into the fresh bundle Zaith tossed me.

"I really thought I was going to die — twice. He can be so stubborn sometimes, you know?" I complained. "But I guess if he hadn't tried to play the hero, he never would have found what he was looking for." I took another long look at the bundle on the throne.

"Well, I never would have found it. Who knows, maybe there's more than one." "Taya, you're babbling. Start from the beginning. How did you disappear?"

I woke to the dim light of the low burning fire. It flickered and wavered in the gentle cross-breeze of our breath. Zaith slept peacefully on one stone bench and I occupied another.

We'd talked into the night, catching up on each other's travels. Zaith couldn't believe the horrors the group dealt with. What shocked her most was looking into the cavernous expanse below the building we stayed in. She wept when I detailed what I put myself through to escape. Actually, I was proud of myself for overcoming the odds. Maybe I could handle this job after all.

Resting my head on the crook of my elbow, I looked at Zaith. Dark eyelids rested even darker lashes on smooth cheeks. Her curved mouth stayed open, ever so slightly. The plum shade of her hair shimmered black in the dimming light.

Slowly, I sat up. My feet made no sound on the floor as I walked, since my treads were made of a soft rubber for distance hiking.

Zaith wasn't accustomed to limited sleep, so I dared not disturb her as I tiptoed over to the throne. *I should wake her, though. We're losing valuable night. I just want to take a quick look at this first.*

Gently lifting the orb into my arms, I sat down on the warm, sun- baked floor behind the throne, my back against the wall. I set the orb on my lap, activated Zaith's light-tube, and grabbed my notebook and pencil to study the Chronicles. I mainly held the pencil between my finger and thumb to avoid aggravating the palm of my hand as I wrote.

The only way to find Dezmind was to translate the ancient text carved into the orb. If a second one existed, his first priority would be to decipher it and learn its secrets. He'd mentioned near the beginning of our journey something about *the chosen one* being able to read the script, but I wasn't worried – well, at least I wasn't worried about the possibility that it couldn't be read. Even though I didn't have a lot of opportunity for code cracking in my daily work routine, I did remember the fundamentals.

Tek's face flared in my memory as perfect as the day he flattened me in combat training. The note he'd left me after class that day used a simple inscription cipher. For the next year, we passed a lot of coded notes filled with taunts and battle strategies. Part of me always wished I'd let him take it to the next level. I couldn't deny that he was gorgeous but if I'd succumbed to his charms I would've been like every other girl at the Facility. The fact that he was smart and tough almost won me over but somehow I knew our relationship would change if we ever addressed our feelings. I don't think either of us was ready to focus on anyone other than ourselves at that time. But then, that always seemed to be the way.

Choosing a section of writing to analyse, I copied out all of the relevant individual symbols in search of an alphabet and numeric system. The writing etched onto the orb was near perfect, so I rarely confused two of the same symbols for different characters. By the time I expanded my search of the basic lettering system, I had five separate groupings of symbols, one of which I was certain represented basic numerals.

Working into the early hours of the morning, when Zaith stirred I set down my work, picked up the fading light-tube and walked to one of the front windows. I put it on the sunlit sill to recharge. *So much for travelling at night.*

"Good morning, sleepy head," I teased as Zaith stretched.

"Been up long?" Zaith asked.

"Oh, since about three hours after we nodded off last night." I laughed at Zaith's sour expression. "Do that again and risk having it stay that way," I joked.

"Kids' rumour. Anyway, why didn't you sleep? We agreed to figure out the next step today."

"I know. I couldn't wait. I've made a lot of progress, but I need to let my brain rest for a while. I'm kind of in a mental block."

"Well, let me look at your work after breakfast. Maybe a fresh set of eyes will help. Go clear your head while I get the food ready."

"You don't have to tell me twice," I said, plunking on my cap. I detached the umbrella from the cart to use as a parasol.

Stepping out into the brilliant sunshine, I focused on exploring the Ancient City – maybe there would be some trace of Dezmind, some sign of where he emerged; maybe I'd even find him sleeping somewhere.

A few feet outside, barren crumbling ruins stretched out in front of me. The structure exactly opposite the Temple, a term I had taken to calling our building, was also made of rock. Its exterior was worn, but the heavily-plastered surface showed no significant cracks or breakages. The same held true with the buildings I could see down the narrow, cobbled street. No other structure was as large as the Temple though.

Anxious to see the city as a whole, I used the open window frame to climb the side of the building. Luckily, the roof's overhang was only a couple of feet wide, nothing like what I'd scaled yesterday. I didn't even need to use my hands to lift me up and risk damaging my wounds. I tossed the umbrella up javelin-style and used my fists and elbows to get me up on top.

Crawling on my hands and knees, I kept close to the edge, not wanting to tempt fate and crash down on Zaith's head.

Zaith had been right; no other buildings in the area were roofed.

I wonder why that is? Maybe they were thatched originally.

The ruins of the ancient city spread out like a bizarre maze with twisting streets and pentagonal junction points – roads met and then scattered again. A person could get lost in a place like this. Time and exposure had weathered the remnants of the buildings my ancestors first resided in. In the distance I just made out the Powder Sands Desert on the outskirts of the City. Slowly, I rotated to get the full view.

The Temple appeared to be a nexus point. It was on slightly higher ground than any other building. All roads radiated out from it, albeit at crude angles, but the pattern was clear.

Odd, how an entire civilization can just pack up and migrate to some new land. What were the repercussions of leaving such a vast empire behind? There's so little about our ancient history that any of us really know.

Crouching down at the edge of the roof, I volleyed off in one arching motion. Arbitrarily walking to the right, I marvelled at the simplicity of the hub. The fierce storms of the Deserts hardly touched the inner mercantile buildings I passed. None of the structures had any furniture.

The further I travelled along the meandering street, the narrower it became. Gradually, the buildings showed signs of storm wear; chipped plaster walls revealed rounded pink tinted Desert stone beneath. A piece of gauze trailed from my hand as I walked. Resting the umbrella on my shoulder, I used the other hand to tuck it back around my knuckles and between a couple of swathes across the back of my hand. The building beside me drew my curiosity.

Leaning through an old window, I noticed the floor was packed dirt.

Maybe these are personal dwellings.

I tried walking in a straight line. As the main street narrowed, multiple other streets, less opulent than the first, trailed off in all directions. The farther I wandered from the Temple, the more ruinous the old buildings became. By the time I reached the outer perimeter of the City there would be nothing left but gaping, toothy shells.

I decided to walk the outer edge of the City, to track its size. Here and there, as I suspected, low-lying foundations sat covered by mini-dunes and banks of sand. Wandering through the rubble, I imagined what life would have been like here thousands of years ago.

It must have been quite the place – when the underground verrin was plentiful with grasses and brush enough to build homes and feed families. I shuddered, knowing that my ancestors walked these very paths.

I wonder why they left. A civilization as advanced as this should have understood basic agricultural cultivation – that can't be the reason behind it – these Deserts didn't happen because of poor soil maintenance. Something abnormal must have caused all this – forced the people north.

Rounding another curve of the City's border, something anomalous drew my attention. I climbed the rough, pale brittle wall nearest to me for a better look. From the ground, what appeared to be a loose gathering of small boulders was a meticulously-positioned arrow marker. It pointed southeast.

"Dezmind–" *He's alive.*

Whipping around, I wound my way back to the Temple through a portion of the City I hadn't explored yet. My line of sight was the raised, lone rooftop, a considerable distance away.

Rounding the back of the Temple down one of the side allies, I stopped short before turning to the front of the building.

Voices? I listened carefully.

"–her progress absolutely astounding. The remarkable feat of climbing, pushed all bounds of standard capabilities."

One voice–

"However, it's not in her character to willingly flaunt her abilities and achievements. Zaith, twelve-nineteen."

The click of a personal mini-recorder snapped.

Already planning her report. I smiled and raced into the Temple. Before I could speak, Zaith stuffed a toasted beef-jerky sandwich into my mouth and a cup of verrin in my hands, taking away the umbrella and returning it to her cart.

"Zaith, he's gone southeast," I muffled out, around a bite of food. Setting down my cup, I ripped off another bite and scrambled to gather the light-tube, writing materials, and the orb.

"Remember Zaith," I mumbled over another mouthful, "it's dangerous out here. You really should consider joining up with the Kahn-lea and heading back home." I finished my meal, took a swig of verrin from the smaller of Zaith's two canteens and stepped up to her, arms extended.

"Thank you. You were right here when I needed you most, but I can't ask you to risk your life following Dezmind and me around in this forsaken place. I don't know how much farther into this wasteland I have to go – I – you – you really should turn back while you can."

Raising her hands to my shoulders, Zaith shook me. "You of all people should know that I can't resist a story like this. If you and Dezmind save us from these crazy environmental disturbances, I want to be right there to get a first-hand account. They don't call me a roving reporter because I have good hair," she quipped and smiled. "Just give me a minute to pack up. I can take a look at those notes while you navigate, all right?"

I took a long, hard look at the conviction in my friend's eyes. "All right. Gear up. I'll take the first shift with the cart. You'll need both hands to get a good look at everything I've done."

Zaith packed in less than five minutes. I led her to the marker, and then passed over all of my notes. It was time to find Dezmind.

Umbrella up, sun hats and goggles at the ready – I was light of step and gay of heart for the first time in a long time.

Chapter Twenty-three
A Dark Light Shines

G amma pulsed faintly on the horizon as the first stars awoke. Zaith and I sat in a small gully between two smaller bumps in the sand – not nest markers. We were at a transition between Deserts.

Having travelled for most of the day and night, fatigue pulled at our limbs. We sat with our backs to a wall of sand, facing the low flicker and waver of the bowl-fire set in a two-foot deep hole. With only the one light-tube, a fake fire was not realistic but Zaith's version was the next best thing. Apparently she liked hot food and I couldn't dissuade her – even with the threat of crawling Desert bugs showing up at random. Since we hadn't seen any yet, she chose to ignore me.

I enjoyed today's walk. We accomplished a lot in relative quiet. Zaith's company was preferable to the constant drone produced by the Kahn-lea. Perhaps the only sound I missed was the melodic sadness of Merik's pipe – the only resonance that mob produced that actually belonged to the Deserts.

The clink of metal on metal drew me from my meditations. Zaith diligently prepared the evening's meal. She'd brought with her a number of vacuum-sealed packages containing meats and vegetables. Emptying the contents of one pack into a pot, she turned to open another. She didn't have access to the ration packs I organised for the Kahn-lea. I got them through a Facility contact who gave me a good deal on a bulk purchase.

"Just use the one. If we keep eating like this, we'll run out of supplies for the journey home. Besides, large meals mean using up more of our internally-stored verrin for processing."

"You still don't look well, Taya. I think you need this more than you know," Zaith said.

I set my notebook on my knees, tapping my pencil on my thumb. "No, not really. I just need sleep – but I won't rest until I've figured this out. We still don't know why Dezmind's going this way. He *must* have found something associated with the Chronicles."

Zaith steamed our meal, adding a touch of water to the mixture. "I've been thinking about it all evening," she said. "I needed the time to let my mind wander over and back again on the stuff you've deciphered so far."

"Got a hunch?" I perked up and stopped tapping.

"Kind of," she paused, concentrating on her words. "What if the squares aren't just decorative or structural?"

"What do you mean?" I asked, pulling the orb closer.

"Well, so far, you've tried reading the symbols line-by-line following the curve of the orb, and a number of similar techniques, disregarding the raised and recessed blocks. What if you've got the lettering system worked out, but the reason it's not translating right is the way in which you're trying to read the text?"

"Try analysing it vertically instead of horizontally…"

"Exactly, maybe then you might find what you're looking for." Leaving the food to simmer over the small fire, Zaith sat back against the base of the dune.

"Block-by-block, chunk the information," I muttered, flipping thorough pages of notes.

I found a thin double line down on one-half of the circumference of the orb. I had used that as a symbol to begin from and wanted to reposition the symbols vertically with Zaith's grouping theory.

Previously, I focused on the horizontal plane because that's how we wrote now. *What if the ancients did it differently?*

Finding the page, I worked furiously on the configurations. My pencil scratched across the paper as I moved, re-translating and adapting – vertical groupings – clumps of words.

"Ha! Yes. You're a genius Zaith. Listen to this: *On the eve of the twenty-first Alpha cycle in the month supporting the maximum light from Gamma, a celebration of solar rebirth and regeneration must commence.* That's the first group of boxes. *The particle generator located at the base of the Canopy Goddess* – whatever that is – *must be ignited when the sky is absent of its twin light during the second hour.*

"This is it! It's an instruction manual for turning something on. If this hasn't been done since the Elders migrated, it's no wonder the quakes are getting worse."

Furiously, I copied more segments of the orb into my notebook. Zaith removed the pot from the fire and nestled it into the sand.

"But it says *celebration*. That makes me wonder if it was just some crazy thing they did to pass the time. I mean, what the heck is a *Canopy Goddess* anyway?"

I sat there, stunned. "I don't get it. What's up?"

"What do you mean?" Zaith avoided eye contact. "Where's that Nutrition bar you told me you had? I still don't think this is enough food for both of us."

"In my belt-pack. Over the push-bar on the cart," I said, still reeling inside. An abrupt change in conversation was not something I had ever experienced in Zaith's company.

"What I don't understand is how you were so hyped-up about this Spoken Truth nonsense, dragging me to all those Rallies, airing segments on their 'many faces' – and now, I've risked life and limb to find this thing, this mechanism, and you, you just slough it off like it's unimportant or irrelevant. What exactly am I missing here?"

Zaith looked at me. "That's exactly it. A mechanism. Did you see the state that city was in? There's nothing technological about it. The closest thing those people had to living above today's poverty line is that orb. What if it was planted in the Temple? What if it's not nearly as old as we think it is? What then?" She paused. "It worries me, Taya. This isn't what I thought we'd find." Turning, she walked over to my belt-pack and rummaged for the food.

"What if... what if there's another city? What if our ancestors migrated twice," I suggested.

Something fell from the pack landing at Zaith's feet. She picked it up. "How could there be another city?" She said. "The history books—"

"Have been tampered with," I said flatly. Zaith looked at me, confusion staining her delicate features. "Merik, one of the Kahn-lea, mentioned it once, or rather, hinted at it. Something about the advice a professor once gave him.

"What if the Elders started further south and migrated to the Stone City? What if there was a reason they had to leave the technology behind? That might explain why the Kronik were so reluctant to encourage innovation until a quarter of a century ago. And why would this have been left in the Temple, of all places, if it were merely a joke or a piece of junk? Think about it. We just don't have all of the pieces to the puzzle yet."

A flicker of clarity flitted across Zaith's face. She lowered her head to examine what she held in her hands. Turning the small book- like object over slowly, then faster, she opened and flipped through it.

"Where did you get this?"

"Get what?" I asked.

Zaith held up what looked like a metallic version of my notebook. The pages Zaith turned were paper thin – even though they clinked together.

The memory of touching something metallic after hitting my head on the stone table returned.

"Oh, I forgot about that. It fell from under the Temple table when you startled me. I just picked it up and stuffed it into my pack. Figured I'd look at it later," I said.

"Maybe you should look at it now; it seems to be a companion to the one you're already working on. Same markings." Zaith tossed it over, pulled out the nutrition bar, and sat down to dish out the meal.

I turned the small booklet over in my hands, flipping through it, just as Zaith had.

"Yeah, but the writing isn't as neat. It gets clearer closer to the end, but it definitely isn't the same hand – doesn't have the same precision as the symbols on the orb."

Flipping to one of the later, neater passages, I tried a translation from memory. *I find myself tracking my thoughts again as – as I – as I'm forced to make a decision about our future."*

"Sounds like a journal," Zaith said.

"Yeah, but why hide it in the Temple? Odd. I'll have to look into it when I'm done with the orb; we still need to find out where exactly we're headed and how this mechanism works."

"Eat something first. I hope you get faster at reading this stuff, you need to rest; and for more than three hours, Taya," Zaith said, stopping me from disagreeing.

"I'm sure I'll manage a few extra hours, *Mom*," I said. Zaith stuck her tongue out as she passed me the food.

Lying still, I stared up at the sky in the very early hours of the morning. At the horizon, Alpha chased away the stars. I'd reached a point, just after Zaith settled for the night, when I stopped translating the orb and found that I could just read it. After the discovery, I crawled onto an extra mat that Zaith had brought with her, intending to sleep for the six twilight hours – but I never once shut my eyes. My mind fogged over for a few hours, causing me to dream the altered dreams of half-sleep, but they kept jolting me awake.

The orb haunted me. The full translation I read remained etched in my mind. The ideas and concepts it detailed explained so much and yet left even more unanswered. It sounded impossible but it had to be true – the Pit existed, the chronicles were real... *right?* Instinct had me laugh at the absurdity of it all; my second reaction was to tell Zaith – but I didn't, because my third and final response was mortification that it might actually be true.

The orb or Chronicles or whatever they were, were kept very secure and hidden for a reason. If what the Chronicles told of was true, the Elders, and in turn the Kronik, kept more than idle mysteries locked behind the gates of the Compound. Exactly how much of this Dezmind already knew, I wasn't sure. *Maybe he's as clueless as everyone else?*

Zaith stirred; I knew she would wake soon. Sitting up, I gathered the supplies to ignite a fire. Thoughts of beef broth for breakfast made my stomach growl. Though I made little noise, Zaith roused faster than I wanted her to.

She stretched, extending herself from fingertips to toes. "So," she yawned comfortably, "what did you find?"

I didn't answer. I debated whether or not to act as though I hadn't heard the question. Honesty won out.

"I – It's pretty much as we assumed. Keep heading southeast."

"How do we know when we've arrived?" she asked, rummaging through her pack for a hairbrush.

"There's a large rock formation we'll have to climb. It sounds considerably bigger than the dunes we've scaled. From there, the directions work according to landmarks from one point to another. It's not very clear though."

"Were you able to figure out what the generator is supposed to do? What it's for?"

"You mean, how a piece of ancient technology is supposed to save Xannia from tearing itself apart?"

"Well, yeah. Did you?"

"There's a reason I'm a Contractor and not a Doctoral Scientist –

I'll have to let it sit with me," I hedged. Zaith didn't notice.

"Right then, what's for breakfast?"

* * *

I grew tired of my thoughts. Going over and over what I couldn't – no – what I didn't want to understand. After walking for nearly an hour, Zaith quieted and the silence surrounding us verged on driving me crazy. Likely, Zaith used the time to plan out the story she'd write when we got back home.

I should have been home by now. I missed Jadis. The big lynx was such a comfort on long lonely nights. She'd lie on my feet or rest her soft furry head in my lap as I read on my tablet or watched the wire. At least I could be certain about her care. Mr. Kerwik, an older neighbour, would occasionally care for the her after our agreed house-sitting time. He was well aware of the unpredictable nature of my work and understood the delays. I just paid him the difference whenever I got home. He teased me once about monitoring the obituaries during bouts of extended absence – not that I was ever gone for more than a week.

I shook my head. This was not the time to be thinking about death. I rubbed my scabbed palms through the layer of gauze with my thumb.

An image of Dezmind walking alone and unprepared flashed through my mind. Likely he was dehydrated and suffering from exposure. *I have to stop these random thoughts.*

Remembering the little metal journal tucked away in my belt-pack, I pulled it from the pouch. A block of writing sat in the middle of the front cover: Ketic's Experiences.

Ketic could be the author's name.

Opening the paper-thin sheets of metal, I found a full page of writing.

Nine left. Klabec and Dorian stayed behind, they professed to be too weak to make the journey. I know they just didn't want more deaths to be in vain, not that it takes vanity to search for hope in our final days.

Maybe something has changed in the last thousand or so years, for the better that is. These dry-lands were not part of the plan, but they're here now and other things could be as well.

Klabec and Dorion are trying to keep the generator active as long as their blood circulates. But it won't be long, not if they're as weak as they claim to be. Really, it's only a matter of time now.

The second entry seemed to be a few days later.

Our water reserves didn't last long with nine of us depleting them – well, eight. Senara hasn't ingested much in the last day or two.

This morning we took turns carrying her. Ballen doesn't seem to be doing well either. The only positive thing about these illnesses is that they don't seem to stem from the Virus, just dehydration and exhaustion.

We caught sight of a civilization of some kind using the Scope. It doesn't appear to be more than a half-day's walk northwest. Maybe someone there will be able to help.

"He must mean the Ancient City," I whispered to myself. Turning the page, I was completely absorbed and nearly unaware of the slow changes happening to my surroundings. The dunes shrank and dissipated as patches of hard sand formed beneath my feet. As long as Zaith kept to herself and stayed in the lead, I kept reading.

All is well now. I wasn't sure at first when the natives held us at bay with their primitive weapons. If our weapons had worked in this magnetic-powder, we would have dispatched them with ease. But conquering isn't the point.

We're having difficulty communicating with them. They're still fairly low in their evolutionary cycle. We frighten them. I don't think they've ever encountered anyone with silver skin before. I noticed later that their eyes are nearly twice as small as ours. Interesting to track the differences and similarities. But they saw Senara and Ballen and realised we were in need of assistance.

The Elders of this species were the only ones to approach us. Senara's always been good with languages, but it took a while to revive her and get a dialogue started. Telna did his best to relay messages with hand gestures. The rest of us listened to them speak – trying to find patterns in their words.

~

We're being kept in a separate dwelling, away from the town's people. We've learned that preparations are under way to leave this place – this desert. The Elders have explained the worsening conditions and the difficulty of surviving here any longer. They are going to look for fertile soil.

We convinced them not to travel south. If our immune systems can't handle what's spreading down there, these beings would be wiped out in a month.

To this day, I'm surprised most of our expanded colony held out after the first case was documented. A year in the face of your extinction is a lifetime of sorrow. The Health Officials were so sure it was nothing to worry about, that it had been contained by a simple pathogen – but to witness the deaths of everyone I ever knew – Needless to say, we made sure they changed their travel plans. The Elders were grateful for the warning.

~

Ballen has almost finished the solar replica. The town's people were astounded as they witnessed the birth of our metals from a mixture of their verrin and various materials we dug out of the ground. By the time Senara teaches the Elders our language, the Solar Replica should be ready.

They now understand that we left our claimed home and something very important behind. We just have to allow the Virus' strain to die out before making the journey back.

I've advised the Elders to consider returning with us in a few years. That way we can train a scout group in the operation of the generator. Ballen is taking care of the details in case we don't live that long.

~

The writing changed after that. It was as though a considerable amount of time had passed as Ketic carefully scripted each character.

The journey north was a success. I travelled much of the distance with Nerroi and his family. The other citizens are still finding it difficult to interact with us. His daughter Danine asks a lot of questions about our home world and how long ago my race of people travelled to this planet. I think she's one of only a few Xannians
who believe our histories.

A different race? A different planet? How is that possible? Only satellites could leave our atmosphere, yet—

Most of the others believe that the Virus affected our minds. Danine's really quite bright when it comes to seeing the truth. I wonder if I could teach her about the other worlds out there.

~

Danine and I are so proud of Annondra, she turned three yesterday. Time has travelled so fast, it's hard to believe we've been Joined for nearly five years. This morning was astounding – Anna and I were able to communicate telepathically. It was only from the kitchen to the playroom, but she has it! She thinks it's a great game.

I was so sure that with all the genetic modifications Nutooi had to make, to both our genomes, there would be nothing to show of any of our extra-sensory abilities. With the positive results Danine, Anna, and I have had, Senara is willing to undergo the procedure with her new mate. She's thrilled with Anna's health and quality of life.

~

Anna takes after her mother in appearance, but it's said that she's the first Xannian to have silvery-white skin and curly hair. Danine is waiting to see if her coliths are going to fill in with age – she's worried the other kids in school will tease Anna. It will be rough, being the first of the joined offspring, but we'll teach her to be strong.

~

It's time. Chief Elder Nerroi has asked that we depart tonight. Danine and Anna are tearful, they don't want me to go – but Senara wants a child and the others are too afraid to return. Only Ballen and his mate, Mirra, will be joining me. I hope enough time has passed. The generator has to be–

"Taya," Zaith whispered.

–has to be restarted before–

"Jutaya Fyce. Look at me this instant!" Zaith snapped under her breath. I looked up, colliding with her mid-step.

"What–" I said.

"Shush. Look." Crouching low, Zaith pointed at something a couple of hundred yards away. "What is it? Do you know? Are they safe?"

I closed the small metal journal and grudgingly exchanged it for Doire's last notes. "I think I remember seeing that image while restoring Doire's work."

Thumbing through the shaded pages, my index finger landed on a picture of a tall bird-like animal carrying a passenger on its back. I whispered the information to Zaith.

"He calls them *Heniths*. They're described as herbivores that enjoy the odd bug. Apparently it took him a while to get friendly with one, but after gaining its trust, he was able to ride it. If you can believe it, he claims they're comparable to a low-end rider at top speed."

Looking at the small group of Heniths, we spotted a couple more of the burgundy, long-necked animals. Gradually an entire herd of them appeared; they were all picking at a small patch of powder sand with their long beaks.

"There's just over a dozen of them. Do you think we could convince two of them to give us a lift?" Zaith suggested.

I met her eyes. "I don't think we'll be wasting time with pleasantries. We'll have to force the issue. Do you have a length of rope?"

"Of course."

"Good. If we get our hands on a couple of these animals, we'll need to hook your cart up fast."

"Right. So, how are we going to capture them?" she asked, poised for action.

I smiled and patted Zaith stoutly on the back. "Creep up on both sides of the pack, then dive in and see if we can snag one apiece. Try to grab a neck – they're probably stronger than they look, but keep a good grip. I don't think we'll get another shot."

As I repacked Doire's notebook, I ran my fingers over the little metal journal. Zaith quickly set up her rope harness and then crept off to the right of the herd. I went left. Within a stone's throw of the closest animal on either flank, we signalled each other among the many legs.

I sprang up, running into the middle of the pack. The Henith closest leapt out of the way, taking off with a squawk. Similar noises erupted on the opposite side of the herd.

Jumping up, I hugged the neck of another as it ran past. Suspended in mid-air for a nanosecond, the beast sprinted as I dangled across its side.

Pulling myself around, I avoided its sharp beak and slowly dragged my heels into the soft sand. In a matter of minutes I had the animal stopped and chirruping frantically in my ear. Its feet impatiently stomped the ground. I looked over to see how Zaith was doing, nearly letting go of my prize.

Zaith bounced wildly on the back of her Henith, desperately clinging to its long neck with one arm and reaching with her free hand to cover its eyes. She succeeded. It hopped around on the spot trying to toss her off. Jumping down, she hugged its neck fiercely and dug her heels into the sand. Stroking its back and neck, she spoke softly to it. It responded well, so I did the same with my charge.

In the space of twenty minutes, we convinced the Heniths we intended them no harm, and fitted Zaith's charge with the rope harness for the cart. We left as much lead as possible to give the animal space to move.

Then, mounting our Heniths, we urged them into a run. With the wind flying past my cheeks, any lingering thoughts disappeared from my mind. Loose sand whipped my face as the animal sprang forward. I leaned into its leathery neck and held my head up to the suns. Now and then, the Henith would spread its wings to catch the breeze and hover. It was then that I truly felt connected with the animal.

After riding for a while, I heard a soft rumble behind us. My breath caught in my throat when I glanced back. The rest of the herd joined us, running along behind their captured brethren. They chirruped from time to time, the sound reverberating in the air like an echo of voices.

We rode side-by-side across the trailing end of the Powder Sands Desert. Resting the animals at twenty-minute intervals, we used the opportunity to water both ourselves and our charges.

And so, the cycle continued – running with the herd and resting – running and resting. Our speed never faltered even as the stars blinked in the heavens. The animals did not seem to tire much and we had no will to sleep.

Finally, though, we could travel no farther.

Nearly four hours of darkness remained as the Heniths slowed to a stop. No amount of urging and cajoling would move them on. I dropped down to study the terrain. My legs wobbled and my head spun. Staying awake for two days and nights destroyed my equilibrium. My mind struggled to accomplish its task.

We were well out of the soft sands and clearly into another Desert. The ground was decidedly packed and hard. Petting the neck of my steed absently, I allowed my eyes to adapt to the steady starlight and carefully scanned the way ahead.

"It gets rocky from here on in, Zaith. I don't think they can travel any farther."

Zaith nodded, unhitching her supplies. She spoke softly, thanking her Henith and praised its patience for dealing with her. I stroked the large silky wings of my beast.

Soft chirruping sounded from the herd in the distance. They had followed us the entire time. I imitated the sound. My steed cocked its head to the side and answered me. I smiled and gave the Henith one final pat. Releasing it, I stepped away. It paused and looked at me with its strange black beady eyes, blinked twice, then turned and jogged away.

Zaith's Henith caught up with mine and the two animals

travelled back to their herd. The sound of chirruping rose when they reached the others. Then, they and their calls disappeared into the heavy velvet darkness of twilight. Zaith looked at me. She assessed my state immediately. It had been a long ride and it was time for bed.

Chapter Twenty-four
A World of Possibility

We slept as late as we could, using the umbrella for shade from the brilliant sunlight. Rousing late in the afternoon, I caught myself staring off into space – thinking, but not daring to open the journal again. Zaith diligently checked the supplies and prepared a light meal. We were desperately low on everything for the journey home.

Yet, I continued to stare and analyse, and attempt to decipher what my eyes were telling me. Uncertainty crept in like the tiny waves of footprints I had seen scattered over the Powder Sands. *How did Dezmind escape the verrin reservoir? Is this really part of a government conspiracy fronted by the Kronik? Where's the orb taking us? What is the Virus Ketic spoke of?* I fought for focus, forcing back the intruding thoughts and worries.

A thin band of deep-brown or grey, like a shadow, lay in the distance. What kept me from revealing this was the fact that, between us and the horizon, lay a completely new Desert to contend with. So far, this one appeared to have a bleached dry-cracked earth and an assortment of darker, sharp rocks piercing up from the ground. It was hard to believe I had imagined torturing Raylan here after reading about it in Doire's notes.

My internal debate focused on whether or not the change in the horizon was due to finally getting somewhere or whether it was a trick of the eye. These tall, sharp staffs of rock could look clumped from a distance. They were numerous, to be sure, but didn't stand much higher than my knee or thigh. Without a doubt, the landscape was astounding. However, I was certain that it couldn't account for the dramatic change on the horizon. Chugging back the last dregs of a cup of water, I stood and returned the mug to Zaith.

"It's not far now."

"What's not far?"

"Something." I pointed. "There, in the distance where the light darkens when it touches the horizon. The landscape... it changes."

"The landscape has already changed, Taya."

"No, I mean significantly. I think we'll be out of the Deserts in a couple of days."

Shielding her eyes beneath the brim of her sun hat, Zaith looked south. "I'll take your word for it. I don't see anything but the same stuff over and over again. I'm just glad we'll be able to walk faster now that the soft sand is gone."

"Yeah, that'll help. Did you want me to lead first?" I asked, reaching for the cart.

"No. I have a feeling you won't be able to concentrate if you've got your nose stuffed in a book."

My eyes widened.

"Don't try to feign ignorance. I saw you tapping that pouch on your belt-pack. I know what you keep in there. Go ahead and finish it off. At least then we'll have something to talk about again."

I laughed. "I don't think there's much left anyway."

Zaith patted my shoulder and smiled before taking the lead. I pulled out the little metal journal and flipped to my spot.

I've promised to return before the month's end with a report. The generator has to be re-started before the Solar Orb's membrane begins to falter and crack. The rays it's shielding are far too detrimental to be left unaccounted for. It should have plenty of stored energy, but why take the risk?

~

I find myself tracking my thoughts again as I'm forced to make a decision

M.J. Moores

about our future. Ballen's wife, Mirra, is showing symptoms of the Virus: she's feverish, with bouts of chills, is experiencing moments of nausea and is having a hard time breathing.

We can't return to the village with her in this state, and we have no cure. Ballen will not abandon her, but he knows he risks contamination if he stays. Tonight, they leave for the old stone city.

If I remain, I too risk being infected – if I leave, there will be no one to activate the generator. If I stay, I'll never see my family again – if I go, they may not have a reason to live. I guess I know what I must do.

~

I flipped the page rapidly – *A deadly Virus – An advanced species – No known cure –*

"Are we walking into an even bigger death trap?" I whispered looking up at Zaith's back, my eyes unfocused.

There was only one short entry remaining. The script though, was in a different, bolder hand.

Mirra Nebula Ballen
Beloved Wife
and
Soul of my Life
2157-2197
Dakturian Years
Long live the last of us;
Cheers, Ketic

"Cheers, Ketic," I said quietly. "Cheers Ballen – let's hope two thousand years of neglect haven't destroyed your generator."

"What's that?" Zaith called over her shoulder.

I waved the question away. There were too many of my own buzzing through my brain. Shrugging, Zaith returned to her path-finding mission. The rock spikes littered the cracked Desert floor like wrappers on the Avenue after a carnival. Only instinct manoeuvred me around the obstacles.

Logic screamed that his words couldn't be possible – as fact stared blankly up at me from the metallic pages. I let the little book fall shut in my hands, looking, without seeing, the name on the front cover.

He stayed behind. Ballen brought the orb and the journal back to the Ancient City. But how – how then were the Chronicles and the Tablets written?

Thoughts tumbled haphazardly over one another, fighting for prominence until, "Senara and the Chief!" I shouted.

"What?" Zaith stopped.

"Senara would have made sure that the Chief and the other Elders recorded what they knew about – but that still doesn't explain the river of verrin and how they would have known about Ballen and the orb – unless – Ketic eventually made it back home.

"Of course! He would have tried to meet up with Ballen and Mirra after surviving the Virus, a second time, but not finding them he would have then returned home with the knowledge that the orb was somewhere in the Ancient City. The Pit of Chance – it – oh! It's all just out of my reach!" I threw my hands into the air.

Zaith moved away from the cart and gripped my shoulder.

"Take your time. Logic problems are your forte. There are a million things I want to ask, but I don't want you to fry your brain trying to figure it all out in the next five minutes.

"Take the lead, focus on something else for a while, and then tell me what you can when we rest for the day. Okay?" she said. Concern ebbed from her voice and flickered in her eyes.

"Okay. But don't expect much." I laughed without joy.

Zaith's lips twitched before letting out a hearty chuckle.

"We'll see about that."

Chapter Twenty-five

Somewhere Arrives

We travelled in relative silence all night. At first I couldn't fathom what I'd discovered, had trouble making sense of it. Then, I didn't want to share – I didn't want to believe it myself. I was certain Zaith wouldn't believe it either, would turn around and leave me. Eventually, I decided to keep it to myself because Dezmind had a right to know first. But in the end, I still changed my mind and decided to relay sketchy details directly related to the quest. Zaith had, after all, journeyed into these barren lands to learn something of significance.

"Okay," I said, staring up at the last few stars after dinner.

"Okay what?" said Zaith, picking flakes of plum polish off her finger nails.

"The orb – the Chronicles."

Zaith leaned toward the fire, back straight, hands on her knees. I couldn't help but chuckle.

"Yeah. It's big. You know all that controversy around Gamma?"

"What? That no one knows if it's some kind of new dwarf star, or moon, or whatever?" Zaith asked.

"None of the above."

"Really?"

The wild flicker of the flames drew me away from my thoughts. The tug of the gauze bandages on my palms told me it was time to change the dressing again. I got up and rummaged in Zaith's travel pack by the cart until I found it. Sitting back down, I used a cap full of water from my canteen to moisten the dried blood gluing the bandage to my cuts.

"Taya, what is it?" Zaith prompted.

I looked up, jolted back into our conversation, "Right." I sighed, determined to reveal at least this much. "Some kind of nuclear device created to imitate a sun. It was launched a couple of thousand years ago to orbit Xannia. The catch is, it needs to be maintained regularly or nasty things happen as it degenerates. Well, there's a heck of a lot of evidence of that now, isn't there?"

"A fake sun? But how? Who could have put it up there – hey, is that what created the Deserts?"

I held up my hands. "Zaith, I don't have all the answers. I've come to many of the same conclusions, but the fact of the matter remains that I don't have all of the details. I have a map and instructions to find a generator. If we can get it started again, we just might prevent Gamma from losing orbit, or self-destructing, or whatever. At the very least we can say that Dezmind was right." I paused.

"The Kronik has been hiding stuff from us." Now I truly was a dissenter. I shivered. I'd been raised by government institutions from the age of ten, and while I knew the Kronik wasn't perfect, I never suspected this.

"They must have known something about Gamma or they'd have squashed The Spoken Truth and Dezmind's quest long before any of the Rallies started. I – I just have so many questions. I need to find Dezmind," I said. *Something drove him out here. Has he known all along?*

I tucked the gauze into my belt-pack before lying back on one arm, trailing my fingertips through the coarse sand. Zaith looked up at the sky too, leaning against a rock spike. She didn't ask any more questions. She did, however, nibble her lower lip. A glint of curiosity mixed with a fraction of understanding and a pinch of compassion made her eyes glow – or maybe it was the fire.

"It's surprising just how truthful the Tabloids can be sometimes. They train you to ignore the impossible – improbable," Zaith mused.

"Maybe the Kronik did try to stop him after all–" I whispered.

"What's that?"

I let out a slow, controlled breath. "I doubt you'll be able to use my suspicions in your report, but mentioning the Tabloids got me thinking. I mean, what if we've been brainwashed into believing they're trash, you know?"

"Where's all this coming from? I didn't know you followed the Tabloids."

"I don't. But I do read the headlines in the market when I'm bored. There was something once about 'sleeper agents' – special agents the Kronik uses to deal covertly with dissenters to eliminate any threat to his power, his ideas. I think I met one."

Zaith inhaled, choking on the dry air. "You met one?"

"Yeah. He tried to assassinate Dezmind during our first dawn in the Deserts."

"What makes you think he was a sleeper agent and not just a random nut job?"

"I'm trained to handle nut jobs. I didn't see this guy coming. His cover was flawless – there were no tells – he lived it and believed it. He looked nothing like an assassin. He was somebody's grandfather – and yet not. I liked him, Zaith. I liked the man who tried to kill my boss. What does that say about me?"

"You have a kind heart."

I shook my head, and threw a rock out into the night.

"It also says you can take care of things when they go awry. You caught him, right?"

"Sort of."

"Do I have to pull it out of you or are you going to tell me what sort of means?"

"I think I killed him."

"What?"

"I killed him, Zaith."

The fist clenching my heart for so long now loosened. Dezmind was wrong when he'd said I was 'okay with death.' I might wrap myself in a hard shell but if it breaks, I bleed like anyone else.

I breathed deeply. It had been too long since we'd talked. I never realised just how much I depended on Zaith's friendship to be able to handle my own life.

"The Whipstaff's ion rope caught him around the neck. I was aiming for his chest but everything happened so fast."

"He suffocated?"

"I think so. I checked his vitals before I went back to Dezmind. Nothing. When I returned to retrieve the body – he was gone. I keep wondering if it was a trick of the Deserts or something I did–"

"Were you wrong? Was he still alive – a weak pulse maybe?"

"No. There were no footsteps, just a pale-powder lining the ground where he fell." My voice cracked.

Grabbing two handfuls of dirt on either side of my legs, I squeezed the emotion out of my body and into the earth. The pressure irritated my palms.

"Taya, just remember – Dezmind's alive. He's alive and we have the Chronicles. Take solace in that."

My fists relaxed, slowly releasing the anger-charged sands. Wiping my gauze-wrapped palms on my pants to clean them, I closed my eyes. Zaith and I didn't speak again that night. My mind bounced from various Tabloid headings, to the orb, to Ketic's journal, to Dezmind, the Kronik, the Facility, and back again. My heart and my mind battled over logistics and lost realities. Finally, a cloudy twilight pressed down on already-heavy eyelids and I slept.

* * *

Mid-morning of the second day, actually day nine since I started on this damnable quest, the landscape altered again. I wasn't sure if this could be called another 'different' Desert or not, but things were definitely changing. The sand steadily took on a darker hue, the spikes graduated into small humps and low flattened hills as the cracks in the ground disappeared. What we stood on was the closest thing to soil since we'd left Vitexid's Lakes.

Patches of brush and smooth, thick-trunked dwarf-trees with rubbery, fan-like leaves grew in the most unlikely places. My odd horizon was no longer just the threat of an illusion. We walked toward a very large, very long, and very high outcropping of dark rock. So high in fact, that it shadowed our progress. It was the strangest land formation I'd ever seen. The closer Zaith and I got, the taller it grew. At times, when one of the suns shone on the curved portion, it sparkled.

A small movement near the base of a tree caught my attention. I stopped the cart. Zaith walked over to me, but I held a finger to my lips pointing to the tree with my other hand.

When Zaith's eyes adjusted to the shadowed light, and the dark silt- like soil, she saw the source of my hesitation. A short, squat lizard the size of my forearms, not including the tail, sat half- burrowed in the ground by the foot of the tree. Zaith mimed laughter at the sight of the strange creature, and stood with her arms crossed, waiting to see what I would do.

Pulling the small knife from my belt-pack, I pried it open as I crept forward. Raising my arm to strike, I scared the lizard off. I tossed the knife. The reptile darted. The blade landed harmlessly in the fine soil.

I needed a better weapon if we were going to have fresh meat. Wanting to save Zaith's Clinex and my Whipstaff in case of an emergency, I fell back on my training instead.

I left Zaith and the cart, walked up to a tree and broke off a branch the length of my arm. Holding either end, I slowly bent it, arching the twig. Both ends nearly touched before it snapped.

"Good."

"What are you planning?" Zaith asked.

"To make a bow."

"A bow?"

"Help me check the bushes. I'll need something heavier for the arrows."

"Wouldn't a spear be easier?"

"But not as fast and not as accurate. It doesn't slice through the air as nicely as an arrow – besides, I'm a better shot when it comes to archery."

We tested a number of different branches. After gathering enough wood, I whittled them straight while describing to Zaith how to form the bow.

We used one of the nylon strings Zaith rolled her sleeping

mats with. By the time she fitted the string to the notches on either end of a new, much longer stick, I'd straightened twelve twigs. I notched one end of each and sharpened the opposite. The only other item needed was a substitute for feathers. Normally I didn't need the extra support to guide the arrows, but I knew the whittled twigs were not perfect.

The leaves on the smallest bushes were the closest in weight and size to a feather fletching. Carefully fitting a couple of leaves into the notched ends of my arrows, I gave them an extra tug just to make sure they were snug. I knew they'd never fly straight, but it was easy to fix a small variance with my aim. It was a matter of getting a feel for it – fast.

When the weapon was ready, Zaith scouted the area in one direction as I walked with the bow in the other. After a few minutes, I caught sight of movement in the shadows of the underbrush. Kneeling down, I silently knocked an arrow. I had no idea how the bow would react.

Pulling back on the string until my bent elbow passed my ear, with my hand parallel to my face I touched my jaw-line.

The string hummed.

Streaking forward, the arrow landed slightly shy and to the left of the vanished target.

Catching up with it again, after a few carefully paced strides, I re-aimed the retrieved arrow; this time a little higher and just to the right of my mark.

The air vibrated. My shot whizzed forward. An audible squeak and a scampering arrow – I hit it. Zaith tracked the lizard until it settled from exhaustion. Grabbing its neck, I snapped it.

Zaith winced.

I swung around and tossed her its limp, scaly body. "That's one. Did you see any over there?"

The beast landed at Zaith's feet. She stared at it, poking it with her left toe, playfully disgusted. "Don't expect me to touch that thing until it looks significantly less like something I can recognise." Motioning with her thumb in response to my question, she added, "We should grab our stuff and look farther ahead. I couldn't see anything my way, even when I rushed the bushes."

Returning to the cart and the orb, we continued south. The rock formation ahead grew taller and larger with every step; that night we would feast on lizard at its base.

Heat-weary, since we'd taken to travelling during the day for several hours, we finally neared the end of our hilly jaunt. I carried three lizards skewered nose-to-tail on a long branch over my shoulder. The soil grew darker the closer we came to the base of the outcropping. It wasn't really richer in the sense of being thick and moist, but its granulation and pigmentation developed a dark charcoal hue.

"Hmm…" My eyes tracked over the earth. "Do I dare ask?"

"It's so dark. I hope the ground doesn't attract the heat of the suns and reflect it back on us."

I scratched at a patch of flaking skin high on one cheek. Zaith's hand automatically touched her blistered nose. Kneeling down, I ran my hands through the top layer of dirt. Leaning over in a mock-bow, I rested the side of my face on the ground. It was relatively neutral, as though the ground had some unknown cooling agent. Perhaps it had something to do with the glittery fragments.

"Nah. It'll be fine. It's no worse than the pinky-beige stuff in the other Deserts – better in fact," I said.

Zaith nodded, reapplying some of the plant extract I'd found nearby to her burn.

As the day steadily came to a close, Zaith and I directed our travels toward a particularly ornate section of the immense rock outcropping. I noticed a significant change in the topography, yet again, recognizing one of the dense bushes from a note in Doire's pocket book.

Gamma's gradual disappearance lit the horizon, bringing night faster as we travelled into the very crook of the outcropping's shadow.

Time no longer seemed aligned with meaning. The change in the landscape marked our progress, but I wondered for the hundredth time if we really were progressing. There was no sign of Dezmind. No sign of anything.

Maybe we passed him on the way? I couldn't afford to think like that.

Zaith broke the silence. "Hey, what do you suppose that is – over there?"

"Where? High or low?"

"Low, actually, just on the face of the last hill before the rock base. The ground looks different but I can't make out why. What do your eyes tell you?"

Focusing on the hill in question, I noticed the odd shapes on it – or was it shape?

"I see it. It's, it's…" Then it hit me, "He's been here!" I cried, running. *A message from Dezmind.*

Zaith followed at a slow trot, dragging along the cart. When she reached me, I circled a broad patch of land piled high with rocks.

"What do you make of it? What's he telling us now?" she asked.

"It's another arrow."

"Where's it pointing?"

"Up."

"Up?"

"Up."

Zaith stood quiet before articulating her next concern. "But it's steep."

"There's always a way," I said, gazing up at the large rock face. "Let's set up camp. We've got a long day tomorrow – we'll need the light to help us climb and every ounce of energy we can muster."

Zaith nodded and unpacked, setting up camp by the large arrow. I pulled out Doire's notebook and flipped to the very end, in search of something specific.

"Zaith?"

"Yeah?"

"There's a plant growing around here *with edible leaves and dry black berries,*" I read directly from Doire's notes. "I don't know if the berries are ripe yet, but I've seen this plant around. I'm going to pick a bunch of the leaves; we can bake our catch in them over the coals of a traditional fire. The lack of large animals in the region means we're probably safe. We'll just need to sleep away from the coals in case they attract stinging crawlers or snakes."

"Sounds good to me, I'll gather up the wood and build a pit. See you in a bit. Oh, and Taya–"

"Yeah?"

"You're taking care of the lizards, right? I don't touch anything that doesn't come pre-packaged in plastic."

I laughed. "I know. I know. Don't worry about it. You'll thank me once your stomach is full and you're drifting to sleep."

We had a fine meal that night, it was no roast ganoo but that didn't matter. I pushed the memory of a dead man I thought I knew to the back of my mind and buried it. Instead, Zaith and I talked like old times about all the stupid things Touf had ever done to embarrass her with his lovesick ways. We didn't mention the quest, or politics, or conspiracy theories, or being on the job, or the Desert isolation – we ate and drank comfortably, two good friends camping out on a nice night under the stars.

I was forced to wait for Alpha to tint the sky red before I could get an accurate look at how to climb the giant cliff of black glistening rock. I wanted to get moving. I anxiously dug a trench in the sand with my foot. Zaith brushed, twisted and clipped her now- mostly-black hair. The plum colour faded, probably from sweat, since we hadn't properly bathed in a while.

As Gamma descended the previous evening, I'd noticed an odd rock configuration three-quarters of the way up the face of the outcropping. At the time, I made a mental note to get a better look at it in the brighter light of the morning. This was my goal, but the dense shadows of the predawn made exploration hazardous.

Large, oblong, rounded shapes peppered the top of the cliff. The small, dark shadows they cast spoke of an interior, but nothing else discernibly helpful. The eroded walkway snaked randomly all the way up to those aerial caves. At times, the path appeared to peter out – still, it was better than free ranging and scaling the entire cliff and leaving behind the majority of our supplies.

Although food problems were solved for now, we were low on liquids. The verrin Zaith brought was now gone, and there remained only a small amount of water. Last night, as I flipped through Doire's journal, I noticed the sketch of a small, round, hopping lizard. As Zaith cleared camp in preparation for the climb, I wandered off, re- reading that section of Doire's notes.

The small beasts lived mostly under the surface of the ground, where it was cool and moist – or at least as moist as a Desert could be.

Somehow I had to convince these things that it was raining, really raining, in order to draw them to the surface. I needed help.

"Zaith!"

"What?"

"Come here."

Zaith brushed her hands on her pants after tying up the cart. Stretching, she wandered over to where I stood studying the ground.

"What do you need?"

"We have to make it sound like it's raining. I think this is a good spot."

Zaith's eyes widened, her eyebrows nearly touched her hairline. "And just what's supposed to happen while we're doing this?"

I flashed the notebook at her. "These guys are supposed to come out. They'll give us this morning's water – and some food for later. Follow me."

Putting the notebook away, I positioned myself a couple of yards from Zaith, knees slightly bent. Slowly, I beat out a low rhythm on the ground with my boot-clad feet. Shrugging her shoulders, Zaith followed.

We trod in place like this for a few minutes. Zaith shook her head and stood up, but when I quickened the pace, she leaned back into it. After establishing a rhythm, I flat out stomped in wide circles. We beat upon the ground, passing each other, circling, and crossing back, arms out to maintain balance. If Dezmind were nearby watching us, his laughter would echo for miles.

Zaith sharply inhaled. I saw them.

Two oversized bodies attached to skinny jumping legs, peered out from under a nearby boulder, in anticipation of rain.

I made eye contact with Zaith. She looked ready to take off. I held her there, demanding with my eyes for her to help me. A couple more jumpers joined the first pair. Zaith blinked, and then nodded.

We dove to the ground. Charcoal dust billowed.

I grabbed one, tossing it down the front of my shirt for safekeeping, and then scrambled after another. Zaith squeaked in protest at having to touch the creatures, but as the fine particles of dirt settled, both of us sat with our catch. Zaith's arms stretched straight out in front of her, each hand gripping a wriggling beast by a leg. My shirt bulged as my catch tried to jump in their confinement.

"I know you're going to hate this, but there's no sense in killing them first then drinking their stores. Doire notes that you kind of have to do it all at once."

"Drink what? I see solid mass here."

"That's exactly it. Seventy-five percent of their mass is captured and retained water. They store it up when it rains and live off it in the cool depths of the soil."

I fished one of the creatures out of my shirt, turned it nose down and lifted it over my upturned mouth.

"What are you doing?!" Zaith shrieked.

"Exactly what you will in a moment."

Grabbing it with both hands I squeezed. A thin, clear liquid trickled out of the creature's mouth – enough for three swallows. When nothing more came out, I tossed its small misshapen body to the ground and pulled out my second catch.

Zaith looked green, a fetching shade almost the colour of the little water-holders. Her eyes wide and glassy, she honestly looked ready to cry.

I tossed the second one down. "Drink up. We have a long climb ahead of us."

"I can't. You didn't tell me anything about how we were supposed to drink their water. There's no way."

"I know it looks terrible. The water's a bit thick, but no worse than pure verrin. It's refreshing going down. Come on. We have to ration what's left in your keg. Who knows what's on the other side of this cliff – for all we know, the Deserts may be endless and I don't know what we'll do if we don't stay hydrated. Come on, Zaith. We've come too far."

Zaith sat for a moment, contemplating her next move. I didn't exactly know what was going through her mind, but it was an ugly battle.

Finally, Zaith tossed one of the creatures to me.

"Turn around. I don't think I can do this if you're looking."

I contained a smile and turned my back to Zaith. The squelch of the little lizard filled the air. A soft *thwup* and its body hit the ground. I turned just long enough to toss her the other one before she lost her nerve.

The second one hit the dirt. Silence. Zaith stood and dusted off her pants. I turned to face her.

"I can't believe you made me do that," she muttered. Then she addressed me directly, "You're going to deal with what's left of them. I don't want to see them again until my fork is piercing their flesh." She stormed off to collect the cart.

Chapter Twenty-six
A Crossing of Fortune

Trudging along the uneven path, we walked first in one direction then another, gradually zigzagging but always climbing up.

Occasionally the path was so sheer we crawled to make it to the next plateau; or so narrow, Zaith had to string the cart and her belongings onto her waist and let them dangle over the edge as she shimmied along.

Hour after hour we moved consistently upward: managing, manoeuvring, manipulating and surmounting. We spoke only to give suggestions and warn one another of impending dangers.

Zaith and I took turns either hauling the cart with the supplies, or the orb. The suns penetrated our protective layers, making skin sizzle and crack as we rose higher and higher throughout the day. We did not stop often, and when we did, only long enough to switch burdens.

My goal was to reach the caves before nightfall, then do some exploring while Zaith slept. I briefly thought about how my time in the later Deserts with Zaith progressed without any incident. This moment of positivity was sure to be my downfall.

In the first shallow cave we came to, we ate an early supper since we'd missed lunch. Zaith was visibly drained and weary; the features of her face drooped in such a way as to match her tortured hair. I warmed up a bit of leftover meat from the night before to give her more time to rest. We didn't speak to conserve energy, but after the meal I couldn't settle. I remained restless and fidgety, waiting for Zaith to fall asleep.

Lying on her side, just inside the mouth of the cave, Zaith savoured her cup of water. I stood up and walked to the small path outside. I stood with my toes over the edge, hands on my hips, and nose pointed north – home.

The monotony of the Deserts spread wide before me.

Sameness scattered with slight variances – life in the wake of extinction.

My eyes trailed from the deep amber-orange skyline, to the hills and valleys of sand, straight down to the base of the mammoth rock I perched on. Dark juts, divots and clumps of shiny solid black earth dropped steeply to the deep shadows below.

Holding my arms out straight to either side, I closed my eyes. Images of balance trials during training flooded my cerebral consciousness; standing on a slim, flat metal bar, perched high above the solid concrete floor of Level 2, eyes closed, praying not to fall – for the lack of a safety net. I smiled ruefully. Within the first week of attending CTF, students were expected to memorise the regimen to which they were to dedicate the rest of their studies, and their lives.

Level 1, the first floor above Main, was devoted to Focus – training in maintaining concentration for long periods of time during physical duress, and mental readiness in a variety of fields. Level 2 was Balance – learning and keeping it in a personal and professional capacity, as well as understanding its importance in mathematical and physical skills. Level 3 was Movement – the harmony and subtlety of physical movement as well as job management and expedience. Level 4 was Commitment – an intense focus on decision- making under various pressures and absences, both physically and mentally.

"5 was Motivation – training in personal and interpersonal drive, understanding how to assess the 'why' of things. Level 6 was Research – a wide variety of job skills and detail-oriented preparation accompanied by senior level reading, writing, and math. Level 7 was Courage, though commonly named Fear by the trainees – testing accumulated knowledge as well as two trial-by-fire examinations of courage in the face of personal fear. Level 8 was Assignment – to search for and receive assignments, and payment for completed work as a full Contractor; the Roof was Track and Field – any level of training had access to the pebble, sand, grass, and concrete running tracks with the permission of the unit Master. Ascension to each level of training occurred only when an individual met or exceeded the requirements of the current level they trained on. If an individual failed to pass Level 7, they would return to specific training levels assessed as needing improvement before taking on that challenge again. Full Contractors had complete access to all training levels to allow for maintenance and growth in expertise, in any area, without trained Masters on hand.

It seemed so long ago and so very far away. Not just my days of training, but even my last visit to Level 1, when I learned about Zaith's advances with reporting on the Facility. I bypassed my time in the sub-basement. Whether I admitted it or not, the terms of my probation were never far from my mind. It was as though my memories belonged to another person who lived my life, but was no longer the same person who stood high above a wild and untamed world.

Zaith roused slightly and set her empty cup aside.

"Taya, what are you doing?"

"Experiencing."

"Experiencing what, exactly?"

I breathed deeply, sighed and opened my eyes – the tight fluttery feeling in my stomach subsided.

"Life." Dropping my arms, I looked up and out into the vast realm before me.

"I don't get it," Zaith said, stifling a yawn.

I stood there, calm and still. I wasn't thinking of an answer, I didn't have to. I wasn't thinking of the question either. Breathing the air of an ancient and forgotten land, I stood – stood in the midst of a crossing between history and the future.

"Life," I said. "Not that fabricated pre-packaged existence of modified living we're subjected to on a daily basis back home…" *I've survived death twice out here.* "But this. A world of possibility. A land more alive in its death than most of us have ever experienced in our safe, cocooned existence."

A heavy silence weighed between us, until finally Zaith muffled out amidst another groggy yawn, "Whatever you say."

Chuckling, I closed my eyes again. Basking in the evening's cooling grace, I waited for Zaith to nod off before checking out the way ahead.

Several moments later, I turned, stepping clear of the edge. Though some light remained, I grabbed the light-tube from the cart and snuck around a dozing Zaith. The next cave opening sat along a more defined ledge just up ahead.

I wasn't entirely sure what I was looking for. I examined the seventh cave away from camp, entered a few paces, shone the light in a wide arc and left.

If Dezmind came this way, he'll have left some kind of signal for me a way of tracking his steps.

All of the caves looked identical. Sure, some went further back than others, but I didn't waste my time with them if they looked undisturbed.

Three tiers up and twenty openings later, I was ready to call it quits. The light was terribly dim, my breath frosted, and my muscles ached – an all-too-familiar sensation of late. If I didn't turn back now, I'd have to grope for the path in the dark.

I made surprisingly quick work of finding my way back. However, I couldn't help but double-check and retrace my steps to the fourth opening – the first cave on the tier above Zaith.

I lifted the faint light, bringing it and my nose less than an inch from the edge of the opening, just above eye level. Because there was no contrast to the rock's colouration, I'd overlooked a palm-sized double-headed arrow carved into the rock face. One head pointed into the cave and the other, the way back to Zaith.

But this cave didn't go back farther than twenty paces.

The light extinguished. Stowing it away, I vowed to set it out for a recharge in the morning. I faced two options: I could easily find my way back to Zaith and we could head into the cave blind in the morning, or I could take a few minutes now and see how far I could explore in the dark.

There really wasn't much of a decision to make. Reaching out my hands, I touched both walls with the tips of my fingers. My eyes cleared to help me see in the dark, I crept along.

Not ten steps in, my foot caught in a crevice, rolling my ankle. I crashed to the ground. Taking a moment to massage my injury before righting myself, I brushed off my clothes and pushed back stray hairs dancing about my face.

At fifteen paces I stumbled again, only this time the wall disappeared. I smacked my knee into the stone foundation of the new passage and bumped the brim of my cap on the lower ceiling.

After tending to my sore joint and muttering about, "just having to do this now," I searched the ground with my hands for my fallen cap.

Composed once more, I spread my arms and followed the narrower walls of the new tunnel. I noticed an incline to the ground. That's a good sign. Finding another passage just ahead, on my right, I felt assured this was the path Dezmind had followed. Turning around, I headed back to Zaith and the camp.

"What in the world did you do to yourself!" Zaith's pitchy voice and boisterous laughter snapped me out of a strange, colour-dominated dream. I rubbed my eyes.

"I wouldn't do that if I were you," she advised, smirking. She clicked the roof of her mouth with her tongue. "Honestly Taya, what am I going to do with you?"

"What are you going on about?" I said groggily.

"I wish I had a mirror to show you. You chose a fine time to take a mud bath – we hardly have enough water to drink, let alone wash with."

I snatched my tinted goggles and angled them to reflect my image. "Oh! I don't believe it." My cap had come off during the night and more strands of hair were mussed, but to top it all off, I was covered head to foot in black sooty dirt.

Stashing my goggles, I looked at my hands. They were filthy

– covered with smudges and smears of black rock dust. My green pants matched them, front and back, and what I could see of my shirt was not surprising.

"Do you have anything I can use to wipe this stuff off my face and hands?" I asked, miffed with myself. Zaith showed me the small cloth I used back at the Ancient City, but I waved it away.

"It's useless without water." I walked over to the orb, knelt down and scrubbed my face with one of the sweater sleeves, leaving the other one for my hands. One look at Zaith's face told me the task had been mostly futile.

"Don't laugh. I found a shortcut through the caves."

At least I hope it's a shortcut.

Gathering the supplies together, we ate on the go – dried lizard meat. We saved the small amphibians for a longer meal. The last of the water was divvied up the night before, so we drank sparingly. Zaith eyed the string of small beasts with contempt as they dangled down my back from the mat string.

Carefully, I manoeuvred us up to the next ridge and into the cave with the marking. We zigzagged through passages of varying diameters, always travelling up. Zaith's cart bounced around on the uneven ground but everything had been securely tied down after we woke.

The tunnels were erratic in shape and size as they were obviously made by some natural phenomena centuries upon centuries ago. Some cavern ceilings were beyond the simple reach of an outstretched hand, while others forced us to walk hunched in single file. But the slope was always twice as steep as the outer-ridge path, tiring our legs after only a couple of hours' walking.

In my haste this morning, I'd failed to keep my promise and we had no light to guide us through the passages.

I stopped abruptly. "What?" Zaith whispered.

I leaned right to let her see.

"What! We can't go in there – how can you be sure it won't stop at a dead end?"

The walls around us shook. Rock sprayed down from the mottled ceiling. Zaith jumped and clung to me, making me fall into the wall. The tremor subsided.

"What... what happens when we're crawling into the bowels of that small tunnel, huh? Then what! The walls are already falling down around us."

"Calm down. We're not going anywhere until the aftershock goes through. In the meantime, we need to disassemble your cart. I don't want to leave anything behind."

"But Taya..."

"Zaith," I turned and held my friend at arm's length, a little awkwardly, since I didn't want to smear her with soot. "Have I ever steered you wrong?"

"But—"

"Have I?"

"But—"

"Zaith—" Nose to nose, I looked straight into a pair of unusually frightened eyes.

"Right. The cart," she said, turning to break it down into its individual components and then latching bundles of supplies to pieces of the cart together in a longer train to be able to pull through the tight opening. Another smaller tremor shuddered the caves. Zaith's shoulders tensed as she worked, but she did keep working. I got down on my hands and knees and crawled into the small passage.

Moving forward, a nagging thought tugged at the back of my mind. I kept pushing it farther and farther back until I'd compiled enough thoughts to completely fill my brain. So far, all the passages we travelled through were created by erosion and the forces of the elements, or lack thereof. But this tunnel, this one was significantly smaller than the others; it had few, if any, bits of rubble littering the ground, and well-defined proportionate walls. I didn't feel cramped in the space – and that's what bothered me.

Ready to crawl back to Zaith and give her an update, I looked up into a larger anti-chamber of some kind; it was naturally brighter in there compared to the other tunnels, as light filtered through something high above me. It only took me a few minutes to get there, so I opted to take a closer look before retrieving Zaith.

I stood up in the circular space, not much wider than the circumference of my arm span. Loose hairs tickled my nose and ears, but I forced myself not to brush them away from my face. *I don't need to be mistaken for Zaith's sister at the end of all this.*

The light alternated and changed in its consistency from somewhere above, indistinct and washed out but a significant change nonetheless. I closed my eyes for a moment and then slowly opened them – allowing them time to adjust to the new light level.

Absently touching the wall at one end of the small chamber, I moved to look up into the faint light. It took a moment to internalise what I touched as I looked up. I focused on the wall in front of me and traced blackened fingers over smooth cut rock.

Smooth cut rock?

Each of the rectangular indented blocks were perfectly chiselled and moulded to fully support a very large foot. There was only one place I'd ever seen craftsmanship like this. It suddenly struck me that no ancient Xannian had ever set foot as far into the underground verrin caves as I had.

A wave of panic engulfed me. I trembled.

What if –

What if – if Dezmind –

Is still out there –

Lost –

Blinding heat surged through my brain like a searing migraine. It compelled me to race up the ladder and run.

But Zaith –

Dropping to my knees, I scrambled back down the tunnel. I burst out the opposite end travelling on pure adrenaline, but the overwhelming sense of desperate anxiety disappeared as fast as it struck. The mental pull to go up and out dissipated with thoughts of Zaith and my responsibilities.

"Zaith–" I looked up to see my best friend filing her nails in front of an organised pile of the pieces of her dismantled cart and supplies all bundled together neatly.

"Well, it's about time. I hope you didn't expect me to follow you blindly?" she griped.

I blinked.

A valve released in my body – relief at finding her safe flooded through every one of my arteries.

"I... I found the way out," I sputtered, feigning aloofness.

"Took you long enough. Still..." Zaith paused in reflection. "I'm sure this route was faster in the long run, but it'll be such a bother getting back home again." She tied one end of the rope to her ankle, the other to the tidy bundle train, and followed me as I rolled the orb down the small tunnel toward the anti-chamber.

Pushing back overgrown mosses and weedy plant life, I heaved the orb up through the hole in the ceiling and followed it into brilliant late morning sunshine. I couldn't make out much as I hauled myself up on to a grassy plateau. Standing, I raised a hand to shield my eyes and scanned the surroundings.

A pale-green grass blanketed the ground with protrusions of dense black rock. Large worn boulders were scattered amongst tall bushes and an assortment of pink wild flowers. The air was still hot, but it had a moistness to it.

I picked up the orb by the arms of my sweater letting it drag as I took a few steps up a steep incline toward the Deserts. The grass here ended in a wide rim of jumbled black rock surrounding the upper edge of the cliff peak. There were scattered trees and bushes a few yards down, but after that, sand was all the eye could see. It felt surreal standing there amidst such greenery and fresh life not more than a stone's throw from the nothingness we'd emerged out of.

I turned south as Zaith scrambled from the hole. At the bottom of a lush sprawling hillside, littered with giant trees and an assortment of wildflowers, stood a dense forest. Spreading wide, it reached a deep blue slice of the horizon. A blue distinctly the shade belonging to the North Seas.

It reminded me of a programme I'd watched a couple of years ago about Darius' and the Magistrate's travels with the dissenters – what everyone else referred to as the Nine Seas Massacre. Now I was beginning to understand why; the Kronik eliminated any threat to the status quo. Salt water was just as much a death sentence as the Deserts. Xannians were not sailors, but the program had outlined Darius' travels and tried equating the ousting of the rebels to a similar grandeur. *How could I have been so blind?*

My eyes hungrily soaked in the bounteous plant life – then my breath caught in my throat – and that's where it stayed.

A fleck of vibrant red splashed against the pale green of a small clearing, not seven or eight hundred yards down the hill and into the forest. The hot fever of anxiety and despair from moments ago in the caves exploded in the pit of my stomach.

"Zaith!" I yelled, "It's Dezmind!"

I pushed the thought out with growing clarity seconds before dropping the orb and dashing full-tilt down the tree-flecked slope.

"How do you know?" Zaith called, scrambling to unhook her baggage and cart train to follow.

How do I know?

Flying past tower-high trees, I hurdled small bushes letting my momentum carry me forward.

Even though he didn't have a stitch of red cloth on him when we started on this fool-hardy quest, the image of a lush red velvet curtain and casual diners wiping chins on three hundred thread-point crimson napkins reassured me my instincts were correct.

My worst fear was now nullified – he definitely came ahead of us.

But at what price? Why did he stop here? Now?

Skirting around the base of an extremely wide tree trunk, supporting vast branches of leaves, I ran through a clump of mature trees – blocking my view of the red flag.

No matter, I could have found it blindfolded running backwards in the dead of night – its image etched my mind.

Crashing through two closely-knit bushes, I stumbled into a clearing – the clearing. Running forward, I snatched the kerchief off the stone outcropping. Scanning the surrounding tree line, I searched for some sign of him – anywhere.

Chapter Twenty-seven
Kindred Spirit

A shadow, slightly darker than the rest, slumped beneath the second row of trees. Its outline far more still than its paler counterparts. My throat constricted at the thought of what I might find.

Intuition told me not to run. I moved carefully toward the unnamed shade, dropping the kerchief back onto the rock. Birds' echoing chirps reverberated in the distance of the dense forest. A light breeze rustled the leaves above, twitching and flipping their pale mimics on the grass below.

Still the dark shadow did not move. The closer I crept, the more defined the shape became. Fear stabbed at my heart.

"Dezmind?" I whispered, dropping to my knees beside his still form, propped against the base of a large tree.

"Dezmind," I repeated – sharper. My head swam. I reached for the base of his neck with a pair of trembling fingers. After everything we'd experienced out here, the thought of losing him shredded my last threads of sanity. Still, I managed to take a few deep, steadying breaths and focused on finding a rhythm from his heart.

A faint but steady pulse flitted at regular intervals. My head and shoulders sank toward my chest as a shudder whipped through my body. *He's alive! Thank the Trinity.*

I exhaled and looked up, tracing my fingers over yellow-brown splotches scattered along his neck and collarbone – all that was left of the attempt on his life nearly two weeks ago.

Cupping his face with my hands, I touched my forehead to his and squeezed my eyes shut. *Oh, Dez, what have you done?*

His lids fluttered before opening to small slits. A slow crooked smile spread dry, cracked lips.

"Taya," he managed over a thick, non-responsive tongue. *Thank the suns.* I sat back and picked up his right hand, holding it to my chest. His skin shifted easily in my grasp, puckering and remaining pinched after a soft squeeze.

"Thought you were ahead of me," he whispered, closing his eyes with the effort. "Dizzy. Thirsty."

An iron wall slammed down on my soul threatening to sever it from my body. Burying all emotion under mountains of training, I said, "And hungry too, I'll bet. Dezmind, you're dehydrated."

A crashing and snapping of branches came from across the clearing. He jumped slightly.

"Don't worry. It's a friend of mine. She… she followed us out here. I'll explain the rest when you're feeling better." I went to meet Zaith as she closed in on the red kerchief on the boulder.

"Is he here? Did you find him?" she asked between gasping breaths. She rested her hands on her knees, taking in great gulps of air.

"Yes, he's over there, but he's in a dreadful state."

I noticed the absence of her cart and supplies. I'd have to go back for one of the kegs.

"I need you to watch him for me while I search for verrin." I gripped her shoulder. "Talk to him. Tell him who you are, why you're here – that kind of thing. Try to anticipate any questions he might have, but *don't* tell him what you know about the orb and the Chronicles. And *don't* let him talk. It'll only worsen his condition."

I looked back the way we'd come. It would take twice as long to run up the hill as it had to come down it.

"I don't know how long I'll be. If he nods off again, just set up camp and wait for me." I didn't linger for a response, but took off to grab a keg and the rope before heading farther south.

He thought he was following me – he thought – he thought I was the one leaving the markers. He has no more sense of what's out here than he did before he went headlong into the pool. Which means – which means Ketic and his friends left those point markers all those thousands of years ago. They are the 'steadfast beacons' mentioned in the Chronicles.

My mind whirled with information, trying to fit the pieces together. Yet, one part of my brain remained clearly focused on finding verrin. I was reckless, I knew, running full tilt through a densely- packed alien forest with no regard for my personal safety.

I dodged another tree, a small rock outcropping – visual key markers for my return. With no idea how long I ran, slowly dehydrating myself, I searched for a body of verrin that might not be there.

After wasted minutes of frantic motion, I slowed to a walk and eventually stopped. Sunlight streamed through the leaves above. My heart beat steadily slowed as I calmed my breathing, and took a moment to close my eyes and listen.

The caw of a large bird carried over a long distance, while softer chirps reached me from high above and not so far away. The wind rustled the leaves overhead, but there was something else that came with it – a rustling, but definitely a rushing too.

The soft babbling of a brook made my chest swell with renewed hope. Opening my eyes, I followed the sound of rippling liquid as it echoed faintly through the trees. Moments later, I arrived at a narrow stream flowing with a surprising current down a slope toward the base of the long undulating valley I saw from the rock-peak.

But it was only water.

Not wasting any more time searching for verrin, I settled for what was here. Kneeling down on the lush embankment, I let the natural flow of the water fill the container. I also re-filled my empty canteen, which had surprisingly remained suspended around my neck.

Finally, I held my breath and submerged my head, rubbing vigorously at unseen smudges. The cool water rushed smoothly past my ears as my face, hair, and cap soaked in the refreshing goodness. But there, under the water I saw myself dropping down beside his lifeless form. My body spasmed as my heart and my mind waged a war I never knew was possible. In the end, the words 'soul mate' quieted the battle – whatever drew me to him was irrational. I was not his lost love, just an unloved child.

I emerged, dripping with a heart aching for something it couldn't have, but with logic restored. Taking off my cap, I shook my head from side-to-side, spraying the surrounding plant life. Mentally readying myself for the return run, I turned to gather my containers.

I turned back – sharply.

Crouching down low, I brought myself within an inch of a white, four-petalled round blossom with vivid purple stamen.

"It can't be," I whispered.

Double-checking the stem and leaf pattern, I took a second look at the area – they were everywhere, growing in clusters. I wiped damp hands on the legs of my pants, resting my shins on the grass. I removed the notebook from my belt-pack.

Scanning the last ten or twelve entries, I found a drawing and detailed description listed under the heading 'Alternative Flora' in Doire's last journal.

The vegetation in front of me and the one he described matched perfectly.

He came here –

I uprooted the flower clusters and stored them in my hat. The journal lay open to the sketch; beneath the image of the flower marked the words *'Restoration Draught.'* The only reason I remembered that plant was thinking that a healing aid like that would come in handy. Trouble seemed to find us with every step in the Deserts.

I forgot all about it after deciphering Ketic's journal – and yet, here it is.

Why in the world would Doire go back then? If he found this place, he should have stayed, built himself a house, and lived the rest of his days healthy and in peace. Why return to the Deserts – why risk death?

I bumped the journal with my left foot and sent it scattering. I turned to retrieve it – a pair of young eyes stared back at me from a faded photograph amid the vibrant greenery. Setting aside my hat, I picked up the picture – the second one fluttered to the ground, from under the first. The young girl smiled up at me from the image in my right hand, the happy mother and daughter from my left.

He must have gone back for them. Time slowed.

The brook quieted.

The birds' voices faded and all other hues bled to grey.

The only vivid image remaining was the one I translated to colour in my mind. I could see Doire kneel down and open his arms as his little girl ran to him – her laughter like music.

I shook my head to break the musing.

A piercing caw sliced the air. Tucking the photographs into the journal, I stuffed it into my belt-pack before gathering up the supplies and racing back to Dezmind.

Zaith sat quietly in front of her empty meal bowl, legs crossed and eyes closed. Dezmind lay motionless where I'd found him. I could make out a slight rise and fall to his chest. The light-tube sat beside the red kerchief on the rock, to recharge.

Zaith opened her eyes. "I was worried. You've been gone a long time."

"You went back for the stuff." I said.

She nodded.

I frowned; she shouldn't have left him alone but it saved me a trip. I dumped the contents of my hat.

"I found a stream of water and a healing plant that could help speed up Dezmind's recovery."

Placing half the pile in front of Zaith, I separated the three main components of the flower: the stem, the roots, and the blossom.

Zaith followed suit.

"When did he fall back asleep?" I asked, instead of being confrontational.

"The moment you left." She gave me a knowing look. The tone of my voice must have given me away. "Well, I was able to tell him who I was, but I don't know if he understood me. His eyes kind of glazed over and he nodded off. That's when I thought I'd make use of the time and get our things."

I frowned. "That's not encouraging – about Dezmind, I mean.

Keep separating these for me, I have to start the fire and borrow your bowl."

Zaith reached for another bunch of flowers.

I picked up the empty vessel beside her and went to search for a few branches since we'd run out of the liquid fire Zaith had brought along. Since Doire had a couple chunks of flint in his bag, I'd slipped one into my belt-pack in case we needed it along the way. It had come in handy for cooking those lizards before we'd climbed the aerial caves. The ancient method was likely to be our saving grace out here.

It didn't take long to find a bunch of wood littering the forest floor. Returning, I lit the dry twigs with my blade and Doire's flint rock. Piling a handful of blossoms into the empty food bowl, I broke a thick branch from a nearby tree – I needed fresh, malleable wood. Cutting it down to the length of a fork, I removed the bark and rounded both ends with my knife.

As the fire flickered in the midst of a mild afternoon, I first dried out and then methodically ground the petals and stamen into a fine dust.

When Zaith finished separating the last of the segments, I asked, "Could you check on Dezmind?"

Zaith knelt down beside him, reluctant to touch his skin. "He's very warm. I don't think he has the ability to sweat anymore."

"Grab the red kerchief, soak it with some water and place it over the hottest areas of exposed skin. You might want to unbutton the front of his shirt and soak his chest too."

Zaith looked at me with raised eyebrows.

"Oh Zaith!" I chided. "Get your mind out of the gutter and help me save his life."

She nodded again, grabbed the tin mug from her pack and moistened the helpless Talian lying beneath the trees.

I'm such a dunce! I should have thought of that sooner!

I continued to curse myself as I placed Zaith's pot on the fire, half filled with water. Boiling a handful of the roots, I watched as Zaith slid her fingers over Dezmind's chest, slowly revealing more of his silvery-white skin. She wet the cloth and traced it over one particularly long colith before sliding it back up to his neck and chin.

I sliced the stalks of the plant more forcefully than I intended and had to pick up the flyaway pieces. I dipped them into the mixture until the milky inner liquid dissolved. My cheeks burned, but not from the fire in front of me. *She can't help herself. She's been eyeing him since the Rally. It doesn't matter anyway; neither of us is fated to be with him.*

I shut my eyes and tried to focus on the herbal mix. I couldn't remember if I was supposed to leave the roots in or not before slowly adding the powdered petals. I pulled out the journal to double-check the recipe.

Roots out.

Trying to jam the book back into my pack, it refused to go all the way down. I shoved my hand in, to shift whatever items were in the way, and pulled out the pure verrin crystal from the Temple. I looked at it, rolling it around on my palm.

"Of course!"

Slipping away the journal, I grabbed my knife. Carefully, suspending it over the top of a now rootless mixture, I sliced off paper-thin wafers of the crystal. After four long thin flakes dropped, the water took on a decidedly pinky hue.

I smiled storing the crystal away. Adding the ground blossoms, I stirred until they dissolved. A light florid scent wafted up with the steam when I removed the dish from the fire and set it on a large flat rock in the shade of a tree.

"Taya!"

I snapped around. Fear laced her voice.

"Taya, something's wrong."

I knelt down beside Dezmind, opposite Zaith. His skin crawled and twittered and twitched. His head jerked from side-to-side, but not violently.

"I don't think it's a seizure, but then, I've never known anyone who's had one before," I said. It was one thing to read about it during my medic studies at the Facility, but another thing entirely to witness one in person.

Reaching over him, I held his head steady between my cool palms. His face flashed fire-hot. Zaith removed the cloth from his forehead.

His eyes popped open.

My heart jumped, but I held firm. Zaith gasped and sat back. "Dezmind. Dez, it's Taya," I said. "It's you," he whispered thickly.

"Yes, but shhh – don't try to talk. I'm here. We're taking care of you now."

"It's you," he said again, more determined. "It's always been you."

"Shhh, try not to talk now, Dez. Save your strength."

"You're the one I've been searching for." His arm sprang up. I caught his wrist.

A picture fluttered in his hand. He let it go. I snagged it as it floated to the ground. Laying his arm across his chest, I turned over a faded photo of a little girl.

Doire's little girl.

In my mind, I watched the image of a young girl reflecting on the surface of a pool waiting to find a lost toy – it washed over and superimposed itself on the picture in front of me.

"It's always been you," he whispered.

I pulled my hand away. The image disappeared.

No.

He's delusional.

His fever and nausea are making him imagine things. Just because I want it to be true, doesn't mean that it is.

"You're not thinking straight. Both my parents are still alive – and well – and Matin." His eyelids shut. His body shuddered in protest. Flipping the picture over, I found a date and a name smudged in the bottom right corner.

Jadis.

"You've mistaken me for someone else," I whispered. Zaith shifted and brought me back to the present.

"He's getting worse, Zaith. Here, take this journal. There's a dictionary of plant-life at the back – see if you can find something that we can have with our meat tonight. We can't afford to lose strength now."

"What are you going to do?" she hesitated.

"Keep him moist until the mixture cools. Then I'll see if I can get him to swallow some."

"Right. I'll check back with you, drop off what I find, let you know

I'm still alive and all that."

The joke didn't register. "Take the bow with you, just in case – I haven't seen any wildlife around here, but I've heard them from time to time."

Nodding, Zaith went to the cart to retrieve the bow, Doire's journal clamped tightly in one hand. I turned my attention back to Dez, pouring a little more water into the tin mug, methodically soaking the red cloth and dampening his forehead. In his delirious state, he'd confused me with someone he'd never met before and would likely never meet.

If Lady Lynnia's daughter existed, he would have found her by now; any man with his tenacity and drive would have found a way. I never believed he'd given up looking for his Soul Mate, the fervour with which he told the Kahn-lea his story showed that this was not something he was going to just set aside – even if the world was coming to an end.

Chapter Twenty-eight
Dezmind's Truth

After dinner that night, I finally realised the severity of my recklessness. I barely tasted the juice-filled fruit Zaith gathered, and didn't even notice until told, that the meat from the small amphibians was tender because she marinated it in the fruity juices. I'm sure this was more to hide the flavour of little beasts than anything else, but it worked out well.

"I'm sorry, Zaith. Dinner was great. It's just–" Zaith waved away the apology.

"Don't worry. I know you're preoccupied. I mean – sheesh, we found him!"

"If you could look after Dez again for a while, I'll do a proper sweep of the perimeter. I won't get any sleep tonight not knowing what's really out there."

"Sure. Just be careful, Taya. It's getting dark and the shadows from the trees don't help visibility," she advised, wrapping the leftovers in some large leaves.

Very true. I couldn't remember if I'd ever told her about my difficulty with dusk, but no matter, we'd spent so much time together she'd probably figured it out on her own.

"Try to drizzle a bit more of that herbal mixture into him too, about a teaspoon every half-hour. You may have to massage his throat to get him to swallow. I just hope it works," I said, blinking back the image of Zaith's long, black fingers caressing Dezmind's throat. Instead, I focused on helping her clean up. The more time Zaith would have tending to Dezmind the better.

I made a couple of wide circles around the camp, moving as quietly as possible. Refraining from using the light-tube Zaith had recharged while I found the water, I tried to keep my movements hidden. But that meant whatever might be out there remained hidden as well.

Working steadily in half-circles, I gradually moved up the grand hill toward the plateau. I had to know every stretch of land we crossed, because at the end of all this we still had to get home – and that was my job.

Finding several different sites Zaith had described to me about the location of the fruit, I tracked her earlier progress. During my search, I found a site she hadn't located yet, but decided not to burden myself with any fruit during the surveillance sweep.

The further up I trekked, the more dispersed the trees were, and the easier it was to see by the light of our false solar sentinel.

Between the Chronicles on the orb and Ketic's journal, the magnitude of the Kronik concealing a two-thousand year old truth threatened to fry my brain. But I couldn't dwell on that now. I had to stay focused. Scouting this side of the hill would be easier and much faster than my explorations to the south.

Reaching the upper plateau, I was illuminated by Gamma against the depths of the forest behind me. Standing resolute, I stared out at a world so familiar and yet so unbelievably foreign – my fears from the Pit of Chance came crashing back unabated. I collapsed. Leaning against a boulder, I finally let myself cry.

Three hours later, I returned to camp, satisfied we were situated well enough out of the dense forest, and away from the creatures that were harboured within it.

I called to Zaith, "Still awake?"

"Yeah, no thanks to you," she yawned.

I walked over, watching her pour water into the mug then swish what remained of the contents of the small keg.

"I won't fill it again tonight," I said. "You're in no state to keep watch if I disappear for another hour. I'll keep an eye on him until the last of it's used, and then get some more before breakfast."

"Did you see anything out there?" Zaith asked, handing me the cloth.

"Small night animals, nothing more. Oh, and I ran across a patch of that spiky fruit just northeast of here. We should check it out tomorrow."

I looked around as I knelt to replace Zaith at Dezmind's side. "We're safe here, Zaith. I'll be up most of the night anyway and can keep watch. I'll sleep no later than mid-twilight. Three hours—"

"I know. Three hours is all you need. I think you're just trying to convince yourself of that every time you mention it," Zaith teased, moving a couple of trees over with her sleeping mat.

"You're just jealous – if you could manage three hours a night, you'd eagerly split your extra time between men and hunting for the next big story."

"Maybe I'd just focus on the men. I've already got my hooks into a couple of really incredible stories and I'm still managing to get my beauty sleep." She gave a tight smile and settled for the night.

She wouldn't be getting her hooks into this man, that's for sure. I brushed damp tendrils of hair away from Dezmind's forehead. At least I was scrupulous enough not to lead him astray. If he'd thought Zaith was his lost love, she'd have eaten him up and spit out the bones when she was done. Luckily, she was also my friend and she knew better than to try something like that under such dire circumstances. Although, I couldn't help but wonder about her sometimes.

I traced one of the thinner wavy coliths by Dez's hairline with the damp cloth. I still couldn't believe he'd subjected himself to this torture – following a series of ancient texts on blind faith until it nearly killed him. I laid the back of my hand against his cheek, and then his forehead.

The fever had lessened since the morning, his skin felt less rubbery, but obviously clammy from the constant attention. The serum mix was gone. I thought about making another batch in the morning as I laid the newly-dampened cloth across his forehead and eyes, settling myself for a long night.

Dez's fever broke early the next day. I watched over him for another hour before getting some rest just before dawn.

I arrived back at camp, from refilling the water kegs just as Zaith started organising breakfast. She held her bottle of oil up to the growing sunlight and shook it.

"We don't have any left."

"I know. There are dried branches scattered all over the forest, we should keep using them," I suggested, setting down two canisters of water beside the cart.

"I hope you're not hungry – this might take me a while," Zaith warned playfully, returning the bottle to the cart.

I smiled at her unfaltering spirit. "I'm sure I'll survive until you get back."

Zaith tossed the empty fire bowl at me – which I caught, as it whizzed past my shoulder.

"Temper, temper. Go blow off some steam, especially the stuff coming from between your ears," I laughed.

Zaith stuck out her tongue, and then emptied her pack to make room for the firewood before wandering off into the forest.

"Maybe I'll find some of that spiky fruit you discovered – I'd like to see you catch that when I get back!" And she disappeared.

I shook my head, poured a cup of water and walked over to Dez. I jumped.

He lay there, watching me. I wanted to run over and crush him in the biggest hug, but I stopped the impulse at the irregular beat of my heart.

"You're awake. How do you feel?"

He gingerly massaged his neck with one hand as he used the other to steady himself, trying to rise.

"Well enough to travel."

I shot him a dirty look.

"The last thing you'll be doing is walking. You nearly killed yourself pushing too hard for too long. I didn't know if we were going to be able to revive you. Tell me, how do you expect to save the world if you can't even take care of yourself?" I challenged, anger biting at my words. That was the last thing I expected to hear coming out of my mouth.

He laughed.

I scowled.

The low baritone of his voice shielded his weakness, but was still detectable in his drawn face and taut features. Sitting down beside him, I helped him find a better resting position before handing him the cup.

He glowered at it and swished its contents. "This isn't more of that poison you women have been forcing down my throat is it?"

"No, you big baby. It's just water. But that reminds me…" I pulled out my knife and the verrin crystal. "Hold out the mug."

"Why? More nasty medicine?" he joked.

"A dash of verrin actually. Something I found after our little swim."

"Don't waste it on me, we might need it later."

"And when exactly would be a better time than now to use it? Just give it here." Holding this vein of hostility helped me keep a clear head. I had to focus on the mission. We had a quest to complete and idle nonsense could kill us.

He obliged and held out his mug.

I scraped a few flakes into the water until it glimmered pink. "Drink up, we need you healthy and you're not there yet."

He snorted into the cup, mid-sip, his eyes smiling back at me. There was more going on in that brain of his than worry over what I put in his drink. *How much does he remember? Will he chock it up to delirium like a good prophet or does he actually believe I'm someone I'm not?*

Putting my things away, I retrieved three photographs from my pack. I spread them out across his lap. He set the mug aside.

"Well, I recognise this one," he said, lifting the least worn of the images and placing it in his breast pocket. "But not these." He looked at me.

"I found them among Doire's possessions. I kept them from you. I don't know why. When I saw the photo you put away just now, I knew I had to show you. The little girl is unmistakably the same."

"Your Doire, Master Desert Dweller, is my Matheson—"

"Your soul mate's banished father," I finished for him. *My own mind finally settling on one point – why an architect would be wandering around in the Deserts.*

I refocused on Dezmind. He had such a strange look in his eyes when they met mine – glassy, happy-sad, and reaching for my soul. No matter what he thought, the man in the photo was not my father. I knew my parents, and that just made my reality more depressing. "Here. You keep the pictures. I don't think I need to worry about finding his kin after all," I said quickly, averting my eyes.

"No, I guess not," he muttered, placing the worn old images with the faded one in his pocket.

"So, tell me Taya – what have you discovered? Zaith mentioned you needed to talk to me. I've noticed there's something in that pile of stuff you look at every time you pass by."

"Hold on there. My story's likely to be longer and significantly more intricate than yours. There's a lot you need to know, but not before you tell me how this happened," I said motioning up and down his depleted body, more so to buy myself time than anything else.

I had yet to organise the mass of information I was safeguarding, although I was interested in the motivation behind his self-abuse. Sighing, he closed his eyes for a moment.

"I knew you'd follow me in, scared as you were," he said, opening his eyes and searching my face for a negative reaction.

"I swam as hard as I could," he continued, "waiting for something to happen. Totally unprepared for what did." The fingers on his right hand massaged the skin behind his ear.

"The pain ripped through my nerve endings as the flesh behind my ears blazed." He let his hand fall to his lap. "The burning just went on and on. I don't remember when I stopped using my lungs. I just felt everything pass over and through my marks." He took a sip from his mug.

"I swam and searched through that stuff until a crack in the ceiling caught one of my fingers. I checked it out, following it as it widened to a sizeable fracture in the rock above.

"Figuring it was the way out, I swam up and into the crevice until I reached a small rocky chamber. I was expecting some kind of grand discovery or giant vault containing the Chronicles – but there was nothing. No majestic hoorah, just a space. I looked everywhere; I couldn't believe that was it. I managed to move part of a rock pile sealing off the only break of light I could find. I hoped it was a neglected passageway – I mean, the Chronicles had to be there, right?

"I crawled from a small rocky area jutting up from the soft pink sands of the same damn Desert that had swallowed us whole. I couldn't believe it. I knew I must have missed something – we were in the Pit after all."

I tilted my head and smiled at his dramatic touches – he'd never have admitted defeat. He rubbed a hand over his face and continued, "Looking around, I saw something on the horizon – the outline of a city. That had to be where the Chronicles were. So, I ran through those awkward sands as best I could." He paused. "But they were just ruins; old lodgings of an even older world. I wandered the streets for a long time. Was this a sign, a message of futility? I yelled at the Ancient City for not giving me what I needed. Then, as I kept wandering I caught sight of a rock-arrow just outside the city walls.

"I knew it had to be a sign from you – that you must have swum past the crack and found what I couldn't. I thought that since you were willing to sacrifice yourself in the silk-sands, you realised what was at stake and went on without me." He quieted then. Looking down, he ran his hands over his face again but this time up through his hair too.

"I should have known you still didn't accept what the Kahn-lea are – were – trying to do. I thought you were ready to die for our Cause – but no. That's not how you saw it at all, was it? It was the job, your contract that you clung to and the promises you made." The timber of his voice was soft with a hard edge at the same time, like the whisper of a knife blade into his heart.

"It wasn't until I'd crossed I don't know how many different Desert- zones when, at the perfectly crafted staircase in the aerial caves it hit me that you hadn't been there at all. Why would you take the time to carve out a ladder in the rock? With your training, you could have scaled it barehanded, I'm sure. All of a sudden the reality of what I'd done crashed in on me. You weren't there... here. I should have known that, for you, this journey was never about what we would find..." He paused.

"Needless to say, by that time I was exhausted and desperate for something to drink. I stumbled down the hill over there." He pointed behind me. "I was hoping to find verrin or water but I was done by the time I reached the boulder. My legs gave out on me and I dragged myself into the shade to die. I lost all hope of finding the one person I needed most to get me through this," he said.

My chest tightened. *You're such an idiot. That's why you hired me in the first place – to be here for you.* I knew he was exaggerating and sloughed-off the compliment by analysing the facts; he'd left the kerchief there, found shade, and lowered his heart rate. Still, I knew what he meant. I'd been that hopeless once and the idea of death has a way of suffocating you, breaking your spirit.

We sat, silent, shoulder to shoulder – just breathing and listening to the distant birds. It was some time before he spoke again.

"Yet, here you are. I underestimated the power of your devotion to your word – to your work. You know, I researched your background after our *introduction* at the Rally. Your superiors warned me of your *flexible* interpretations of contracts. I was even told of the Ethics hearing, but not the details – so you can understand I had my doubts you'd stick around. I also knew there was no one else to accept the contract."

I was right, he hadn't given me up at the Rally – but who else could have known it was me? Who would have told the Master Keeper? I could've walked away from all this if I hadn't been on probation... but then, the Chronicles exist after all. I do believe that this is exactly where I need to be...

"You were right," he broke into my thoughts. "I should have trusted you. Doubt in your ability is what makes the contract weak, not the lack of your will to follow it through. I thought you were just showboating at the Rally, giving me a hard time at the restaurant – I've learned a lot from you, Taya, working with you out here." I felt the telltale heat of embarrassment creep up my neck and into my cheeks.

"You promised to keep us alive – to my knowledge, you've done exactly that. And really, that's what I clung to. It's all I had left. For nearly a day I lay through a rainstorm waiting for you to show up and yell at me for being an idiot." I smiled and bumped his shoulder with mine playfully. He'd learned a little something about me after all. "Luckily, the last time I consciously opened my eyes I knew I'd be safe – you were looking back at me."

Something restless stirred deep in my stomach – I wanted to punch him and hug him all at once, but I didn't do either. I sat there, looking into the surrounding forest, green life bursting around us. Finally, I stood up and looked back at Dez.

"I found the Chronicles," I whispered, and disappeared from his sight.

Returning, I held the orb in my arms. I set it down between us. It took no less than ten minutes to describe my terrifying ordeal: the disturbing flood of memories during my unconscious state, the sheer climb of pure will over impossible odds, finding Zaith, and the breaking of the code during our search for him. I even drew him a picture of the Heniths we rode to track him down, since Zaith had Doire's latest note book at the moment.

Then, I slowly turned the orb to the double parallel lines etched into the metallic object. I read for him the words written so long ago, in a time of such pain and despair.

"On the eve of the twenty-first Alpha cycle in the seventh month of eighteen yearly supporting the maximum light from Gamma, a celebration of solar rebirth and regeneration must commence. The particle generator located at the base of the Canopy Goddess must be ignited when the sky is absent of the twin light during the second hour." I didn't dare look up from the orb. I remembered my own confusion at this point, so I read on.

"The regeneration cycle must be maintained at least once yearly. In recognition of the orb's regenerative capabilities, the Dakturian settlers of this world adopted a monthly schedule in the hopes of new life and new land development, for the eventual expansion of our race elsewhere on Xannia." I felt him stiffen beside me and risked a glance. His eyes looked at me but he wasn't seeing me. I licked my lips and continued.

"It is essential to this world's survival that the Solar Orb – Gamma – be maintained and cared for regularly. Its very composite requires respect and reverence as we mourn the premature passing of those citizens whose forefathers made it possible for this colony to survive and thrive on new land." I had to stop myself from reading too fast. I wanted the insanity to be over, to be a lie, to be anything but the truth – and I could only imagine how Dez felt listening, learning.

"Gamma was carefully designed to be a self-contained solar unit. Metlemar Netlek's vision enabled us to create the embodiment of a sun without the egregious effects that a nuclear mass would bring at such close proximity to this world. He and three great scientists: Deniadrek Plenni, Suerainin Beldanis, and Tchertok Ramnar, worked on a theorem to alter the apparent resting state of metallic matter from our home metal, Kieumnium, into a regenerative active state.

The results of this active state would allow the metal to form a protective shield around a small nuclear mass projected into orbit. Its high-grade illumination and terra-forming capabilities were for the future of our people."

Every time I read about the terra-forming I shuddered and thought about the void under the Temple in the Ancient City, where the pure verrin should have lapped up to the plateau I'd climbed – of Professor Denali's research and his findings about the desalination of verrin into water – the fact that there seemed to be no verrin in this alien forest. I stumbled over the next line.

"Th-the only flaw in Ramnar's eventual breakthrough was that, without yearly regeneration, the seal of the Tchertokium, the shape memory metal, would degrade causing micro-fractures in its membrane. Should this happen, it would allow harmful x-rays and radiation to reach the surface of the planet. Extended exposure and continual neglect of the membrane will lead to an environmental disaster, causing severe land disruptions, inflicting permanent damage on all life forms." *The end of the world.*

"The activation sequence for the particle generator is marked uniformly around the perimeter of the device. In order to find the Great City of Augitmein, follow the path of the first solar rising into the shadow of all living things – a rock formation that touches the sky and severs the land. One must follow the steadfast beacons to meet and scale this natural creation. At the falls of Essence and Renewal, the wings of the Kiki will lead to the Goddess' resting place – for this plane of existence and the next. The song of those now silent surrounds the Well of Regeneration and the source of continuing celestial peace in the Dia Quadrant."

A large bird cawed overhead. The leaves above us rustled in the breeze, and the long grasses in the clearing swayed with the wash of the wind. Every thought I had been fighting and pushing aside – wanting to share but not daring to, flowed between us like waves crashing against a rocky shore.

"These – these aliens, they all died," I whispered. "An incurable Virus swept through their cities in under year.

"I found a journal written by one of the last Dakturians. They formed a search party and met up with our early ancestors in the Ancient City shortly before the great migration.

"I'll leave you with my notes – there are a few passages in particular you'll want to read. I think you'll learn a little more about why Talians are so different from the rest of us."

His face remained blank. No trace of emotion.

The impact of this knowledge had been severe on my schema, but Dezmind came into this with so much more at stake, so much hunger for truth. I'd been happy enough to support the government effort, I'd always believed they would find a solution to the quakes and the climate change. But if they were lying to themselves about their own past in order to maintain genetic superiority, the well of deceit ran deeper than even I guessed.

And yet, some part of me knew that they'd forgotten, that they strove to forget why they kept the ancient artefacts Dezmind found. At some point in the history of the Kronik it hadn't been about absolute power – it had been about ruling for the betterment of the people; something Dezmind's race forgot about when the last of the pure-bloods died. I was sure of it. That Seer set Dez on this path for a reason I was certain only he could understand.

"I'll catch up with Zaith. Maybe she's found that fruit."

And I left him, with half a cup of verrin and a world of trouble on his mind. I knew he would need time. *Time to think. Time to breathe. Time to form his own conclusions, laugh until his sides hurt and bleed tears. His truth would be his pain and our salvation. He won't have as much time as I did to comprehend it all, but it'll have to be enough.*

I felt better now, in a way. I'd held this information inside for so many days – struggling with the reality of it. Now that Dezmind knew, a suffocating weight lifted from my chest.

Listening for Zaith working in the woods, I walked up the side of the long hill. At least, there on the plateau, I would be able to enjoy the rest of the morning. Breakfast, it seemed, could wait until I'd studied the landscape one last time before leading us toward the Great Alien City of Augitmein.

Approaching the crest before the plateau, I caught snatches of Zaith's voice but as I started to call out, the words died in my throat.

Chapter Twenty-nine
Skeletons in the Closet

Fragments of hurried words spoken in hushed tones reached my ears as I walked up the hill. Creeping around to one of the rockier bracings of the plateau, I settled to listen behind a few large boulders.

"I repeat: the Gamma sun is fraudulent – the reconstruction of a small-scale compact nuclear combustion enclosed in an alien shielding device. This device is failing. Without a way to regenerate this solar orb all hope is lost."

I never told her that.

"As for the conclusion on the matter of Jutaya T. Fyce – I must concur with Council that she has indeed come to show herself as the threat so outlined in Pact Agreement 4 1 7 8 and, therefore, must be eliminated."

Eliminated?

Zaith? But–

I shook my head and rolled silently onto my knees. Skulking low around the edge of the boulder, I kept to its slight shadow. I locked both eyes on Zaith.

Zaith, the Betrayer…

She clicked off the mini-disk recorder and knelt to rummage through her empty pack. The sound of a zipper from the base of the bag sliced the air. Her hand emerged clutching a small mechanical device. Glinting dully in the mid-morning light, she opened a tiny compartment. Setting it in her lap, Zaith removed the micro-disk from her recorder.

It was a mierimek, a metal version of the small, delicate, red and black culturally protected bird. The compartment she slipped the disk into was the belly of the device. I watched as Zaith pried back its little metal head and turned a key-crank inside.

The gears of a perpetual motion system turned as its paper-thin metal wings beat with a hum. Zaith closed it up, and pointed it northwest before lightly tossing it into the air. As it flew out into the Deserts, I could only think of how such devices were scoffed at in my circle of trainees as they read from the pages of the Local Inquisitor – a tabloid newspaper snuck into the Facility.

My blood surged. Fire raced across my cheeks.

Zaith's an imposter – a sleeper agent for the Kronik. She lied about our friendship, she lied – she lied about everything! Anger flashed white hot behind my eyes. It consumed me. It controlled me.

Eliminate me, will you?

I sprang out and pounced.

Silent as a mountain lynx, lithe as a threstix, and faster than a Henith; I crashed into my prey.

"Traitor," I growled into Zaith's ear. "Who are you working for?" I spat and shook her by the collar. I had ignored all the signs: that day at the Facility, her excuse for not joining the quest, arriving in the Deserts 'just in the nick of time,' even the supposed report I overheard at the Temple – all lies.

Zaith's surprised eyes shadowed as her training kicked in.

"You know nothing about it," she barked. Zaith reached under my body and pushed me over – threatening me with a hunting knife, double- serrated for a clean kill.

I caught Zaith's blow with the light-tube. The casing shattered. She twisted and sliced at me a second time. I counter-manoeuvred, catching her head in the vice of my legs – switching places yet again. Zaith kneed me in the back, rabbit-kicking me into an outcropping of rock. My skull cracked against a boulder as it whipped back from my shoulders. I slumped, winded, fighting for consciousness and blinking through the pain.

Zaith hopped to her feet. I kicked out my legs.

She crashed to the ground.

Shaking off my nausea, my head still ached, but I pounced again. Clutching Zaith's ribcage between my knees, I slammed her arms down over her head onto the ground. Pounding the knife out of Zaith's hand, I smashed my forehead into the traitor's nose – squeezing her ever tighter. Blood poured from her nasal cavity as she twisted to reach for something suspended around her neck – inches away from consuming it.

I released an arm and snatched the chain.

"No!" she screamed. I jumped up, kicking her in the stomach. I looked carefully at the charm suspended from the chain and snapped it off. Inside the little metal heart rested a tiny capsule with a thin purple band. I shook it and a powder of fine particles shifted inside.

I shoved it under Zaith's nose, "What do you want this for?"

She snatched at it, her face and hands smeared with blood from her nose. I kicked her again. Breaking open the capsule, I scattered its contents to the ground.

Zaith shrieked.

Her eyes followed the fine dust as it drifted to the grass. Turning her chin to her chest, she held her arms over her face. Lying there, she hugged herself, shaking as she sobbed.

I'd never encountered a blubbering foe before. If I'd been Taya – Contractor, and Zaith had been Best Friend – Reporter, my heart would have shattered. Instead, my eyes now clear of the lies, all I saw was a weeping deserter bent on destroying my life – although that didn't make it any easier to deal with.

But why?

"Who are you?" I said. Zaith continued to cry. "Who are you?" I snapped. The sobbing grew louder. I sprang on her. Wrenching her arms back, I held her against the nearest boulder.

"Who are you?" I growled.

"Just kill me. Get it over with. I can't go back – just kill me."

Something's not right. She should be begging for her life, not pleading for her death. I released her. Moving back slightly, I rested on my haunches, ready to strike. Perhaps another question might goad her into talking.

"Why do you want to die?" I said evenly.

Zaith's tears waned but she breathed heavily, still in pain. Likely her winces were due to a few bruised ribs, her nose should have been numb by now.

Zaith sighed, "If they find out I failed, they'll torture me. They – they'll…" she gulped. "It's said that they keep you alive until only the fear of living causes your heart to stop." Her eyes stayed focused on the ground. Her fingers twitched in her lap.

"Who?"

"My employers," she said quietly, hedging the answer I already knew but needed to hear.

"Why does it matter what you say if you're never going home again anyway?"

"It's–"

"And don't say it's your training."

Zaith shook her head. "It's what you'll think of me."

What?

"What are you talking about? Why should that matter? A moment ago you wanted to kill me."

"If I really wanted to, I could have – any number of times, both you and Dezmind."

"You were gathering information – you needed me – us – alive for some reason," I countered, balking at the thought that Zaith cooked our meals and helped nurse Dezmind back to health.

"My job was to verify information, not gather it. My employers have known about you for a very long time, Taya. You've been tracked and watched and studied since before you were born."

"What? Why? There's nothing special about me."

"Ohh, but there is – to them anyway." Zaith gasped as she tried to sit. I released her arms.

"Again, I ask, *who?*"

Zaith paused and pursed her lips.

"The Kronik."

I was right. *Zaith is another sleeper agent.* Standing up, I paced as I watched Zaith. My mind constructed one barrier then another, not wanting to processes the relevance of her employer in my life.

"What's your mission?" I stepped in front of Zaith.

She sighed again, "After the death of my parents, I was approached by a secret division of the Kronik, an agency created for the capture and recovery of someone important many years ago. My parents were the product of this secret service and remained under their command after most other agents had been officially disbanded."

"Why?" I asked, crouching again.

"Because they were among the few who eventually found this special fugitive. They were thought to be competent. You were somehow connected to the original search and so their new assignment was to keep track of you.

"You were linked to a possible crisis, so you retained the Kronik's interest. When I took over, I was told only what I needed to know; the rest I picked out from conversations in my presence or documents I deciphered from my father's private files.

"There was something wrong with you – or rather, there was the potential for something to be wrong with you. I had to watch for abnormal capabilities, bizarre markings or any alterations to your outer appearance."

I looked at my hands. The thin black outlines around my red coliths were suddenly glaringly obvious.

"My parents' records showed that you were capable, but basically normal as an infant at the adoption agency–"

"I'm not adopted – you've got the wrong person." Something inside me released.

Maybe all this is just a misunderstanding, an oversight.

They have the wrong person.

"Taya, do you honestly think your biological parents would have abandoned you like that?"

"What do you know about my parents? Something happened after Blain was born – something snapped."

"Yeah, snapped into place: why were they spending all that Foster Care income on a child who wasn't even theirs?"

"No–" I shook my head.

"Taya, my parents received a letter. I found it in the encrypted documents about you; it was from the Society. The gist of it read, *make sure no one finds her, maybe she'll just die.*"

Silence hung thick as fog in the air between us.

"But you didn't. You did the one thing that's continually kept you alive – you went to work for the Kronik. You laboured in the mines for years before enrolling with the one institution where differences like yours are celebrated and rewarded. A Contractor is expected to go above and beyond the standards of commoners – they are expected to excel in the service of the Kronik, and you did exactly that."

I looked at her, baffled.

"Your speed, your agility, your sensory perception – I was to track the abnormal excess of all these things, but no one questioned them to your face because you were being trained to use them on behalf of the very institution that previously wanted you dead.

"This excursion was to be my last mission. If, in these extreme conditions, in an outstanding circumstance, you went beyond all expectations – I was to intercept you and interpret your actions before sending word to the Kronik – if I found you in breach, eliminate you."

Zaith threw her hands into the air, hopelessly, wincing slightly. "We could have remained friends until the end of time, but you had to go prove them right and survive drowning, muscle exhaustion, and extensive heat exposure. You see in the dark when my eyes are blind and you hear things no one else can sense – don't you see? These abilities you take for granted are abnormal. They weren't so noticeable in the Prime when you were doing standard assignments and sticking to protocol. But out here... you passed their tests with flying colours. What was I supposed to do?

"All along I've been trying to convince myself that my job didn't matter, that at the end of all this I would be Zaith – up and coming star reporter, best friend to one Taya Fyce – adventure seeking Contractor. But you blew it for both of us."

I held my head and shut my eyes tight.

I'm adopted? My best friend is a spy for the Kronik. I've had my mortality balancing in someone else's scales for something I know nothing about, all while on a stupid quest to save the planet and the very establishment that wants me dead.

The world went black.

Chapter Thirty
The Root of Deception

A voice came from very far away. "T-ya, T-ya-"
Was it calling me? I tried to push the haze from my mind
to focus on the voice.

"Taya," it started soft.

"Taya," it rose.

"Taya!" Zaith shrieked in my ear.

I ripped my eyes open and grunted.

I lay there, flat on my stomach, sprawled out on the grassy
plateau. Zaith must have noticed me waking, she didn't say more.
Burying my forehead in the soft grass, I clutched at the long
blades, intending to use them as an aid to lift my body. *She's using
disinformation to confuse me.* One hand caught air and fine particles.
My focus shifted to the anomaly. I lifted my chin to get a better look
at the substance in my right hand.

I let the pale granulated particles fall idly to the ground. An
image flashed to mind.

*The Valley of the Dunes – Dezmind's lifeless form – soaring through the
hot air – a flash of light from my Whipstaff, and an impression left in the
sand coated in fine dust.*

"Werks," I said, pushing myself to a sitting position.

"What's that?" Zaith asked, relief flooding her nasally voice.

"Werks, an older chap who worked for the Chalklin Pond as Master Chef."

"Oh."

"He was the one I told you about – the sleeper agent for the Kronik. Only, he wasn't after me. Is that why your dossier changed? They found out his mission failed and sent you in as back up – the only person who wouldn't raise suspicion?" I was on to something. This wasn't about me, this was about Dezmind and the damage he could cause. I lifted a handful of the dust.

"And what about this? He disappeared, and this is all that was left when I went to collect his body. How can a person disappear that fast? I chalked it up to some natural Desert phenomenon, but it wasn't, was it?"

Zaith sat, visibly drained. She'd been beaten, humiliated, and forced to betray her secrets, but I wasn't done with her yet.

Wiping away some drying blood from her upper lip, she nodded.

"Yes, he was a spy. I don't know all the details of his mission, only what I was told to be able to replace him and still conduct my *original* mission."

I ignored her emphasis and waited for her to explain why she was really here.

"When Dezmind left the sanctuary of the Compound, it was decided he was a liability and therefore dispensable. Werks had been keeping an eye on him but he was obviously given the go-ahead to terminate and felt it best to do it out here, away from prying eyes. When headquarters learned of Werks' death I was ordered not to let Dezmind return – at all costs, but..."

"But you believe in him," I finished, recalling Zaith's jubilation at learning that an elite Talian would be speaking at a Cause Rally about the truth. "You still believe in him," I said.

Zaith sighed in resignation. "I thought if I could convince him to stay out here after he'd found what he was looking for – this alien solar regenerating thing you told me about–"

"That you eavesdropped on our conversation about," I said.

Zaith flinched. "Yes. I figured nothing untoward would come

of the excursion; I could go home with you, give my final report, and everything would go back to normal."

"How did they find out Werks was dead? How could they have known he failed? Nothing can be traced, tracked or transmitted through the Deserts."

"Not quite. Remember, it's pockets of dead space. The communication block is caused by the magnetism."

"I thought so," I said under my breath.

"That capsule you destroyed worked on reverse magnetism, the repulsion of atoms. It releases a pulse when the seal is broken. The pulse is received by an orbiting satellite and then redirected to a central database. Within its encryption is a binary code displaying our identification tag.

"If we fail a mission and are compromised, or are simply in mortal peril, we swallow the capsule – and then we're gone. The powder is an acid-based oxidizing agent that takes effect when the seal is broken. The contents dissolve in liquid, or out here in the heavy moisture in the air. The chemicals devour you from the inside out. Apparently the process doesn't take very long," she snorted disdainfully, wincing at her miscalculation, holding her nose.

"So, when you couldn't kill yourself – you wanted me to do it for you, so that you couldn't be found and tortured," I said.

"What are you going to do? I woke you because I wasn't sure how long you were planning on leaving Dezmind by himself."

Dezmind.

This was too much for me to handle right now.

"You can't go back, right?" I said.

"Right."

"Dezmind can't go back, right?"

"Right."

"I can't go back, right?"

"Right," Zaith said, catching the link.

"If we all agree to stay, no one has to die, right?"

"Right."

I didn't like it, but it solved a lot of immediate problems.

We returned to camp and walked into the clearing side-by-side. Zaith carried firewood and sported two black eyes. Luckily, her nose wasn't broken and we had enough sense to clean ourselves up before retuning; I carried spiky fruit and a sizeable lump on the back of my head.

We dropped the supplies by the boulder.

Dezmind stood, leaned really, against his tree watching us approach. We raced over to him. Zaith and I each cradled an arm, sitting him back on the ground before he could get a word out.

"I'm fine," he said, repositioning his back against the tree.

"No, you're not," I said.

"You still need time to recuperate," Zaith added.

When he was sufficiently settled, Zaith organised the firewood and prepared brunch. I was going to retrieve the fruit, but Dezmind caught my arm and pulled me close.

"Does she know?" he asked.

I nodded, wincing at the pain. "Not before I told you. Well, I hinted at a couple of things because she helped me crack the code, most of the rest she found out just now, though I didn't go into detail about the journal." I shrugged. "She's a reporter – I had to give her something to keep her quiet."

He smiled. "She's also your best friend."

I forced a smile for his benefit; an invisible knife ripping open my chest at the thought of the bond Zaith and I once shared. That tie was forever broken.

I turned to leave, but he pulled me back again. "You two look awful. What happened?"

I didn't know what to say.

"Hey Zaith," I called in an overly-friendly voice. "Dezmind wants to know what happened to us."

Zaith laughed a nervous sort of laugh and tossed another branch on the fire. "I fell out of a tree; Taya played hero and tried catching me! Needless to say, she isn't getting a medal for that one."

Dezmind chuckled. I forced another smile before tending to the fruit.

I guess it's better that we wait to tell him – keep him on a need- to-know basis. He's got enough on his plate as it is, what with recuperating and sorting through the truth of the Chronicles.

Stripping first one, then another piece of large fruit from its spiky protective exterior with the blade of my small knife, I licked a trail of juice from my forearm to my wrist; the yellow meat inside smelled sweet and inviting.

After our meal, I had big plans to attend to. It was time to find the Great City, but I needed Dezmind mobile.

Chapter Thirty-one
Follow, Follow, Follow

"This really isn't necessary," Dezmind protested for the umpteenth time that afternoon.

"Have a piece of fruit or I'll find another way to keep you quiet," I said. I'd reconstructed and converted Zaith's cart into a stretcher of sorts. Adding a back support of long, heavy, woven leaves. I extended both the width and length of the flat bed using branches and more weaving.

Dezmind sat with his back to us as Zaith and I shared the burden and pulled him along. He was surrounded by baggage and supplies, not a luxury transport by any means, but it would keep him rested as we followed directions to a city and a generator built over two- thousand years ago.

I reserved the length of rope to employ as an extended twin-pulley. It provided less strain for any one hauler and made for swifter mobility. The only bad part was remaining so close to someone I despised. Pulling the cart was no longer an easy task. Inclines and rough terrain meant two capable bodies instead of just the one Zaith and I utilised while in the Deserts.

After discussing the directions with Dez that were left by Ballen, the Dakturian chronicler, it was at least obvious we needed to stick to our southeast trajectory in order to find the next "steadfast beacon" – the falls of Essence and Renewal. We travelled down a path, if you could call it that, following the rise of the Alpha sun into the depths of the dense forest. I had no idea what the falls of Essence and Renewal looked like, but I figured they'd be grand if Ballen had used them as route markers.

Long after Dezmind's last protest about the cart, I picked up on a rush of water. There didn't seem to be any verrin around these parts, so I didn't get my hopes up. I adjusted our path to intercept whatever water source it was; at least we'd be able to replenish our supply.

Shortly after altering our course, Dezmind and Zaith picked up on the strange sound too.

"But what is it?" she asked hesitantly.

"Probably water. I hope it's the falls we're looking for."

The rushing sound grew louder until it felt as if the roar in our ears had always been there. Breaking through particularly dense brush, we found ourselves steps away from the most awe-inspiring landscape imaginable.

Zaith and I unhooked the lead lines from the push-bar, letting the rope dangle between us. We turned Dezmind's cart around and the three of us stared for what seemed like an age. A majestic, five-storey waterfall tumbled gaily over sparkling black rock and across a causeway of three main tiers, surging down in a ballet of froth, to a pool nearly three hundred yards in diameter.

There was no beach, but there were rock outcroppings of various sizes encircling the dark blue-green liquid filling the pool.

The trees surrounding this area swooped slender, pliable branches with tiny leaves down into the calmer waters lapping against the embankment. Blue-white lacy lichen hung at random from the bows of these graceful trees, giving the area an ethereal presence. But, high atop the peak of the falls guarded a stately bird of gigantic proportions. It was made of the very rock it perched upon. Even from this distance, I could see how each individual feather was lovingly carved and chiselled to perfection. Its head rose up and its long rounded beak pierced the glow of the Alpha sun.

I never wanted to forget this moment. It was an image my heart clung to. There was so much power and beauty in such a small corner of this wide world, I felt honoured to witness it.

"If this is just a route marker, I can't wait to see the Great City," Zaith whispered.

It was almost a shame to pierce the perfect serenity of this special place, but we were all in need of a bath, and an extended soak would do wonders for Dezmind, verrin or not.

As we waded at leisure and cleansed our travel-weary bodies, I carefully monitored the movement of the marine life, scanned the banks, and kept track of the time. We were, after all, here for a very important purpose. Besides, if I let my thoughts stray for any length of time away from the task at hand, doubt crept in. Not about why we were here or whether or not we'd actually find this generator; no, I knew it was out there somewhere. It was Zaith's mission; her insistence that I was wrapped up in this twisted government conspiracy in some way. There was no proof. Only the word of a liar and a Secret Agent sent to kill the man I – no, I wouldn't go there either.

As Zaith helped Dezmind swim smooth, steady strokes on his back across the width of the pool, I searched the cliff-face on either side of the waterfall for a path leading up. *The wings of the Kiki bird will lead to the goddess' resting place.* I made sure to keep Zaith and Dezmind well within sight; there was no way I'd ever trust Zaith again.

He caught me glowering at them once. Well, not *them*, Zaith. I just turned away and didn't say anything. I'd let him attribute it to my early foolishness with Jantice and Tamaine in the Deserts.

I hoped the Kahn-lea were all right. Syvis had a copy of my map with a few notes on springs and edible plant life Doire had found. I could rely on him to get them back home – he just had to get them safely out of the Powder Sands first. I shook my head at the vulnerability of the group and splashed water on my face. I couldn't think about them now. The Chronicles were real and we had a mission to complete – I could trust Syvis to do right by them.

This place was, without a doubt, the falls of Essence and Renewal. That automatically made the statue dividing the water at its peak the Kiki bird. Its wings swept up and back, away from the split in the water fall and the rock on which it was perched. Thus affirmed, our next route lay on a more vertical plane.

At the end of an hour's time, we were thoroughly rested and refreshed. I'd spotted what looked like severely overgrown stepping-stones leading up a gradual, tiered path. It was going to be a rough ride for Dezmind, but a ride it would be. I would rather him have a sore ass and sleepy legs than wear himself out on a climb he wasn't ready for.

He continued to sulk and when I mentioned my observation about the Kiki bird he'd just waved me off and said, "Whatever. I know you'll get us there."

I wasn't going to let his moodiness change my mind. He'd stay on that cart until we lugged him up to the goddess' nose, and he knew it.

Travelling alongside the falls, I used the blade I took from Zaith to cut a path through the overgrown thicket. What shouldn't have taken more than an hour, turned into two, as I first hacked a small path, then helped Zaith lift Dezmind to the next level – hack, lift, pull – hack, lift, pull.

But all our muscle strain and effort were rewarded once we reached a small clearing near the edge of the stream that fed into the falls. Just over a city block's travel to the south, loomed the peak of a great tapering tower, several tens-of-yards above the treetops. Its black colouration gave it the appearance of a shadow.

Fitting really, as we're journeying into the heart of a shadowed and forgotten realm.

The deeper we went into the depths of the lush forest, the taller and more densely packed the trees grew. I continued to utilise Zaith's blade, trimming a path through centuries of overgrowth and neglect. No one spoke. It was not about conserving energy or keeping the small flying bugs out of our mouths; we just had nothing to say. Delicately spired black tower gates appeared abruptly, as a result of the extensive growth in the area. Here, slimmer trees grew where once a transit route had likely thrived.

The gates stood closed.

Fine spindles of what I thought were rock, turned out to be a solid metal, flanked either side of the gates. Each spindle, approximately two feet from the next, mimicked the spire of the tower itself. The expanse these gates guarded spread nearly fifty yards – twenty-five for each wing.

I pushed on one, then the other side of the gate to great resistance. A brief search to either tapering leg of the tower revealed evidence of a wall several yards high which gradually extended lower, the farther from the gate it went.

We could walk around it, but then who knows where we'd end up or how much time we'd waste backtracking.

I returned to the main gate. "There's no obvious locking mechanism. I don't think they feared invasion or conquering. Likely, this is just a piece of art."

I pushed it again. The large hinges groaned, but didn't budge. I relented.

"Zaith, help me out here. I have a feeling they've just lost lubrication. We only need to open them wide enough to pull Dezmind through."

"I'll help," he said, making to stand. Maybe he'd heard the hesitation in my voice.

I turned to him. "No you won't. Who knows what kind of effort we'll need from you to get this generator going once we find it. I'll not have you waste your strength on a silly hunch. We can always walk around if we have to."

Perhaps my demeanour came across a bit on the overzealous side. I could only hope he didn't wonder if I was overcompensating for something.

Settling himself back down again, he crossed his arms, watching Zaith and I struggle with the gate. We focused our combined strength on the right wing. It wailed in protest without budging. Taking a moment to catch our breath, we attacked the left wing next.

It creaked.

It shifted a couple of inches.

Progress renewed our vigour and we assailed the great metal beast with a fuelled frenzy. It helped for me to imagine that it was Zaith's skull I was pushing in. *I am not adopted. I am not on the Kronik's radar. Spies lie. I'm helping Dez, that's why they issued the kill-order. I'm not an anomaly.*

Anger charged my blood when I least expected it, and with no way to expel the rush and keep up the charade, I made the best of this damned situation to bleed my wound.

Ten minutes later, the gate stood ajar. Zaith and I leaning against the now-open wing. Taking a few long pulls of water from our canteens, we pushed off the gate to collect Dezmind. He did not acknowledge our success. Instead, as we pulled his transport on and through, he sat frozen staring straight ahead. I was glad he was miffed at me, then maybe he wouldn't notice my behaviour toward Zaith. I knew I had to keep up the sham, but that didn't mean I had to like it.

"This overgrown path follows the same direction as the wings of the Kiki." I said to no one in particular. Zaith nodded and Dez ignored me. *So be it.*

At first, there was a never-ending stream of trees: thick rough trunks climbing to absurd heights supporting vast upper limbs and a mass of leaves. Gradually, the thick grasses padding our footsteps gave way to satiny black-pebbled rock, worn smooth with age and weather. The cart travelled easily and Zaith silently agreed to take the first shift pulling it.

The tree trunks receded and lessened in frequency even as the full branches overhead grew together, thicker, blocking out all but the thin, soft streams of sunlight smattering the path. The first sign of the lost civilisation came with the appearance of a small, rounded, metallic hut.

From a distance, it looked smooth and solid, absent of any windows or doors. As we passed, we noticed that the metal was decorated with small dents and markings. It stood almost entirely covered in this fashion except upon certain dark, circular areas I could only guess were windows.

"Why don't we check it out?" Zaith suggested.

Dezmind answered, "Anything sealed that tight wasn't meant to be disturbed. It was left that way for a reason."

"But if it's been – what'd you quote, Taya – two thousand years since anyone's been here... what does it matter?"

Dezmind explained as I searched for signs of our destination, "Respect for the dead." He paused. "An enormous devastation racked and destroyed a once-great society. But, for all their advancements, the only cure they would have clung to was the isolation and segregation of those who were infected from those who weren't.

"Not only would we be disturbing the resting place of ancient spirits, but we'd be placing ourselves at risk. The Virus they faced was merciless. It could still be lying dormant in an undisturbed corner of the past, waiting. Do you see?"

Zaith shuddered. "I didn't think of it that way." She looked around with quick jerky movements like a trapped animal.

Soon, the rounded huts became more frequent and more elaborate. We now walked through the city proper. Zaith travelled closer and closer to Dezmind and me on an ever-widening road – waiting for a sign that it was safe to breathe.

Since I had taken over pulling Dezmind shortly after passing that first small dwelling, Zaith didn't know what to do with herself. I ignored her as much as I could without being obvious, but Dez had a keen eye and nothing else to do but observe. I tried to think of a suitable explanation for when he asked me about it.

On the outskirts of the city between the spired gate and the first house, I had noticed various fruit trees and bushes. Those, coupled with the identified 'edible plant life' Doire had catalogued in his last journal, settled my mind on our food supplies.

The river that fed into the falls swung west, away from our destination and I hadn't noticed any other tell-tale signs of water between there and the city. Many of the suburban dome housing had patches of identifiable plant life growing around the dwelling or in clumps, like gardens gone wild. If we were planning on staying here for the rest of our lives, I had to be sure we could survive on the native food sources. I made a few notes in my own book regarding locations to check on later, once we found the Canopy Goddess and the generator. As much as I despised it, we'd need to cultivate several of our own gardens.

The sheer density of the city core was overwhelming. While any one building remained below even the most modest of apartments in Darzeth-Prime, the three and four storey domes looked like mounds of dark metallic ice-cream piled up and crammed side-by-side. Open shop windows lined the lowest levels of these hulking buildings with what were likely many levelled apartments above for extended family living. Quite frankly, they reminded me of space ships written about in children's stories. Who knows, maybe that's exactly what they used to be. The Dakturians didn't just blink their eyes and appear here one day; they *arrived*.

Abruptly, we came upon a stupendous glimmering, bubbling fountain adorned by yet another majestic Kiki bird. We'd reached the centre of the Great City. Who knew over what vast land the original colony had spread, but here – I felt sure – was where it all began.

Stopping just short of the large babbling fountain, I surveyed our surroundings. We stood on the same worn, black pebbles that started near the gate with layer upon layer of domed store fronts and apartments reaching up into the high cover of the trees but not breaching them. There were several gaps between buildings – some wide enough for a couple of riders to pass through as they might on the streets in the Prime but others looked only big enough for one or two people to walk between.

It was time to communicate. I put on a good face and forced some energy into my voice.

"Zaith, why don't you and Dezmind take a look at these buildings; likely we'll be bunking down here for the night."

Zaith looked hesitant. She knew I didn't really want her alone with Dezmind but I didn't want her coming with me either. I'd made it obvious enough for her to read my body language. Our fight on the cliff-side plateau destroyed everything between us. I could finally see recognition of that fact in the set of her mouth and the tilt of her head when she looked at me.

Our pact to remain here and live was a logical conclusion, not an emotional whim as she had hoped. She got used to living a double life once before, she'd just have to do it again – this time without a best friend.

"Don't worry, they look like merchant shops, and besides, they're wide open to the Common here. There's one more clue to deciphering the whereabouts of the generator – I'm going to explore the area and check it out."

"The song of those now silent." Dezmind recited from memory. "I'm coming with you." He made to stand.

"No." I stood with my hands on my hips. "I know how much this means to you but—"

"Do you?" Now standing, he leaned against the handle of the cart.

His words in the forest as he described his journey alone ricocheted around in my mind. *For you this journey was never about what we would find...* but he knew that wasn't true anymore, right? I held the proof in my hands, read in the words of an alien language long dead. I believed now – we had a chance to do what was right, fix what was broken when no one else could. I tried to convey all this in a look but he refused to meet my eye.

"Dezmind, you feel stronger right now, but your time alone has taken its toll. If we find the Well of Regeneration, the generator, and you collapse—"

"Call out if you need us," he said cutting me off.

He dropped back down onto the cart with his arms crossed over raised knees and turned his head away from me. Zaith pulled the cart and Dez over to the nearest building. I touched the peak of my cap in salute, and then set off down the cobbled road before he changed his mind and followed me anyway. He looked as though he would run down the road with me. The only thing keeping him with Zaith was knowing I'd find a way to make him stay put.

I knew I'd said the wrong thing again, but what I wanted to say wasn't meant for Zaith's ears. I wasn't even sure it was meant for mine, but regardless, it would have to wait.

The burbling of the fountain was far too loud for me to hear birds calling to one another from the treetops. The orb mentioned following a song. I didn't know what else could be singing in this desolate place.

The farther I walked, the quieter it got and the smaller and less dense the buildings became – though none nearly as small as the first one out by the gate. They were clustered together, ranging in shape and style – another suburb. I gazed as far as I could down the road. Other, narrower streets branched off the main one. It was eerily silent back there, all alone.

But I don't want to be alone. My thoughts breached forbidden, half-formed, and discarded ideas. *If we're staying here forever, Dez will never find his Soul Mate. Lynnia moved past the death of her Soul Mate and had a child with Doire. There's obviously a connection between us, maybe we could – maybe there's some remote chance that we might...* but I couldn't go there, couldn't make that leap of faith; couldn't live with the thought that I would perpetuate a lie. *Zaith is wrong, Dez is deluded. I'm not the one.*

The oppression of my thoughts collided with the heavy air and increasing density of trees. An absence of wind left trees lifeless and still. Boughs were barren of songbirds. The humidity climbed. A thin bead of sweat slipped down the side of my nose and over my lips.

I stopped moving, closed my eyes, wiped away a trail of moisture – maybe sweat, maybe not – and waited. Not even the hum of insects or the patter of animal paws broke the weight of this soundless place. But I was close.

Something thrilled inside me.

My heart climbed ever higher toward my throat. Clearing my mind and deepening my breathing, I shimmied my shoulders to relax my muscles from my forehead right down to my toes.

I stood that way for a while. Behind the dark of my eyelids, I could sense only space – where it was filled and the absence of something. The soft whisper of a breeze kissed my burnt and peeling cheeks.

There it is!

Like an undertone in the air currents, a soft, far-away tune played at the edge of my hearing. I snapped my eyes open.

Turning, I sprinted southeast in the direction of the unknown sound. Careening around lone buildings, I scrabbled over the walkway intent on finding the source. The echo of scattering stone clattered with every stride, until tall grasses pushed up in patches as the road thinned.

Buildings disappeared into the background. Tree trunks grew more tightly packed, though still large. Hanging mosses, lichen, and lolling branches choked the light streams until only a haze illuminated long-used animal paths under the thick boughs.

The faint sound dwindled as the breeze broke, but did not falter entirely. The more dense and overgrown the trees and bushes grew, the more reassured I was that the sound actually existed. I crashed through a high hedge of obstinate branches – and into a world of sleeping spirits.

Here, layers of leaves blocked the direct suns' light. Instead, a filtered pale green haze floated as though suspended in time. The cooler air of this protected place caused light wisps of moisture to cling in patches to the tips of long, thin blades of grass blanketing the ground.

The trees were easily the oldest I'd seen yet. Enormous trunks of shadowed wood dug deep into the ground with massive vine-like roots. Layer upon layer of heavy, solid branches flooded the view of the sky with pale blue-green leaves. Here too, lichen clung undisturbed in great wisps of purple, blue, and smoke- grey.

But there, in that intimate clearing surrounded by aged trees, stood one alone whose bark was heavily scarred by a millennia or more of growth. It stood twice as grand as any other tree, boughs blacker than ebony, leaves deeper and richer in their tones with a powder- blue dusting. The branches spread out and intermingled with those of the other trees; it covered more than half the expanse above the clearing.

Even more amazing, though, was the very source of the sound that had called to me – thousands upon thousands of wind pipes suspended in clusters or hung solo up in the trees. They were strung from branches and attached to poles driven into the ground near the base of the trees. Filling the space, they looked like raindrops frozen in mid-descent.

Another breeze brushed past my cheeks. This sacred place danced with voice and song, harmonising its choral tones – like an ancient dialect sprung to life calling from beyond.

One delicate pipe twirled in circles from a nearby low-hanging branch. Its solo, higher pitch drew me to it. It nearly touched my brow. Its rotation slowing with the ebbing breeze, I could just make out something inscribed down one portion of the barrel –

'Maenene,
1st Born, House of
Qualyn ~ 7th Generation'

Memorial Grounds – I shouldn't be here.

But just as I thought it, I caught sight of something metallic hidden amongst the overgrown grasses and mist. I cautiously walked toward it, crouching low, feeling as though thousands of eyes bore into my soul, demanding to know the meaning of my presence.

Approaching the spot where I saw the flash of metal, I realised that short, thick green mosses covered an area spanning close to twenty- five yards in diameter. I lightly brushed aside the grasses and uncovered the outer rim of something nearly two feet high. Tracing my hand around the edge, I felt something cool and solid. Bold swaths of writing marked the exterior of the ring.

I looked directly overhead at the treetops –

Or, is it Canopy?

An identical circle, without windpipes, showed me what I could not see from my former vantage point.

This is the answer.

A distant cry rang out. It had to be from the Common.

I jumped to standing. *Sister Zita, don't tell me she's killed him!* Several other cries followed. I tore away from my discovery. Racing, I sped back to Zaith and Dez.

Chapter Thirty-two
An Unexpected Surprise

I shot past trees and skirted around dwellings, bursting breathless into the Common. Dezmind and Zaith stood surrounded by a mass of people.

"Jutaya!" called a voice, "You're safe too!" Tamaine's voice filtered over from across the crowd. The circle of bodies split, widening to a crescent. I walked, dumbstruck, to stand with Dezmind and Zaith.

"I was just introducing them to Zaith – after the initial shock of the gathering of course," Dezmind said, beaming. His flock had been returned to him.

Four different conversations were going on at once. My head spun.

"Syvis!" I called.

The others quieted. He stepped forward.

"Here."

I locked eyes with him.

"And why exactly is that? You should have taken these people home."

A rise of muttering and gruff contesting settled only as Syvis explained.

"We were going to return. In fact, we were just settling the camp for a day's rest when Raylan caught sight of a figure moving toward the path we'd fallen from. I asked him to take Deltek and look into it. Fifteen minutes later, they came back with a report of footsteps in the sand.

"Not knowing what to do about them, we held a meeting in the tent to confer on our next course of action. Again, we were divided. So we sent a small scouting party ahead as the rest of us ate and slept. I stayed on guard until the volunteers returned the next morning.

"The footsteps, it seemed, travelled to the edge of an old city. The Ancient City, Merik pointed out. It was decided then that we would travel at least as far as the ruins before planning our next step. If the footsteps, by some miracle, belonged to either of you – well, we had to be sure.

"Once there, we found two sets of footprints leading out of the City, past an arrow made with rocks. It was agreed that the two of you survived the fall and likely made it through the Pit of Chance during your travels back to the surface. Lutrice pointed out that if those sands could envelop a small cave, then why couldn't they cover a Pit? Raylan noted that you'd probably convinced Dezmind to leave us if the Chronicles said to travel on.

"So, seeing as this entire journey was brought on by our belief of the truth in our fate, we decided to follow you – why else would you have marked your path if the anticipation of our arrival hadn't crossed your mind? Besides, the map you gave me showed that we were nearly out of the Powder Sands. Once we got packed dirt under our feet again, the extra four days of travel were relatively easy. We even found another spring. We're out of food now, but judging from the vast growth of this place, I'm sure we can restock without a problem."

I smiled ruefully, astounded by the tenacity of these people. Looking into their waiting faces, I was taken aback at their dedication to Dezmind and their belief in the Cause. From day one they trusted him, believed in his mission and desire for the truth. Even Zaith's faith had never wavered.

"That was my friend Zaith you saw checking in on the camp. She was searching for Dezmind and me. She decided to follow us the day after we left, when she finally got permission from her boss. You see, she's a reporter."

I took a deep breath and did my best to condense what seemed a lifetime of experiences into a simple, straightforward account of what happened.

"To put it plainly, yes, we did fall into the Pit, but we were separated. I managed to find the Chronicles. I stumbled upon Zaith, and together we tracked Dezmind across the remaining Deserts.

"He's still recuperating from considerable dehydration. Even so, we've managed to decipher the Chronicles. They led us here, to this place, to complete an important task described in their writings." I looked at Dezmind trying to decipher just how much to reveal.

"Dezmind will explain the contents of the Chronicles to you in greater detail tonight, but right now we need to assess the situation and get ourselves settled. We can't relax just yet; time is no longer on our side. I located what the Chronicles wanted us to find, but now that you're here, we'll need everyone's help to get it operational." Dezmind's eyes held mine. His silent questions would have to wait.

Taking advantage of their confusion, I divided them into three groups without receiving any complaint. Zaith took a renewed Jantice and Tamaine scavenging for food. They brought the bow, the larger knife and several packs to fill with fruits and plants.

I took Raylan, Syvis and Deltek to fill the several kegs they'd brought along – the basin of the fountain in the Common wasn't large enough to accept the bigger kegs, so I had to bring them to the water source. The hauler and AHT were left at the base of the cliff with the rest of the kegs, near the arrow. We'd likely leave it there until a scouting party could be formed to bring back whatever was portable. One thing was for certain, we were going to be here for a while. Two assassins and a two-thousand year old secret did not bode well for any of us.

I left Dezmind with Merik and Lutrice to scout out the buildings in the area and gather up whatever materials they could find to use as tools and general resources.

As the men and I walked, the humidity remained, making the air moist, but the canopy of trees kept us sheltered from the suns' hot rays. Everyone pitched in to organise a working settlement, with dinner to look forward to.

I knew the Kahn-lea would be eager to learn about the Chronicles, just as I was sure Dezmind and Zaith were stewing to hear about my discovery.

The men followed me, each carrying an empty keg. *I can't believe they're actually here. It's just my luck Zaith was spotted. Still, other than the risk of heat exposure, the few remaining Deserts we crossed were relatively monster-free. I haven't read enough of Doire's later notes to know for sure though. At lest they made it without incident.*

Syvis cleared his throat – twice, "Um, Jutaya?" He caught up to me. "We're going to the falls, right? There's nothing closer?"

I didn't look at him. "I don't know, Syvis. We've only been here for maybe an hour and my top priority when we arrived was to find what we came for. There's a working fountain in the middle of the Common. Zaith's smaller kegs will fit just fine under the spouts in the basin. It's easier for me to look for a stream or river later, on my own."

"Wouldn't the four of us be able to cover more ground?"

"Syvis, if I wasn't a Contractor, I would agree with you. But the simple fact of the matter is—"

"That you're a selfish woman who doesn't know how to use her resources," Raylan growled.

"Wow, now big guy." Deltek said. "There's a lot on everyone's minds right now and you can't take to heart Jutaya's words. She's explaining the best she can. Be patient. We don't know what they've been through." Raylan huffed but stayed quiet.

"Yes," I continued, "I don't particularly care to relive the near- death experiences I've had to deal with. Dezmind is the storyteller. As I was saying, I am a Contractor and while you may be unfamiliar with my specific capabilities, you should know a little something about the profession. Needless to say, I can hear water moving at greater distances than you could cover, with three times your ability to run. I'm not here to boast, I'm just trying to explain why it's more efficient to leave the tracking to me. Now, let's focus on getting what water we can in order to be comfortable for the next couple of days."

Syvis dropped back to walk single file with the others. Passing through the black gates, the rush of the water from the falls hovered above the sparse trees. My rigid back and fast pace kept me out of further conversation.

Why did fate bring them here? It's bad enough that I'm stuck with Zaith for the rest of my life operating an alien generator. When am I supposed to get these people back home? Their lives are intrinsically tied to ours now and we're all facing a death sentence. If the Kronik want Dezmind dead and me by proxy, the same holds true for these people. They know the secret.

Chapter Thirty-three
The Cycle Continues

That's right. Two self-supporting ladders that reach the canopy and one to span them at approximately twenty-five yards," I said.

Syvis looked at me, perplexed. I'd led him along an invisible path into a desolate area of the dead city.

"With the less than basic tools we have, it'll take all day to build solid, reliable structures," he said.

"The day is fine, and if you follow my directions, it'll just be time-consuming and not laborsome. Take all the men along with you and create an assembly line. It won't be that bad." I stopped walking and stood beside a lone dwelling near a copse of trees – the edge of the dense foliage I'd raced through yesterday. "Meet us here when you're done. Call out and I'll bring everyone the rest of the way in."

Taking in his surroundings, Syvis fell into step beside me, heading back to the Common. "Dezmind and the women will be with me on site. We have to prepare the grounds for your arrival this evening." I patted him briefly on the shoulder. "I realise how overwhelming this is – just remember, you were able to bring the Kahn-lea halfway across the Deserts. This should be easy in comparison. I know first-hand how difficult they are to keep in line." He nodded, smiled and jogged ahead to gather his team, along with the few useful tools found the day before.

When I returned to the Common, shortly after Syvis, I signalled to Zaith. She came over to where I stood by the gurgling water fountain. Her mouth was set and her forehead furrowed slightly. She stood with her arms crossed, just as I did. This didn't look good, so I forced myself to punch her on the shoulder and stood beside her with our backs to the fountain.

I leaned back and rested my hands on the edge of the basin. Zaith did the same with an uncertain glance – she wasn't sure if I meant the friendly greeting or not – if I'd started to 'come around' and accept that she had only been doing her job, just as I was mine. I don't know how she managed to delude herself so willingly. It only left me more saddened at our loss than angry right then.

"I think we should tell him now," I said.

"Why? It'll just upset him. He should be focused on the generator, getting it running again. If we tell him about the Kronik now, he'll get distracted."

"Zaith, the man's life is on the line. He's not going to stay here forever." *He has a civilisation to lead and a Soul Mate to find.*

A keg clunked against the other side of the basin. Zaith and I turned to look. Dezmind was walking away from the slowly filling canister to gather the troupe of women together. I looked at Zaith. *How much did he hear? Maybe nothing.* The water bubbled and gurgled out of several spouts surrounding the central fountain, it might have been enough to cover our conversation.

"Don't say anything," she said. I sighed in frustration and went to join Dezmind while Zaith grabbed the canister. As I approached, the eyes of those in our little group glistened and moved rapidly in spurts of nervousness. Their faces clearly stated that they still weren't sure if this was an ongoing dream or not.

The previous evening, Dezmind had explained everything that happened from the time we woke up in the Pit, to the very point of the frenzied reunion. Everyone was up, long hours into the night, asking and answering questions – even Zaith had played her part, never letting on that she was anything other than a reporter.

Zaith's betrayal, her lies, twisted my stomach and brought bile to the back of my throat. I realised, during the tale, that it was Zaith who'd reported the incident at the Rally to her superiors.

Since the Facility was supported and maintained by the Kronik, the Ethics Committee found out through backchannels what had happened. My skin crawled thinking of the weeks, months and years ahead – trapped. Between Zaith and Dezmind, the spectrum of confusion my brain dealt with wouldn't leave me sane for long.

My shoulders felt permanently affixed to my ears and my back ached from the constant tension. I couldn't wait for the day when I would finally be numb to it all, to the day when we could have an unrelated argument and stop the pretending, stop the lies and face the truth.

As Dezmind reassured the women, Zaith and I grabbed some supplies for lunch. My thoughts drifted back to last night when the orb passed slowly around the circle after Dezmind's explanations. I made my notes available for anyone who wanted verification – only two did: Merik; for posterity's sake, and Raylan; for his own sake.

Since the Kahn-lea had passed through the same Deserts we had, little needed to be said of their unique features, but Zaith offered up the story of the ground-stomp and the hopping water-lizards. Her humour and ease talking with other people who shared her passion for the Cause and the truth, bound her seamlessly to the group as a sister-in-arms. Her description of the Henith corral brought more smiles and laughter. Dezmind continued to make notes and scribble in his journal all the while.

I escorted Dez, Zaith and the other women through the centre of the City to the edge of the dense shrubbery just on the outskirts where I'd shown Syvis to meet us later. We stood there listening to the hollow, serene whispers of the windpipes wavering beyond. I spoke low to the group.

"Don't rush when we enter. Pace yourselves and speak quietly. There's no sense disturbing its rest until it's absolutely necessary. Dezmind and I will enter first then I'll come back for you. When everyone's present, I'll show you what I need your help with."

Dezmind walked slowly between the women, from the back of the group, toward me. I warned him not to over-exert himself before it was necessary, but he refused to be dragged around on his cart today. He was among his people now and he had an image to maintain. As we slipped through the brush, I reached for his arm, but he shifted it and caught my hand in his. Boughs bent gracefully aside as leaves caressed cheek and chin. My spine tingled, but not from the haunting melody of the grave markers.

We stood shoulder-to-shoulder under the boughs of the Canopy Goddess the great ebony-barked tree. Our breath flowed in and out, in time to the beat of our hearts, in time with each other. It was the strangest sensation. I could only wonder what thoughts reeled through Dez's mind. This was the most sacred of places for his ancestors – ancestors not of our world.

He turned to face me and clasped my other hand. Raising both to his chest, the space between us evaporated.

"Do you feel it?" he whispered, touching his forehead to mine. *Feel what? Confused? Excited? Delirious? Lost? In love? The last time we were this close I nearly lost my mind… what am I to lose this time?*

"Dez–" *I'm not who you think I am.* The walls shot up around my heart. He jolted back as if he'd heard me, released my hands, and turned to face the Goddess. I shivered. I shouldn't have been cold.

I turned and left him standing on his own. I was not the woman he'd searched for in his youth and as much as I wanted to, I couldn't pretend that I was. Quiet gasps expounded as I returned with the women through the tall mist-laden grasses. I led them to Dezmind and the ring of low green mosses.

"We need to uncover this site. Position yourselves equally around the perimeter and work your way toward the centre. Try not to rip or tear up the mosses. Instead, pry them gently away – work at making a clean surface. When your pile warrants it, spread it evenly beneath the large black-barked tree over there." I gestured toward it.

"The Canopy Goddess," Tamaine whispered reverently.

"Dezmind and I will work on deciphering the inscription around the frame. Don't rush. Zaith and I brought lunch if you get hungry – the others won't be finished until close to supper anyway.

"Remember, you can speak, but softly – this used to be a place of celebration long ago. A few light words and some pleasant conversation might help ease the tension." *Or it might not.* Dezmind refused to look at me.

No one said much at first, but as the minutes dragged on, one brave voice spoke up; Lutrice. "The moss seems to have woven in amongst itself. It's surprising how soft and spongy it is, yet it's almost like little sucker feet on the roots that grip the metal."

"Yeah, you can't just pull at it from the top," Jantice remarked. "But the weave is so tight it's hard to get my fingers at the roots." She favoured her wounded arm, but still said nothing of the incident to anyone. Her demeanour had changed since her recovery, even toward Tamaine, and I wasn't sure it was for the better.

"You almost need to tease it up, like volumizing hair," Zaith offered. "Then I'm using my fingertips to massage the roots before I slip my nails underneath."

"Hey, yeah. That works," Tamaine said, lifting up a clump of moss.

It was surprisingly peaceful listening to them chatter – as if the trees embraced the new life. Dezmind worked directly opposite me. He'd spent much of the previous night with the orb, Ketic's journal, and my annotations. I may have been 'the chosen one, granted the sight of old' but he was making damn sure to use my notes and study up for the big day. We made separate analyses, slowly and methodically, moving clockwise around the ring several times.

A series of formulas and instructions on opening the aperture of the generator gradually built structure within my mind. A completely separate set of figures appeared to describe the steps for activating the generator – which had to be done approximately two hours after the setting of Beta.

After an hour of deciphering this early dialect in the language, I sat back on my haunches and looked at Dezmind. His head was down as his fingers traced over the carvings. Opening my mouth to call his name, I startled as he looked up at me. Startled by his intuitiveness, I motioned behind me with a tilt of my head. We stood, meeting by the bushes where we'd entered.

"What do you make of it?" I asked, sitting beside him on a

moss- covered log. He linked arms with me. Tilting my head, I squinted a second silent question at him.

"I'm a bit unsteady," he replied. I didn't believe him and yet part of my brain said that it was entirely possible.

He was different.

He'd settled something in his mind during the last hour scrutinising the alien text. The air between us softened. It was a comfortable compatibility but different from the one we shared in the Deserts.

I'd never felt this before and didn't have time to analyse it. "Two sets of instructions, yes?" he said.

"Definitely," I replied. "The script is an even earlier version than the orb. It took a bit to work through it. What did you come up with?"

Dezmind ran the fingers of his free hand through his wavy black hair. His skin, extremely pale of late, shimmered silver in the misty half-light. "One set describes how the generator needs to be re-sequenced every hour until Gamma *passes below the Canopy Goddess' embrace*. But I don't think we'll see any progress until after it's been activated regularly for the next month – even then I'm not sure if there's any permanent damage to the membrane around the nucleus."

"Yes, but first we need to activate the iris the second hour after Beta sets. There are so many calculations that need to be taken into consideration–"

"Did you bring your notebook? It'll be better to write it out than trying to re-read it off the ring's edge while we work tonight."

"Yeah, I brought it." I hesitated. "How long before it has a global effect, do you think? I mean, healing Xannia after it's healed itself?"

"I honestly don't know. I hope the super quakes will stop in a week or so, but it'll take several years, maybe even dozens of years, before the environment finds balance again. This technology is beyond anything I imagined and the terra-forming element is troubling to say the least."

"I guess it'll be the same before Professor Denali's research becomes obsolete, then. I just hope people realise that it was your vision that healed Xannia and not some stuffy, ignorant scientist working in secret for the Kronik."

It wasn't a fact but as far as conspiracies went, it made sense. The Kronik would want to control all information related to the source of the environmental disturbances. They wouldn't allow Denali to fracture civilian life but they would want to know as much about it as possible to try and fix the problem. That seemed to be their approach with all things, covert and controlled.

"I mean, his theories are sound – it's just the idea that the Kronik is secretly funding his research for their own endgame that makes me so furious."

"Denali? Isn't he the one who was nearly exiled because the Kronik thought he made up his research results? How do you know him?" he asked.

"Doesn't matter – it was in another life."

"You're being evasive again."

I smiled. "Yeah, I guess I am. I worked with him for three weeks out in the field. In fact, I quit the Contract with him the morning I first introduced myself to you with my plasma gun."

"Ah, yes, the Clinex episode at the Rally. It seems like a lifetime ago. I'm surprised the Facility let you get away with that – walking off a job I mean."

"It seems that trying to shoot you with a Facility-issue weapon was the more newsworthy of the two incidents. While I don't think they would've been happy that I left Denali's employment, I think they would have ultimately understood. Being the youngest Contractor to ever graduate hasn't made me exactly popular. Not that it matters now." I bit my lower lip and slipped away from his warm body before I said too much. I retrieved my notebook from one of the picnic packs.

By mid-afternoon, the aperture was clear and the sequence for the generator identified and recorded. After resettling the space, we returned to the Common to help the men with any finishing touches needed for the ladders – and to prepare an early dinner. Likely the guys would be ravenous.

But, as my group walked back up the black-pebbled path in

the lilting shadows of the branches, we discovered that the men were already done.

"We're thinking of going for a quick swim, did you want to join us?" Merik offered, after taking a swig from his canteen.

The women were anxious to go, and the men were done ahead of schedule. "All right," I agreed. "But only for an hour. We'll have an early dinner then move on to the next phase of preparation." *Before the twin lights are shadowed.*

I wished we could have spent the rest of the afternoon lounging in that water paradise. Raylan and Merik caught fish for dinner down an adjoining stream while Deltek and Lutrice found wild fungus matching a description in Doire's guidebook. The soil here was rich and fertile. I'd have to enlist their help with tilling a few gardens before I found a way to get them home again.

After a sumptuous meal, that even Raylan agreed was sufficiently filling, the group manned their three ladders and marched toward the Goddess' Realm. The guys were forewarned by the ladies about the sacred nature of this space, and I reinforced that, while we were conducting an extraction, we were in no way to destroy its splendour. Our task was two-fold: it would serve as a means to a very important end and would restore function to beauty.

Tamaine took Merik's arm, Lutrice took Deltek's, Jantice took Syvis', Zaith surprisingly took Raylan's, and I linked arms with Dezmind, following the others through the shrubbery and into the memorial garden. We carried the ladders in our free hands.

Entering the space, the men felt the presence of thousands of silent beings, for on this night the air was calm – absent of the usual ethereal whisperings. The women and Dezmind stood a little taller and breathed a little deeper. The two-foot high metallic ring and aperture of the generator stood low and clear of moss and grass, a poignant reminder of the long-awaited close to this erroneous quest.

"Set them up on either side of the generator. Be sure to span the middle ladder across the greatest height possible. Utilise us whenever you need to, otherwise we'll stay clear of your work," I said in my strongest voice, though my nerves refused to settle and my stomach threatened to bring back my meal. It was like waiting to go on a date for the first time – or so I assumed. Had I considered having a life outside my duties, things may have been different between Tek and me – but that was long ago and far away.

Dezmind took the opportunity to be involved. His idleness of late made him fidgety, if not downright impossible to deal with at times. He suddenly looked strong and healthy, more vibrant even than that first night in the Deserts. To watch him hauling, lifting, and interacting without a trace of excess effort to belie his ailment – gallivanting around the site unaided – it was no wonder the others thought me overly cautious. I caught myself staring, and got back to work.

But maybe – just maybe he really is fully recovered. Maybe there's something in that alien blood of his that enhances recuperation.

He faltered in his steps handing a hammer to Syvis.

Or maybe he's just playing it up to save face, putting on a good show for the Kahn-lea? I just couldn't tell.

As the makeshift scaffolding rose, bodies were called in to hold, sit upon, and climb the ladders. By the end of it all, two people sat on either lower leg of the supporting ladders – utilising four bodies in total. One person sat at the very top of each A-frame, and another out the rear of the extended cross-section. That left me and Dezmind to climb up opposite ladders with the cutting utensils to prune the central area above the aperture.

"We should start a few feet from the ring of memorial flutes. We don't need to be tidy about it, just delicate. The last thing I need is to be haunted by any of these ancient spirits," I said. Dezmind balanced on his shins, legs resting along the width of the rungs.

Reaching overhead, twenty-five feet off the ground, he closed his eyes and whispered.

"What are you doing?" I asked. "You're going to fall."

"It's a prayer. Insufficient I'm certain, but necessary." Lightly running his fingers over the smooth bark of the branch, he caressed each leaf as if lips to a lover's throat. My spine tingled. He snapped the wood.

The crack of it tore at my heart. That first bough slipped from his palm and floated to the ground. The finality of it made me shiver. Ceremony complete, he broke three branches at once snapping me back to the daunting task ahead. Raising my own hands, I cracked three more boughs and let them fall.

As much as I tried to focus solely on the trimming of the Canopy, my eyes continued to wander to Dezmind – to check on him, make sure he didn't grow tired, and for other reasons.

After clearing what we could of the centre of the canopy, Dezmind and I sliced clean the remaining breaks. We'd agreed during the planning stages that what remained after opening up the canopy should not appear ripped or torn. The fine pruning took twice as long as the initial removal, but with only one quarter rotation of the ladders, and Zaith stepping in for Dezmind on my insistence, we completed the endeavour as Beta set. The sun balanced on the horizon when the last of the scaffolding descended to the ground. I pulled Zaith aside.

"I want you to shadow Dezmind."

"Why?"

"He won't last."

She frowned at me.

"He's putting on a good show. You've already stepped in for him once today, I guarantee you he won't make it to sundown."

"What if he complains?"

"Tell him it's for your article, for posterity's sake – we're making history after all, though I hate lying to him."

"All right, I'll think of something," Zaith said, slipping among the deepening shadows to stand almost directly behind Dezmind. He tracked with his eyes the patterns of the shapes we would depress for the activation sequence. Each one was the answer to a mathematical problem etched into the ring. He didn't acknowledge Zaith's presence.

Night fell in relative silence as Gamma's pale light streamed into the new clearing two hours later. Lightly snoozing individuals were roused as movement around them quickened with anticipation.

Dezmind stood opposite me, once again. We had to depress the same symbols at exactly the same time in the predetermined sequence – and I wanted to get it right the first time. We called out simultaneously–

"Sigma–"

"Theta—"
"Omega—"
"Delta—"
"Pi—"
"Alpha—"
"Beta—"
"Gamma—"

A deep groan beneath the ground switched to a churning and hissing as invisible cranks moved gears in chambers somewhere below.

Gradually, the symbols flickered then glowed with a faint white light. The aperture split across its diameter. It steadily pealed back like the lid of a closed eye. The thunder of it rumbled through my bones and chattered my teeth.

"Now!" Dezmind called over the sound.

Time for the second progression. One word to sequence —

"I – l – l – u – m – i – n – a – t – e," we called in unison.

An echoing clunk reverberated among the trees. A brilliant light, a thousand times more intense than any known spotlight, broke free. It sped trillions of illuminated particles toward Gamma, the pale solar orb currently encircled by the ring of boughs freshly opened in the canopy above.

I put on my tinted dive glasses and still had to squint. Those who hadn't brought their eyewear along shared with others or snuck peaks between fingers.

It was truly magnificent.

Chapter Thirty-four
Man on a Mission

I slept late the next morning. Rolling idly onto my stomach, I opened my eyes to an empty sleeping mat and footprints in the dust. Other than the stairs and a double set of open windows flanking the door, the expansive main floor where Zaith and I bunked held nothing more than a large worktable and some chairs. Zaith had chosen this place for us the day before, until further exploration could be done. I would have preferred sleeping under the stars, alone, but it was probably better I stayed close to the Betrayer.

Zaith had kept her word so far, and in some small, dark place, I knew she wasn't a risk to anyone anymore. She seemed genuinely prepared to start a new life out here. Things between us, however, would never be the same.

Zaith had taken over from Dezmind after three hours of maintaining the Light Sequence. He'd wanted to finish the last hour but exhaustion claimed him. Instead, he led the others back to the Common and got them comfortably settled for the night. By the time Zaith and I returned, morning was six hours away and the darkest hours of twilight reigned. My eyes were weary after such a long, bright night. Likely, Zaith would need to take shifts with Dezmind before he'd have the stamina to work a full cycle.

Pulling myself up, I walked to the round metal table on the other side of the room. Zaith had left a brief message written in the thick dust: *Hunting for lunch – back soon.*

Smiling grimly, I sat in one of the four round-backed chairs surrounding the table, and picked up Zaith's hairbrush. I indulged in a moment of quiet contemplation as I fixed my hair for the first time in what seemed like an age.

After wandering into the Common, I took a quick drink from the central fountain and refilled my canteen. Deltek and Lutrice had thought to bring my backpack and Doire's satchel along when they scaled the aerial caves. It was a good thing.

Our engineered verrin drops would last us a while but not forever. Doire's stock of verrin crystals would come in handy. I spotted one of the thick, orange- skinned fruit near a pile of unopened spiky fruit – *I really ought to give them proper names* – and had a light snack.

The day of the Kahn-lea's arrival we'd dragged a bunch of tables out of the shops in the area to circle the fountain and act as a central location for food, tools, and other resources. It became our hub, just as the fake fire had when we were out in the Deserts.

It's awfully quiet around here. Poking my head into Dezmind's dwelling, I saw a few tidy pages stacked on his table, undisturbed. One sheet sat apart from the others with a stone paperweight holding it down. Curiosity got the better of me, so I snuck a quick peak.

It was one of the maps he'd drawn, back when we first started on this journey. Except, where he'd neatly printed *Pit of Chance* he'd scored through it and written *The Amphitheatre*. My eyes drifted to the stack of pages, likely the notes he'd written and referred to throughout the quest. I slid around the table to look without disturbing them.

I snatched up the pile. *Is this what he's been doing?* I rifled through the pages. I wanted to believe that I didn't understand – but I couldn't. They were sketches: a cheek, a shoulder, a braid, an eyebrow – individual aspects. I didn't need to see the last complete image to know who had captured his eye.

Me.

Zaith's voice shouted in my mind, "You're adopted!" *Was she telling the truth after all?*

Dezmind's voice echoed, "It's always been you." *Was his delirium at the height of the fever actually a result of something he'd already discovered? Already knew that I didn't?*

Zaith's voice penetrated, "My parents helped intercept the fugitives... tasked to keep an eye on you." *Lynnia had been captured outside an adoption agency...*

Dez, "The Oracle was wrong once before, why not a second time?" *If Lynnia could have a child with another race, why couldn't his Soul Mate be a half-breed?*

Zaith, "We could have stayed friends, but you ruined it all."

Zaith never intended to kill me – she wanted it to be a lie just as much as I did but my strength, my hearing, my night vision, all of it meant so much more.

The Kronik secretly watching me, my foster family running away from me, the Ethics Committee putting me on probation right when Dezmind requested me as a guide into the Deserts: I could no longer call these coincidences. I stared at my hand holding the sketches, the bronze skin, red coliths, and that faint black outline around each one.

What race was Matheson Doire? His ID badge and the family photo were faded and dull. He was clearly not of Jeridan, Nirian, or Metek descent but that left four other races to consider. *Dez truly believes I'm the lost child – Lady Lynnia's forbidden offspring. Why? What more does he know that I don't?*

I had to find him.

I left the hut and passed through the Common. He wasn't there. *Maybe he went for a swim?* I walked to the falls.

Striding past the last dwelling before arriving at the gate to and from the City, I met Merik as I hurried down the winding path to the falls. He nodded a greeting. I nodded back. Then, a thought struck me.

"Hey, Merik. Do you have a moment?"

He turned. "Many moments actually. Which one would you like?" He smiled.

I smiled back. "You mentioned spending a great deal of time

reviewing Xannia's history. Did you happen to study much about the Ancient City?"

"Quite a bit actually. I did a number of papers on the topic. What do you want to know?"

"Well…" I folded my arms. "Are there any records of the citizens building or using an amphitheatre or coliseum?"

His eyes lit up. "It's a wonder you should ask. Dezmind spoke with me early this morning on that very topic."

I quirked an eyebrow and cocked my head to the side.

He continued, "There was one natural structure they used, very much like an amphitheatre – I was actually hoping to catch sight of it as we passed through the outskirts of the Ancient City."

"Why the outskirts?"

"Well, it would have been too big to keep a place of that magnitude in the middle of the city. Besides, it was only used twice a year."

"I see. Why was it so important that you spent time researching it?"

"Its purpose was purely functional. The Ancient Elders would hold 'The Ceremony of Truth' there. It was a large enough space to accommodate the entire population, and everyone was expected to attend.

"At the crossroads of a citizen's life," he quoted. *"The roads of Fate and Destiny must be appraised before the Truth of one's life can be revealed.* It was spiritually and politically based. No one could be considered for the position of an Elder until they first bared their soul to the congregation. The current Elders would identify for that individual which aspects of their life happened for a reason, and then guide them toward understanding the truth of their destiny."

It keeps coming back to the truth of fate and destiny.

"It was mandatory for every citizen to endure this before entering their late ageing process. The idea was that their spirit would be at rest during and after passing, but it could be done as early as the age of twelve and as often as life presented trials that couldn't be understood. One time of the year was set aside for the mandatory ritual, and the other was made available for any citizen to participate if they wanted advice.

"They interviewed no fewer than twenty Truth Seekers at every mandatory gathering, and generally saw well beyond that during the volunteer gathering. One of my papers focused on the kind of advice given and whether there was a pattern or a prerequisite the Elders followed."

"What did you find out?" I asked, suddenly needing to know. This sounded so similar to Dezmind's Oracle and the foundation of the Talian culture that it couldn't be a coincidence. That and a few phrases he translated from the Tablets made me wonder if there was a connection.

"That every case was indeed unique. Even those who presented similar life trials seemed to have very different destinies to follow."

I considered what he said for a moment. "Were there any rituals observed using verrin?"

"Yes." He looked at me quizzically. "The details have been lost but there was a rite of passage that was connected to a sacred verrin site."

The pool we found. "Thanks, that was helpful." He turned to leave, but I asked, "Have you seen Dezmind recently?"

"Not since this morning."

I nodded my thanks and continued down the path to the falls. My mind raced.

It fits too well. Almost perfect in fact. The Pit of Chance – three Trials – a natural structure large enough to accommodate the entire population. It was all linked.

That, coupled with my memories as I floated trapped between two worlds, and Dezmind's insistence that the Oracle held the answers to his future, explained what the Pit of Chance truly was. But how could the Oracle know Lynnia would betray their race and still give birth to a daughter? *She wouldn't have known, so she didn't make a mistake, but she did supply Dezmind with all the clues he needed.*

Where is he?

I searched for the better part of an hour before stumbling back to the Common amidst the commotion of meal preparation.

"Jutaya," Lutrice called to me. "Do you have that herbal list you promised me?"

I ripped a couple of pages from my notebook. "Yeah, here you go. I haven't had time to note where I've seen the plants, but we can go over it after lunch. Have you checked out the wild gardens in the suburbs?"

"Thanks for the notes and no, not yet. But I'd like to hear more about your plans for them. I have a small garden back home. I'd love to help you."

"We'll need all the help we can get, Lutrice. You'll have to convince your husband and anyone else not afraid to get dirty to join us." I made to pass her but turned back and asked, "Have you seen Dezmind?"

"I heard him arguing with Zaith earlier before she went hunting, then I got busy."

"Thanks." I nodded. *Why would they be arguing?* I caught sight of Syvis dropping a pile of dry branches by the side of the fire ring just outside of the hub in the central Common; he knelt to arrange the wood. I joined him.

"Have you been in the forest all morning?" I asked.

"Mostly. Zaith asked me to join her hunting, but I kept scaring the animals away. I went off on my own after that. Figured I'd collect some wood and explore a bit."

"So you haven't seen Dezmind?"

"I thought I saw him talking to Deltek around the north-west side of the city this morning."

"Did Zaith say anything about him while you were with her?"

"No. She wanted it quiet so she could catch stuff."

"Right. Of course. Thanks."

Deltek stood at the preparation table set out as part of the hub. He skinned and filleted fresh fish. I backtracked and walked over to him.

"Try angling the blade so that it's nearly parallel with the table," I suggested.

"Is it that obvious I've never done this before?" he chuckled.

"You have a good blade and you're not afraid to touch the fish – you'll be a master in no time. Syvis mentioned he may have seen you talking with Dezmind this morning."

"Yes, we bumped into each other out and about."

"Did he say much?"

"Why do you ask?" He chopped the head off the next fish, sliding it over to the pile of guts.

"He's being awfully mysterious today and I need to find him. I'm hunting him down, so to speak."

"He was gathering supplies. Those healing flowers, herbs, and stuff. He didn't say much."

Volleying from group, to individual, to group – no one had seen Dezmind since that morning. I returned to his hut – one last-ditch attempt to find him – and there lay the map.

No Dezmind. No pack. No papers.

He's gone.

I raced through the Common. At the prep table, I lifted the lid on the metal box and counted the verrin crystals. One missing. I skirted around the buildings to the side of Zaith's hut. No travel cart. I ran to the central fountain. No mini-kegs.

Dammit! Why now?

I knew what I had to do. Bursting into my shared bunk, I plotted out my needs and resources. Collecting the belongings returned by the Kahn-lea, and anything else I'd accumulated, I packed in a fury. I eyed the orb. It sat on a chair in the far corner of the room.

It'll slow me down. But it's proof... Speed was of greater importance. Dashing for the door, I ran headlong into Zaith.

"What are you doing? Lunch'll be ready soon."

"I'll take what I can, but I can't stay."

"Whoa, what are you talking about – you're not leaving?" She walked me back into the room.

I don't have time for this. "I can't find him, Zaith. He's going back. We should have told him the truth – about everything."

"I know," she said, her voice tight.

The argument. "Lutrice said you two argued this morning. Why?"

"He wanted to know what was wrong."

"Wrong with what?"

"With us." My heart twisted itself into a million knots.

I gasped, "No. Tell me he doesn't know."

"He heard more than we thought at the central fountain yesterday. He wanted to know what happened between us."

"What did you say?"

"That it didn't matter so long as we didn't go back."

"Dammit! Zaith. The second you tell that man he can't do something he'll do the exact opposite. We don't have weeks to keep him here and convince him not to leave any more – he's gone. The last time anyone saw him was this morning. Don't you get it? I'm half a day behind him. He's walking blind into something he doesn't have all the facts about. The Kronik are going to kill him!"

"But your job is done. If he goes back home, what does it matter? Maybe he won't say anything and it'll be all right," Zaith tried to convince herself as well as me.

"Because of us, that man's life's in danger. I swore to protect him. I saved him from Werks, I saved him from you, and I'm damn well not going to let him walk into a trap now. Not when the truth is so close. Besides, I think he's planning something. He's following the words some woman prophesied of him as a child – I should have known from the start that he wouldn't have stayed, even if we'd told him," I realised.

He'd sensed the tension between Zaith and me – saw that something wasn't right and knew who was the weaker link between us to confront. Then there was his calm acceptance at the generator, not saying anything when Zaith shadowed him or took over the sequence – I closed my eyes and shook my head.

He didn't want me to stop him. He knows I'm the only one who could.

"They'll kill you, Taya." Zaith's words brought me back.

"Is my life worth more than his?"

"We need you here – I don't know these people and we have a generator to keep running. Do you realise what you're leaving behind? What you're risking by returning?"

"I have to leave. I have to know the truth. Dezmind said something I would have disregarded as nonsense if you hadn't told me I knew nothing about my childhood."

"Oh, so now it's my fault? Who's to say any information I was given was the truth? I've worked sliding between lies and deceit for most of my adult life."

"So I might not be adopted?" I accused.

"Well…" Zaith faltered. "No. I'm pretty certain you are."

"Do you know who it was that signed my life away? Who my real parents are?"

"No. That was privileged information."

"Therein lies the crux of my problem. My whole life has been a lie and the one man who seems to know more about me than I do is walking back home to his death."

"What does it matter now? The only problem I see is if you leave, the next time we'll meet is in the afterlife! I bet Dezmind knows Werks was an operative of the Kronik, not at first but after, you know? He's not an idiot."

I shook my head; deep down, Zaith still thought things could go back to the way they were. I took hold of her shoulders and looked her in the eyes.

"I have to know who I am before I can even begin to understand why I'm here. It can't be a simple coincidence that the very paths I chose in life were the only ones that could have kept me alive. The missing piece of the puzzle is back there – with Dezmind and the Kronik, so there is where I have to go."

"I didn't think you believed in all this destiny nonsense," she countered.

"I didn't believe in the Cause or the Spoken Truth either, yet here we are, standing in a house made by an alien species, on the brink of rejuvenating a fake sun that we never would have come to rely on, if they hadn't bothered to settle on our planet in the first place. Something big is about to happen and Dezmind's in the middle of it. He needs me. And I need to know."

I walked past Zaith and out into the expansive Common. My actions drew curious stares from different members of the Kahn-lea. I filled my pack with whatever food I could find already gathered at the hub, remaining steadfast in my task. When I turned to go to the falls, Merik blocked me at the edge of the Common on the road to the spired gate.

"Where are you going?" he asked, the joviality we shared earlier gone. A crowd gathered. Zaith remained on the outskirts.

"To find the truth about my own destiny and to save an idiot," I said. Understanding registered in his eyes.

Raylan shouted, "You can't just leave us here – abandon us – I'm going with you." Several other voices joined his, until a commotion erupted. I climbed up on a large boulder by the path.

"Listen to me," I said. Several voices quieted, but other remained angered.

"Everybody, listen." I commanded.

The reality of Dezmind's decision to return struck me anew. This was never just about saving Xannia from tearing itself apart – it was about saving the citizens. The Kahn-lea were merely a microcosm of the society he meant to bear witness to – to tell the truth to. *Why didn't I see this before? He was always going to go back. The mission didn't end here. The Oracle foretold…*

The voices ceased.

"You can't go back," I said. I still couldn't bring myself to temper the truth.

Raylan spoke first, "What are you talking about?"

"Jantice, what does she mean?" Tamaine fretted. "I'm getting married next month!"

Syvis asked, "Jutaya, what's going on?"

I held up a hand to silence them. Vicious glares and tear-streaked faces stared back at me.

"At least, not yet." I took a deep breath to steady my nerves. "Dezmind's in danger. Zaith brought me news that a spy from a secret society organised by the Kronik wanted to silence him for good.

Dezmind was not supposed to return home – ever. He – we – were never supposed to get this far."

"Werks – he worked for the Kronik?" asked Deltek.

"That's right," I said. "Werks was the person Zaith mentioned; only she didn't know he was no longer with us."

I glanced over my shoulder, down the path to the falls.

"We kept this from Dezmind hoping he'd want to stay here, in the safety of this place – watch over the generator with our help. But now he's gone home to finish his mission and fulfil his destiny. He means to expose the Kronik and spread the Truth of what we've learned. Anyone he's come in contact with is at risk of being killed too."

Gasps erupted from the group. Tamaine wept freely. Jantice held her tight.

"But there's still hope." I reminded myself of Dezmind now – here I was trying to give them an ounce of ground to stand on, something to grasp hold of in the face of adversity.

"Dezmind truly believes in the prophecies of the Seer he told us about. Completing this quest was just one phase of a plan he's had tucked away in the back of his mind for several years. Think about it – about the stories by the campfire." I paused.

"My decision is final. I'm going back to warn him about the Kronik, and help him if I can. We will send for you when it's safe to come home again. "Right now, what you need to do is learn about the generator from Zaith. She's going to stay here and help you. Explore the city under her guidance. Learn all you can, stay safe, be well, and keep hope. We will return, but now I have to go."

I jumped down from my perch. Zaith stood face-to-face with me. I pulled mine and Doire's notebooks from my belt-pack and gave them to her. I had memorised them long ago as moments in time and pictures scanned by my brain. I just never trusted myself with the knowledge until now. She strung her full canteen around my neck and it rested beside the smaller one she'd given me back in the Ancient City. I turned and ran down the path – never once looking back.

Chapter Thirty-five

Back

Five days later, I crept along a back road to an alley that would lead me home again. The pitch black of twilight fell over the Prime an hour ago, but I remained on full alert – watchful of myself and my surroundings.

The low-rise apartment buildings near my house absorbed the shadows cast from street and building lights. They dulled my vision and amplified my footsteps. It was a good neighbourhood, but there was so much at stake I couldn't take anything for granted.

The only chance I'd taken was travelling into Vrazeth, the town bordering the Expanse, before Beta had set. I knew I couldn't afford to wait until the fall of Twilight to catch the public transport; it went through town before Gamma's dominance. Waiting would have set my timing off for reaching Darzeth-Prime in total darkness.

As much as I wanted to find Dezmind, I was exhausted. I would confront him in the morning. Likely he was using the Chalklin Pond as his base of operations again.

There'd been no evidence in the news, electronic print, or on the wire about his return or any arrangements for a Rally. He'd need time to reach out to his supporters and make plans. That wasn't likely to happen at the end of the day with the grime of travel on him and weariness in his bones. I should know, having kept pace with him the whole way back.

Weary, my feet ached and my body pleaded for more than three hours' rest. The thought of sleeping on my own soft mattress, or even just falling onto my couch and closing my eyes with Jadis at my feet, drew me on through the last leg of my return.

It took ten days to reach the Alien City, and find the generator; our homecoming was cut in half. No longer required to look out for anyone but myself, riding the Heniths through two of the Deserts, and only sleeping for the minimum three hours, helped me gain momentum. But Dezmind had also found the Heniths, and must have cut time by skipping several watering holes marked on his copy of Doire's map.

Since I only had the two canteens, I was forced to track down every spring and reliable food source. I was never more than an hour or two behind him – the fresh footprints at various landmarks throughout the Deserts said as much – but gaining even that much ground was enough to wear me down.

I scooted silently between my house and Mr. Kirwik's place, until I reached the side window. The last thing I needed was to draw attention to myself by walking in the front door. I had to be fast. My alarm delayed for one-minute before arming the silent warning and then the audible alarm. The second I cracked the sill, I'd be on the clock.

Reaching into the leg of my boot, I pulled out my Whipstaff. I aimed a thin ion beam at the space between the windowsill and the frame – right where the lock was.

A quick flash. The energy rope licked out. The lock released.

Pushing up the window, I threw my pack inside. Springing onto the sill, I balanced on my stomach before sliding in. Jumping to my feet, I ran to the front door. Entering the code with one hand, I used the other for the palm display. The counter reset at twenty-five seconds. My knees wobbled. I rested my forehead against the cool wall. *I'm home – but where's Jadis?*

Grabbing my pack, I slid the Whipstaff back into my boot. The digital clock on the coffeemaker glowed pale blue in the kitchen. My stomach growled. Opening the fridge, there was nothing but energy drinks. Opening the cupboards, there was nothing but nutrition bars and coffee beans. Real food would have to wait. My legs would take me no farther. I dropped onto the couch. Jadis lay curled up at one end resting on her large paws. She lifted her muzzle as I dropped the pack onto the floor and lay beside her.

"I'm home, Jadis. Yes, I can hardly believe it myself. And you know what?" I asked, giving the Lynx a thorough scratch behind the ears, "You can sleep with me all night if you want."

I stroked her back idly, breathing in the lavender traces of the large animal's shampoo. Any remaining strength ebbed out of my limbs, pooling on the couch beneath me – at least it felt that way. Ignoring my boots, I flipped onto my side, rubbed Jadis' tummy, and buried my face in her thick mane – then I stopped. I ran my fingers over her coat. She gave a low growl. Large patches of fur were missing. The only time Jadis had shown signs of moulting was when a burglar broke into the house last year.

Come to think of it, Jadis didn't run to meet me. She'd have heard me come in – she must have been worried it wasn't me –

"They were here."

Hauling Jadis into my arms, I dragged the two of us over to the window. Setting her down on the floor, I scrambled back through the opening. My muscles screamed. My brain fought against the impending fog of sleep.

"Come," I said, quick and sharp.

Jadis leapt from the sill into my arms. She lay limp and unmoving in my embrace. A red dart protruded from the back of her neck.

"No," I whispered, tearing it from Jadis' unconscious form.

I fled down the back street, tears whipping from my eyes as I slung the large cat around my shoulders and across the back of my neck.

Jadis' chest rose and fell sparsely but evenly.

Now where? I desperately tried to think.

Racing down narrow back allies and up hidden streets, I hurdled small fences and dashed across backyards. No matter where I turned, I knew they were close behind.

I heard the wisp of fabric against fabric, the faint slide of boots running on concrete, and heavier breathing than mine. I didn't know where my feet were taking me. My body worked on autopilot. Street lights blurred as a chill wind snapped at my sun-scorched face. Every time I crossed a major road, I risked being shot.

Jadis was heavy; the extra weight of my beloved lynx reduced our chances of escape. I turned down the side avenue of a posh culinary district, and ran to the back window of a long, low building.

Zapping the window latch, I pushed aside a crimson velvet curtain and carefully lifted Jadis through the opening. The potent scent of roast ganoo clung to the tapestry, invading my senses until the drapes fell shut with the window. I sped off down the side alley of the building.

Dodging garbage canisters, parked riders and bikes, I deked in and around dark houses and tall buildings – running for the sake of running with no clear destination. I jumped onto the fire escape of a low-rise condominium.

I'll hide on the roof.

A hard sting bit my neck.

Everything went black.

Chapter Thirty-six

Enigma

My head throbbed, my back ached, and my feet were numb. A metal door slammed, ricocheted inside my head. I tried to swallow – but couldn't. I tried to move – but couldn't. The haze in my brain thickened – darkness returned.

I shrieked!

My eyes popped open as a second bucketful of icy water crashed down on my head. I tried to move, but my hands were tied behind a pole and my ankles bound straight out in front of me.

Raising my parched mouth, I shut my eyes as a third and final shower poured over me, this time including the metal bucket. It hit my mouth and my lower lip split.

Tin laughter echoed around the room. A calm, deep voice filled the space.

"Got wise, did you?" he said.

I blinked the water from my eyes. I felt it mix with the Deserts' dust and slide down my face. My cap was gone. So were my boots.

A man dressed in grey stood by a table with a black case on it. The grey metal walls surrounding us were pock-marked and stained. The floor beneath me was cold and now wet and muddy.

I saw no door and no body belonging to that voice.

Warehouse district? I tried to jolt my brain.

"Why – Why am I here?" I asked around a thick tongue. More laughter echoed from somewhere behind me.

"Because you're not dead – yet," came the reply. The man in grey stood facing the wall, his back to me. He didn't speak. It was someone else.

"Then why am I alive?" I growled.

"Oh – feisty are you? Good. Maybe this'll be more interesting than I anticipated."

"You haven't answered my question."

"You only get one – and that I did answer. Now, it's your turn." He paused, and then quietly asked, "What is your name?"

I sat, dumbstruck. *What a stupid question.* "You know what my name is," I spat. "Why else would I be here?"

He chuckled. I was tired of his sense of humour. "Yes, I do. Perhaps I need to rephrase the question." He cleared his throat – another long pause. "Do you know what your name is?" he asked.

I sat quiet a moment. "Yes."

Excessive clapping filled the room, bouncing off the walls. "Very good," he drawled. "I'm sure your training never covered interrogation tactics – and yet here you are, doing so well. Although, perhaps you need a little more time to think before you give me your next answer."

A door clanged open behind me. The man in the grey uniform picked up the black case and metal bucket. A second set of footsteps joined his and they walked out of the room. Whatever light source there was shut down.

I was alone in the dark – I hoped. But where was I? And how long had I been out for? Without windows or direct ventilation to the outside I couldn't see or hear anything that would give me a clue. The dark here was absolute. My eyes couldn't adjust without a light source. It was just as bad as dusk – no, worse. Not only was I blind but I was trapped, too. My fingers traced over my bindings.

Standard rope. There were no tears or catches I could use to pick the threads apart and I had no nails left to dig between the creases of the overlapped bindings.

I slid my feet in close to make wings with my legs. I leaned forward but couldn't quite reach the rope on my ankles with my mouth. I shifted my ass to one side of the pole to gain a couple of inches.

Using my teeth, I worked on loosening my bindings and fraying the strands of rope.

Time passed inside an eternity. My mouth was sore. My gums bled. What seemed like a normal piece of rope had a metal core that the fibre strands wrapped around. I couldn't bite through them and I couldn't snap them apart. I spat over my shoulder again. The metallic taste of blood mixed with fibres from the rope in my mouth taunted me with thinking I could have escaped.

I sat.

I stood.

I slept.

I waited.

Vicious blue-white light flashed blindingly bright, out of sync with an echoed ticking from a dysfunctional clock. That started shortly after my failed attempt with the rope. They probably had infrared cameras watching me. The clock sped up and slowed down with no apparent rhythm. The fierce light etched itself onto my retina. Even with my eyes closed, the flashing refused to leave me.

I tried to block out the erratic ticking that bounced off the metal walls of my prison, but I was never able to draw far enough into my mind to block it all out.

There was no way to monitor the time, the eternity I spent alone – was I alone? I couldn't be sure. The flickering room weighed on my patience and my nerves. At every third flash, I tried to use the glimpse I got of the room to build a better mental picture of my cell.

Standing and hobbling around the pole my arms were affixed to, I saw the metal door, a single steel chair in the far back corner of the room, and some industrial ventilation dropping from the ceiling in several places.

Eventually, the bright flashes blinded me just as the black had. I needed to let my eyes rest. I sat down, pulled my knees close and rested my eyes against them. I still saw the echo of the flashing light but in time I knew it would dissipate.

The metal door clanged open. I was ready for him this time. I opened my mouth. Hot, scalding water splashed down, scorching my skin.

"Ahhea," I yelled, then clamped my mouth shut – tongue blistering.

I opened my eyes. The white light flashed incessantly. I still couldn't see.

Another wave and another bucket crashed down on me. I snapped my eyes shut again. My skin prickled, burned. That familiar deep voice echoed in the room – a long low chuckle. Through the slits of my eyelids, I watched the man in grey stand with his back to me beside the table with the black case. My stomach growled audibly. Oh, shut up.

"Three days. In case you're wondering. I'm not often generous with my information, but I've taken a liking to you, Girl."

"Then set me free," I croaked.

"Now don't get the wrong impression, my dear. Freedom will come, but only as a form of release…" He chuckled.

I knew what he meant. As much as I tried to steady my breathing and calm my pounding heart, I couldn't do it. It followed the rhythm of the erratic clock. A sound piped into the room as I never once caught sight of an actual clock.

Tick-tick, tick, tick, tick-tick –

"Shall we skip the formalities for today? Or are you ready to answer my question?"

Tick, tick, tick-tick, tick-tick, tick-tick, tick, tick –

I waited, then said, "In what form are you looking for my response to be?" I coughed. Dry breath scorched my throat. "I've already answered your question as simply as possible and yet it doesn't satisfy you."

"A good question, and one that I'll allow, for it pertains to the matter at hand – which is so very rare that I cannot afford to pass it up."

Tick-tick, tick, tick, tick-tick-tick – Silence.

My eardrums pounded against my skull, trying to make up for

the void left in the wake of the ticking. My breath echoed like a haggard wind.

"I'm enquiring into the name or names which identify you for the person you are. Your formal birth identification."

He came prepared. He'd clearly stated his intensions this time. My mind rattled about in my head, causing me to chase semi-coherent thoughts.

There's no reason why I shouldn't answer – but what if that's the only information he wants to know? Maybe it's a trick or a trap – or maybe if I give up a little bit of information he'll, he'll –

I really didn't know what he'd do, and the stress of the situation combined with my fitful sleep and lack of food didn't help.

"I'm not sure. That's why I came back." Laughter filled the empty space.

I wanted to cover my ears to cancel out the reverberation. It grew like a mass, a physical manifestation that took up and suffocated the space around me.

"Well, now you're just giving information away. Don't get ahead of yourself, Girl. What do you mean you don't know?"

Did I already give too much away? Was I in danger of revealing information about Dezmind or Zaith? Would this somehow get back to the Kahn-lea? I needed time to think. Time to figure out how to get out of this mess. Time; time I really didn't have.

"Who can really say they know themselves before they've found the truth of their existence?" I rasped.

He didn't laugh.

He didn't clap.

He didn't say anything for a long time.

"You speak wiscly. I know you're fighting to choose your words. But there's much to be said for the art of reading between the lines." Tick-tick, tick-tick-tick, tick, tick –

The door creaked open and once again, two sets of footsteps walked out. I looked up sharply, scanning the ceiling before all was lost to the blinding flash of light and the echoing tick, tick.

I noticed an air vent in the ceiling above me. With renewed spirit, I worked at snapping the bonds around my ankles. The metal bit into my skin through my pants and into the soles of my feet. I rocked my ankles to step on the metallic bands and sliced my flesh time and again, in order to find the right counter weight to break or weaken them and crease them in some way.

I buried the pain, knowing I would have to endure much more before I'd breathe fresh air again. Hunger pangs stabbed my stomach. Drawing my legs to my chest, I rested my forehead on my knees. However drained I felt, I would not give up.

There was no way it had been three days. The pittance of water I'd taken in would not have sustained me and after three days without verrin I wouldn't have the strength to stand – Dezmind could attest to that statistic. He was trying to confuse me, test me. The Facility taught me all about testing.

I heard the door open. I still sat in the original position they'd placed me in with my back to the door. This time my knees were together as I sat on my feet. Some part of me knew that the door wouldn't open unless I faced away.

I braced for my 'welcome' drenching – mouth closed. The water hit me square in the face. It was tepid. I licked my lips – a strange aftertaste remained on my tongue.

Tick, tick-tick-tick, tick, tick, tick-tick – The second blast hit.

"Come now, surely you want to quench your thirst, my dear?" came his voice.

I kept my mouth shut as the third wave and the bucket fell on me. "You disappoint me. Here I was looking forward to each new encounter with you – but you've turned the tables, haven't you?"

Tick-tick-tick, tick, tick, tick –

"You're playing me instead of the game – and I don't like it." I sensed a change in the space in front of me when the ticking thankfully stopped. I cracked my eyes open. The man in grey approached, masked with the same material as his uniform. He worked at untying the bonds around my wrists.

"I've never met a subject quite as advanced as you, Girl. The defiance and mental acuity you have maintained inside of a week equals that of a trained agent."

"You're lying. I'd be dead already if I'd been here a week."

He laughed. "What? You think I tied you up without a backup plan? You are naive, aren't you? Let's just say we have ways of keeping you alive. There was more than just a sedative in that dart. But no matter. You've effectively pushed me into this position far sooner than I would have liked – you're stubborn and I'm on a deadline." Relief flooded with the release of my arms – but not for long.

Harsh, cold metal clamped around my burning, and irritated wrists. I shifted, only slightly, to touch the inside of my new bonds. They narrowed to a point, encircling the entire space – not piercing, but definitely sharp. *Some new form of torture?*

"Since you chose not to drink your water this morning – you'll need to take my 'un-inhibiter' another way."

Between the severe flashes of light, I saw the man in grey opened the black case – its contents beyond my view. I knew what to expect. He wasn't wasting any more time. The cuffs were to prevent me from struggling.

"I want answers, Girl. Now, sit tight."

The lights momentarily dimmed to a steady, low wash. The grey man turned to me, holding a small needle.

White spots flashed in front of my eyes. I tried to gain my bearings. As grey Man stooped to kneel within arm's reach of my neck, I sprang up. Jumping, I kneed the syringe from his hands catching his jaw with the bloodied metal core of the rope I'd finally snapped; landing on him, I crushed his head between my legs.

My breath was quick.

My flesh quivered.

My heart beat as if to burst from my chest was the only path to freedom.

The man lay limp beneath me. Three quick, polite claps echoed.

"I knew you had some spunk left. Let him go. I'm the one you want, because I am the one pulling his strings too."

I held firm, reducing his air supply just enough –

"No?"

Silence.

"How many shall I send for then? Do you want to see if you can break the record?" He snapped. "Shall I call for just enough to have them put you in your place? Is that what you would prefer?" His voice was hard.

I've got him on edge.

"Will it be a surprise?" I asked, "Or should I ready myself for a particular combat formation? One-on-one until there's no room left to pile them?"

I worked rapidly to slide the keys from Grey's hand with my bare feet.

"In threes perhaps, so that I can only see two at a time, or will you send in the hoard and give a bonus to the first one who marks his strike?" I barked, kicking the alive-but- unconscious grey man away. I slid up the pole with keys in my hand and adrenaline fresh in my veins.

Silence.

"Or were you only bluffing?" I twisted, striking out behind me as I hugged the pole. I connected full on with another grey man's chest. He collapsed, gasping. My binds clattered to the floor with the keys.

The door shut.

Mr. Voice was gone.

In the space of a breath, five figures stepped from the shadows. They slowly fanned out, surrounding me.

I blinked in rapid succession trying to clear the flashes from my eyes. My knees wobbled as the slices in my feet shot pain up each leg.

The men surged forward.

Darkness descended.

I scrunched my eyes. There was a particular reason I woke up. It was miraculously dark. I rested the back of my heavy head against the pole and sighed audibly. Still stuck. A soft, faint glow above caught my eye; I looked up. My head swam with the rush. I leaned back on the post.

I shivered. My pants had been reduced to shorts and my shirt a torn, shredded rag after the fight. My hands were tied, no, were back in those sharp metal cuffs. I shifted my feet.

They're still free –

I tried to think back – but it hurt too much. My mind refused to focus. My senses dulled.

Maybe, if I close my eyes—

There it is again.

The flickering light reminded me of a spark-fairy, the ones from children's tales; a small creature, helpful to wayward travellers.

"Help me little spark-bug," I whispered.

Something registered at the very depths of my haze – the fairy wanted me to follow it. It was urgent, blinking faintly above in delicate patterns of pale light – familiar, wonderful patterns.

The pole, it wants me to climb the pole.

"That means I'll have to turn around, spark-bug," I whispered.

I spent little time thinking; it only clouded my mind. The image of a diver flashed into my thoughts.

Yes.

I would reverse-dive out of my current position and shimmy up the pole backward.

I lay down flat on my back and rested my head beside the post. I balanced my upper back and shoulders on the floor. Crunching one knee tight to my body, foot flat on the floor, I extended my other leg straight out beside it.

I exhaled.

Throwing my straight leg into the air, I pushed off from the ground with the other leg simultaneously. Rolling from my back and shoulders onto the crown of my head, I pushed up at the same time.

Something popped.

Hot, spiky pain threaded its way like needles through my right shoulder and down my arm.

I didn't falter.

Something kept driving me forward.

Something – or was it someone – the idea that He might somehow be monitoring the room in the dark. That *He* was always watching.

Balancing on my forearms, my legs stuck straight up in the air. I clamped bare knees onto the pole and pushed my torso up. The metal cuffs bit hard into my wrists as I clutched the post near its base.

A trickle of liquid slid down the back of my right hand. The bruises on my arms and legs throbbed in time with the soles of my feet, but I ignored them. Slowly, methodically, I inched my way backwards up the pole – from a springing crouch to a graceful dive, stretch and crouch, stretch and crouch.

As my feet touched something cold, a pair of hands guided them through an opening. I pushed myself the rest of the way up on a slant as my lower body disappeared into the ceiling. I arched my back.

Finally, I was suspended from my back-waist and the cuffs. The helpful hands held me in the tunnel. As I lay somewhere inside the ceiling, my hands still attached to the pole – a long, flexible device snuck out past my head. It found its way to the key-disk slot on my cuffs – they disengaged.

"Catch them," said a voice by my ear.

I snatched them and was pulled into a different kind of darkness.

Chapter Thirty-seven
Drezek for Your Thoughts

I may or may not have woken several times within the course of who knows how many hours or days since the spark-fairy rescued me. But I knew I was somewhere safe. My head was clear and I could hear the steady rhythm of a heart monitor coupled with the wash of friendly voices behind my closed eyelids.

I wonder if they know I'm awake?

A cool hand tested first one, then the other cheek before resting momentarily on my forehead.

My eyelids fluttered.

I sighed. *They know now.*

Squinting, in case the lights were overly bright, I opened one eye and then the other. I found myself in a dimly-lit room. The double-framed glass doors looked out onto a cheerily-lit nurses' station. Several bunches of white, yellow and orange wild flowers adorned the counter.

I felt my face, and then ran my hands up and down my arms.

Nothing's stuck into me–

The only device attached to my body was the heart monitor. I stared up at a ceiling painted several shades of blue. Scattered across it were large fluffy white clouds, resembling an early spring morning. The wall to my right was a deep russet orange and the one across from me was painted pale yellow. Darker images of tall grasses blew in an unseen breeze.

This was like no hospital I'd ever stayed in. A soothing voice came from behind and to my right.

"Good morning J.J. How are you feeling?"

An older man, a Glaaon-Balanis cross, with silver-streaked dark- brown hair, walked calmly away from a small writing desk. "Better," I said, caressing my tender, bandaged wrists and feeling the tightness of similar bandages on my feet and ankles. I flinched. Pain pierced my right shoulder. Foggy images wavered behind my eyes.

"The spark-bug," I whispered.

He chuckled. It was a light, pleasant sound – intimate, for my ears only. Leaning over the bed, he rested his pale pink hands on the metal rail. Unlatching it, he slid the safety bar down. Waves of deep purple coliths showed briefly as the cuffs of his white jacket slid back from his wrists.

"Yes, Gerrund mentioned you called him that the other night." He smiled and set a chart to hang from the end of my bed.

A flash of images exploded:

- Jadis jumping out the window
- A bright room
- A grey man
- Echoing walls
- Ticking
- Five masked figures

"Where am I?" I shouted, springing up from the bed. "What happened? Who are you?" The heart monitor followed me on its casters to the foot of the bed, beeping rapidly. "What's going on?" I demanded.

The glass doors slid open and a tall Nirian male, of grey skin and jade-green coliths with a shock of vivid blue hair, walked into the room.

"All of your questions and many others will be answered by Mr. Kipling." The doctor motioned to the man in the black button up shirt and charcoal-coloured pants – the Nirian.

"Is she stable? Can I check her out?" Mr. Kipling asked casually.

"She's back to her old chipper self," the doctor said, clapping him on the shoulder and pulling the curtains shut as he left the room. "Just sign her out when you leave."

"Here, put these on," Kipling said. He tossed me a paper bag full of clothes. "You won't want to be seen in that gown out in public. My name's Gerrund. Gerrund Kipling. I'll answer everything you need to know—"

"Just stop the cloak and dagger act and tell me one thing," I said. "And what's that?"

"Why should I trust you?"

"Ah," he said, slipping through the curtains to stand by the door. "Because I'm an old family friend. Now get dressed and meet me in the lobby." And he was gone.

An old family friend?

That was the last thing I'd expected to hear and likely the only thing he could have said to motivate me. I unwrapped the bundle he'd tossed me. Clean underclothing, a hairbrush, mirror, and deodorant fell to the bed tumbling from a one-piece jumpsuit. It was black with a slight sheen and had a long, wide, mauve belt to complete it. *Not exactly my style – but at least it's stylish.*

I walked out into the reception area cradling my left arm. I felt refreshed yet still very confused. The speed with which things happened lately left me reeling. Gerrund stood speaking with a couple of flirtatious nurses. He appeared to be enjoying himself.

"Shall I show myself out then?" I asked walking past him toward a door marked 'stairs.' I didn't see an elevator nearby, but that didn't bother me.

Gerrund caught up with me. He tossed a sling around my neck and replied with a cocky, "If you're going to show me around, the least you could do is give me a moment to gather a few things."

He handed me a small paper bag with stiff twine handles.

"What's this?"

"Is that really the first question on your mind or are you just teasing me?"

I punched him in the shoulder then looped my sore arm into the sling.

He staggered and rubbed his arm.

"Okay, okay – enough joking. It's your medication."

I stopped mid-stair, "For what?"

"Well, if you bothered to look—"

I narrowed my eyes at him. He held up his hands in surrender. "Right, okay. One is a painkiller for your recently-dislocated shoulder; there's cream to soothe and relax the tense muscles around the inflamed joint; and a bottle of sleeping pills."

"Well, I won't need *them*." I put my hand in to remove the pills from the tote.

"When's the last time you had a restful night's sleep, J.J.?" I stared at him.

"Close your eyes. Tell me what you see," he suggested. I shut and opened them.

"Longer."

I sneered but closed my eyes completely. *Nothing but the back of my eyelids – or is it? There's a metallic sense about the darkness – a shadow of movement – a distant pulse of ever brightening light and –*

I opened my eyes, blinking twice rapidly.

"I rest my case. We've seen it often enough – happens like clockwork."

I flinched as a faint ticking echoed somewhere between my ears. I noticed his gaze.

"What does? Seen what? You know, I still don't know who you are or where I am. Are we about to waltz out into the street? I do have to be a little more cautious than that." We exited the stairwell and crossed a small reception area.

"No street you've ever lain eyes on – within the last seventeen years or so anyway."

"What are you talking about? Is that some sort of vague reference to knowing my family?" My temper rose unchecked.

We walked out onto a cobbled street lined with stone lampposts and turned left. A small café with only a few patrons nestled itself between two brick façades. He guided me into a back booth, eyeing the owner as we passed the counter.

We sat down across from one another. This all seemed so surreal, like I was walking around in a dream I couldn't wake up from. Maybe I was. The walls felt like they tilted in near the ceiling, which looked like a slab of rock or stone.

"Do you know why you were taken captive?" Gerrund asked in a low voice.

I looked him in the eyes. "I'm not in the mood for twenty questions."

"There has to be some give and take here before the whole truth can come out," he said.

I'd come back looking for answers, now I wasn't so sure I wanted them. I fiddled with the cap of a spice shaker left on the table. "I have an idea."

His silence prompted me to continue. For a moment I just listened to the low conversation around me, the faint clink of forks and knives – the normality of it all.

"The Kronik wanted Dezmind, this Talian I was working for, to disappear while we were out journeying the Deserts. They sent two secret agents out to finish the job; both failed. Dezmind's back in town and anyone he's connected with is now under suspicion." Gerrund looked at me, knowing I knew just a bit more.

"They also want me dead." I paused. "For being too good at what I do. Zaith really couldn't tell me any more than that," I muttered the last.

Recognition flashed in Gerrund's eyes. "And that's all she told you?"

I hesitated. "Yes, but it was said under pain-of-death with a final promise that we'd remain..." I faltered. "We'd remain alive, away from known civilisation. Do you know Zaith?"

He smiled, "In some ways better even than you do – in other ways, well, we never really had a chance to just sit and chat about the weather."

It was my turn to wait for an explanation.

"You obviously know about her part-time job with the Kronik's Secret Agency."

I nodded.

"You must also realise then, that she valued her friendship with you above all else."

I nodded, recalling how easily I'd brought Zaith down – it really hadn't been much of a fight – short, vicious, but predictable.

"You're more like her than you realise, J.J. Whatever

information she wasn't bound to by law or the Agency, she gave to us. She wanted to see that certain knowledge reached the public."

"The Tabloids," I whispered.

"Exactly. But we'll speak more on that later."

The owner approached our small table carrying two enormous stainless steel trays. He set them in front of me and left. A host of food steamed on warming plates. Jugs of verrin and mixed juices sat next to a personal size pot of tea and a frothy mug of cocoa.

Gerrund spread his arms over the feast. "My gift to you as a symbol of friendship – from us spark-bugs," he chuckled.

My stomach growled. Snatching two pieces of freshly-cut bread, I piled on roast gelluf, smoked meat, and a pair of fried eggs – topping it all off with a drizzle of syrup before closing the sandwich and stuffing it in my mouth. I took a sip of verrin from a small glass, another bite, and then a chug of hot cocoa. The frothy ring around my mouth was the only sign that any had existed in the mug.

"Enjoy your meal – but don't over indulge. You know it's not good for you after being depleted for so long. Berik brought you a variety to pick and choose from, not knowing what you'd prefer."

"How long have I been MIA?" I asked around another mouthful.

"We caught wind of your imprisonment several hours after you arrived at the Agency Warehouse. It took us four days to find your compartment. We devised a plan on the fifth day to contact you by flashing code through the ventilation shaft on the sixth night. We were shocked to find you already on week three's treatment – the serum.

"If you hadn't performed as you did, there's no telling what you would've said the next day. As it is, this is the second morning you've been with us, equalling approximately eight days since you got back to town."

I choked down my last bite, "Oh Zola, I have to find Dezmind." I stood up, prepared to leave, looked around and sat back down again. "How do I get out of here? Where is here? You keep avoiding that question."

"Dezmind is fine for now. And I wanted to wait until you'd

eaten before answering your last question. Take a moment; make sure your appetite is satisfied. Then we'll go for a walk and I can show you where you are."

I eyed the table, reluctantly reaching for a berry muffin and some more verrin. "What do you know of Dezmind then?" I relented.

He smiled. "You're a focused woman. Quite a bit actually." He paused. "He's been keeping to the public eye; he held a few small Rallies to spread the word of his return but he hasn't revealed what he found in the Deserts, yet."

Gerrund held up his hands to silence the coming query. "He's fine J.J. The public has turned him into a hero – *the man who survived the Deserts*. The Agency can't afford to make their targets public and since that's exactly where he is, he's safe for now."

I wiped my mouth with a napkin. "Why do you keep calling me J.J.?" Gerrund's eyes widened. "Because, that's what your parents called you when you were here."

A whole swarm of emotions and questions exploded in my brain. "Umm, there's only one 'J' in Jutaya, and how exactly do you know my parents, or more precisely, who were my parents?" I asked, confused all over again.

"So, you don't know the whole story? I guess Dezmind doesn't realise who you are yet either?"

"I'm Jutaya Tannya Fyce – Contractor Extraordinaire."

"You are Jadis Jutaya Doire, daughter of Lynnia and Matheson Doire."

I sat bolt upright.

"No."

"Yes. Your parents came here for protection because your mother was a–"

"Talian." I gulped. "How do you know that's me? You said yourself you haven't seen me since I was a baby."

He held out his hand across the table. I hesitated. "Give me your hand and I'll show you."

I gave him my hand palm up. He rotated it over and traced the black outline of the colith that runs from the inside of my thumb, over the bandage, on my wrist and up my forearm.

"This black outline is unique to Lynnia and Matheson's child – to you."

"He wasn't delusional." I buried my face in my hands; my long hair falling forward like a curtain.

"So, you did know – deep in your heart." His voice came softly from outside my inner space.

"It was something Dezmind said before he returned. Something about me being *the one all along*. And Zaith–" I looked up. My eyes remained unfocused. "My father's dead."

I'd been trained to override the pain of exercise and exhaustion – physical meeka that meant nothing but the fact that I wasn't good enough. But my shredded heart, the one muscle I walled myself off from, just couldn't take this new loss. My eyes lost focus, rolling randomly in their sockets. I couldn't handle this emotional stuff. I couldn't handle being abandoned twice – an unwanted child, an anomaly the government wanted to destroy.

Gerrund leaned forward. "How do you know? He could be anywhere out there." His question grounded me. I could deal with cold facts.

"No. We found his body – in a hidden cavern." I shook my head. "I was drawn to a picture he had in his wallet – a family – I couldn't understand why he'd return to the Deserts after going where we've been."

I blinked the haze from my eyes. Two wet streaks painted my cheeks down to my chin. Gerrund leaned forward and cradled my trembling hands in his.

"Your father was deeply in love with your mother. They were caught at the Adoption Agency. A spy spotted your mother waiting in a rider two blocks from the building. Your parents wanted you to have a normal life – one without lies and deceit where you could play in the sun and be with other children."

"But that never happened," I whispered.

He sighed. "Likely your father was returning to be as close to your mother as possible. He didn't think it right that they kept her locked away. We published his journals whenever he returned to the outskirts of the Expanse."

I nodded.

"Gave him food and verrin and some basic supplies, but we

never had any good news for him. He kept hoping she'd be released someday."

A thought returned from seven Deserts ago. "If I'm their daughter, then that makes me Dezmind's—"

"Soul Mate?" he finished. "So he told you about his search, did he?"

"He told the Kahn-lea early one morning – the story of little Lynnia, the Lost Lady, and his own missing pieces – the prophecy – he seemed almost lost as he spoke, lost of hope. Is it true then?" I asked.

He sat back folding his arms across his chest. "I'll tell you what I told him. The prophecy that the Seer made was likely based on Lynnia mating with her true Soul Mate – a Talian. You, although female, were not a product of that union. So, this leaves some room for faith and interpretation.

"He chooses to believe that any daughter Lynnia gave birth to would fulfil the prophecy, as long as that birth happened within the first twelve years of his own childhood. He feels that the Seer didn't specify a particular union Lynnia would have to follow.

"But, J.J.…." He leaned forward. "Your path in life, your soul, have always done as you willed them. If you don't believe in the old ways, that we're all destined for a particular purpose – only you can see the truth of what lies ahead – not an Oracle you've never met, not a man you hardly know, and not a Talian on a personal quest to fulfil his own fate." Gerrund rose from the table. "Come."

I let him lead me away from the table of food.

"You wanted to know where you are and who I am – let's walk."

He brought me out onto the street. I looked up. The light was tempered, shining down in an even band the length of the road. "We're not outside are we?" I asked.

He smiled and led me down a cobbled road only pedestrians and cyclists travelled.

"That's right. Take a closer look at the shops along the way here. What else do you see?" As we walked, side-by-side, I looked intently at each shop in turn. The interiors of some places didn't change, no matter from what direction I viewed them. Yet others, sporadically configured, were small cramped spaces not much bigger – or smaller – than the café. The entire street conformed to that slight curve I noticed back in the cafe.

"Some of them aren't real," I surmised.

"Good eye. These walls have been plastered and painted by great artisans. These lampposts were chiselled by some of the most skilled craftsmen to walk these streets. We're deep underground in an intricate tunnel system that spreads like spilt water throughout the base of Darzeth-Prime and beyond.

"A great ancestor of mine worked for a developer nigh on a thousand years ago. As new buildings were constructed and new land claimed, this architect kept track of all the honeycombed pockets of caves he discovered below ground. On his deathbed, he willed his journals to my ancestor – his faithful apprentice.

"Now, it has long been known why, twenty-two years ago, our Magistrate was sent to cross Darius' Nine Seas. But what people don't know, is that wasn't the first account of unrest among the commoners.

"For hundreds of years, small instances of aggravated farmers and business people challenged the Kronik's authority. However, their voices – their very presence – was always quelled and subtly silenced. The only reason such a big deal was made about the Magistrate's departure was that we'd grown too numerous to be silenced. So, the Kronik used the Magistrate and the rebels to set an example. My entire family was aboard that ship; all except for my youngest sister and me. We were too little to join the uprising and were never caught.

"For generations these passages and caves have housed those who seek an alternative rule under the Kronik, or sanctuary from its wrath – like your parents. I carried on in my father and grandfather's absence. I kept the news leaflets circulating among the commoners so they would never forget what happened and why. Eventually, I built up a network of my own to keep tabs on the Kronik and those loyal to him.

"The leaflets grew to magazines and newspapers. I made sure my staff mixed our message with nonsense reporting, creative stories, poems, and artwork – anything else anyone living down here felt like submitting that week. For them, it gave their families above ground hope of their continued survival; for me it provided a means to an end."

We walked in silence for a while. Gerrund's passion for his cause, his destiny, was mind numbing. I'd spent so much of my life simply focusing on surviving, building walls to keep others out, that I'd come to take so much for granted.

The Facility, an institution of the Kronik, was my home, my shelter – but it was just an elaborate lie. *I wonder how many of them know the truth? The Master Keeper? The Ethics Council? Do they know who I am? Surely if they do, I'd still be working the mines?* I'd carved out an existence for myself, brought meaning to a meaningless life, or had I? Within the space of a few weeks, I was first hit with Dezmind's convictions, then Zaith's, and now a man I barely knew described a generation's worth of mindset and beliefs.

I still don't have a firm conviction of my own truth – why I am still here – still alive. With every answer, two more questions pop up.

I spent so much of my life searching – without even realising it. Searching for something remarkable to believe in, to live for – taking on dangerous or challenging work in the hopes of finding something true. And now, here I was, in an underground city, mixed up in the affairs of a whole host of people I'd never heard of before, or met until recently.

I just wish I knew what to make of it all. I've been slowly losing control of my life since I graduated.

I ran a hand across the smooth surface of a lamppost, touched the sill of a painted window and again, looked up.

How is this possible? There's so much I still don't understand.

The bell of a bicycle chimed behind us. Gerrund stopped and turned. "Expecting someone?" I asked.

"He's a messenger. My people have tracked me down. Must be urgent."

A black-skinned man with red coliths jumped from his bike and swiftly handed a dark-purple envelope to Gerrund, who tore it open and flipped out the inner message. I read the words in reverse as he held it to the light.

The Kronik have plans set in motion to extricate Dezmind during a major Rally this evening. He will not survive without intervention.

"Where's the Rally? I have to get to him first," I demanded.

Gerrund quirked an eyebrow and looked at the back of the page. "You do realise that this won't be something as detectable as an assassination attempt? Whatever they've got planned is going to be immense and will likely affect a large number of people – the Kronik know this can't lead back to them, but it has to have a big enough impact to draw away his followers."

"All I know right now is that I swore to protect him." This was the one aspect of my life I had control over – the choices I made. And I made the choice to come back and save a friend. "If I'm not out there, he doesn't stand a chance. Where is he? I need to warn him."

"Hold on there. You can't go back to the surface looking like that – you'd be spotted in no time."

"Looking like what? You gave me these clothes—"

"No, no. Look, we won't do Dezmind any good warning him about what's coming. You must know by now that he'll do it anyway – it's his calling – what gives him a reason to live."

He was right.

"No, right now what you need to do is meet a friend of mine. She'll take good care of you."

Chapter Thirty-eight
Split Personality

"How much farther?" I asked.

"We're almost there. Slow down. We don't want to attract any undue attention. Try not to think, J.J.," Gerrund advised, strolling casually with his hands in his pockets, nodding at the occasional pedestrian.

There were no sidewalks. Other than the feeling at the edge of my mind that something wasn't quite right with outside, the caverns we walked through easily held two- and three-storey houses and shops carved out of the rock and crowded together like the network of places in the Ancient City. Only here, the streets were wide, empty thoroughfares with painted façades and a sense of safety. Whatever the light source was and however it worked, the soft diffused glow made it feel like a perpetual spring day.

"How many people are down here?" I asked, noticing only a smattering of walkers and cyclists.

"Oh. Well, I don't keep official count with births and all, but I would say somewhere in the realm of two or three thousand."

"What?" I spun in an arching circle as I kept pace. "Where is everybody?"

He chuckled. "Working, of course. Or going to school. What – did you think we just sat around all day moping about our banishment?" I staggered a little with the accusation. He smiled.

"We've grown to be our own microcosm of civilisation. We function because we have to. While I would like to say that visits here are brief, most citizens choose not to return to the surface. Many can't return because of their political views or some terrible misunderstanding, but people build new lives for themselves. Nobody willingly wants to be a target of the Kronik."

Nobody except me. Gerrund obviously thought so too, with my insistence about returning to the surface. "So, this place is huge then? What I'm seeing–"

"Are a few streets of a very large town. Now, see that shop up ahead?" he asked.

"The pastry shop?"

"No, the one beside it. We're not here to slap an apron and some flour on you."

"The one with the image of male and female silhouettes almost mirrored?"

"Yes. When we enter, she's likely to have customers, so just sit by the front window in one of the chairs until I give you the signal."

I didn't have time to respond, to ask who she was. Gerrund allowed me to step through the wide entryway ahead of him – most of the shops were bereft of actual doors. Entering, I turned to the waiting area: three small orange cushioned armchairs and a tiny table.

Gerrund sauntered past the salon-style row of chairs and partitions to a black door at the back of the shop – a real door with a peephole. He knocked lightly, twice. The older Metek woman in the second styling chair was having her silver-streaked hair placed in hot rollers. A toddler, a boy with the same dark-green skin and gold coliths, played with a small electric passenger train. As the youthful stylist wrapped another shoulder-length tress, the woman stared at me.

I sat down. Averting my eyes, I reached for a magazine from the small round coffee table. The back door opened and closed. Gerrund was gone. I ignored the pages in front of me and closed my eyes.

Jadis leaping out of my living room window flashed in my mind. I felt her limp body cradled in my arms – I pushed past that night and instead let myself bury my face in her imaginary fur and listen to her deep rumbling purr. Someone coughed. I opened my eyes, sat forward and flipped through the paper; it was not a magazine as I had first thought.

Forcing myself back into the present, I scanned the table: it held only backdated issues of the Tabloids and various pamphlets echoing much the same information. *Data Tracking for Population Control* topped the headline of the print in my hands.

The back door re-opened. Gerrund walked out with a woman of no race I had ever seen: shimmering gold from head to, well, finger tips – she wore a simple black short-sleeve blouse and pants. Her multihued, multilayered red hair contrasted with her solid black coliths.

"This is the possible new hire," Gerrund pointed indifferently at me. "Send me word about her skills. If I need to find her another job, I'd like to know as soon as possible." He nodded to me and walked out the door.

I stood, dropping the pamphlet back on the table. The woman held out her hands, taking hold of mine. She ran her forefingers lightly over my scarred palms.

"Welcome, my dear. I have a doll in the back room you can test with." The woman led me by one hand and an arm around my shoulders. "I'm Magda, the owner of Twin Faces."

She smelled of wildflowers in the breeze; that scent that always seemed close but floated just out of reach. Each mirror we passed reflected our image. Her confident face and my scared one. We walked into the back room. Magda closed the door.

A work desk hewn from the rock of the wall held a variety of papers. Three rock shelves above displayed plastic sample bags and small dishes filled with a myriad of colours. A simple wooden stool served as an office chair. On the far side of the desk stood a four-foot metal filing cabinet with a large, fake, leafy plant in the back corner. On the other side of the room stood another stool beside a brown love seat.

What dominated the back corner of the space was anything but inviting: a torture device of chrome and black leather. It was at the same time both a stripped-down version of a styling chair and one of the most advanced pieces of salon equipment I'd ever seen. It had padded manoeuvrable arms, a metal footrest, and variable height controls with a foot pump. My dentist would drool. What stood out the most was the lack of a doll. I clearly wasn't here for a job interview.

"I guess I'm the doll?" I said quietly, scrunching up the thigh of my jumpsuit in one hand.

Magda smiled. "No, my dear. You are the canvas." I shivered. "We should begin. The timeline is short."

"Something tells me this is so much more than just a makeover." Magda guided me into the chair.

"You're getting the Transformation package. Did Gerrund not discuss this with you?" She opened the filing cabinet and took out colour palates, sponges, scissors, brushes, and a number of jars and tubes.

"No. He said only that I needed to meet you."

"Sometimes I wonder about that man," Magda tisked. "A complete body transformation is the only way to be unrecognisable. You are going to resurface, yes?"

"Ah, yes?"

"You're wanted by the Kronik but you still want to go topside?" she clarified as she arranged items on the desk, both stools, and the sofa.

"Yes."

"The only way to return to the surface incognito is to give you a new look and a new identity. I handle the looks department. Gerrund is working on your identity. Now, what is your favourite colour?"

"Wait. Did I hear you right? I can't just walk out of here?" I jumped out of the chair. "Am I a prisoner here too?"

Magda cringed and whispered, "We are all prisoners down here. Each and every citizen is in mortal peril of the wrath of the Kronik.

Gerrund saved you – he had a hand in saving all of us. But this is the price we pay to live our lives unfettered by Kronik rule. If you leave without our help, you will be killed. Not by us, but whoever the Kronik assigns to assassinate you. What will it be?"

What will it be? I was exhausted and laboured with Jadis the first time I ran. But I am the best of the best – first ranked among my peers at the Facility. But if the stories are true about the Master Keeper and the Sleeper Agents and the special abilities of Talians –

I sat back down again.

"Is it permanent?"

Magda swept her hand gingerly around the side of my face – temple to chin. "No. Some of the pigments I use, and some of the techniques, will last longer than others, but the effect is only as good as the shortest reapplication sequence. Now, what's your favourite colour?"

"Um, purple I guess. I like blue as an everyday colour but purple has always been the stand-apart one."

"Not that we want you to stand apart," Magda chuckled. "That's fine. Purple works well. I need to test a variety of hues on you to get the right one, but I'll make it work. We may as well have a bit of fun with this. It will be the body you see in the mirror every morning."

"My whole body?"

"Yes, dear. The gold I'm sporting doesn't just stop at my undergarments – one of the reasons so few people choose to return to the surface. If you want to be in the public, you'd better be prepared to wear a bikini and get a little intimate." Using a large flat paintbrush, Magda applied pigment to my arm.

"Won't the different shades look odd?"

"These are water soluble, Hon. I don't add the permanent until I get it perfect."

My eyes swept over the office, the normalcy of it all: the desk where an easel should have been, filing cabinets instead of art drawers for supplies.

"If you're an artist, why do you run a salon?"

"The body has long been my canvas. My drive to perfect that art is what put me on the Kronik's radar. I was warned in writing about tattooing, but I kept experimenting, altering, and enhancing the beauty of the body."

"What did they do? Why couldn't they let you work in peace?" Magda spread different base colours on my forehead with a sponge.

"They blew up my house."

"What?"

She smiled ruefully. "I was delayed by a businessman interested in sponsoring my work," she laughed. "Later I realised it was Gerrund in disguise. The Underground had learned of the Kronik's interest in me. Apparently the government sees my work as traitorous and not as art. If I have the ability to hide a person's identity, they do not have the ability to track that person. I would have said it was a conspiracy theory if everything I owned hadn't burned to the ground. Since I could not be found, I was assumed dead. I've been living down here, helping the Cause ever since."

"Magda – your family?"

"My family knows that I'm alive and that I'm safe. They read the Tabloids regularly and see my drawings. They will stay safe as long as I never resurface."

"But if you can transform yourself, why not go back?"

"My dear, I would have to erase who I am to accomplish that. I cannot be anyone else. I would falter. My craft is my life and so I chose to live." Magda worked silently for a moment. "And you, my dear? Who did you used to be?"

Chapter Thirty-nine
Finding Truth?

Emerging from an old tool supply shed on the back lot of a local scholastic institution, I scanned the perimeter. Luckily, it was after hours. Hidden behind a bank of trees and shrubs across a large field from the main building, the site was perfect for a secret access point to the Underground. I kept to the edge of the tree line so as not to draw undue attention. Gerrund promised me I'd only be a couple of blocks away from the Rally point, once I found my way to the main road.

Although I still donned the same black jumpsuit and mauve sash, I was now equipped with a matching carry-on bag. I'd begged for a belt-pack, but Magdalene insisted it would draw attention to me – it was too much like my old self.

After four hours of intense treatment, I was literally unrecognisable. My skin was now pale pink, like Tamaine's, and my coliths were a deep purple. My body itched from the alteration creams and injections, but I couldn't risk scratching for another twenty hours.

I was released only because I threatened bodily harm. My hair, I ran my hands over absentmindedly, was shoulder length and layered from the top of my ears down the nape of my neck. And the colour – well it was the only one that appealed to me at the time because Zaith hadn't tried it yet. It glistened coppery-bronze all the way down each strand to the tips, where Magda had painstakingly bleached each layered end white.

The only trace of *Taya* was what remained on the inside – and that scared me because I still wasn't sure who that was. Understanding the truth, at least what I knew of it, eluded me like a shadow flitting about in the darkest reaches of my mind. What I did know was that Dezmind was indeed destined for something greater – not because some Oracle told him so but because of his passion to unite all the people of Xannia under the same banner of truth. I didn't know how he was going to do it, but I knew he would.

Walking past mirrored windows on the street, I kept reminding myself that it was my own image travelling beside me and not that of a stranger. A few curious eyes looked my way; I exchanged smiles or a polite nod – no one suspected I wasn't who I appeared to be.

Being the first evening of a three day weekend meant that the stores and cafés were full of eager people wanting to spend their credit. I passed a series of row houses with perfect lawns. *I wonder if I'll ever own my own house again? If I'll have a yard big enough for Jadis to race me in. Zola, I miss her.* I couldn't dwell on that now. I had to focus on the Rally and Dez.

But my mind dragged me back to that first Rally. I was so determined to prove Dezmind wrong, to prove the status quo, and keep order and sanity in my neatly packaged world that I didn't let myself see past the day. There was so much more happening between the black and white of my government upbringing – so much more to know. A shiver travelled down my spine. I gave my head a quick shake. Focus. I had to find Dezmind.

I approached Darius' Square, an enormous park courtyard marked by a near life-sized bronzed statue of his once-great sailing ship. A throng of people stood packed between me and a makeshift platform over a hundred yards away. Balloons floated in the hands of children and adults waved streamers. The trees were littered with festive ties and the atmosphere fairly sizzled with excitement.

No one stood alone. No one looked lost or frightened. Laughter and light chatter filled the air. The closer I manoeuvred to get to the stage, however, the tighter the weave of spectators grew. I was swallowed by the crowd.

"The Kronik's message stands—" I heard a tinny voice say. I looked over the shoulder of a woman holding a small portable wire, tuned into *Network News Now*.

"Here again is the clip from this morning's live address from the Kronik himself," the reporter announced. The face of an aged Talian, likely in his early hundreds, took full precedence of the small screen.

"Again, I would like to reiterate: everything that can be done about these disturbances will be done, and it will be accomplished by scientists and engineers. A rogue Talian has hinted that writings from a bygone era led him to a place where harmony is currently being restored to our celestial heavens. Be assured that if anything were amiss in the heavens you, the people, would be the first to know.

"Remain calm, disregard the rogue's claims and do not fall victim to his false promises. We are working towards a freedom from these ongoing and escalating disturbances."

"What a load of crock!" I said. "It'll take months before the quakes die off—these things don't just cure themselves overnight!"

The woman holding the portable wire turned to me. "Isn't that the truth. Mr. Lisle's being permitted to speak only in small venues, but he exposes a bit more of the Spoken Truth every time. This is the largest crowd I've seen yet. I think he's gonna tell us everything this time."

"This notice from the Kronik has been running all week?" I asked. "How have they proven what he's saying isn't true?"

"Where've you been? The Kronik hasn't appeared this often since the Magistrate's departure over twenty years ago." The woman eyed me critically.

"I've – been – visiting family – out of town. They don't have any modern conveniences – don't believe in them," I scrounged.

The woman nodded. She grabbed hold of my arm. My heart flew into my throat.

"Look, look. There he is. Now you listen up, Lady, and listen well. He's a man who's seen our future."

What an odd thing to say.

Shrugging off the woman's comment, and her hand, I looked up at the stage. My stomach flipped.

"Dez," I whispered. He stood there, not in his tan travel fatigues, but in a white summer suit with a pale-blue button up shirt. There was something very different about him now – he still held himself straight and tall, but the angle of his chin had changed, and the way he held his shoulders.

He exuded confidence but no longer the arrogance I challenged not so long ago. This was the man who befriended a sceptic – a man who looked at me as his equal, his partner. *If only I can keep him alive.*

I moved forward, manipulating my way through the crowd. Dezmind tapped his microphone twice; the loudspeakers crackled.

"Good evening friends," he welcomed and spread his arms wide. The crowd cried out and surged forward – eliminating more of the precious pockets of space. My heart beat like a pickaxe against the walls of my chest; chip, chip, chipping away the emotional barrier I used to keep us apart. I felt a surge of triumph and fear.

He's too exposed.

"I see some familiar faces among you today." Part of the crowd roared to life. "And some new eager ones, too." The other portion of the crowd responded.

The attentiveness of the public was astounding! I'd never witnessed anything like it. I tried to squeeze between the backs of two tall strangers.

"For some of you, my words may come as a shock. You may recoil with the weight of them. Some of you are here to listen to them again because you weren't sure you heard right the first time. And still others of you have joined us today because you've heard the word pass from mouth to mouth and needed to hear it for yourselves.

"What I am about to fully impart to you reveals much of what we have forgotten or buried about our Ancient past. Ten of us travelled into the forsaken Deserts in search of the truth, and I have returned to share our findings with you."

Dread slid through my veins, swelling like a poison as Dezmind described the fading magnificence of the Ancient City. He spoke of the deciphering of the Chronicles – not by any one person, just that it happened.

"A crucial part in our search for the truth. And this document, thousands of years old, yet preserved in the material it was forged with, describes in detail a solar device activated and placed in orbit around our equator, out in space, by an alien species not of our world."

Conversation broke out in the crowd. A young Danieth girl, of deep-orange skin and black coliths, turned to me, "Another species? A solar device? What's he saying?"

"That there's a lot of information the Kronik has kept from us and he's the first Talian to admit it. Keep listening." I never thought I would hear myself speak those words – speak against the Kronik and everything I once held dear. The blind trust was gone. I pushed away the uncertainty that remained as I forced my way through the cramped crowd. A wall of bodies, huddled in conversation, blocked me from my goal.

My patience waned. I burst forward through the group, elbowing and clipping, pushing and weaving though the crowd.

A large hand clamped down on my arm not fifty feet from the stage. I turned to the stranger and grovelled. "Oh, please, he's such an inspiration. I have to get closer to see better. You don't know how important this is to me."

The mysterious person attached to the large hand released me. But I only got about thirty feet from the edge of the stage.

I have to tell him of the danger.

I screamed in my mind, closing my eyes in fit of fury. *Dezmind!* I opened my eyes. He stared right at me, still speaking but clearly confused. He wasn't the only one. Was there more to this connection between us? Was it something in my blood?

"As a result of their efforts to find help, they eventually integrated themselves into our society, forming the basis of the genetic code for all Talians. Because of their close connection with the Elders, those who they bonded with tended to be of that class and sect. Slowly, the Kronik and Compound of the Society evolved and their power and prestige has grown to divide our people."

The onlookers and listeners gaped openly at the one man willing to tell them the truth. The silence between his sentences weighed on me. *I'm not close enough.*

"This is the first step to reuniting our brothers and sisters – our kin – this is the first step to reclaiming our heritage and the truth about our world!"

The ground shook. An all-too-familiar rumble travelled through my feet, up the bones of my legs, and echoed amidst the excited onslaught of hollers, yells and screams that erupted with his final words.

The enthusiasm died.

The earth jolted once and exploded. Ground debris: chunks of dirt, rock and grass blew out and rained down on the crowd. Massive clumps of caked earth landed on unsuspecting bystanders; young children ran screaming and wild, searching for their parents. Shrieks of terror rode like a wave as mass panic gripped the crowd.

The earth fell and rose alternately, creating enormous chasms. The innocent were knocked from their feet. Hollers escalated as bystanders fell into crevices, disappearing into the void below. A child wailed at my feet, clutching the long grass. My arms ached to hold her, find her parents. A man fell back into the void surrounding the stage. I froze. I could be swallowed up too. *Move!* I yelled at myself.

Dezmind scrambled to get off the sinking platform. Six more succession-bursts hit.

The stage groaned.

The ground beneath it caved in. The platform, everyone on it or near it, fell several hundred yards down as the earth opened up and swallowed them.

I can't save them all. I pushed the heels of my palms into my eyes. The stabbing pain from the pressure cleared my mind. *But I can save our future.*

Scrambling against the surging masses, I was lifted off my feet by the crowd and dragged backward. Instinct told me to dig my heels in and fight – intelligence told me I'd only end up getting trampled. They carried me farther and farther away from the chasm.

No! I have to reach him. There's no time left. If I couldn't go through them, or under them, I'd have to go over them.

Gripping the arms of two people, I hauled myself up onto shoulders and heads. Struggling to walk on the crowd toward the void, the bodies surged apart. I jumped to the ground and ran to the edge of the crevice. I looked down. My eyes darted back and forth.

Groups of people huddled on their stomachs, hand-in-hand, covered the floor of the stage and what ground remained. I focused on a lone man dangling from the bow of Darius' ship at the edge of the divide. Scuttling around to the stern, which still rose above the crater, I pulled myself along by the metal rigging.

Tears stung my eyes as the new skin on my palms burned and blistered against the coarse statue. The wave of pain that surged up my arms blinded me. I stopped. My palms cramped. I screamed. Forcing my blood to boil as frustration flashed across my neural pathways, I opened my eyes. I worked my way toward the mast, suspended several yards above the ship's floor.

Blood streamed down my arms as freely as the water from my eyes. There was nothing between me and Dezmind but more rigging and a severely tilted deck.

The ground was unstable. A tremor vibrated up through the metal statue. My teeth chattered as I fought to clamp them shut. My arms went numb from the constant shaking. My right hand slipped off the rigging. Relief and fear battled my senses – one hand relaxed as the other threatened to cramp up again. I wiped the free one on my pant leg then swung it back up. My left hand slipped off, tearing open more wounds that would never heal.

No!

I dropped a foot and caught hold of another section. I dangled like a leaf ready to fall.

"Whhoooahh!" I hollered from my gut, wiping my left hand and then swinging it to grab the woven metal. Biting my lower lip to distract me from the pain, I walked hand-over-hand until I reached the main mast. Sliding down from the upper rigging, red streaks of blood marred the bronzed finish of the ship.

My feet slammed into the floor with a boom from the hollow hold below. My knees quivered. I hugged the mast tight. Calm warmth teased the edges of my consciousness. I grabbed hold of the unexpected sensation and took a deep breath – the warm pulse penetrated deeper into my psyche.

Flattening myself to the ship's floor, I shimmied across the space separating me from Dezmind.

I touched his hand. He looked up. Grabbing his arms, I hauled him back up onto the deck and then spread my limbs out across the sheer surface.

"Use my body as a ladder over to the mast and the rigging!" I called over the thunder of feet and voices refracting from above. The ground rumbled and quaked again, but something wasn't right – *it's happening at patterned intervals.*

Dezmind grabbed my wrist. He slipped off. My heart twisted. He tried again. Catching my breath, I braced for the pull of his weight.

Slowly he dragged himself along my body until he could find solid footings. At the mast he gripped my bloodied wrist, helping me up. The ship pitched and swayed with the next volley of blasts. We clung to the mast and one another for support. I motioned with my head to go up the rigging. He jumped for the lowest section of the grid and looked back at me. I waved him on. Red splattered his perfectly- pressed white pants.

I clung to the mast with my body and shimmied up to the rigging. Every swing of my arm accompanied another wipe of blood on my jumpsuit. The nerve endings in my palms were fried and I gripped without feeling. Envisioning my practice climb on Level 1 at the facility, all those weeks ago, the blood turned into sweat and the weight of the digital timer tracking my progress pushed me up the last of the rigging. Dezmind hauled me to my feet on the edge of the open crow's nest. Our bodies became one as he held me steady.

Another tremor shook the ship. Dezmind lost his footing and plummeted over the edge. I landed on my stomach as he dangled from my arms. My breath vanished. White spots flashed in front of my eyes. I twined my legs around what was left of the top of the mast.

"Climb." I forced out as I gasped for breath.

He obeyed, careful to avoid hurting me further. When he stepped free of my body, my lungs kicked in and my vision cleared. He helped me up. My legs buckled from the rush of blood.

"Get out of here!" I yelled. "My legs are numb. Jump over to solid ground." This visage meant nothing to him. He could leave me and I could die knowing that by saving Dez, I saved our future.

"No. We jump together."

"There's no time. Go without me."

Grabbing me under my arm he hauled me back up to my feet. My toes spasmed, exploding like mini-fireworks in my shoes as the blood returned. Draping one of my arms around his shoulder, he bent his knees and shouted.

"Now!"

I pushed with every ounce of strength I had left and we launched ourselves from the ship to the grasses above. I slipped from his arm. He landed on his stomach with his feet dangling into the precipice. My hand went purple as I dangled from his grip. I swung my other arm up. He snatched it, swung his feet up over the edge and dragged me up beside him.

He lay on his back, panting. I pushed myself off my stomach onto my fists and knees. Forcing myself to stand, I pushed Dez's shoulders up and away from the massacre. The ship went down into the expanding ravine.

"Hurry, it's you they're after!" I shouted, my body working on adrenaline alone. We sprinted away from the chasm.

As I searched for a quiet residential street, I split my sash with my teeth and wrapped my hands. My fingers barely responded. Dezmind moved ahead. A smear across his shoulders and two perfectly-formed red handprints flashed like beacons against his white jacket. Rescue vehicles sped toward us heading for the scene. *We're too exposed.*

Dropping to my knees by the side of a public transport, I dragged Dez under with me – temporarily out of the sight of prying eyes. We lay locked together, struggling to control heaving lungs and rapid breathing.

"You're injured," he said, his brow wrinkled with concern. "You need to go to the hosp—"

"Hospital? No. The Kronik wants *me* dead just as much as it does you. They'll have spies on the lookout for us. Besides, the blood is starting to clot. I just need to rest for a while." He angled his head to look at me better.

I explained the situation, "That was no quake. Those ground tremors were caused by explosives. Gerrund–"

His eyes shone with recognition.

"Gerrund received a message that the Kronik were planning to kill you – except we didn't know any specifics and I couldn't get to you sooner." I couldn't believe I was still alive. *I should be sinking with that ship, but somehow I'm here.*

We lay there breathing – listening as the charges dissipated and the sirens wailed. I brushed stray strands of hair from my eyes and caught sight of my pink skin and purple coliths through the drying blood.

I grimaced, and then gave myself a mental kick. "Perhaps I should introduce myself?"

He quirked an eyebrow and rested his chin on a free hand.

"My name is Aelonia Dione Trellice aka Jadis Jutaya Doire – but you can call me Taya."

His eyes crinkled smiling back. "I knew who you were even before I laid eyes on you." He drew my wrapped hands to his chest.

"How?"

"The same way you knew I was in trouble when you were scouting the Desert Caves."

That sudden jolt of fear and the need to race on flashed through my veins a second time. A remark Ketic made about his daughter echoed as well: *Anna and I were able to communicate telepathically – only from the kitchen to the playroom, but she has it.*

"I don't understand. If you could speak to me with your mind, why didn't you sooner? Why didn't you reach out to me in the Ancient City? Why–"

He touched a finger to my lips. "Think about it, Taya. The Dakturians might have been capable of doing that, but not a modern Talian. Distance plays a factor as well as knowledge, individual ability, and–"

"And what?"

"And willingness." He lightly traced the colith that ran from my temple down just below my ear. "In addition to being half-Talian, your mother's DNA was obviously diluted. With you not knowing your true heritage, why would you open yourself up to something you didn't even know existed?"

He rested his forehead against mine.

"You built up so many barriers around your heart, your mind, and your soul that I never stood a chance of connecting with you. Only when you let your guard down was I able to detect the possibility of your ability. You only let me sense you in your greatest moments of agitation."

"So, that's really how you knew I was coming to see you after the first Ral—" but I didn't get a chance to finish. Dezmind's lips found mine. I closed my eyes. His body pressed against my every curve. His fingers slipped up the back of my neck and into my hair. The tingling fire in my heart sizzled through every vein as I gripped the back of his shirt.

Soul Mate or not –
Destiny or not –
Really, what did it matter as long as this felt right?
We belonged together.

We parted with a shared breath. Our eyes met. The sounds of commotion had lessened, but they were by no means gone. We were only temporarily safe from prying eyes, secret agents, and spies.

"So, what now? I know our fates are connected – but why this? Why now?" I asked.

Dezmind smiled. "That's like asking 'why me?'" He shifted to get more comfortable. "Try to look at it as Fate might – why not? With everything that we've been through in our lives, to finally be together here and now to face what's next – it couldn't have happened any other way."

"But so much of it was awful – it tore at us – at me –" The words choked my voice. The double abandonment, living on the street, working in the mines...

"Would you be the same person you are today, if you hadn't been challenged, hadn't been forced to make certain choices?" He paused. "The truth, Taya, wouldn't have been revealed any other way."

We remained there under the public transport until the fall of night. We spoke of plans and hopes; how Dezmind found my lynx eating the stuffing out of his office chair at the restaurant, and the state of his apartment after he'd left Jadis alone for more than eight hours one night. And what our future might hold.

If you enjoyed Time's Tempest, check out:

Cadence of Consequences

Book 2 in
The Chronicles of Xannia Series

Available Fall 2015

**Time's Tempest:
The Lost Chapters**

Prequel to Time's Tempest: The Chronicles of Xannia

eBook available for free through most major distributors

About the Author

Growing up in Ontario, Canada, M.J. was the only child of a single mom. M.J.'s passion for the arts ignited at a young age as she wrote adventure stories and read them aloud to close family and friends. The dramatic arts became a focus in high school as an aid to understanding character motivation in her writing. Majoring in Theatre Production at York University, with a minor in English, she went on to teach in both the elementary and high school divisions.

M.J. currently lives with her husband and young son. She keeps busy these days with her emerging authors' website Infinite Pathways: hosting writing contests, providing editing services, free publicity tips, book reviews and a myriad of opportunities for authors to build their writing platform and portfolio.

Connect with M.J. online:

Author Website – www.mjmoores.com
Facebook – www.facebook.com/AuthorMJMoores
Twitter – www.twitter.com/AuthorMJMoores
Goodreads – www.goodreads.com/author/show/8104388.M_J_Moores